Cara Colter shares her life in beautiful British Columbia, Canada, with her husband, nine horses and one small Pomeranian with a large attitude. She loves to hear from readers, and you can learn more about her and contact her through Facebook.

Christine Rimmer came to her profession the long way around. She tried everything from acting to teaching to telephone sales. Now she's finally found work that suits her perfectly. She insists she never had a problem keeping a job—she was merely gaining 'life experience' for her future as a novelist. Christine lives with her family in Oregon. Visit her at christinerimmer.com

Discover more at millsandboon.co.uk

CINDERELLA'S NEW YORK FLING

CARA COLTER

IN SEARCH OF THE LONG-LOST MAVERICK

CHRISTINE RIMMER

MILLS & BOON

First Published in Great Britain 2020
by Mills & Boon, an imprint of HarperCollinsPublishers,
1 London Bridge Street, London, SE1 9GF

Cinderella's New York Fling © 2020 Cara Colter
In Search of the Long-Lost Maverick © 2020 Harlequin Books S.A.

Special thanks and acknowledgement are given to Christine Rimmer for her
contribution to the *Montana Mavericks: What Happened to Beatrix?* series.

ISBN: 978-0-263-27886-6

0720

MIX
Paper from
responsible sources
FSC™ C007454

This book is produced from independently certified FSC™
paper to ensure responsible forest management.

For more information visit: www.harpercollins.co.uk/green

Printed and bound in Spain
by CPI, Barcelona

CINDERELLA'S NEW YORK FLING

CARA COLTER

To Ally Blake and Sophie Pembroke.
There was a knock on my door one day,
and two lovely strangers stood there and said,
'Can you come out and play?'

PROLOGUE

IT ALL HAPPENED so quickly.

But then, that is probably what most people would say of a catastrophe. One hardly gets out of bed in the morning meticulously planning for disaster. No, it has a tendency to spring on one when it is least expected. At my advanced age—seventy-four—things going awry should hardly take me by surprise.

But they do, and it did.

I was walking through Faelledparken, delighted with both my escape from my tiresome head of security and with how the famous Copenhagen park had been transformed for the Annual Ascot Music Festival, held in a different country every summer.

The park had been turned into a lovely little village of colorful tents that featured all kinds of drinks, food, trinkets and souvenirs. There were smaller stages scattered throughout for some of the less well-known singers and bands to perform. Street performers juggled and did cartwheels and magic tricks.

This year's festival was titled *Carlene to Celine and Everything in Between.* I thought it was very catchy and modern, though one of the PR men—they prefer the term "marketing executive" now—had the audacity to roll his eyes when I suggested it. I wished, for a very brief moment, that the super suave, *I'm the expert on everything* man, with his hyphenated name, was walking with me to see how that title was displayed everywhere, eclipsed by the much larger *Ascot Presents*.

The name Ascot even eclipsed Carlene, which, of course, was my intention, though I would act properly horrified if anyone pointed it out as the shameless publicity move for Ascot that it was. When I took my inherited family fortune to the next level—the Ascot brand was now a household name in products that ranged from pharmaceuticals to kitchen faucets—I learned that women in business had to be shrewd and smart, and very careful not to let anyone know just how shrewd and how smart they were.

Carlene herself, the headline act, would be performing in about fifteen minutes and throngs of people were heading through the park to the stadium. Certainly no one took any notice at all of me, a gracious elderly lady in a colorful head scarf, sunglasses and a sweater that was…er… perhaps a touch bulky.

It was all very exciting, and there was a kind of energy to the crowd that was invigorating. But little by little I began to feel that familiar bombardment that reminded me why I avoided crowds.

That man needs some vitamin C.

That woman needs a baby.

The thoughts were coming faster and faster and were followed by a heightened perception of the crowds being quite crushing and the evening being very warm.

I hadn't exactly counted on the heat when I thought of Denmark on a summer's evening or when I stuffed Max under my sweater.

People are always so quick to offer their judgments, and I'm sure many people would say having a dachshund snuggled under my sweater at such a crowded venue was practically inviting trouble.

But Max suffers from separation anxiety and it had been

made worse by jet lag and a hotel room he was unfamiliar with. The poor little fellow could hardly go pee he was so discombobulated. The only place he seemed to settle was under my sweater. I felt a bit like a mother kangaroo with her joey, a nice feeling, since I had never had children myself.

That nice feeling lasted precisely until I walked by a performer who chose the very moment of my passing to clank a pair of oversize cymbals together.

Max let out a yelp, scrambled up my belly and chest leaving, I'm sure, a trail of red welts that marked his desperation.

He exploded out the neckline of my sweater, leaped onto my shoulder and hesitated for only one brief moment before he launched himself over my back.

I whirled in time to see him hit the ground and tumble. He was wearing the most adorable little sailor outfit and the hat fell off. He found his feet and raced off, in the opposite direction of the crowds heading to the stadium.

"Max!"

You would think the desperation in my voice would have been enough to stop the little bugger, but no, he cast one glance back at me, looking distinctively pleased, not frightened in the least, and quickly lost himself in the sea of legs marching toward me.

I practically risked my life to rescue the hat from the crush of stamping feet before attempting to follow him. I can't describe the pure panic I was feeling, clutching his jaunty little hat to my chest. That little dog is my whole world. I practically own the earth, and in that second, I was aware I would trade every single bit of my fortune for him.

The futility of trying to follow him soon became apparent. I could not make my way through the crowds. Frankly, it was like being in a nightmare where you are trying to run and you cannot move.

My invisibility was terrifying. It was as if no one saw me at all as I pushed the wrong way. I got only brief, annoyed glances, as if I had been drinking too much. As if to confirm the worst suspicions of all these strangers, I suddenly stumbled and felt my ankle turn. Pain shot through it.

I allow myself very few vulnerable moments, but there I stood, paralyzed and trembling, wondering if my ankle, which felt as if a red-hot poker had been thrust through it, was going to give out on me. If it did, surely I would be trampled.

And then she appeared, like an angel. A young woman stopped in that endless push toward the Carlene concert, and looked at me. People flowed around us unceasingly, as if we were two rocks in a stream.

I knew right away she was a good person. Her eyes were huge and brown and probably the gentlest eyes I had ever seen.

"Are you all right?" she asked me. She spoke English, without an accent, which made me think she was North American. She touched my shoulder.

I practically threw myself into her arms and instead of pushing me away, as if she was being accosted by a crazy person, her arms folded around me.

She was very slender, and yet she felt ten feet tall and enormously strong.

"My dog," I sobbed. "He's escaped. He went that way."

Feeling foolish and old I stepped back from her embrace, wincing at the pain in my ankle, and pointed a quavering arm in the direction Max had gone.

It was then I noticed she was with a man. He was one of those supremely attractive types, who have an inborn knowledge of their own superiority. He had that way about him, of a very good-looking man, as if he was doing this woman some kind of favor by being with her. Even though she was being protective of me, I actually, despite my distress, felt very protective of her.

"Ralph," she said, pronouncing it in the German way, *Rolf*, "this poor woman has lost her dog. Can you go find him?"

He gave her an astonished glare and looked, rather pointedly, at his very expensive wristwatch. It was clear he didn't want to miss the opening song of the concert, had probably put out a lot of money for front row seats.

The woman gave him a look.

I saw right away that she was seeing things about him that she had not seen before or maybe had seen but, in the heat of romance, had dismissed. I think he saw her blossoming awareness, too, because he turned begrudgingly to me and with the outmost reluctance asked after the dog.

"What kind of dog?"

"He's a dachshund. He's wearing a sailor suit."

The man—I decided I hated him in general, and him for her in particular—raised an eyebrow at her that spoke absolute volumes. *We're going to miss Carlene's opening set for a crazy old lady who probably doesn't even own a dog.* But he set off the way they had come.

"His name is Max," I called out helpfully, but I realized that man was not going to go through the crowd shouting for the dog.

I began to tremble uncontrollably, partly from the pain in my ankle, but mostly from thinking of Max lost out there in this absolute sea of people.

"Are you hurt?" the young woman asked me.

"I seem to have turned my ankle."

She quickly had her shoulder under my arm, and again I realized she was much stronger than she appeared. She practically carried me out of the press of the crowd and off to a tea stand set up under a colorful yellow-striped awning, with a scattering of mismatched plastic tables and chairs under it.

A young woman was just getting up from a table. She was clutching her Carlene ticket as if she had waited her whole life for this moment. She saw me, crying, and she saw my angel, and she hesitated, and then made a decision.

"Is everything all right?" she asked, approaching us. She had short dark hair and she was quite petite, like she could be cast for Tinker Bell in *Peter Pan*. She had some kind of instrument slung over her shoulder in a case—perhaps a violin or a ukulele, making me think that, as well as being desperate to see the Carlene concert, she might be one of the lesser known performers here. She was British, like me, and for some reason I found that quite comforting.

"Not really. My friend has lost her dog. And hurt her ankle, I'm afraid."

Friend.

Not *Crazy lady keeping her from the concert.*

"Oh, dear," she said, and then I had *two* angels, as she rushed to support my other side. The tent café was empty—of course it was, everyone was heading to the concert—so we had no problem finding a nearby table.

"Do you think you need medical attention?" the British girl asked.

"I need my dog!" I said and my voice came out in an embarrassingly quavering wail.

"What kind of dog?" she asked gently.

Again, I was so grateful not be asked why I had brought a dog to the event. Even though Denmark is one of the most dog-friendly nations I have ever visited, obviously bringing Max this evening had been pushing it just a wee bit.

"A dachshund."

She won me forever when she smiled at me, her green eyes sparking with good humor, and said, "I adore dachshunds. What's his name? I'll go have a look."

"His name is Max." I hesitated a moment, thinking of the man's reaction, but anything that would help had to be divulged. "He's wearing a sailor suit."

"A dachshund in a sailor suit," she said. "Honestly, you have made my day. Maybe my whole week."

This from someone on her way to the most coveted concert of the year! But she put the Carlene ticket in her pocket, as if it didn't matter a whit to her, and was soon lost in that crowd, shouting after Max.

My remaining angel went and fetched me a cup of hot tea.

She was just the loveliest girl in an understated kind of way. She was dressed in a rather unexciting pair of capris and a knit tank top I could only describe as the color of porridge. Aside from her eyes, which were quite astonishing in both the doe-darkness of them and their size, she was what I might call plain. She had shoulder-length, light brown hair, and even, but unremarkable features, and the willowy build of those disinterested in food.

She obviously intended to distract me, because she chatted, even though she had that reserved air about her of the type who would not enjoy being chatty with strangers. She told me her name was Jessica Winton, and that she was from a small town in Canada, where she owned a bookstore named, adorably, The Book and Cranny.

"Difficult to compete with the online giants," I commented.

"Not really," she said, "because my view is that a bookstore is no longer just about selling books. If anything, the online world is creating an even deeper need for connection."

She went on to say that people thought brick-and-mortar bookstores were going to go the way of the dinosaur, but she disagreed. She felt bookstores needed to reinvent themselves as the hub of the community.

I could see she did have a gift for connection, because I felt connected just talking to her. I could also see that she was an astute businesswoman, and she reminded me, just a bit, of my younger self. She had succeeded in taking my mind off both my missing dog and my throbbing ankle.

I indulged my curiosity about her. "Do you travel a great deal?"

She gave a little self-deprecating snort. She told me she had never traveled abroad before, and that this was her first real adventure. She said that all her previous adventures had been between the covers, and then added *of books* and gave a little laugh. I could tell, even as distracted and panicky as I was about poor Max, that her adventure might not be turning out exactly as planned.

"Is that man your boyfriend?" I asked, putting unnecessary emphasis on *that*. One of the few perks of being old is you can be as direct as you want.

Jessica hesitated, and then looked uncomfortable. "We've been back and forth online for nearly a year. This is our first actual time together. I thought…"

She let her sentence drift off, but I'm afraid I could tell exactly what she thought, poor thing.

With an ocean between them, and his rather stellar good looks, she had thought he was her Prince Charming.

I had nearly finished the tea, and despite how much I might have enjoyed my companion in other circumstances, I felt deflated and exhausted, and as if I needed to go back to my hotel room, to the inevitable finger-shaking of my head of security, and to begin to mourn the loss of my beloved Max.

But just as I had given up hope, that girl who had put her ticket in her pocket emerged from the crowd, and she was with another girl. They could have been sisters, they looked so much alike with that spiky, very short hair, and both of them with petite builds.

The other girl's hair was lighter, and she had freckles, and it was she who had a squirming Max held firmly in her arms. Both the young women were laughing, and they looked so vivacious and full of life. It was such a beautiful thing to see—plus the miracle of Max being returned to me—that I started to cry all over again.

I suddenly found Max in my arms. The little monkey— his outfit utterly destroyed—licked my face as though he had not deliberately run away and was delighted to see me. The two young women who looked like sisters introduced themselves. The British girl was Daisy, which is a name I find very old-fashioned and completely lovely.

It turned out the third girl—her name was Aubrey and she was Australian—had scooped up the loose dog as he had continued his mad dash through the crowd. How appropriate is that, that my little joey had been snagged by an Australian? That girl had a "life of the party" way about her.

And then Daisy had come upon her as Aubrey stood there, not quite sure what to do with her find, and brought her—and darling Max—back to me.

We ordered tea all the way around, and I found out a bit about each of them. Daisy was, indeed, a budding musician who would be playing some of the minor stages at the festival. Aubrey, despite being so outgoing, had something faintly fragile about her, that made me feel concerned about illness. She was involved in some kind of custom painting family business with her brothers. She sounded less than enthused.

I was enjoying visiting with those young women so

much I nearly overlooked the fact I was keeping them from their concert, which would be starting momentarily.

I gathered Max, and stood to go. The delight of being in the company of all that vigorous youth had been so lovely I had forgotten the injury to my ankle. But when I stood pain shot through it, and I sank back down with a defeated yelp.

I caught sight of *that* man, Ralph, on the edge of all those moving people, craning his head, obviously looking for Jessica. He saw her and came to the table, casting a terrible shadow on it.

"I see the dog has been found," he said tightly, not at all humbled by the fact there was a *real* dog. He was obviously more than annoyed that his time had been wasted in the search, and that he was about to miss Carlene's show. "Jessica, let's go."

She tilted her chin at him, and I was happy to see a spark of pure fire in those soft, dark eyes.

"Actually, my friend is going to need some help getting home. She's hurt her ankle."

I could have protested that I did not need help, but it really seemed far more important to see how this played out.

"We're missing the concert," he said.

"Yes, we are," she returned, calmly.

"These other women can help her."

"So our enjoyment of the concert is more important than theirs?"

The other two girls sat, wide-eyed, eyes going back and forth, as if they had front row seats at Wimbledon.

Ralph drew in his breath, gave Jessica a withering look and stalked off in the direction of the stadium.

It seemed like all of us had been holding our breath.

"Well," Aubrey said, breaking the silence. "What an ass."

And then we were all giggling like schoolgirls. It made

me feel a part of things, something I certainly had never felt when I was an actual schoolgirl.

"I can manage," I said. "Please go enjoy the concert."

"I don't see how you can manage, at all," Aubrey decided. "I'm going to go see if I can flag down one of those golf cart things that are driving around."

The lady who was running the tea stand came out to collect dishes and I ordered a crumpet for my dear little Max.

The lady brought Max his treat and said, "I'm going to close up now, if you don't need anything else?"

I looked at her and realized she looked exhausted, and also, of course, I knew exactly what she needed.

She needed to feel like everyone else in the park tonight, as if life could have some happy bits in it, and things to look forward to, not just be a sea of endless drudgery.

"Here," I told her. "I don't have any need for this."

I gave her my ticket for the Carlene concert.

Jessica said, "If you've got a friend who can come on short notice, you can have mine, too."

And then Daisy chimed in, and the waitress was suddenly holding three tickets to Carlene. The weariness evaporated from her face and she stared at the tickets as if they had fallen straight from heaven.

"My kids were dying to go. We live close. They can be here in a blink. These tickets are impossible to get," she breathed.

"Nothing is impossible," I told her sternly. She looked hopeful, as the evidence of that very thing was resting in her hand.

Daisy was smiling at me. "I like that. Nothing is impossible."

"But you could still have gone! I don't need all three of you to miss the concert!" I told her, but she was watching that waitress, and I could tell she would not have traded anything for the look on that woman's face. In a world where "self" seems to reign, how had I been lucky enough to run into these three women?

A golf cart came careening down the path, Aubrey in the front with a young man who had on a first aid attendant uniform.

He grabbed a bag, and peeled off my sock and shoe, and poked and prodded at my ankle.

"I think it might be broken," he said. He took a radio off his belt and, ignoring my protests, ordered an ambulance to meet us at one of the exits.

Even when I insisted, my angels, bless their hearts, refused to leave me, even Aubrey, who still had her ticket.

"What will happen to Max at the emergency room?" Daisy asked, practically. "No, we'll come and take turns staying outside with him until you're released."

And so, we all ended up in the golf cart, though it hilariously overloaded it.

Aubrey said, "I feel as if I'm in a carload of clowns heading for the center ring," and we all laughed, and despite my ankle throbbing, that golf cart ride through Faelledparken felt very spontaneous and joyous. There was an ambulance waiting at the exit, manned by two swoonworthy Danish men. Jessica came in the ambulance with me, and Aubrey and Daisy followed with Max in a cab.

Hours later, outside the hospital, with my ankle bandaged—thankfully just severely bruised, not broken— we exchanged hugs. We were beaming at each other as if we had known one another forever, the most delicious little bond between us, the kind that only a closely averted catastrophe can create.

Finally, I was able to look at the young women who had put their own agendas so selflessly aside to help me.

Really look at them.

I've had this unusual gift since I was a child.

My mother was appalled by it and called me *fey*. She went as far as to discourage my use of it by saying she thought maybe I wasn't a *real* Ascot, after all, but an Irish traveler baby, fallen off the caravan.

I'm afraid the thought of *really* being an Irish traveler, instead of a member of a very stuffy aristocratic family, bound by rules and customs and most especially by *what will people think*, gave me many fantastic hours of make-believe and much needed respite from my mother.

I certainly wasn't fey in the way most people would think of that. I was unable to speak to dead people, an enviable talent that has become so popular there are now entire television programs about it.

It was just that I could look at people and sense what they needed.

In my younger years, it had been quite overwhelming, especially in a crowd. People's needs, both large and small, swarmed around me like restless bees, buzzing...

She needs to see a doctor...he needs a long walk in the forest...he needs glasses...she needs a new life...he needs a new wife...

As I had gotten older I'd learned to keep my observations mostly to myself. People didn't really appreciate a complete stranger approaching them with life advice. I'd also gotten better at shutting off some of it, and had learned that knowing what someone needed—even when sometimes they did not know themselves—gave me quite a sharp advantage in business.

Looking at my rescuers right now, I knew with startling clarity exactly what each of them needed.

Still, you didn't attain the incredible successes in business that I had, by relying on your instincts alone.

"I have ordered a car for Max and me. I'll make my way

back to my hotel." Jessica was going to protest, but she had done enough for me, so I held up my hand. "But I would so love to keep in touch. I'm brand-new to social media. Would you mind if..."

Of course they saw me as entirely adorable, and wrote their full names and all their social media contact information—Facebook and Twitter and Instagram—on a scrap of paper I provided. They had already exchanged information with each other, but they had put that directly into their phones. No scraps of paper for their generation.

Having all that information meant I could spy on their private lives shamelessly—young people were so oblivious to who was watching what they revealed online—to confirm if what I thought they needed *really* was what they needed.

And then, I was in the unique position of being able to give it to them. I felt no rush, at all. They were young, and at that age where their needs could change in a heartbeat. I would be patient. Bide my time. Wait until I was 100 percent certain.

I realized, gleefully, all the girls had accepted me introducing myself simply as Viv, and not one of them had any idea who I really was—Vivian Ascot, one of the sponsors of the music festival and CEO of one of the largest and oldest corporations in the world.

"What a good little boy you've been," I told Max. "You've brought me this wonderful opportunity."

I watched the girls walk away, arm in arm, lifelong friendships appeared to be budding. Jessica was going to stay with Aubrey tonight instead of running the risk of running into Ralph at her hotel, and then they were all planning to go together to watch Daisy's "gig" at the festival the next day. I contemplated what those young women, my rescuers, needed. They were so young. So filled with hope.

So confident that they knew everything they wanted and needed for happiness. Naturally, they had no idea.

Of the three of them, I had gotten to know Jessica the most. I loved the way she had described Timber Falls, the small resort town in the Canadian Rockies where she had grown up and ran her bookstore, and where her parents still lived.

But, while it had sounded like a great place for aging parents, and possibly for a short holiday, and while Jessica undoubtedly felt safe there, what longing had led her to Copenhagen? Whatever she had told herself, I felt her journey to the music festival was not so much about a romance as it was about a longing for a larger world. Young people need challenges to make life seem fresh and interesting.

The small town had to be quite stifling for someone so smart and ambitious. And single. But now, after the Ralph fiasco, it seemed there was a possibility Jessica would go back there and be more reluctant than ever to explore all life had to offer.

Well, not if I had anything to do with it.

Waiting for my car to come, I felt the most delicious wave of happiness. I decided playing fairy godmother to those three young women was probably going to be just about the most fun I had ever had.

CHAPTER ONE

JESSICA WINTON STEPPED out through the Customs and Immigration doors into the full flurry of the arrival area of John F. Kennedy International Airport. Her hand tightened on the handle of her wheeled carry-on.

She had not seen a crowd like this since that summer night of the music festival in Copenhagen. Could that be two years ago, already?

Yes, almost to the day.

And look at how that had turned out: her grand virtual romance had been exposed as horribly naive and shabby when the harsh light of reality had shone on it.

This was going to be more of the same. Jessica could just feel it. Yes, there it was, the panicky sensation rising in her chest.

What moment of madness had made me agree to this?

Right now it felt as if, after that initial glance, it would have been better—so much better—if she had just junked the email that had brought her to New York City as one of those endless variations of the Nigerian orphaned princess scam.

Dream job this time. Dream man last time. Did she always have to be the sucker for a dream?

She cast a desperate glance back at the doors that had just whispered closed behind her, but saw that reentering the Customs area was strictly forbidden. What would she do if she managed to go back through the doors, anyway?

Demand to be sent home, like a child who had found summer camp not to her liking?

She'd been invited to a job interview here in New York City. Of course, she already knew she couldn't take it. Even if it was her dream job, which it most definitely was. She had her life and it was a totally satisfactory life. She was successful, she was a respected member of the community. Who was always the keynote speaker at Career Day at the Timber Falls High School?

No, a job in New York City, at this point in her life, was out of the question.

And yet, here she stood, as if pulled by an invisible cable. She'd been up front with the marketing firm Jensen, Henry and Ascot that she wasn't in a position to take the job. But they had been persuasive. Why not just come? Have the initial discussion? See some of New York City? And then, an airline ticket, and a reservation confirmation for three days at a posh Manhattan hotel had been sent, as if that was all settled.

No one could say no to that. Could they?

And yet, standing here, exhausted—it took longer to travel from Timber Falls than the time she would spend in Manhattan—and not quite knowing what do next, Jess felt regret at being so impulsive. It never paid off for her. Other people could embrace spontaneity, but it seemed as if it just wasn't a good fit for her.

Something wasn't ringing true about all this and she should have paid attention to that feeling instead of being persuaded by Aubrey's ever chipper Australian voice coming over the line, chiding her.

Is something not ringing true, or do you just believe good things can't happen to you?

Daisy, while pleased that Jessica had decided to accept the trip to New York, had said rather gleefully, *Looking at a new job is like going to the pet store and looking at puppies. You're already partway committed to taking one home with you.*

What if it proved harder to resist the temptation than Jessica anticipated?

It wasn't going to be that hard to resist if her first few minutes in New York were any indication. The Customs lineup had been slow, the official had been unnervingly unfriendly and, now that she had been admitted to the country, the crowds were crushing, and her stomach was growling. And as far as she could see, there was no one here to greet her.

Her tablet case and her purse were strapped securely to the pull handle of her carry-on bag. She turned to it. She fished the piece of paper from the outside pocket of her purse and looked at it.

The letter instructed her she would be met at the airport by James Gilbert-Cooper, Chief Operating Officer of Jensen, Henry and Ascot, a marketing firm that had a division that exclusively handled bookstores. The man could potentially be her new boss!

But not if this was his idea of making a good first impression. Leaving her hanging.

It's been two minutes, Jessica chided herself. She forced a deep breath, and a change in attitude. She was sure Aubrey, her irrepressible Australian friend, would invite her to turn it all into a game.

Okay. What would someone with a name like that look like? Old, she decided. And very proper. A vested suit and a bow tie. Definitely glasses. Round-framed ones.

Jessica looked around nervously. She couldn't see anyone who looked like she expected Mr. Gilbert-Cooper to look.

What if he didn't come? Should she wait? Call the number on the letter? Surely the office would be closed. Should she take a cab to the hotel she had the reservation at? Didn't cabdrivers take advantage of people like her? Despite her best effort to look sophisticated, Jessica felt she was probably telegraphing that she was from a different country and a small town. Did cabdrivers have to pass some kind of test of their driving skills? What if she was killed in traffic? And what about their character? What if she was driven to a remote location and—

Stop it! Jess ordered herself.

She made herself think of Aubrey and Daisy, and the wonderful connection the three of them had enjoyed since Copenhagen—thank you very much, WhatsApp. Both women had encouraged her to come, and hinted that maybe they thought Jess tended to play it too safe, and make her world too small. It was funny what close friends they had all become, despite the fact they came from different parts of the globe and had very different lifestyles. Still, Jessica confided things to them that she would not have dreamed of saying to any of the people she shared a life with on a daily basis.

Take a chance, Aubrey had insisted after Jess had received the intriguing email and determined it was not a hoax.

Too late, Jess was remembering almost those exact same words—from other well-meaning friends—had led her to the disaster in Copenhagen with Ralph.

Jessica took a deep breath, and searched the sea of faces waiting in the arrivals area. None of them seemed to fit her idea of James Gilbert-Cooper, and none of them seemed particularly interested in her.

I'll be wearing a red jacket.

Thinking about it now, that could be left open to some interpretation. The jacket in question leaned toward burgundy. She should have been more descriptive: the color was like sun filtering through a bottle of merlot, which was what she had thought when she splurged on it.

Why hadn't she thought out the intricacies of being met by a stranger in such a large airport a little more thoroughly? Had she been expecting someone to be waving a sign with her name on it?

To be perfectly honest, yes, she had.

And then she saw him.

It felt as if the sea of people around her had been storm-stirred waves that suddenly went still.

He was standing, leaning one shoulder, casually, against a post, long legs crossed at the ankle. Unlike almost everyone else in the terminal, he seemed to be neither waiting eagerly for someone nor rushing off somewhere.

He seemed, while not exactly indifferent to the controlled chaos around him, above it, somehow, untouched by it.

He was wearing a suit of the lightest charcoal gray, the jacket open, the cut showed off both his broad shoulders and the length of those powerful legs. The shirt was a crisp white, a tie, in an unlikely shade of pale pink, was knotted somewhat carelessly at his throat. Jessica's gaze rested on his shoes—leather, buffed to a soft sheen, a shade of tan that shouldn't have worked with the suit, but did.

Not one man in all of her hometown of Timber Falls could carry off any shade of pink, in any circumstances, and certainly not in combination with those shoes. The man's sophistication—his absolute confidence—was underscored by the color of his hair.

It was gray—*not fifty shades,* Jessica scolded herself—but certainly a dozen, from several startling variations of silver, to strands of white, and tiny hints of black. Rather than aging him in any way, his hair, and the superb cut of it, made him seem distinguished, in control and fabulously sure of himself.

He was scrolling through his phone, and she had a ridiculous desire to know what was holding his interest like that.

Photos? Of his children? He somehow did not look the type. Wife? No ring on his finger. Girlfriend? Ah, probably plenty of those.

He glanced up, as if he'd sensed her gaze on him. Jessica saw his eyes were darker than her own, coffee as compared to chocolate, and his gaze was intense, and stripping.

Embarrassed by feeling such a pull to a complete stranger, Jess looked quickly away and scanned the crowd for the far more dowdy Gilbert-Cooper of her imagination. When she didn't see anyone, she cast another longing glance over her shoulder at the firmly closed Customs doors behind her.

And then, disgusted with herself for the weakness, Jessica found she could not resist glancing back at that man one more time. He was scanning the crowds now. She noted his brow was furrowed in a frown, almost as if he was irritated. And then it appeared he saw whomever he was looking for because he tucked his phone away, and moved. Straight toward her! She could feel herself holding her breath.

Jessica didn't know if she was relieved or sorry when he stopped in front of the woman beside her.

Who happened to be wearing a red jacket.

Paired with a rather hideous flowered skirt.

With jet-black beehive hair and too much makeup.

"Jessica Winton?" he asked the woman.

Jessica felt the insult of it, and also her wariness increased. Was that how he pictured a small-town bookstore owner, then? If that was the case, why had his company gone to such lengths to get her to come?

Still, the inquiry did mean that *he* was Gilbert-Cooper. Her potential boss!

"Honey," the woman said, eyeing him as if he was a hot fudge sundae on a sultry July day, "I'll be whoever you want me to be."

Jessica understood the polite thing to do would be to go correct this, but some little devil made her want to see him pay the price for his misconception.

"I believe it would be a yes or no answer," he said after a pause. "Jessica Winton?"

The woman extended her hand. "And you are?"

Jessica's mouth fell open. Was this stranger beside her really going to pretend to be *her?*

It obviously was time to say something, she knew that. But she was inappropriately tickled to watch Mr. Suave and Confident's hand disappear inside a ham-like grip. The woman didn't let go, either. In fact she blinked, eyelashes so heavy with mascara that it looked like she had spiders glued on, at him.

He extricated his hand with difficulty. "Jamie Gilbert-Cooper."

If they had said Jamie, instead of James, in the letter, Jessica might have been better prepared for him. She would have been prepared to meet the hero of *Outlander* not someone dowdy and old and in a bow tie! Still, she was guiltily aware she had let this go far enough.

"I don't see a wedding ring," the woman said boldly. "A guy like you not hitched?"

His discomfort was acute, and really Jessica could not have him believing for another second that this woman was *her.*

Well, maybe one more second. Just until she heard his answer.

"Not *hitched*," he said, only the tiniest tightness in his tone indicating he was irritated, "and not planning on it, either."

"Well, that makes you exactly my kinda guy, Mr. Gilbert-Cooper."

Jessica cleared her throat. "Did you say Gilbert-Cooper? That's who I'm waiting for."

Jessica looked at them both innocently, as if she had just noticed them.

The woman swiveled her head, and gave her a glare as if Jessica was an uninvited guest at a private party. Then she turned back to Jamie Gilbert-Cooper. "Honey, you are one long, tall drink of handsome. You can't fault a girl for trying. Can you?"

Apparently an answer was required.

He did not look like he was caught off balance often, but he definitely was now. Casting Jessica a faintly accusing look, he muttered, "Enjoy your stay in New York."

"I'm here for the Gidgets Widgets Convention," she said, not so easily dismissed. She fished in a large red handbag that missed matching her jacket by a shade or two, and handed him a card. "I'm Debbie, a sales consultant."

He glanced at the card and actually blanched before quickly handing it back to her.

She pouted prettily, cast Jessica another dark look. "Now you look like a gal who could benefit from—" she held out the card that he had returned to her.

He intercepted quickly. "No," he said, with such firmness even Debbie was dissuaded. Miffed, she put her card back in her purse and then marched off through the crowds.

"Your loss," she called over her ample shoulder, before disappearing from view.

"What is a Gidgets Widget?" Jessica asked, watching her go, trying to contain her glee at his discomfort.

"You don't want to know," he told her firmly. He turned his attention back to her. "So you are the real Jessica Winton, then?"

"Guilty."

"It seems to me you might have stepped in sooner."

"Um…"

"You enjoyed that."

"Just eager to clear up misconceptions about small-town bookstore owners everywhere." *Potential boss*, she reminded herself sternly. Even if she pretty much had already decided she was not taking this job, she needed to be professional.

Her potential boss cocked his head and studied her. He was much taller than her. Close up, the chiseled perfection of his features was even more evident. He had the faintest hint of gray-and-black stubble on his face. Deliberate, obviously. Sexually potent, terribly.

The most subtle fragrance came off him, faintly spicy, faintly exotic and strongly masculine.

"It was the red jacket, not any kind of preconceived conception about small towns or bookstore owners."

His voice was as smooth and smoky as the twenty-one-year-old Glenfiddich her father broke out once a year at Christmastime. She did not think she wanted to be having a conversation with him that included the word *conception*, no matter what the circumstances.

She had worn the red jacket that she had purchased for her trip to Copenhagen two years ago. It was, easily, the best item of clothing that she owned, the only time she had ever splurged on a designer name.

But suddenly she was *so* aware it was two years old, and it didn't feel as timeless as she had told herself it would be when she had indulged her desire for it. Her blouse felt wrinkled and her black pants felt travel-rumpled. For the first time in her life, she felt aware of the importance of shoes, and sorry that she had chosen the loafers she had on for their comfort and practicality.

Meeting a man like this, one wanted to have on four-inch heels.

Jessica Winton, she chided herself, *you've never had on four-inch heels in your life!*

She'd been concentrating on how to look businesslike this morning as she had prepared for the flight, and so her hair was held back in a clip, and her makeup was minimal.

"Jamie," he introduced himself to her, as if she wasn't already 100 percent aware of who he was! His voice was deep and had an entirely too sensual rasp to it. "Gilbert-Cooper."

She let loose the handle of her suitcase. Her fingers actually felt cramped from holding it so tight, and she extended her hand to him.

"How do you do?" she said, and then could have kicked herself for how ridiculously formal and stilted she sounded.

He took her hand.

The feeling of stillness, of all that activity around her fading to nothing, increased. His handshake was firm, strong and sexy.

How could a handshake be sexy?

"Mr. Cooper. Mr. Cooper!"

He let go of her hand, and turned, frowning. Jessica could see Debbie, the Gidgets Widgets gal, steaming back toward them.

"I forgot to give you the free sample!" she bellowed. She was coming at them brandishing something that looked like a large green cucumber. People were staring at her, startled and wary.

Jamie actually tucked Jessica behind him, putting his

body between her and the charging saleslady. There was something so entirely protective about it that it could completely dissolve that potential boss barrier.

Jessica felt, more than saw, a movement out of the corner of her eye. Someone jostled her. Hard. She lurched into Jamie's back, and he took a startled step forward then turned around.

"Hey!" Jamie cried.

She realized, stunned, someone had grabbed her suitcase. As she watched, frozen in horror, what appeared to be a businessman—nearly as well dressed as Jamie himself—darted through the crowds with her suitcase, her purse and tablet case still attached to the handle. He wasn't running, just moving fast, like someone late for a connection.

"He stole my things!"

Jamie took both her shoulders in a strong grip and scanned her face. The strength in his touch, the calm in those dark eyes—he had thick sooty eyelashes that the women of the world would die for—had a way of making the calamity unfolding fade into a distant background.

"You're all right?"

As soon as she nodded, he released her shoulders and took off at a dead run after the perpetrator.

Even with it being such an awful moment, some despicable part of herself insisted on noting how athletic he was, and insisted on seeing this as somehow intensely romantic. She would have to share this story with the romance genre fans who met at the bookstore once a month. The members of the Smitten Word would be delighted! And so would Aubrey and Daisy. They had told her life could be full of unexpected adventures, and here you had it. She had been in New York less than fifteen minutes, and she was being rescued by a stunning hero.

Not that she should be thinking about her potential boss like that. It was highly inappropriate.

It occurred to her, almost peripherally, that Debbie had disappeared. That seemed impossible. She had been charging straight toward them. How did someone that size, that colorfully dressed and that loud, simply vanish?

Without the calming effect of Jamie's touch and gaze, Jessica could feel the full implication of the theft. She felt rattled and off balance.

She took a deep breath, then found an uncomfortable seat.

Jamie was just the kind of man you could rely on in a situation like this, she told herself. He radiated an ability to control the world. He would catch the perpetrator, return her belongings to her and the ice would be broken between them. He would forgive her for having not stepped in sooner to reveal Debbie as an imposter, and she would choose to believe that it was the red jacket that had caused the mistaken identity, and not a stereotypical idea of what a female business owner from a tiny dot on the map in the Canadian Rockies would look like.

In a few minutes they would be sitting in a cab—or maybe he had an extraordinary car—but either way, they would be laughing about her introduction to the city. She could picture those firm, sensual lips tilted with laughter, the dark eyes sparking, and that picture made a very improper shiver run up and down her spine.

She craned her neck to see, but the crowds had swallowed up both Jamie and the thief making off with her suitcase.

Seconds ticked by, and then minutes.

Finally, she saw Jamie coming back through the crowds toward her. She leaped to her feet but her relief at seeing the only face she knew in all of New York was short-lived.

His hands were empty and there was a look like thunder on his handsome face. He was breathing hard.

Reality collided with fantasy. As he approached her, he loosened his tie with one hand, and held his phone to his ear with the other. Obviously he was talking to the police or airport security.

It occurred to Jessica that instead of mooning about, making up stories, she should have been calling the authorities. They could have been setting up traps at the exits, watching security cameras...

Except her phone was in her purse.

He ended his call as he came back to her. "I'm sorry," he said, running an agitated hand through the multicolored gray silk of his hair. "He's obviously very skilled at this. The Artful Dodger. I couldn't catch him. I lost him in the crowds. He probably has some favorite getaway route, and some little hole he ducks into."

She could feel the tiniest prick of impending tears behind her eyes. She would not be a country bumpkin in front of this super sophisticated suave man. She would not! But the enormity of what had happened was hitting her. Hard.

It wasn't an adventure. It was a catastrophe. Trust her to mix the two things up!

"I called the police," Jamie said, his voice soothing, despite the anger on his face. "Unfortunately, there are nearly two hundred claims a day of baggage theft at this airport."

"Two hundred thefts a day?" she gasped. So much for a team of people scanning the exits and the security cameras in search of *her* stolen items.

"Most of the stuff is grabbed from the luggage carousels, but there's been quite a sophisticated ring operating lately. Teams. One distracts, one grabs the goods."

He lifted an elegant shoulder in apology.

"In Timber Falls," she said, "we probably don't have

two dozen thefts in a whole year. I've had two shoplifting incidents in the four years that I've had had my bookstore. Poor Mrs. Webber, who was getting dementia, and Sonny McGill, a teenage boy who had been going through a rebel-without-a-cause phase."

She realized she was babbling nervously. She realized she had probably revealed all kinds of things about her life that he would find quaint and amusing.

On the other hand, maybe she didn't have to say a word to reveal secrets about herself. The theft team had obviously targeted her as hopelessly small-town from the minute she had come out those doors.

"I'm really sorry," he said. The genuine distress in his voice made the cold, hard reality of what she was dealing with intensify.

"Did they peg me as naive?" she asked softly.

"Hey, don't say that as if it's somehow your fault you were robbed. Honestly, I feel as if I should have twigged in on Debbie's over-the-top performance." He turned his attention back to his phone. "As I suspected. No Gidgets Widgets Convention in New York this weekend." He scowled as he scrolled. "No Gidgets Widgets, period."

"Too bad you didn't keep the business card," she said forlornly.

He raised an eyebrow at her.

"Fingerprints."

"Uh, yeah, I somehow doubt this crime would have rated fingerprinting. Sorry. Apparently, we can file a police report online, though. And we need to get your credit cards looked after. Your phone plan canceled."

We. Because *she* no longer had a computer. It felt somehow insulting that the crime that had been committed against her did not even warrant a face-to-face visit with authorities. His suggestions for dealing with practicalities made her face the grim truth of the matter.

"I'm not getting my things back, am I?"

He looked uncomfortable. "Um—

The prick of tears intensified behind her eyes. "I don't have my phone," she stammered. "And no cash. No clothes."

It occurred to her that her reliance on this formidable specimen of a man, a person she barely knew, and her potential boss, was 100 percent.

It was shocking, and yet her mind insisted on itemizing things of no importance at all.

No makeup. No perfume. No favorite shampoo. No pink frosted nail polish. No novel to escape into.

She glanced one more time at the Customs and Immigration door she had exited from. Even if she could go back through there, she needed proper documentation to go anywhere.

"My passport," she whispered. "How am I going to get home? How do I go about replacing it?"

Jessica realized she was trapped in New York City. With Jamie Gilbert-Cooper.

Such a dreadful, dreadful mistake to come here.

Just like her ill-advised adventure to Copenhagen.

The noise and activity around her seemed to rise up to almost unbearable levels: the intercom warning people not to leave their luggage unattended, a shout of laughter, the constant hum of busy people moving.

Jessica suddenly longed for the comfort of Timber Falls: for her charming bookstore on Main Street, and for her little cottage in her mom and dad's backyard. She longed for the turquoise waters of the nearby lake, for the cool green of a forest just getting ready to welcome summer. She wished she was sitting beside Timber Falls, that thunderous noise filling her every sense, her face lifted to the spray.

"We'll get it all sorted out," Jamie told her, his voice solid and reassuring.

Something in the utter strength of that voice made her look at him. Really look at him. He was gorgeous, yes, but there was an underlying calm there, a man, who despite all the sophisticated trappings, you would want at your side if the bandits were coming at you with knives in their teeth.

Unfortunately, there was something about his composure, his strength, that allowed her to let hers slip, just a little bit.

She felt her throat close.

And then, even though she ordered herself not to, the first tear slipped out of her eye. And then the second one. And then, the floodgates opened. There. She could be grateful that, in her rush to get the plane this morning, she had not bothered with mascara.

It was of little comfort that James Gilbert-Cooper's colossal self-confidence seemed to evaporate, completely, in the face of her tears.

CHAPTER TWO

"DON'T CRY," JAMIE ordered Jessica Winton, a little more sharply than he intended. The order seemed to have the exact opposite effect of what he had intended. Her face crumpled a little more.

"Please?" he added, trying for a softer tone. Instead, he could hear desperation in his tone. Jamie's father had died when he was eighteen. There had been so many tears from his mother and his sister, so much emotion that he had been powerless to stanch. He *hated* the memories of that period of his life, and couldn't believe he'd been plunged into them by the vulnerability—as understandable as it was—of a complete stranger.

Despite a terrible start, this was still a business association. One of the things he *loved* about business was that it was a black-and-white world. Pesky things like emotions—feelings—could be left safely outside the perimeters of the work environment.

His relief that she was the real Jessica Winton—that he didn't have to spend three days trying to be civil to that obnoxious barge in a dress—was not standing up to the challenge of the stolen luggage. He could handle crass and vulgar over soft and vulnerable any day.

He realized, since the feeling thing had crept in, exactly what he *was* feeling.

Guilt.

He had failed. That barge in a dress had tricked him into

letting his guard down, and the woman who had suffered the consequences of his failure was trying not to cry and failing as completely as he had.

Guilt was also a residue of that period in his life when he had been powerless over the pain of those he loved, where he had also felt the agonies of failure.

This, Jamie told himself firmly, has nothing to do with *that*. But as he watched, first one little tear slid over that exquisite cheekbone, and then another, and then those slender shoulders heaved, and the storm came.

He had lied to Jessica Winton. He *had* entertained preconceived notions of what a small-town bookstore owner would look like. Young had not been part of that equation. Neither had completely adorable.

He was not prepared for huge brown eyes the color of melted milk chocolate, the lush fullness of a bottom lip, the little mole on the tiny lobe of her ear.

Of course he was not prepared for any of that! Jessica Winton being offered a job was all part of *the joke's on you*.

Jamie had been part of the internationally renowned marketing firm of Jensen, Henry and Ascot for seven years, the last three of them as the Chief Operating Officer. Until two and a half years ago, he'd been unaware that the Ascot part of the corporation name was anything more than a silent partnership. The Ascot name was, after all, in everything, from nuts to bolts to concert production. He'd been a bit surprised there was an actual person attached to that iconic name.

And what a person. Auntie Mame on steroids.

Vivian, herself, had descended on the office, at a meeting concerning the promotion of the annual Ascot-sponsored music festival. Despite being diminutive, she had been larger than life in oversize Gucci sunglasses, a fur hat unapologetically made of some endangered species and with a fat little sausage dog in a jeweled collar stuffed under her arm.

Jamie thought all her ideas were dreadful, and he might have rolled his eyes at the worst of them: something to do with the name she had come up with for that year's festival to be held in Copenhagen.

She had lifted her sunglasses and cast him a flinty look that could have stripped paint.

"Uh-oh," Phil Jensen had said in an undertone, "she never forgets."

At the time, Jamie had thought Phil was ribbing him. It had been the smallest thing, really, and Jamie had dismissed it within minutes of leaving the meeting.

But fast-forward to a few weeks ago, and there he was called into Phil's office. Vivian Ascot, whom he had never seen or even heard of since that day, had resurfaced, not in person, but in the form of an order.

Apparently, she had discovered some small-town bookstore owner whom she thought would be ideal for representing some of JHA's publishing, author and bookstore accounts.

Bookstores were a tricky marketing business these days, but apparently an independent owner had caught Vivian's attention by making her tiny town bookstore extremely viable, by making it, according to the letter Phil had read from, *the hub of the community.*

No matter that the publishing and bookstore accounts were Jamie's particular cup of tea, or that one of his genuine delights was working with authors. Miss Winton was being offered a job opportunity, sight unseen, and she wasn't to know Vivian Ascot was behind it.

And what's more, Ms. Ascot-Who-Never-Forgot, had specifically requested that Jamie be enlisted in the recruitment of Miss Winton.

"We're supposed to seduce her," Phil had said, dryly. "And that's a quote."

"Like some small-town bookstore owner wouldn't jump for joy at this opportunity?"

"Uh, my initial contact would make it seem like Ms. Winton is not exactly jumping. I'm not prepared to risk Vivian Ascot's displeasure. But it's more than that. Before you came on board here, we had hit a bit of a bump in the business road. Viv bailed us out. Failure is not an option."

We're supposed to seduce her. That had seemed like a very casual term of reference a few days ago.

Not so much now with Jessica Winton standing in front of him, crying.

She really could be a poster child for the small-town girl with her undyed hair pulled primly back, her basically makeup-free face, her guileless expression.

Despite the red jacket—he thought if it had been called burgundy the barge mix-up could have been avoided—there was something very understated about her. He moved in a world where people, and particularly women, drew attention *to* their assets, not away from them.

She had, he could see, a beautiful figure, and yet if he was to describe her look, he might call it *spinster librarian.* She'd probably be hurt to know it was *exactly* the look, had he not been distracted, that he would have assigned to a small-town bookstore owner, though one who was twenty years older than her.

Her expression was one of pure vulnerability: those huge dark tear-filled eyes, her thick lashes studded with diamond tears, the trembling of an unexpectedly tempting mouth.

Everything about her—except maybe that mouth—said wholesome. Fresh. Untainted. Easily hurt.

Which had made her a pretty natural mark for the likes of Debbie and the Gidgets Widgets team, unfortunately.

"It's going to be okay," he said and felt something he rarely felt: clumsily inept.

Not unsurprisingly, she was not at all reassured. He recalled he might have used that same expression *often* in that terrible year after his father had died, and his sister and his mother had not been reassured then either.

Jessica buried her face in her hands and wept.

He froze.

Do something, he snapped at himself.

What? a voice asked back.

Anything.

So, he patted her shoulder. The curve of it was so delicate that it felt as if he had whacked her. He withdrew his hand hastily. She hiccuped noisily. People were glancing at her. And then at him. As if he was supposed to know what to do.

He wanted to protest. *She's a job candidate, not a love interest.*

He ordered himself to back off and let her have her cry. It was not unnatural for her to be crying. She was ten minutes into her visit to one of the largest and most sophisticated cities in the world, and she'd been robbed.

"I'm sorry," he said, "I know it's a nasty turn of events."

The wrong thing to say—no surprise, underscoring what he had already deduced, great businessman and emotional moron that he was—as her sobs, muffled by her hands, became louder.

"It's going to be okay," he repeated, even though those very words had had no effect on any of the many occasions he had used them.

It occurred to him words—or at least not any he could think of—were simply not going to cut it.

To his own shock, some instinct moved him closer to her, instead of farther away. To his own shock, he tugged her hands from her face, scanned her tearstained cheeks, and then, with a sigh, folded his arms around her, and pulled her to him.

She did not resist, but snuggled into him like a wet kitten rescued from a storm. Nothing could have prepared him for that, either: the softness of her, the warmth of her, the way she was making him feel, well, manly, in a way he was not sure he had ever experienced before.

She sobbed against his chest, her tears leaving a warm patch that was threatening to melt even his ever cynical heart.

He could smell a heady scent coming off her hair, which was tickling the bottom of his chin. What was that? Lavender? Since when did he know what lavender smelled like? And yet it seemed as if he could picture a field full of those tall purple blooms, with her walking through it, her hand grazing the top of the flowers like a blessing.

He gave himself a mental shake and wondered if he should say something to hurry this along before he ended up picturing himself in that field of lavender with her.

There, there seemed too grandfatherly. *Pull yourself together* seemed too hard and *I understand how you're feeling* would have been a stretch.

After what seemed to be at least an hour, the length between the sobs—he was timing them, though he thought that was probably supposed to be for contractions—lengthened and then lengthened a little more, until they stopped and she drew in a long, shuddering sigh.

Finally, she stepped away from him.

His eyes went to one of the airport clocks. Three minutes, not an hour. He looked back at her. Her face was blotchy, her hair was mussed and the front of her blouse, where it had been pressed against him, was creased. Three minutes of crying could cause quite a look of dishevelment in a woman!

"Thanks. I'm sorry." She looked mortified with herself. She gazed in the region of the wet blotches on his shirt, appalled, and then said, again, "I'm sorry."

"Don't be."

"I'm tired. And I'm hungry. And basically, I'm a mess. How do you like me, so far?"

Thankfully, she did not seem to be waiting for an answer, because the truth was, he did find her oddly appealing at the same time that he did not think she was cut out for the high-pressure world of JHA.

It was harsh judgment, but there it was. Despite the fact he was supposed to seduce her to take the job, he could feel himself planning the exact opposite. He'd show her around the city, as per plan, gently dissuade her from a career at JHA, then put her back on a plane as soon as they got her passport sorted out. He'd announce his failure to the powers that be, and then get on with his life as if she had never happened.

It occurred to Jamie, with just a bit of shock, that maybe it wasn't all about her. That maybe he felt a need to protect himself from this small-town girl and the things she could coax out of him without half trying.

She sniffed. "I don't even have a tissue."

He wasn't sure if she wanted the tissue for her little red nose, or to try to repair the damage to his shirt.

"I don't even have a tissue," she repeated. The issue of the tissue as a sign of her complete destitution seemed as if it might push her over the edge again, so Jamie hurriedly pulled the pocket square from his suit and handed it to her.

Thankfully, she dabbed delicately at her nose and left the front of his shirt alone. She had a very cute nose, small and a little turned up at the end. Her bottom lip was trembling a bit, and it was more than cute. Full and plump. Jamie gave himself an annoyed mental shake.

Even though he was determined she would never work for him, a little propriety was in order. Which meant not trying to guess what those lips would taste like.

She was vulnerable. He did not take advantage of the vulnerable. Or sweet girls from small towns.

Embracing her had been a mistake—visions of lavender fields proof of that—but it was one he now intended to quickly rectify.

"Let's get you settled," he said, his voice a touch on the curt side, more to remind himself than her of the nature of their relationship. "I have a car outside."

She stepped out the doors with him, and flinched as they were plunged into even more madness; horns honking, tires squealing, the smell of hot engines on a summer night.

"It's dark already," she said.

He glanced at his phone. "Ten p.m."

She nodded. "I'd forgotten. A three-hour time difference."

JHA had several cars and drivers at their disposal, but when the uniformed driver held open the door of the Bentley for Jessica, she took in the well-appointed opulence inside the vehicle with little pleasure. In fact, she seemed to sink even a little more into herself. By the time he got in the other door, she was squished up against her own door and staring straight ahead. She looked very pale. And fragile. She was clutching his pocket square as if it was a lifeline.

The car pulled away from the curb, and headed for the Grand Central Parkway, Jamie realized he needed to take charge of this situation.

"We've got a forty-minute drive into Manhattan. Let's make use of it and get you started on canceling credit cards and your phone," he suggested, and pulled his tablet from a pouch in the door. "Maybe contact your bank about emergency funds. You can use this, and I'll make some calls to see what the procedure is to have your passport reported missing and then replaced."

He quickly put in his password and handed her the open tablet. He was entering his comfort zone—take action—but she was staring numbly at the computer on her lap.

"Bring up your credit card company," he directed her, and then plunged into his own calls. He covered the phone with his hand for a moment. "Maybe try the chat feature if they have one."

When he disconnected from his calls, she had closed the computer.

"The bank's website had a number I can call tomorrow about emergency funds. Meanwhile, the cards are canceled," she reported, "and my phone. Thank you for realizing how important that was. I think I'm so shaken, I would have overlooked that and had a billion-dollar phone bill to who knows where on top of everything else."

"Great." He ticked off their accomplishments on his fingers. "Credit cards canceled. Phone canceled. We'll work on your bank and the passport tomorrow. The Canadian Consulate isn't open right now, but we'll go see them first thing in the morning. From what I could tell, it looks as though there is a procedure for issuing emergency travel documents or a temporary passport."

"Thank you, again, for taking charge."

He smiled at her, the kind of reassuring smile, he hoped, that said, *See? No more tears are necessary.* "I'm in the zone. Solving problems is my specialty. So moving on, are you up to tackling the police report?"

"I'm sorry, no."

He lifted an eyebrow at her. A more sophisticated companion would have gotten it: *I'm trying to take your mind off things. Play along. Don't make it any more awkward than it already is.*

But she shook her head. "I'm exhausted. I've been traveling for two days. Timber Falls is not close to a major airport. You have to drive for a day to get to one. And then I chose a hotel close to the airport, and couldn't sleep for planes and sirens and noise. And then, this."

See? It was going to get awkward. That luscious bottom lip was trembling again.

"I should have never let go of my suitcase handle. What was I thinking? What kind of idiot lets their guard down in New York City?"

He wanted to tell her the crime rate in the city had been dropping since the 1990s and it was now considered one of the safest large cities in the United States, but it seemed she might not appreciate that insight at the moment.

"Would it be a mugging, would you say?" she asked. "I mean, I guess I would assume some violence in a mugging. It felt violent. He did push me."

"Are you hurt?" The hospital! Good grief, here he was looking after all the business details, solving problems, and she was in need of medical assistance. It made Jamie realize, surprised, that he might be feeling a little more off balance than he was prepared to let on. To her, and even more, to himself.

"Oh, no, I'm not hurt physically. Just shaken. Badly."

She held out her hand. He could see it was trembling like a leaf in a breeze. Without asking her, and propriety be damned, Jamie pushed a built-in panel in the back of the driver's seat that opened a minibar. He poured her a generous cognac and handed it to her.

For a moment she stared at it silently, as if she planned to refuse. Then she grabbed it, took a sip, wrinkled her nose and then tossed the whole thing back.

She shuddered, from her toes to her head, then held out the glass.

Clearly, she wanted more. Clearly, that would be a dumb idea. Still, her hand had stopped shaking and the drink seemed to have dried up the tears.

Besides, who was he, in this age of equality, to tell an adult woman she should not have another drink?

He poured her a second shot, hoping she wouldn't notice it was not quite as generous as the first one. She downed it, handed him back the empty glass and then leaned deeply back into the seat, tilted her chin up, sighed and solved the problem of distracting her by closing her eyes.

Jessica did not open her eyes for the rest of the ride, even when the driver slammed on the brakes to avoid colliding with a cab that was darting in and out of traffic and blasting his horn.

Apparently, if she'd had interest and curiosity about the sights and sounds of New York, she had totally lost that interest now. Jamie suspected any slight interest she'd had in the job was also gone, and he felt too sorry for her to even be gleeful that pushing her toward getting back on that plane was going to be so easy.

Now what? It occurred to Jamie, even to get through a few days until they got the passport sorted out, she was going to need absolutely everything, from toothpaste to a temporary phone.

He could sense the most curious feeling rising up in him. Panic?

Or maybe it was something else. That old feeling, near the surface anyway, because of the tears, coming now with a vengeance. The weight of the almost unbearable responsibility of becoming the provider for the family way too young, feeling he was totally in charge of the well-being of his mother and sister.

Once his sister was safely through college and then married, and his mother in the apartment that had been his first big purchase to celebrate his business successes, he had sworn he would never feel that way again.

Still, he was glad he had thought of it. Because little sister, Sarah, owed him a favor or two.

He had actually never thought his sister owed him anything, but desperate times called for desperate measures, as the old adage went.

He didn't realize he'd said it out loud until Jessica, without opening her eyes, said, her voice just a tiny bit slurred, "Hippocrates."

He was not sure he'd ever met a woman who could pin a quote to Hippocrates before. A woman, who by the way, was going to need everything...including underwear.

Hey, Hippocrates, can it get much more desperate than that?

Casting a glance at her, it seemed like, despite the reference to Hippocrates, she might be sleeping—or at least trying to shut out the world, not that he blamed her—he fished his phone out of his pocket and hit the message icon.

He tapped in the first letters of Sarah, and the box came up. He realized he hadn't talked to his sister since his nephew, Jared's, second birthday. A month ago. Now was not the time for guilt, however. He'd already felt guilty once today, and that was his quota for the month. Maybe the year. He didn't see any point beating around the bush, either.

Hey, I need your help.

There seemed to be quite a long pause, and then:

Who are you and what have you done with my brother?

Don't be smart. I'm serious.

What's wrong?

Just leaving JFK. I picked up a…

Jamie glanced at Jessica. Her eyes were clamped tightly shut, like a child pretending to be asleep. Some of her hair, light brown and wispy as an angel's feather, had fallen out of the clip and was lying across her cheek. But if he was not mistaken, a little purr, almost like a snore, was coming from her.

Maybe he should have given her champagne instead of cognac? This was why he needed his sister. He had a feeling, with an unknown entity like Jessica Winton, he could do everything wrong.

A business acquaintance. Her luggage was stolen. And her purse.

What? Oh, no!

She has nothing. No computer, no phone, no cash, no credit cards, no clothes.

He decided not to put the *no underwear* part. His sister was clever. She would figure it out.

What do you need from me?

He'd ignored her for a month, and yet, there she was, no questions asked, ready to do what family did. He had thought he was going to have to play his *you owe me* card but she was volunteering willingly. Really, he wasn't worthy of her, not that he planned to let that stop him from asking for her help.

But suddenly, he wasn't sure what he was asking her. He suspected it was to not let him be alone with the burden of Jessica's distress. He suspected it was to get rid of the terrible sense of failure he felt for not catching on that he was being skillfully distracted and then for not catching the thief. Now, he felt a terrible responsibility for making it all better for the small-town bookstore owner who had just experienced the very worst that New York had to offer.

That was a responsibility he could not trust himself with. At all. His sister he could trust with it.

Maybe you could take her shopping? If we could get her set up with a few basics until we figure out what to do about...

Getting rid of her seemed a touch harsh so he put:

...everything. I'll pay.

You're paying? For a shopping trip? I'm in. Is she young or old? Big or little?

Considering he was asking his sister to go shopping with a stranger, these were probably not unreasonable questions, but he felt annoyed by them. Surreptitiously, he snapped a picture of the snoozing Jessica and sent it.

The pause between texts seemed unreasonably long.

What have you done to her?

Nothing! She's had a long day. And a terrible shock. And a shot of cognac.

She's cute.

It was his turn to be silent.

In an understated way.

He remained silent.

She doesn't look like a cognac drinker.

Did that sound faintly accusatory? That was the problem with texting. The nuances of communication were completely missing. He refused to respond.

I'll get a sitter. Tomorrow morning?

Perfect.

Jamie disconnected, and thought, way too late, it might have been a mistake to involve his sister. Jessica let out a long sigh that blew a tendril of her hair up off her cheek. Her hair was coming out of the clip that held it. He had thought at first her hair was nondescript, a shade of light brown he was pretty sure they used the term "mousy" for. But there in the darkened car, only the lights from the dash and his phone screen for illumination, her hair lying across her shoulder looked as if it had been spun from unrefined gold nuggets. He was aware of that scent, subtle and sweet, a field of lavender, wrapping itself around him.

He suddenly had more misgivings about his plan. Was his sister's arrival to rescue him tomorrow enough? What about tonight? What was Jessica going to sleep in tonight? Would the hotel have a shop that was open and that sold something suitable?

He could feel a little throb beginning behind his eyes.

He realized he didn't want to think about what she slept in, not tonight or any other night either.

He'd give her his credit card. She could buy something to sleep in. He wouldn't know what it was, thank God, until the bill came. She could order food, too. It would be nice if he did that for her, but he had a feeling she was the kind of person it could prove dangerous to be nice to.

Mistake or not, he was going to be very glad to turn her over to Sarah.

CHAPTER THREE

JESSICA WOKE SLOWLY. She didn't open her eyes right away. Momentarily, she had no idea where she was. There was a lovely scent in the air—leather and spice. She wanted to just snuggle down into the deep seat, sleep, shut out the world. She was aware of noise outside, a constant hum, but in here it felt soothing and quiet.

A hand touched her shoulder, and she opened her eyes. There was a man leaning toward her. A very handsome man with gray-and-silver hair and sexy stubble and animal-dark eyes. It was his scent that was tickling her nostrils.

She smiled at him. He looked nonplussed.

And then it all came flooding back to her.

Little sleep.

No supper.

John F. Kennedy Airport.

Jamie Gilbert-Cooper.

A robbery.

Two shots of cognac.

And, added to the equation, she was pretty sure her hair was falling out of the clip she'd held it back with, and that she was sporting a pool of drool on her lovely red jacket.

Her smile faltered and then died.

The jacket that she was going to have to wear for days. Since she did not have one other thing. Not even a tissue. Oh, wait. She still had Jamie's pocket square clutched in her hand. She dabbed surreptitiously at the drool spot.

"We're at the hotel," Jamie, her potential new boss, who had now seen her bawl her eyes out, glue herself to him and pass out, told her. "We'll get you checked in, and you can do what you need to do to rest up. I'll give you my credit card so you can pick up anything you need tonight. In the morning, my sister is going to take you shopping for a few…ah, necessities."

Did the faintest wave of color move up those cheeks when he said that?

Oh, *necessities.*

Somehow it was nice, though, that he was capable of discomfort even though he looked like the kind of man who would handle a woman's *necessities* with a certain suave aplomb. It was also nice that he had a sister. A family made him a little less cover-model-for-*GQ* and a little more human.

Which was actually more dangerous than cover model!

Jessica wanted to protest the shopping trip with his sister, but really? She was not in a position to protest anything, and his sister shopping with her was a relief, given the *necessities* part of the shopping equation.

She contemplated the plight she found herself in, and the phrase *beggars cannot be choosers* took on new meaning.

Beggars, like her, who had only the clothes she wore and a borrowed pocket square. The driver held open the door of the vehicle, and the quiet of the car was invaded by the sounds of the city. Jamie exited easily, a man in his element on streets crowded with busy people, even at this time of night.

She wanted to shrink away from the sudden bustle, but Jamie was holding out a hand to her. She hesitated, then took it. His hand closed around hers, and she could feel his strength and his confidence. She also felt a little thrill of excitement that had nothing to do with her first glimpse of Manhattan.

It was in reaction to that sensation that as soon as she was free of the car, she pulled her hand out of his, unfortunately staggering a little bit when she did so. She couldn't possibly be drunk. Could she?

To her utter embarrassment, Jaime was looking at her as if he was wondering the same thing!

When was the last time she had had anything to eat? She remembered soggy eggs on toast at a hotel—that was not at all in the same league as this hotel—early this morning.

She looked past Jamie, and the streams of people enjoying a warm summer night, to the hotel. The sandstone was lit up with a floodlight and glowed like polished marble. A black awning stretched out. A uniformed doorman already held open the door in anticipation of them stepping through it.

Jessica's legs felt suddenly wobbly, and when Jamie offered his arm, she had no choice but to take it. Again, she could feel strength and confidence radiating off him.

The hotel lobby was refreshingly cool and relatively quiet after the warmth and activity outside, and it was jaw-droppingly posh. Soaring ceilings were plastered with a motif, and lit by gorgeous chandeliers, dangling crystals dancing with light. Deep rugs lay over highly polished dark hardwoods, and there was inviting furniture groupings in subtle, elegant neutrals. Under different circumstances she might appreciate it more.

Now, she wanted to say goodbye to Jamie. It would be too easy to get used to leaning on him. Jessica was not a leaner! She needed to collect herself. She wanted to go to her room and shut the door. She'd call her parents and not let on that a single thing was amiss. She'd act breezy and happy and as if she was having the adventure of her life. She'd take advantage of being in the big city and order room service. She'd have a bubble bath.

When she was feeling solid again, she would email Aubrey and Daisy. Or maybe, depending on the time differences, call one of them on WhatsApp.

They'd make her laugh about it. They'd let her know it was not the end of the world. They'd encourage her to see a fun side of it.

Then it hit her.

Email.

WhatsApp.

Part of the life of someone who owned a little something more than the rumpled clothes they wore and a damp, borrowed pocket square.

She and Jamie approached the main desk. Ever sensitive, she felt the look on the desk clerk's face seemed to change ever so slightly when he saw them. Did his nose tilt toward the air, just a tiny bit?

No luggage, she realized. And a splotch on her jacket. Her hair spilling out of the clip in an untidy mess. Her walking was just a little wobbly, despite the solid strength of the man beside her. Good grief, the desk clerk thought—

She stopped dead, and Jamie stopped beside her and looked askance at her.

"I think he thinks we're, um," she lowered her voice to a whisper, and stood on her tiptoes, "having an evening… er…tryst."

"A what?" Jamie lowered his ear to her lips.

She had a horrible temptation to nibble it. Which would confirm the clerk's worst suspicions. She wasn't drunk. She wasn't. But had the two shots been enough to lower her inhibitions? Was she looking at Jamie with the same naked avarice as Debbie had?

She could feel herself blushing thinking about it. "We don't have any luggage. And I might look a little come-hither."

"Come-hither?"

"You know what I mean."

Clearly he did not.

"He thinks we're having a dalliance," she whispered.

Jamie reared back from her and stared at her. "Who thinks that?" he asked, a warrior look on his face like he wouldn't mind knocking some sense into someone.

She nodded toward the clerk. Jamie scowled in that direction, but didn't, apparently, reach the same conclusion as her. He looked back at her.

"Look," he said, his tone very quiet and obviously aiming for a patience and failing somewhat, "this is not the opening chapter of a Brontë novel, filled with dalliances and come-hithers and trysts."

She frowned at him, and said stiffly, "You obviously are not familiar with the opening chapters of any novel by either Charlotte or Emily."

"And thank God for that," he returned. "I'm just trying to make the point this is the big city. I'm sure in Lumber Falls people might be making note of who is checking into the local hotel with whom, but people here don't really take that kind of interest in each other."

"It's Timber Falls," she said, correcting him on the only point she could, as the other was very accurate.

He lifted a shoulder with insulting indifference to the nuances between Lumber and Timber.

And the snooty clerk was still watching them.

"He takes that kind of interest," Jessica said stubbornly.

Jamie apparently didn't care what the desk clerk thought. With a formidable expression on his face, he took her elbow, guided her up to the desk and presented a business card.

She saw the attitude shift again as the clerk skimmed the card. He glanced at her again.

Like she was the main character in *Pretty Woman*. Pre-transformation. Not that she looked anything like Julia Roberts.

"He's an evil little person," she said, standing on tiptoes to whisper that information into Jamie's ear. Too late, she realized to the clerk, it may have looked like a love nibble.

I am drunk, she decided. *No, not drunk. Tipsy.*

"Mr. Gilbert-Cooper, how may I assist you?"

"This is Miss Jessica Winton. You have a reservation made for her by my company?"

"I've lost my luggage," she said, as way of explanation, to erase the possible perception of a nibble of Jamie's ear and any remaining *tryst* thoughts from the clerk's mind. It occurred to her, as the clerk tapped furiously on his computer, that her breath might be boozy, and the word *lost* might be a trifle slurred. Those facts probably overrode her explanation for her lack of luggage.

Still, how she envied him that computer! On the other hand, the hotel would have one, wouldn't they? A business center, with computers in it? Or was that old-school? Did everyone travel with their own computer now?

"Here you are," the clerk crowed, as if he was surprised to find her. "Miss Winton, if I could just have your credit card and a matching photo identification, I'll complete the booking."

"There's been an incident," she said. "I'm afraid I don't have that."

Did the clerk smirk? His every suspicion confirmed?

Jamie's tone brooked no nonsense. "The room is confirmed already on the JHA credit card. As for ID, I'll have to show you mine. Miss Winton experienced an unfortunate event at the airport. Her luggage and purse were stolen."

"I just said lost for the sake of expediency," she added. Jamie shot her a look that suggested she might not be being helpful.

"Oh," the clerk said, and his discomfort in the face of Jamie's tone seemed genuine enough, "that is very unfortunate, but I have to see the identification of everyone who stays in the hotel. It's mandatory."

"I just told you I would show you mine instead."

"Are you staying in the hotel?"

"Are you being deliberately obtuse?" Jamie asked dangerously. "She's had her identification stolen."

"Sir," the clerk's voice was actually trembling, but Jessica could not help feel he was secretly pleased by this turn of events. "I can't. Check her in. Without ID."

"My company booked the room, I'm sure you recognize the name?"

"I do, but—"

"I can give you a generous deposit against any damages."

"It's not about damages. It's a legal requirement. Homeland Security. Medical emergencies. What if, heaven forbid, the hotel caught on fire? Or what if the maid went into the room in the morning, and she was lying there, comatose?"

Was that a dig at the boozy breath? Jessica wondered, narrowing her eyes at him.

"We have to have proof on file of exactly who every person in the hotel is."

It was just like a scene from that movie. Jessica realized she, most unlikely person to ever be mistaken for a miscreant, was being refused a hotel room. The worst possible thing was happening inside of her, a slow giddy trembling. It was worse than her crying.

Jessica giggled.

Jamie and the clerk both turned to stare at her.

She put her fist to her mouth, but another giggle escaped.

And then a snort of laughter. Despite her pressing against her mouth harder with her fist, more laughter.

Okay, it had a hysterical edge to it, enough so that Jamie was staring at her with concern—the *Is she going to make a scene?* kind of concern—and the clerk with an *I knew it* expression on his face.

Jamie was suddenly at her elbow, completely composed, guiding her out the door the way they had come in.

They got back in the car that had been waiting for them.

The door whispered shut and she sank into the silence, feeling as if she'd been rescued from a close call with crocodiles.

Jamie was looking straight ahead. His lips were twitching. She couldn't tell if it was with suppressed amusement or suppressed annoyance.

"I'm sorry," Jessica said. "I can't imagine what made me laugh."

"The cognac?" he suggested.

"Nerves," she insisted, trying to sound very sober. And then she added, hearing a certain defensiveness in her tone, "I haven't eaten for quite some time."

"Maybe just the absurdity of life," he suggested, rolling his shoulders back. She suspected he much preferred the burst of laughter to her earlier tears. The driver was waiting for instructions, but Jamie was obviously considering his next move.

"My place," he told the driver, finally.

Jessica felt suddenly and instantly sober. "Your place? I'm not sure. I don't think—"

"If you can think of some other options, let me know," he cut her off, his tone reflecting a souring mood. "I can drop you at the homeless shelter, if you prefer."

He groaned at the horror on her face and tilted his head back against the seat. "Sorry. Kidding."

Their choices seemed limited, indeed. But, still, his place? It seemed wildly inappropriate.

Though, just under her resistance to the idea, was a shameful curiosity. What did a man like Jamie Gilbert-Cooper live like? She was willing to bet no socks on the floor or dishes in the sink. It would be a rather intimate glimpse into his life. Under normal circumstances, she would not give in to the temptation to know a little more about him. But these were not normal circumstances.

"It will probably be just for tonight," he said. "Tomorrow, I'll have someone at the office start to figure out the details of getting your identification replaced. And getting you home."

He sounded quite eager about that, she thought.

"It's very kind of you to offer, um, your place," Jessica said. "I just don't want to put you out." She had heard people lived small in New York City. Even very well-to-do people, which he obviously was. Was he going to sleep on the couch? Was she?

"My place is not a studio walk-up in Greenwich Village," he said, as if he could read her mind. "You won't be on a roll-out sofa for the night. I think you'll find it quite comfortable."

"Oh. It's just that—"

"You're concerned about trysts?" he asked dryly. "Dalliances?"

She blushed. "Of course not," she protested.

He, apparently, was not convinced.

"The perception of trysts? This is strictly business."

Why would she feel faintly insulted by that—as if he would never even consider a tryst with her! As if *she* needed to be reminded it was strictly business.

"I can go get a hotel if it would make you feel better," he offered. "Though I'm just not sure if it's the best idea to leave you alone. I think we should order some food as soon as we get in, since we've determined cognac is not an answer."

"Oh, I don't want you to go to any more trouble," she said, a trifle stiffly. "Just a couple of slices of toast would be fine."

"I don't cook," he said.

She cocked her head at him. *She'd been right about no dirty dishes in the sink, then.* Still, she had to ask.

"You consider toast cooking?"

"I do."

"Oh."

That should have made the differences between them more than apparent—a chasm they could not cross—but she felt, crazily, more curious about his world than ever. Perceptions of trysts aside, she realized she was *glad* she was going to his place, as if she was a science fiction fan being offered a glimpse into a world that was unimaginable until you had actually seen it with your own eyes.

"What do you think you'd like to eat?"

Toast, she thought stubbornly, but decided not to press the issue. "I bet you can get good pizza in New York City."

"I'd say the best in the world."

"My luck is changing!"

He actually smiled at her.

In that smile, she saw something you could rely on and lean into. She had nothing. To add to her other losses today, she had just, humiliatingly, been refused a hotel room. And yet he was just the kind of man who made it seem like everything would be all right.

That *he* could make everything all right.

Tentatively, she smiled back at him. And then, before he took it as an affront to his strictly business attitude, she quickly turned her attention out her window, watching with interest as New York City unfolded before her.

He pointed it out when they passed through Times Square, and the famous Theater District. She recognized Macy's and the Metropolitan Museum of Art, the Empire State Building. The traffic was chronically snarled and it seemed to take forever to move a small distance, but the constant noise and activity outside the car held her interest. New York City was a constant swirl of movement, light and sound.

His apartment building, across from a park, impossibly seemed fancier than the hotel they had left behind. When they got out of the car, she didn't know what to look at first.

"Is that Central Park?" she asked.

He followed her gaze, and said with affection, "None other."

"I thought it would be scary. Especially at night."

Instead, she saw that even though it was now after 11:00 p.m., the park was a well-lit beautiful space. Young couples were strolling…people were walking their dogs. A runner in colorful spandex flew by. A horse-drawn carriage was clopping along in the distance.

A horse-drawn carriage ride through Central Park was on her secret list of things she wanted to do in the short period of time she was here.

"One of the many misconceptions about New York is that Central Park is not safe," Jamie told her. "The park is closed between 1:00 a.m. and 6:00 a.m. but most of the rest of the time it's pretty well populated. Naturally you would want to stay to the well-traveled paths, but it's quite beautiful at night."

In Timber Falls everything was closed after six at night! Except Wilbur's Watering Hole. Somehow, Jessica didn't want to share that with him, though.

A doorman opened the door, greeted Jamie by name and tipped his hat to her, supremely indifferent to her business with Jamie. Did that mean he came through here with women frequently, not as unfamiliar with dalliances and trysts as he was letting on?

None of your business, Jessica told herself firmly. She turned her attention to the lobby of the building, which was more understated than the hotel lobby had been, but every bit as opulent.

The lobby should have prepared her for his apartment, but it didn't. He had a special key for the elevator and it opened directly into his apartment, which made her think of something out of a James Bond movie. Lights whispered on automatically as soon as the elevator doors opened. There was a bank of floor-to-ceiling windows that looked out over the park and made the nightscape of the city that surrounded it look like a sparkling painting.

The living room, kitchen and dining room were all one large open space.

She could not stop herself from moving toward the kitchen. She ran her hand along the leathered granite of a huge kitchen island and then turned to look at the banks of white cabinets and the shining stainless steel appliances.

"It's incredible that you don't use a kitchen that looks like this," she mused. "Look at it. Double ovens!"

"What does one use a double oven for?"

She shot him a look to see if he was kidding. He was not.

"Thanksgiving dinner. Christmas dinner." She could not contain a sigh of pure longing. "Turkey in one. Pies in the other. It's always a problem."

He was giving her a look as if she came from another planet. That look should have been enough to stop her exploring, but no, she might never see anything like this again.

She shamelessly oohed and ahhed over the wine cooler,

a built-in barista-style coffee maker, the cleverly hidden pull-out-drawer-style dishwasher.

She stopped at the fridge. "It looks big enough to park a Volkswagen in," she said. "Can I peek inside?"

He nodded, watching her with *that* look, the one she couldn't quite decipher. The one where she didn't know if he found her annoying or amusing.

The fridge had zones in it! And yet, it was relatively empty. A few condiments, a container of cream, three bottles of imported beer.

The fridge seemed to mirror the rest of his space. Nothing had a "used" look to it. The polished counters were bare of the clutter of daily life. There wasn't even a sugar bowl or a paper roll out. Where were the dish towels?

She turned her attention to the rest of the space. No books out, not even a newspaper tossed carelessly. No family pictures. Definitely no socks. The artwork was gorgeous, but all abstract, revealing nothing about him.

The space should have cemented him in her mind as what he was: cosmopolitan, busy, not home much.

Instead, the perfection of it, the ready-for-the-posh-interiors-magazine-cover-shoot, made her feel oddly sad. His home was beautiful, and yet it did not have any soul.

When she turned to study him, it was obvious to her that he was beautiful, too, but that he did have soul, a great strength of character, a composure that rose above the inevitable chaos of life.

"Your space is gorgeous," she said, quietly.

"Why do I sense a *but*?" he asked, cocking his head at her.

"It doesn't really suit you," she ventured, feeling as if she was being way too personal, and at the same time that honesty was called for.

"Ah. I'll have to speak to the designer about that." She

could tell he wanted to leave it there, but curiosity got the better of him. "In what way doesn't it suit me?"

She did not know him well enough to weigh in on that. He could be her future boss, after all. Still, she couldn't stop herself.

"It doesn't feel like a home. It feels like a hotel."

For a moment, he looked stunned. And then he raised an eyebrow at her. "But that suits me perfectly," he said.

No, it doesn't. For just a moment, she could picture him tossing a child in the air, toys on the floor, the space filled with the good smells of things cooking and laughter and motion, and his vitality.

That imagined picture brought a tinge of color to her cheeks.

It had just been a too long and eventful day that had brought on this flight of fancy. You did not picture the man who could be your boss—obviously single and successful and not willing to change one thing about his glorious playboy lifestyle—in a scene of domestic contentment.

Was she in that scene with him? Good grief! Was that *their* baby the Jamie of her imagination was playing with?

The renegade thoughts were stunning. She had put away such longings what seemed to be a lifetime ago. To hope for such things was to reopen a place in herself that was completely barricaded from the possibility of ever hurting the way she had once hurt...hadn't she known, even when she met Ralph in Copenhagen, he could not touch that place inside of her? But this man...

"I have to call my parents," she blurted out, as a way of grounding herself.

"Sure. Let's just get the pizza ordered first. Have a seat," he invited with a careless sweep of his hand. He was unknotting the tie from his throat, and it felt enticingly intimate to witness that moment. She scurried over to a deep leather chair that looked toward the view, instead of at him.

"Pizza," he said, still taking charge, still solving problems. Of which, she reminded herself firmly, she was one. "Any preferences?"

"The wilder the better," she said.

When she cast a look at him, she could see his mouth had dropped open, and she was happy to have surprised him.

He was studying her with interest. "You are a walking contradiction, aren't you? The big family gathering dinners, and then the wilder the better taste."

Her happiness at his surprise dissolved as she realized the possibility for double entendre. "I was only talking about pizza!" she stammered.

"Of course you were," he said soothingly, but not before she saw the wicked satisfaction cross his features. She had caught him off balance by weighing in on his style, and now he was enjoying catching her off balance, as well.

"Don't you have traditional family celebrations here?" she asked him, remembering he had mentioned his sister, the one who would be shopping with her tomorrow.

"No," he said, a little too curtly, as if by asking about his family, she had crossed a line.

"I have to call my parents," she reminded him—and herself—again. And she could see the fact she was going to check in with her parents negated, completely, any wild thoughts he was having concerning her.

As if.

He ordered pizza first. When he handed her the phone, she said, "Please keep track of the costs, for the pizza and the long-distance call. I'll pay my share when I have funds."

His lips twitched. Again, she could not tell if it was amusement or annoyance. He didn't address her offer to pay at all, just handed her the phone.

"Let me show you the guest room and you can make your call there in privacy—"

As if she would have anything *private* to say to her parents.

Hey, Mom...hey, Dad. It's been a crazy introduction to New York City. I've been robbed, but rescued by this gorgeous man who might be my boss someday if I abandon you and Timber Falls, and by the way I'm staying in his apartment with him.

Her mom would have a heart attack and her dad would be on the next plane to New York.

"—and freshen up. By the time you're done, the pizza should have arrived."

Jessica trailed him down a wide hallway, taking a peek in the master bedroom as they went by. It faced those same Central Park city views, and held a massive bed that made her think, to her eternal horror, *the wilder the better.*

The guest room was gorgeous. The views did not face the park, and yet the cityscape was utterly breathtaking. He showed her through to the attached bath, and she saw it had a stand-alone tub and a deluxe Italian-tiled shower stall in it.

Bubble bath? Or shower? Somehow, she was not sure she could stand having a bubble bath in the same space he was in, even if walls did separate them. Besides, she was hungry, and a proper bath required a commitment of time.

Shower it would be, and she could not wait!

"Do you suppose I could borrow a T-shirt to use as a nightie?"

"Of course," he said smoothly, but something had flashed, just for a moment in the dark depths of those eyes, when she mentioned a nightie.

Or maybe not, because he continued speaking, the ideal host, unruffled by mentions of nighties. "Meanwhile, there's a canvas bag on the back of your bathroom door, if you put your clothes in that and set it outside, I'll have the concierge pick them up and have it laundered."

"At this time of night?"

He lifted his shoulder. Obviously anything was possible here, at any time of the night or day, and he didn't give it a second thought.

"So, you don't cook *or* do laundry?" she asked. The truth was that the thought of someone else doing her laundry was embarrassing to her.

"I'm often short on time. I cheerfully delegate anything I don't enjoy doing."

He left her, and then came back a few minutes later, knocking softly on her door before coming in and placing a selection of neatly folded T-shirts on her bed. Then he laid a plaid bathrobe—obviously his—beside the shirts.

He gave her his security code and left her his phone, then closed the doors behind him. Jessica unlocked the phone and called her parents. How high school crush was it that she was aware that her mouth on the phone was very close to where Jamie's mouth had been on that same phone?

I do not have any kind of crush on Jamie Gilbert-Cooper, Jessica told herself sternly.

He was her rescuer in a bad situation. Naturally, there would be some feelings of transference, like a hostage might feel for the Navy SEAL who saved her from a certain and horrible death at the hands of bad guys.

When her father picked up the phone, he wanted to know, immediately, why she was calling from a strange number. Her mother had started to worry an hour ago, and had been texting her. They were on speakerphone now, her mother denying she had been worried.

"I seem to be having trouble with the international phone plan I ordered," Jessica said. "It might be better if you didn't text me for a bit. I think I have to pay per text, and I'm not getting them anyway."

She hated lying to her parents, but she hated the thought of them worrying even more. She told them, breezily, she had been dropped into an episode of *Lifestyles of the Rich and Famous*. Without mentioning she was in a private apartment, she described the room she was in to her home decorating channel obsessed mother.

"Send me a picture," her mother said. "Or put some on Facebook."

"Um, I will when I get my phone plan sorted out. I don't want to use any data just yet."

"Doesn't the hotel have internet?" her mother insisted.

"Oh, it's late here. I'll try to do some Facebook updates tomorrow." From the computer at the public library. That was on her list of must-sees. The New York Public Library. "I haven't eaten yet."

"Don't go out by yourself!" her mother warned.

"Don't worry, I'm ordering pizza."

After listening to a long list of instructions from her mother about opening her hotel door to the deliveryman, she tried to hang up. But her mother had to give her quite a lengthy description of her father fiddling with a lock system for the house and her store that could be operated from a cell phone. Jessica was finally able to disengage. She wondered about her impatience. Was it because Jamie would be waiting for her with pizza? She couldn't help but also wonder what he would make of an adult woman getting those kind of instructions from her mother.

Maybe Daisy and Aubrey were right when they weighed in that perhaps her life was too small.

Suffocating.

The word, popping into her head, stunned Jessica, and

made her feel guilty. She quickly turned her thoughts in a different direction.

She had his cell phone. She had his security code. She could sign in and send a quick private message to her friends. Or she could have a quick look through his photos. It would tell her all kinds of delicious information about her host.

She was not that kind of person! Snoopy and deceitful. *One little look...*

No! Before she could change her mind she took his phone back out to him. He pocketed it with a quick nod, as if it had never even occurred to him that she might have a peek at the information on it.

Did that make her trustworthy? Or just plain boring?

She retreated back to her room and to the bathroom. She stripped off her travel-rumpled clothes, and the water from the shower pounding down did literally wash away all her cares. Jessica was not sure a shower had ever felt quite as wonderful as this one. The hot water alternated, blissfully, between pounding, spraying and misting. She accidentally touched a button and was bathed in soothing light. And then, more purposefully, she touched another button. Music flooded the shower stall.

Coincidentally, it was Daisy's first number one hit single, "Nothing is Impossible."

As the water massaged her skin, and the music spoke to her as if Daisy was right here coaxing her to dream big, Jessica was aware of feeling not frightened and not put out, but finally, relaxed and safe.

But it was more than that. And it was more than the contortions of the water coming from that showerhead that were making her skin tingle.

She became aware she felt fully and completely alive.

The sensation increased as she stepped out of the shower

and toweled off with deeply luxurious pure white Egyptian cotton towels, and then padded out to the bedroom and chose one of Jamie's T-shirts to slip over her head.

Despite the crispness of it, it smelled of him: clean and spicy, fragrant in an exquisitely masculine way that made all her senses vibrate, as if the air itself had taken on a quality that stroked her.

Feeling life so intensely begged the question: How did she feel most of the time? Asleep? Operating on some kind of autopilot?

Was it a reaction to overcoming a crisis that was bringing her this sense of being exquisitely and intensely aware of everything? Absolutely every single thing that could have gone wrong had, and yet, here she stood, more than a survivor, life handing her completely unexpected gifts.

Or was it from being in Jamie Gilbert-Cooper's space, surrounded by his things and his scents, his powerful energy permeating the very air she was breathing that left her feeling so aware? Perhaps when you had his kind of energy, you didn't have to decorate a space to reflect who you were?

She had a thought even more troubling. Was this sensation of being so alive, so open to what happened next, so ready for the strange adventure she found herself in, a message from her life?

Aubrey and Daisy had been hinting almost from the beginning that Jessica was in a rut, was playing it too safe, was not open to the truly sensational experience that was life.

It was true. Since her fiancé, Devon, had died what she had wanted, more than any other single thing, was for life to feel safe again. But in this moment, she was aware she didn't want that at all.

Jessica felt suddenly powerful, as if, just as Daisy's music had suggested, nothing was impossible. As if she could change her whole life and her whole outlook right now, right this very second.

For the first time it occurred to her that maybe she was going to accept this job offer.

And then, she eyed the bathrobe he had brought in. It was a man's, huge and plaid, and way too bulky for a summer night.

She shoved all her dirty laundry into the bag Jamie had provided. Let someone else do her laundry! The new Jessica Winton—bold, embracing the adventure of life—threw open her bedroom door and walked out into that luxe apartment in nothing more than her future boss's oversize T-shirt.

Well, she might have been hiding behind the laundry bag, just a touch.

CHAPTER FOUR

WHILE JESSICA WAS in the shower, Jamie waited for pizza—the-wilder-the-better-be-careful-what-you-ask-for-sweetheart-pizza—to be delivered.

Pizza. She was in New York City. She could have had anything. He had a list of favorite high-end five-star restaurants that were happy to deliver. But no, she wanted pizza, and insisted that she would pay her half when she had some funds.

Who walked into an apartment like this one—at one of New York's toniest addresses, the three-block stretch that formed Central Park South—and demanded to pay for half the pizza?

The same woman who had seen something here—or a lack of something—that no one else had ever seen. Seen something about *him* that people did not see.

The same woman who looked at his quarter-million-dollar kitchen remodel and did not see *arrival* but wondered about Christmas dinner. He had a feeling that she would not approve of the fact there had never even been a Christmas dinner here. There had never even been a Christmas tree.

She wouldn't approve, either, that the last female guest to his apartment had not had turkey on her mind. In fact, she'd had quite an interesting idea of what the kitchen island could be used for.

He had sent her home without testing her idea. He realized, now, something he had not realized at the time. It was probably the influence of his guest that made him articulate, within his own mind, what he had felt when his last disappointed guest had left the apartment.

Jamie was sick of the kind of women he had deliberately populated his life with. Fast and sophisticated, they liked all the trappings of success that this apartment represented. They didn't complicate his life.

Not a single one of them had ever suggested, of his space, *it doesn't really suit you.*

Why did he care about Jessica Winton's approval? *I do not* he told himself, but he was aware it was not quite the truth.

That very same woman who was worried a hotel desk clerk thought she was sporting a come-hither look was the kind of woman who could complicate a man's life before he knew what had hit him.

Jamie decided to entertain himself by looking up the phrase *come-hither.* It turned out the saying dated back to the 1800s. It indicated a look of sexual invitation, flirtation and seduction.

Even though he could not think of one person less likely than her to have such a look, he put down his phone as if it had burned him.

Who used a phrase like that?

A bookstore owner, apparently. One who also was familiar with quotes from Hippocrates and the works of the Brontë sisters.

Down the hall, he could hear the shower running in the spare bedroom en suite bathroom. She—Jessica Winton, of come-hither fame—was in his space.

But there would be no come-hithering of any sort. He was a professional. She was a professional. They had been dealt an unexpected hand. They would deal with it professionally. He heard the shower turn off. He imagined her dressed in nothing but a cloud of steam.

She had borrowed his phone to call her parents, he reminded himself. Not one single woman who moved in his circles called her parents to check in. Not under any circumstances.

She wouldn't be calling her parents if she had a boyfriend, or significant other. She'd be calling him. She wouldn't have come to New York to investigate a job opportunity, either.

Why was his brain insisting on acting like it had uncovered a very important truth about her? That she was single?

All he needed to know about Jessica Winton was that she was wholesome and innocent and in need of protection. And professionalism. Until he got rid of her. He was probably going to be struck dead with a bolt of lightning for even thinking of her dressed in only a cloud of steam.

When the doorman rang to let him know the pizza was here, Jamie nearly jumped out of his skin. He hated it that his unexpected charge had him wound up tight in some way he was not accustomed to. He elected to go down to the lobby and get the pizza, rather than have it brought up. He took the stairs.

When he came back into the living room, puffing slightly, Jessica was standing at the floor-to-ceiling window, in one of his T-shirts.

The value of the take-his-mind-off-Jessica run down the stairs was instantly dissolved. He might as well have saved his energy.

The T-shirt was falling off one of her shoulders, leaving it completely bare. The shoulder seams came down to her elbows, and the hem of the shirt ended past her knees. She didn't have on a speck of makeup or a piece of jewelry.

She hadn't put on the bathrobe he had provided, and

though that was completely understandable—it would have been way too large for her and it was summertime, not winter—he resented it.

Because there was something about her standing there, in only a T-shirt, her legs long and bare and slender, her body faintly and femininely curved against the thin fabric, that made his mouth go dry.

Jamie chided himself that he saw much more provocative outfits in the office daily. Really, she should have looked like a child playing dress-up.

Jessica turned and looked at him. Her hair was wet and curling, her face flushed pink from the shower. Her eyes looked huge, as seductive as the chocolate that they matched. She did not look like any kind of child at all. She did not look like she was innocent or in need of protection, either.

Her expression was about the furthest thing from come-hither that he could ever imagine. And yet he was unbelievably aware of her.

"The view is amazing."

He thought it was, too, and he didn't mean the park.

"Thanks," he said, congratulating himself on his professional tone, "I like it."

"I had no idea that Central Park was so huge," she said turning back to the window.

"It's eight hundred and forty acres. Forty-two million people a year visit it." He congratulated himself on the utter safety of a tour-guide-to-client conversation.

Forty million, nine hundred and ninety-nine thousand and ninety-nine of whom, had they seen his apartment, would have just taken it at face value. They would have seen arrival and success. Not a vague emptiness.

But she hadn't used the word *empty*. So where had that come from, that indictment of his life?

He glanced at his dining room table. Would he sit next to her? Across from her? Which would be less dangerous?

"It's a nice night," he said. "Do you want to eat pizza alfresco?" Side by side, on his deck, an end table in between them, less chance of those naked little toes touching him, or shoulders brushing, or eyes meeting. They could look at the view, instead of each other.

She laughed and he raised an eyebrow at her.

"In Italian," she explained, "that phrase means 'in the cool.' Usually, when an Italian says it, it refers to spending time in jail."

"You speak Italian?" he asked, incredulous. He had a sudden, totally unwanted vision, of her leaning in to him whispering, *Voglio fare l'amore con te.*

As if Jessica Winton would ever say something like that! It was wrong to even think it. It was right up there with come-hithering. Thankfully, she did not speak Italian.

"I just seem to collect information," she told him.

"Dibs on you for my Trivial Pursuit team." The weird thing was, he could picture playing Trivial Pursuit with her. At the Christmas celebration he had never hosted. Jamie gave his head a shake in an effort to clear any vision of Jessica Winton inhabiting any part of his future.

Not Christmas dinner. Not sexy Italian phrases. Not playing a game at the annual office party. Not come-hithering.

He slid the patio door open and the sounds of the city, along with warm summer air, rushed in. He held the door back, balancing the pizza in his hand, letting her go out first.

As she brushed by him, the lavender smell—the one that invoked visions of her, and possibly him, in a purple field together—was, thankfully, completely gone.

It was, unfortunately, replaced with something even more tantalizing.

Soap. Skin. Squeaky-clean hair. Something so purely feminine, it took his breath away.

He held the pizza box closer to his nose, hoping to banish all else. He pulled out a chair for her with his toe, and then set the pizza box on the table and took a chair on the opposite side of it. The park was growing quiet—it was probably close to midnight.

"Look! There's still a horse and carriage."

"I think they book the last rides at eleven thirty."

She got up from the table, and went to the railing. "It's a young couple," she reported. "Oh, my gosh, I think he's asking her to marry him. Come see."

Though it was against his better judgment, he joined her at the railing. Sure enough, eleven stories below them, a young man was presenting what looked to be a ring box to a young woman. Her squeal of delight rose over every other sound in the night.

"It's like something out of a fairy tale," Jessica said, with a happy sigh. As she turned back to the table, her shoulder—the naked one—brushed his arm.

Cue the music, he thought, to banish any red-hot thoughts that accidental brush, the one he had been hoping to avoid by choosing to dine alfresco, might cause. *Someday, my prince will come.* That was it *exactly*. Jessica Winton had the starstuck look on her face of a woman in search of a prince.

Scary.

Even scarier was his curiosity about why she hadn't found one.

He opened the pizza box, and offered her a slice. She took one, took a delicate bite and closed her eyes.

"Wild enough for you?" he asked.

She opened her eyes and glanced at him. He kept his expression deliberately bland. *Professional*, he congratulated himself.

"Definitely wild. And delicious. I come from a pepperoni-only family and I always seem to cave to the majority. This is a treat. Some kind of Mediterranean, right? Olives? Onions? Feta cheese?"

"Plus anchovies and hot pickles. Here. I'll show you how to eat it like a New Yorker."

"New Yorkers eat pizza a certain way?"

"Of course." As she watched, he took the crust and rolled it neatly toward the triangular tip of the pizza.

"But now it's a sausage roll, not pizza!" she protested, watching him.

He took a bite, aware of her eyes on his lips, before they skittered away. "Try it before you knock it."

And so she did. She closed her eyes with pleasure as she bit into it. Now his eyes were on her lips!

"And so practical, too," she decided.

Considering how aware they both seemed to be now of each other's lips, he wasn't so sure about that.

"So," he said, after they had both staved off the worst of the hunger and were working on their second slices, "tell me why you think you might like to work for JHA. Because you don't really seem like the type who ends up in marketing."

Terrible timing for a job interview.

And yet he could not think of a better way to get his mind off the lusciousness of her lips closing over that roll of pizza. When he dragged his eyes from her lips, he noticed her naked leg sticking out from under his T-shirt. Her toenails were painted the palest shade of pink.

"The type?" she said. "What type do I seem like?"

The type who was targeted by thieves looking for an innocent. The type who phoned her parents. The type who harbored a belief—however secret—in fairy tales.

"I guess you don't seem like the type who would leave everything you know behind to find a new life," he said carefully.

"Really?" she said, the deliberately light tone of someone who was hiding something, "This pizza alone is enough to make me toss my old life."

"Pizza preferences aside, you seem like a picket fences kind of woman. And a solid guy who adores you and whose world revolves around you. Babies. A golden retriever. A summer cottage on the lake. A big Christmas tree, only real will do."

He was pretty sure, according to the employment standard act, you weren't allowed to say anything like that to a prospective employee. It was probably sexist as all get-out to offer conjecture about her lifestyle but he was deliberately trying to provoke her.

"Are you reaching these conclusions because I think your oven is ideally suited to the preparation of traditional feasts?" she asked. "Or because I think your house is more like a hotel than a home?"

"Traditional," he said. "That's what I'm trying to say. You seem more traditional than career oriented."

"And yet," she said calmly, "I've enjoyed great success in my career. I assume that's part of why I was invited here."

Sitting here on his deck, the sounds of New York calming for the night, the warm summer air embracing them, it felt as if he needed to know *more* about her than the career synopsis that had been put together for him by an office assistant. Admittedly, he had not even glanced at it until he got to JFK to pick her up.

"Though I did grow up with very traditional values and a lifestyle very close to what you described," she said, after a moment. "It's the life my parents had, and the life I always thought I would have, too."

"What made you change your mind?"

She hesitated. "That solid guy who adored me died."

"I'm so sorry." He looked at her face. He hadn't turned on the patio light, and it was alabaster in the subdued secondary lights from the city and the other apartments. Really, his intent had been a kind of casual job interview, not a prying into her personal life. But suddenly, he *had* to know. "Will you tell me what happened?"

"The world I grew up in, and that I always wanted—safe, predictable, traditional—was shattered in a second. Devon died in a skiing accident." Softly she said, "I don't want to leave myself open to believing in happily-ever-after again."

But he had the feeling she did, she just didn't want to believe she did.

"Tell me about the two of you."

Really?

Good night, Miss Winton, nice to make your acquaintance would have been the wiser choice!

Jamie did not have these kinds of conversations with people. And especially not female people who might be working for him someday soon.

"We grew up together," Jessica said. "I started preschool the same day Devon did. We had the same friends. Our parents were friends. We lived down the block from each other. We enjoyed all the things that growing up in a place like Timber Falls had to offer—hiking and camping, skiing and snowshoeing.

"We never really *fell* in love. We were always in love. We always knew, both of us, that we had been together forever and we always would be. But then, we weren't. He died our senior year in high school."

"He asked you to marry him in high school?" He couldn't keep the shock out of his voice.

She nodded, and tilted her chin at him, with faint stubbornness that said, *Just because we were young doesn't mean it wasn't real.*

Jamie grappled with what he was hearing. He knew from the fact sheet he had been given about her that she was twenty-six years old. That meant high school was seven or eight years behind her. It troubled him that even before high school she had been making huge choices. It sounded awfully young to be mapping out the entire course of your life, and choosing a life partner. It seemed criminal, somehow, that she had missed out on the experience of falling in love.

Not that he was one to talk about that! He'd avoided the complications of falling in love like it was a plague.

So, instead of saying any of that to her—that she had been too young, that she had missed something—he was shocked to hear himself saying, "I was only eighteen when my dad died, so I know how tragedy shapes a person."

She cocked her head at him. A man could fall toward what he saw in her eyes: someone who *knew* what it was to have your heart break in so many pieces it could not possibly be put back together again.

It felt imperative he get this back on track—that he not fall toward the respite offered by her eyes—so he carefully rephrased his original question. "So what makes a woman like you leave everything she knows in search of a new start?"

"I do have a really good life in Timber Falls," Jessica said hastily. "I have my bookstore and my family…" Her voice trailed away.

"But?" he asked her.

"You're probably absolutely right. I don't think of myself as the marketing type, but there must be a reason I came to

JHA's attention. I made it clear that I'm not at all sure about this position, but I love bookstores, I love books, I love authors and I love readers. I've come up with an equation for putting all those elements together successfully. I can't take it any further in Timber Falls and sometimes I feel a longing for *more*, even though I don't know what that *more* is."

She had thrown that *love* word around pretty casually, but what if that was what she was really longing for? What if that was her *more*? The one she wasn't admitting, even to herself.

Jamie could feel a longing, unknown to him before this very second, rise up in his own soul.

"A couple of years ago, I met a guy online," she admitted, embarrassed. "He was from Europe. We met for the first time in Copenhagen. It was a disaster."

She was telling him it wasn't *love* she was after, after all. It should have been a relief to hear it, and yet…

"So when the invitation from JHA came, 95 percent of me said *don't be ridiculous* and 5 percent said *just go see*. And here I am." She smiled at him. "Seeing."

In the darkness her eyes seemed luminous, and her lips lush. He could smell the scent of her above the scent of the pizza.

It felt as if he was seeing something, too.

He had every trapping of success, and yet she was making him aware, again, of some dangerous emptiness. There was something about her that was fresh and tantalizing and as foreign to his world as all this was to hers. He felt a pull to see where the merging of their two worlds could lead. It felt utterly dangerous.

And irresponsible, as well.

It must just be the lateness of the hour making him think these uncharacteristic thoughts. The lateness of the hour, the oddness of having a stranger in his space, in his T-shirt, munching pizza with a most delectable mouth.

He glanced at his phone. "It's gotten very late," he said. "Would you be more comfortable if I got a hotel for the night?"

"No, of course not!"

He considered the possibility that *he* might be more comfortable, and then dismissed it. He found her refreshing and attractive. Disgracefully, there was something he wanted to challenge about her belief in that teenage love. One taste of adult passion—the wilder, the better—could break her out of that almost childish loyalty to old memories.

Jamie drew himself up short. He could handle her under the same roof for one night. He was not a Neanderthal, not a *me Tarzan, you Jane* kind of guy, at all. And there was nothing he could teach anyone about the complexity of human relationships.

"I had some things arranged for you for tomorrow, but I'm going to have to rearrange them," he told her, all professional, again. "Getting you a few necessities and getting your paperwork in order seems like it should be a priority. I'll look after it first thing in the morning."

"Thank you," she said.

There, he congratulated himself, very businesslike, indeed.

The moment of temptation had passed, and he would hand her off to his sister and other assistants so that another moment of temptation did not rise up to take its place.

"Good night, then," he said, got up and quickly went back inside. He dispensed her laundry to the lobby with an urgent tag on it, and had just gotten in his bedroom and closed the door when his phone lit up, an incoming text from Sarah.

Sorry, it's late.

It's okay. I'm up.

Jared's sick. He was at a birthday party. I think he might have overdone the cake and ice cream. All the evidence points in that direction.

If he encouraged her, he was going to get a picture of the evidence, so he typed in:

Spare me the details.

Not going to be able to make the shopping trip tomorrow. Take her to Hennessey's on Fifth. Ask for Meredith.

He contemplated that. He'd been planning on turning Jessica over. Getting away from her.

How is she holding up?

Fine.

And then, before his sister could ferret out the fact Jessica was staying here, in the same apartment as him, Jamie quickly typed in that he was sure Jared would be okay.

You always promise that.

He stared at the phone, thinking how odd it was she would say that when he had thought of it today for the first time in a long time.

And you're almost always right.

That part surprised him. Had those paltry words he had offered his family really brought anyone any comfort? He focused on the *almost*. It was a good reminder, in the emotional support department, he had nothing to offer.

A case in point: thinking that kissing a young woman, who still held a torch for a long dead young man, could somehow bring her back to life, like a princess who slept.

Jamie shook his head. Fairy tales, now? It wasn't the Brontë sisters, but it was evidence that the small-town bookstore owner who had invaded his apartment really was a bad influence on him.

He contemplated the unfortunate turn of his life: he was going shopping at Hennessey's. No, he wasn't. He was turning Jessica over to some capable shopping person named Meredith, presumably an expert. Then he was walking to his office, which was just off Fifth, and he was assigning one of his assistants all things Jessica-related: police report, passport replacement, a little New York sightseeing, meetings with a few selected clients. He would make sure it was on the assignment list that as soon as she had replaced her ID, they would get her into her own hotel room.

But at the same time Jamie was making plans to distance himself from his guest, he was aware of a little voice in the back of his mind, warning him: from the first moment he had laid eyes on Jessica Winton not one single thing had gone according to his plan.

CHAPTER FIVE

JESSICA SAT OUT on the deck for a while longer, drinking in the sumptuousness of the night. She wasn't quite sure what had just happened. Jamie's departure had seemed abrupt.

Had she said or done something? She shouldn't have told him so much about Devon, about her personal life. It was the long and eventful day that had encouraged uncharacteristic confidences from her.

And yet even with Devon freshly in her mind, she could not help but wonder if Jamie was just as aware as she herself was, that as unlikely as it seemed, there was a chemistry between them.

After a long time of thinking about that, she got up and went to bed. She was still on Canadian time, and it wasn't that late in British Columbia. There was a television in the room, but she felt no desire to turn it on.

Oddly, she was not missing her internet connection, either.

She felt no need at all to report on the circumstances she found herself in, but rather she wanted to keep them to herself, as if they were a secret she was nurturing. There was something freeing about just allowing herself to have an experience, instead of feeling a need to divulge it to her online world.

She slid between luxurious sheets and snuggled under the lightweight down comforter. It occurred to her she should be worried: she was no closer to having cash, replacing her credit cards or getting a passport so that she could travel home at the scheduled time.

Oddly enough, when she closed her eyes, she realized she had rarely felt less worried in her entire life.

How much did that have to do with Jamie Gilbert-Cooper taking charge? She was asleep before she could answer the question.

Jessica awoke in the morning to a soft rap on her door. When she opened it, there was no one there, but the laundry bag was outside and her jacket, enclosed in a thick paper wrap, was on a hangar that had been put on the doorknob. There was also a small bag of toiletries: toothbrush, toothpaste, deodorant.

For one mortifying minute she considered that he was trying to tell her something, but then she realized that was the *old* Jessica, too sensitive and too serious. Of course he wasn't trying to tell her something—like that her breath was bad, though after the pizza last night that did seem like a possibility—he was being considerate!

Brushing her teeth felt exquisite. But when she pulled her hair back into its clip, put her freshly laundered clothes on, and looked at herself in the full-length mirror behind the bathroom door, she came face-to-face with that *old* Jessica.

How could she have changed so much in less than twenty-four hours? She *hated* the outfit. It seemed dull and conservative, appropriate for the floor of the Canadian House of Commons, perhaps, but for a few days in New York City? Not so much.

When she went shopping with Jamie's sister today, she was going to choose items that were appropriate business attire, but not quite so staid. But she still had to be practical. She still had to choose things she could wear in Timber Falls.

Could you choose clothes that were practical *and* sexy? It was a dilemma she had not found herself in before, not even when she was shopping for her trip to Copenhagen. Shouldn't she have known something was off with her first face-to-face meeting with Ralph when, instead of thinking of items that would be attractive, she had been thinking of travel practicalities, like wrinkle-free?

She realized she was looking forward to meeting Jamie's sister. She wasn't going to pry, but she was sure his sister would drop all kinds of clues as to who Jamie really was that his apartment was not giving away.

Jessica also hoped Jamie's sister was good at fashion. She herself sucked at it. There was nothing about the growing up in Timber Falls experience that encouraged fashion-forward thinking. It was an outdoorsy lifestyle that lent itself to plaid shirts and khaki shorts and sturdy shoes for both genders. Business attire at the bookstore was blue jeans and a blouse in the summer, blue jeans and a sweater in the winter.

Jessica had a book-themed sweater collection that children adored. She felt embarrassed just thinking about it! There would be no sweaters with embroidered cats on them today. No, it was summer and she was in New York. She wanted her style to reflect something a little bolder.

Fashion-wise, would she recognize those things? She didn't want to go over the top, after all. Once again, she longed for her phone. With it, she could have consulted with Aubrey and Daisy right from the change room, time differences notwithstanding. She could have snapped selfies and sent them, a virtual fashion show and consultation.

She stepped out of her bedroom. At the last moment, she pulled the clip from her hair, and ran a hasty hand through it.

The apartment was flooded with light. The kitchen island had on it a selection of pastries, croissants, bagels, breads and spreads.

"Good morning." He looked at her only briefly. Did his eyes rest, for a moment, on her loose hair, before he looked hastily away?

Jamie Gilbert-Cooper was standing there, sipping coffee from a take-out cup and leafing through a newspaper he had on the counter in front of him.

She used his concentration on the paper to quickly study him. Yup. Her first impression of him was confirmed: gorgeous. He had obviously already showered: his silver hair was damp and impossibly shiny, his skin had that tender, touchable look of being freshly shaved.

He was dressed, more casually than yesterday, but still in the kind of clothes that in Timber Falls would have been reserved for a wedding. Or a funeral.

Which suddenly struck her as faintly pathetic, though she felt instantly disloyal to her hometown.

He was wearing a white shirt, with a subtle pattern in it. It was opened at the throat and rolled at the cuffs. It was tucked underneath a belt that was threaded through the loops of gray, knife-pressed pants. He had on loafers, with no socks. In Timber Falls no one ever wore shoes in the house.

"This one's for you," he said, pointing at a coffee. "I didn't put anything in it, but I brought creamers and sugar packs."

"You have a coffee maker like that—" she gestured to the machine built into his cabinetry "—and you pick it up?"

He glanced at the coffee maker. "I'm not sure I've ever used that. I pick up coffee and breakfast on the way to work. There's the best little shop just down the street. Taste it and tell me if you think I could do as well."

She picked up her coffee, removed the lid and added some cream to it. The aroma was heady, and she took a sip.

"That's not coffee," she said. "That's ambrosia."

He smiled. "Welcome to New York City. A better welcome than yesterday."

She decided she had not experienced too many things as dangerous as Jamie Gilbert-Cooper smiling at her as she drank the best coffee she had ever had. After a minute, she chose a croissant. It was so flaky, light and buttery, she thought she was going to die. Sensory overload!

"I had a quick look online this morning," he told her. "You must have travel insurance, right?"

"Yes, I do."

"I'm sure they'll cover your losses. We'll need to file the police report in order for you to make a claim, though."

Her mouth fell open. "I hadn't even thought of that."

"Have some breakfast, and then give them a call."

"Thank you, I will." She hoped it wasn't a weakness to feel so good about having someone to lean on, someone to take charge, to help her navigate all the messy details of putting her life back together.

And it wasn't just the current messiness. After Devon, she had never really put her life back together. Maybe, just maybe, this was her chance. Maybe this was why she had been drawn to New York as if tugged by an invisible thread.

"Which do you want to do first?" Jamie asked. "Canadian consular services, or shopping?"

"What's more convenient for your sister? What's her name, by the way?"

"Sarah." He looked uncomfortable. "My nephew was sick last night. I think she's going to bow out."

"How old is your nephew? Is he okay?"

"Jared is two, apparently suffering from a birthday cake overdose, the little oinker."

She heard the affection in his voice, and again, could imagine him throwing a laughing child in the air.

As sorry as she was for the missed opportunity to ferret out the family perspective on Jamie, and as sorry as she was that his nephew was sick, she felt the tiniest little tickle of pure anticipation.

"Let's go shopping first," she decided, aching to get rid of the clothes she was wearing the way she assumed a snake must ache to get rid of its old skin.

"Shopping it is," he said with so little enthusiasm she burst out laughing.

And then he was laughing, too.

And it felt, oddly and beautifully, like one of the most glorious moments of her entire life.

Which, she told herself sternly, just meant everyone was right. She had been far too sheltered. She had lived way too small. She had used a dreadful event to cling to safety, as if the whole world was a life raft that could capsize at any time.

Jamie was a charming man, used to these kinds of intimate little interchanges with the opposite sex.

She needed to be very wary of being enchanted by him.

But the new her insisted on poo-poohing her wariness. It wasn't as if they had posted banns for marriage. They were going shopping. She needed to loosen up and learn to have fun.

A sensation of freedom overcame her. Not a single person here knew her. There was a lovely anonymity to being here.

Not like Timber Falls, which was akin to living in the proverbial goldfish bowl.

Suffocating, a small inner voice offered helpfully.

For the second time.

She shrugged it off, finished her coffee and her croissant, and felt ready, not for a shopping trip, but for the adventure of her life. Her eyes met Jamie's.

Nothing is impossible, Daisy's voice sang inside her head.

Together on his computer, his shoulder nearly touching hers, they filled out the police report, and then she borrowed his phone and called her insurance company.

When she hung up, she was beaming. "They'll cover everything, even the costs involved in getting my passport replaced. They are being extraordinarily generous." She couldn't resist telling him how much they had offered her. "Shopping just became a lot more fun!"

But her confidence flagged a touch as their driver dropped them off on Fifth Avenue, arguably the most exclusive—and expensive—shopping area in the world. As they joined the throngs of people enjoying the early-summer warmth and strolling the famous street, familiar names vied for her attention: Tiffany, Gucci, Versace, Hugo Boss, Luis Vuitton.

"Isn't there a Woolmart?" she asked Jamie, only partly kidding. She was getting a *Who do you think you are?* feeling. Glancing in the windows, she doubted, even with the insurance money, if she could afford a pair of socks on this block.

Jamie looked at her and smiled. "What do they sell? Wool?"

He was teasing her. It felt nice, but he wasn't getting the point.

"Look, I just need a few things, temporarily. This seems—"

"Fun?" he suggested.

Fun. A reminder of her goal for the day. A reminder of the new her. But new her or old her, she was going to have to be careful not to get carried away.

"There's nothing fun about bankruptcy," she said firmly. She stopped at the window of a jewelry store, and looked at the watches on display. She gasped. One of them was worth more than a hundred thousand dollars! And it looked quite a bit like the one on Jamie's wrist.

This suddenly didn't feel fun. Not at all. She felt so far out of her depth, she could soon drown.

As if sensing her sudden discomfort, Jamie swept his hand toward the rings that were displayed next to the watch.

"Which one do you like?"

They were obviously engagement rings, diamonds winking and blinking as the morning sun hit them. "That one," she said. It was as different as the sun was to the moon to the small promise ring Devon had once given her.

And perhaps, unfolding without her awareness, she had become as different from that long-ago girl as the choice of that ring would indicate. The thought was vaguely unsettling, but she shook it off and reminded herself of her goal to just let go, have some fun and relax a bit.

Jamie bent nearer to have a closer look. "You have good taste."

She looked at the discreet price tag displayed beside the box. "What kind of man would spend that on a ring?" she gasped, shocked.

"One who is very much in love?"

She slid him a look. Did he have a secret romantic side, then?

He took her elbow and steered her away from the jewelry store window and through the crowds.

"My sister recommended this place," he said and stopped at the black-painted door of a posh storefront. He opened the door, placed his hand on the small of her back and thrust her through it as if he sensed her desire to bolt.

Jessica stood there, letting her eyes adjust to the light.

The space looked like a hybrid between a living room and a boutique. It looked expensive. It even *smelled* expensive.

And here came the saleslady who looked more like a wealthy heiress than a clerk. She was dressed in understated elegance, a single string of pearls at her neck, her makeup and hair and manicure absolutely perfect.

Jessica braced herself, ready to get kicked out. But then she could feel Jamie's presence behind her, and his hand resting on her shoulder, that solid warmth reminding her she was not only not alone, but also that she had a great guide for navigating his world.

"We're looking for Meredith," he told the woman.

"I'm Meredith."

"My sister, Sarah Stately, recommended you."

"I adore Sarah!"

"Don't we all?" he said dryly, "My friend here, Jessica Winton, is in New York for a few days and has had all her luggage stolen."

Meredith turned to her, and the genuine sympathy Jessica saw in her face belied whatever she had expected from the big-city shopping experience.

"You'll need absolutely everything." She couldn't hide her delight.

"Just for a few days," Jessica said quickly, resisting the temptation to go and start turning over price tags.

"I love your jacket. Clarion? The Canadian designer? You're Canadian, aren't you? I recognize the accent."

Jessica nodded. "The Clarion was a splurge," she said as a hint the jacket wasn't in her regular price range.

"Can I just say, that even though I love it, it seems, um, a bit mature. How old are you?"

"Twenty-six. I am here on business, so I need items that are appropriate." She wanted to add, *and not too expensive*, but she'd wait until Jamie was out of hearing.

"Got it. You are safe with me." Meredith stood back, tapped a manicured finger against her lip. "You are going to be a dream to work with. Look at that figure."

Jamie seemed to take it as an instruction. He looked at her, she blushed. She looked at him, he blushed. That super suave man blushed! It was one of the most endearing things Jessica had ever seen.

He looked hastily to his expensive watch. "If an hour will work, I'll just duck out…"

Jessica felt oddly abandoned. Had she really thought he would stay? He was a busy man, and important. He wouldn't have time for something so frivolous as all this.

"You're not going anywhere," Meredith told him firmly. "We'll need your opinion if we want to get it just right."

Jessica shot Jamie a look. His mouth fell open, and then he slammed it shut. He ran a hand through the silver of his hair. Obviously, he was not used to being ordered about by a saleslady, no matter how high-end the shop.

But when he looked at Jessica, something shifted in his face. His colossal composure was rattled, but only briefly. He cocked his head at her, and then lifted a shoulder.

He was staying!

Jessica felt like a deer caught in headlights. When she had originally assumed he would stay, she hadn't considered modeling outfits for him. She supposed he would take out his phone and settle in one of those deep leather chairs at the front of the store.

It was a nightmare. Or a dream. She wasn't sure which.

Meredith showed her to the change rooms. Actually, more like a change *suite*. They entered a private enclave with a sitting area and a change room bigger than her bedroom in the tiny cottage she had in the yard behind her parents' house. It was certainly more well-appointed than her own lodgings, which suddenly seemed to lean more toward shabby than chic.

"In you go," Meredith said.

"But I haven't even looked at any clothes," Jessica protested.

"I'm going to choose things for you." She wagged a finger at her. "No dull colors. No safe but boring styles. No clothing that does not show off that super figure of yours!"

Jessica looked down at herself with a frown. Super figure? In Timber Falls they called it skinny. Still, it had made Jamie blush. She shot him a look. *Rescue me*, but apparently he was all done rescuing her for the time being. Because he wagged his eyebrows wickedly at her when Meredith mentioned her super figure, and then sank down in one of the chairs and pulled out his phone.

He could have had the decency to look a little uncomfortable—he was a man in a woman's clothing store, after all—but he looked terribly at home.

Jessica went in the change room and Meredith slipped in with her, closed the door and studied her. "Did you lose everything?"

"Everything. My luggage was stolen from me at the airport."

"So, you don't even have makeup?"

This said with a faint shudder, as if no makeup was a catastrophe beyond measure.

"No lingerie? Pajamas?"

"Everything's gone."

"How many days do we need to get you sorted for?"

"Three," Jessica said, firmly. "If I can get my temporary passport, or travel documents, I'll be here for the three days I originally planned. But just in case it's a bit longer,

I'll need things I can mix and match for slightly different looks."

"We'll get you fixed up. It may be a blessing in disguise. I'm going to send my assistant to get you some makeup. Your face is amazing. I can't wait to show you. It's going to be a makeover."

"Um, I'm not sure—"

"Your current bra, by the way, is a disaster," Meredith said.

"Pardon?"

"You'll see what I mean when I bring you a good one. Do you mind if I measure you?"

"Yes, I mind!" She crossed her arms defensively over her chest.

Meredith sighed. "All right, just give me a size then."

Jessica did. "And nothing fancy," she whispered, so that Jamie, sitting just outside the door, couldn't hear her. "I don't like underwires in my bra. And I don't like lace on my underwear, at all."

Meredith was looking mutinous.

"It's scratchy!"

Meredith left, and Jessica sank down on the Cleopatra-style pink tufted chaise longue. What had she just let herself in for? Another woman was choosing underwear for her. It was appalling. She should have protested more strenuously, instead of agreeing to be Meredith's hostage.

Shoot, she'd forgotten to mention that all important word. *Budget*. She looked at the ceiling. She'd worry about that later, when it came time to make final selections. She'd have to put her foot down then.

Jamie waited until Jessica had closed the change room door after Meredith left, then got up from his chair quietly and followed the sales associate out into the store.

"Can I get you to take the tags off things before you bring them in to her? I want her to get what she wants, and not be influenced by the price."

Jamie told himself that giving this instruction to the sales associate was why he had stayed. But it was a lie. There was something about being a witness to Jessica discovering some of the treasures of being in New York that he found himself unable to resist.

"At the end, if it could add up to her insurance settlement that would be great." He named the amount. "I'll look after the difference, if you can slip me a second bill."

What on earth was he doing?

"Love that!" Meredith said, grinning at him, a delighted coconspirator. She held up two dresses. "Which one do you think she would pick?"

One dress was a subtle gray pinstripe with straight lines and a longish skirt. The other was a sundress style with a full skirt. It was white with huge red poppies all over it.

"She'd go for the gray," he said. "Very businesslike."

"That's what I thought, too," Meredith said, and with a wide wink at him, hung the gray dress back up on the rack. "This other dress can be for business, too, with the right sweater and shoes. What do you think of this one?"

And so, somehow he ended up being on Jessica's personal shopping team. It was all fun and games until they came to the underwear section.

Meredith, unabashed, held up a pair of shapeless beige panties. "What do you think?"

He didn't want to be thinking about Jessica's panties, obviously!

"This is what she told me she wanted," Meredith said with barely concealed scorn.

Somehow, it made him feel oddly sad for Jessica that she didn't celebrate her femininity. On the other hand, if she did? Danger zone! He had to remove himself from this situation.

Meredith smiled at him, held up another pair.

He felt his mouth go dry. Thankfully, his phone pinged. He glanced at it. Not at all urgent. But he wagged the phone at Meredith, anyway. "I have to take this."

"Chicken," she mouthed at him, adding a generous supply of froth and film to the already gigantic pile over her arm. "Okay," she sang, "this will get us started."

You had to like a woman who loved her job.

"I haven't had a chance to tag these yet," Meredith said to Jessica as she went through the door of the change room. "I'm raiding our brand-new summer stock, just for you."

"But I need to know—"

The door closed on Jessica's protest, which Meredith must have managed to assuage, because Jessica emerged from the change room in the first outfit. It was the poppy-covered white sundress and she looked absolutely stunning.

If he was not mistaken, she had makeup on. It was subtle and yet the changes to her face were extraordinary. Her eyes looked huge, her cheekbones high and sculpted, her mouth a sultry pout of pure temptation. Her hair had been put up in casual knot, instead of clipped back, and tendrils were escaping and curling wildly around her face.

Despite the sophisticated woman-of-the-world look of the clothes, Jessica looked as shy as a young woman going on her first date.

Meredith had paired the dress with a short white cashmere sweater and white high heels, and the look was professional, yet hinted at a playful side at the same time.

"Give a twirl," Meredith ordered. "You have to see the movement in that skirt."

Jamie wasn't sure if he was ready for the movement in that skirt! Jessica hesitated.

"Pretend you are someone else," Meredith advised. "Elise Hollander on the red carpet."

Jessica hesitated, and then obviously made a decision to get in the spirit of things. She put a hand on her hip and cocked it. She twirled. He expected she might be awkward, but nothing could have been further from the truth. She was as graceful as a ballerina, and her legs were toned, tanned and looked a mile long as the skirt swirled around them. He was pretty sure he caught a glimpse of a pair of panties that were about the furthest thing from boring beige that a man could imagine.

She finished her twirl, set her legs wide apart, put her hand back on her cocked hip and winked at him.

"Fun, flirty and youthful," Meredith declared approvingly. "Yes or no?"

Jessica held his gaze. He nodded his head, unable to speak.

Next she came out in a straight-lined plaid skirt, that should have looked librarian—or bookstore owner appropriate—paired with a pair of stilettos and a loose white blouse that was, by design, semitransparent. He could see a lacy outline beneath it. It was about the sexiest thing he had ever seen.

"These shoes…" she said hesitantly.

Shoes?

"Are perfect," he growled, without even looking at them.

Meredith was an absolute wizard at her job. The clothes she had chosen showed off Jessica's amazingly lithe but sexy figure. Jessica made the transformation from a small-town girl to a supermodel before his very eyes.

He loved seeing the change in her. It wasn't just the clothing, though obviously the cut of expensive clothes made a huge difference, and obviously Meredith had supplied a little something that had transformed Jessica's some-what athletic figure into something far more beguiling.

With each outfit change, Jessica's confidence grew, her hips swinging, her eyes glowing with a soft luster as she began to unveil who she really was, certainly to him, but also to herself. By the time she tried on the last outfit, she was reveling in her femininity, enjoying the effect it was having on him.

He couldn't believe he was disappointed when Meredith opened the change room door, and announced, "Last one."

Jessica emerged in a dress that was light blue, a confection of gauze and spiderwebs. The dress clung in all the right places, and it made her seem mysterious and alluring.

"I certainly don't need the cocktail dress. I don't even know why I tried it on."

But the expression on her face belied the words she had just spoken. She *loved* that dress.

"You're in New York City!" Meredith said. "Surely you're going to go out for a gorgeous dinner at Le Bernardin and take in a Broadway show."

Jessica cast him an uncertain look. "I don't think there's anything like that on the agenda, is there?"

Jamie could hear the wistfulness in her tone, and just like that, Le Bernardin and a Broadway show was on the agenda. He was being bewitched!

He had to stop it, though. He'd turn her over to an assistant for the rest of the day. Get his head on straight—and the boundaries back in place—before he took her out for dinner and a show.

Jessica cast a glance at herself in the bank of mirrors. "It's going to be impossible to decide what to take. Not this, obviously."

"That one, especially. You should take it all," he said.

"I couldn't possibly. You think this one? Really?"

"Absolutely that one," he said.

"I guess find me the price on this one," Jessica said. "And the white-and-red sundress. I'll figure out from there if I can afford anything else."

"Let me figure out what it would cost if you took it all," Meredith said smoothly, "and if you can't handle it, we'll start editing."

"But—"

Meredith swept up all the clothes and left them.

"I feel like Cinderella," Jessica said, sinking into the chair beside him. The dress hitched up on a slender leg. He tried not to look. Failing in that, he tried not to be obvious about looking.

"But it's just about midnight. The glass slipper falls off, and I see what it all costs. I probably can't even afford one thing from here."

He looked at his watch so she wouldn't see the pleasure in his eyes that he was going to play a part in her fairy tale.

Not the prince part, of course. Though something about seeing her in all those clothes could tempt any man to play that role, even one as cynical about fairy tales as him.

Meredith came back. She held out a piece of paper to Jessica.

Jessica took it, looked at it, and blinked. "Oh," she said. "It's so much less than I expected. Still, I don't need two skirts. So, I should probably take out the pencil-line one and keep the navy pants."

Meredith snatched the paper back from her. "I forgot to add Sarah's preferred customer discount."

Jessica took back the paper with the adjusted price. Her mouth fell open with shocked surprise.

"All right," she cried, beaming, "I'll take it all!"

As Meredith handled the transaction—giving the one bill to Jessica and putting the real amount on Jamie's credit card, Jamie realized this was probably the most duplicitous thing he had ever done. But Jessica was absolutely radiant.

"I'll pay you back, of course. The insurance representative said I'll have some money by this afternoon."

How could something feel both so very wrong and so very right at the same time?

When they left the store, Jessica was wearing the brand-new sundress. Jamie couldn't help but notice that, in a city where no one paid any attention to anyone else, Jessica was receiving subtle—and deeply appreciative glances—from the men of New York.

A man on a construction site whistled at her. Jamie threw him a warning glance, and then noticed Jessica was blushing as though she had been propositioned.

How could he turn her over to an assistant when it was so complicated? Jessica now *looked* like a sophisticated woman of the world. But she was the furthest thing from that. He couldn't just cast her out on her own. A still small voice, somewhere in the region of his heart, whispered to him, *Admit it, pal, you don't want to.*

CHAPTER SIX

WALKING DOWN FIFTH AVENUE, with Jamie beside her, his arms laden with the parcels he had refused to let her carry, Jessica felt amazing. Like a sleeping princess who had been brought to life.

Not with a kiss, of course, though the thought made her take a quick look at the sensuous turn of his mouth and realize that kissing Jamie Gilbert-Cooper was not as impossible as it had seemed just this morning. Their worlds were intersecting.

The funny thing about the impromptu makeover, her astonishing new look and awesome new wardrobe was that she hadn't felt out of her element.

As Meredith had expertly applied that makeup—making Jessica's eyes look huge and dark, her cheekbones look amazing, her mouth look sensuous and faintly sultry—Jessica had not felt like Cinderella, dressing up as someone she was not. She had felt more like duckling to swan.

With each stroke of Meredith's hand on the makeup brush, and with each outfit she had tried on, something about herself, that had always been there, was being revealed. When she had stood before Jamie in that final outfit, the cocktail dress, Jessica had felt as though she had become who she really was.

At that time she hadn't known what that dress was worth—still didn't know the prices of individual items for that matter—but the look on his face had made her decide it was worth its weight in gold.

"So," Jamie suggested, as they exited Hennessey's, "let's go look after things at the Canadian Consulate office, and then I'll surprise you for lunch."

Jessica was not really sure if it was Jamie's presence, or her own growing confidence, but things went far better than she had anticipated. Though they could not replace her passport immediately, they would treat her case as urgent, and contact her through Jamie as soon as they had temporary documents available so she could travel.

Unfortunately, until they had completely verified her identity, they could not give a photo ID.

Which meant she still could not get a hotel. It meant she would be staying with Jamie one more night, at least. She was appalled at how thrilled she was by that!

After that, the rest of the day was a whirl of delight: the Russian Tea Room for champagne high tea, a stroll through Central Park, where they paused and watched little boys—and one little girl—race remote control boats on the reservoir. The little girl kept ramming the boats around her, and then giggling fiendishly.

"Was that you as a little girl?" Jamie asked.

"No, I'm afraid I've always been the good girl." Then she realized how it sounded and she blushed.

He took in her blush, and the smallest smile, just a touch wicked, crossed his features, as if he were having wayward thoughts about rectifying that.

It occurred to her she would let him!

"What were you like as a little boy?" she said, to ease some of the sudden tense awareness of each other that tinged the warm summer air around them.

"Pick one," he said, nodding toward the boys.

She studied them for a moment, and then pointed to a

solemn-looking boy who appeared to be dismantling his boat to diagnose a problem. Jamie laughed. He was one of those men who threw back his head to laugh. A light came on in his face, making him—impossibly—even more attractive. His laughter was so deep and rich and genuine, that Jessica noticed it brought smiles to the faces of those passing by, New Yorkers generally famous for being oblivious to one another.

"Maybe more like that one," he said, pointing to a lad whose hair was going every which way, and who had his pants rolled up and was in the water up to his ankles. "If he catches a frog, tomorrow it's going in the desk of the girl he secretly loves."

The thought of Jamie secretly loving someone sent tingles up and down her spine. "You don't seem like that at all," she said hastily, not sure if she was talking about the little boy, or the ability to secretly love someone. She remembered when they had looked at that expensive ring together she had wondered if he had a secret romantic side. It was dangerous—and thrilling—to be thinking of him in such a personal way.

"Like most boys, I've outgrown my desire to put frogs in girl's drawers."

The way he said *drawers* made her think of her sexy new underwear, and from the wicked look on his face, that was exactly what he intended. Jessica was fairly certain that the only part of that equation he had lost interest in was the frog part.

"My mother claims every gray hair on her head was caused by my *shenanigans*—her word not mine—between the ages of two and eighteen."

"Ha! I think gray hair may be hereditary in your family." He rewarded her with a smile, but then she remembered what he had told her last night. "The shenanigans stopped at eighteen because of the death of your father, didn't they?"

He hesitated, and looked off into the distance. "I was suddenly the man of the family. It was a role nothing in my life, to that point, had prepared me for."

Unlike her, shrinking away from life when Devon had died, she had a feeling he had handled it differently.

"You rose to it, didn't you?" she asked softly.

She laid her fingertips on his forearm, where his shirt was rolled up. She thought he might pull away, but he didn't. If anything, the touch connected them at a deeper level.

"I think I pretty much sucked at it," he said, some emotion in the sudden hoarseness of his voice.

"I don't believe that," she said firmly.

He looked at her, deeply, as if there was something in those simple words he wanted to hang on to. "It was just a tough time. Along with the shock of sudden loss—he had a heart attack—I was suddenly plunged into the world of adult responsibility. He left some insurance and savings, but for a while I wondered if I could find a way for my mom to have a home again and let my sister go to college as she had always dreamed."

"You did find a way?"

"I did," he said.

"You don't sound as proud of yourself as you should."

He lifted a shoulder. "I managed the *things* that they needed. But I couldn't take the pain away."

"You're very hard on yourself," she said softly.

"I had a sense of failing them almost every day."

She could tell a man like him would not like anything he perceived as failure. She knew it was probably uncharacteristic for him to reveal something like this of himself, and she could feel his trust in her trickle warmly down her spine.

"I think you held yourself to an impossible standard."

"Do you, now?" he asked softly.

She nodded, and he seemed to take that in, before he shrugged it off, as if it was absolution he felt he was undeserving of.

"If you ask my sister, it soured me."

"You don't seem sour!" She finally, reluctantly, took her hand away from his arm.

He smiled at her. "Thanks. Sarah thinks everyone should be happily married and producing children, like her, otherwise it is not a life well lived. She says all that shouldering the family responsibility so young killed that for me."

"And did it?" Jessica whispered.

"Oh, yeah. She has gone as far as to call me hedonistic."

"That seems mean. After all you've done for her."

"We like to tease each other. I call her DD for Domestic Diva."

Jessica liked these little glimpses into who Jamie was. She liked it that he and his sister teased each other. Still, she felt a need to defend him. "Anyway, you are not! Hedonistic."

"Yes, ma'am, I am. Self-centered and selfish. I work hard. I play harder. I'm allergic to domestic activities and responsibilities, hence the reason no turkey has ever filled my oven."

Despite the lightness of Jamie's tone, it was a warning to her, that was clear. He had already told her he saw her as a picket fence kind of girl, and he was letting her know he did not fit that kind of dream.

He was painting a picture of himself as the quintessential playboy.

And yet, looking at him, his shirt open at the throat, his sleeves rolled up, the sun on his silver hair and the exquisite lines of his face, she didn't feel he had shown her one sign that he was selfish or self-centered. Still, she was aware a girl could change her dreams to fit his.

A girl could loosen her hold on the concept of *forever* and be willing to just take whatever he offered. It might actually be fun to not be the good girl, for once. She was in New York. She was a long way from home. Who would ever know if she had a little fling with a sexy man? She experienced a shiver of pure *wanting* when she thought of Jamie in those terms, when she thought of his lips claiming hers, his hands…

Stop it! She ordered herself.

Given their circumstances—his potential to be her boss, her forced stay in his quarters—she was entertaining very perilous thoughts, indeed.

When they turned away from the young boaters to walk again, she went over on her ankle ever so slightly because of the unfamiliar shoes. Despite the fact she knew she was flirting in general and flirting with danger in particular, when he reached out to steady her, she did not return his steadying arm to him when she should have.

No, she looped her arm though his—felt the surge of delight at being linked to him—as they moved along the pathway toward his building.

"I hope you don't mind," she said. "I'm not used to the shoes. I'm going to skin my nose if I don't have you to lean on."

He looked down at her for a long moment. He looked as if he wanted to warn her not to play with fire. Instead, he took a deep breath. "We wouldn't want you to skin a cute little nose like that," he said.

Cute. He thought she was cute. Or that her nose was. Cute was a long way from pretty. Or gorgeous. Or beautiful.

And yet she liked it very much that he thought her nose was cute.

And then he started humming, *lean on me*, and Jessica was glad she had silenced her good girl because she was not sure she had ever experienced a more perfect moment than that one, walking through Central Park on a sun-drenched day, in her new dress, with a gorgeous man on her arm.

One perfect moment was determined to follow another. She wore her new cocktail dress for the most exquisite dinner she had ever had. Whether it was the food, or Jamie's company she wasn't sure. He was so at ease in every situation, radiating confidence and good humor. Maybe his sister was right about him! He certainly seemed practiced at entertaining the opposite sex. Conversation with him seemed so easy. They talked about everything: books, recent movies, music they liked, travels they had experienced. Her travels were limited—only Copenhagen—but Jamie had been many places, both professionally and personally.

His anecdotes revealed him as a man with a rich sense of humor and a great verve for life.

He had gotten tickets to *The Phantom of the Opera*, which he told her was the longest running show in Broadway history. She was thrilled. But somehow, just as thrilling as going in to the show was standing in line with him at the Majestic Theatre, and seeing the admiring gazes he garnered. Jessica realized she was very much enjoying being mistaken for a couple.

She was also enjoying the sheer variety of the crowd. There was everything here from elderly couples to families, and even a school group.

"The variety of what people are wearing is amazing," she whispered to Jamie. It was true, there was everything from men in tropical print Hawaiian shirts and shorts, to women in evening gowns.

"The really dressed up ones are tourists," he whispered back.

"Am I overdressed?" she asked, feeling a bit of the magic slip away. "I haven't had on anything this fancy since my prom."

He cast an appreciative look over her, long enough and male enough that she felt herself starting to blush.

"You," he said, softly, "are perfect. Ravishing."

Just like that, the magic was back. Jamie Gilbert-Cooper thought she was ravishing!

When she shivered from the gruesome makeup on the phantom, Jamie assumed she was cold, and she found his suit jacket settling around her shoulders. It felt so nice that she did not correct him.

Jessica was not sure what she had been expecting from the show, but it was incredibly sensuous in places, and terrifying in others. When the chandelier "fell" into the audience she shrieked very unbecomingly. Jamie's hand found hers and then he lifted her hand to his lips and kissed her wrist.

Jessica was pretty sure her heart stop beating. She turned and looked at him, and very deliberately, he lifted her wrist to his lips again and kissed it.

It was not, to be sure, a wildly passionate kiss. It was more a reassurance: See? Nothing to be afraid of. I'm right here beside you.

And nothing felt frightening after that except maybe the wild beating of a heart going down a pathway it had never been down before.

Jessica Winton was not his type, Jamie told himself, for the umpteenth time. She was a small-town girl in a big-city world. Even dressed up in *that* dress, even with her makeup applied expertly, even with her hair piled on top of her head in a sophisticated bun, there was a quality about her that was wholesome. It was not exactly naive, and yet it was not worldly either.

Whatever that quality was it had coaxed him to tell her about the death of his father, and to confide in her the effect that event had had on him and the course his life had taken.

He wasn't accustomed to sharing confidences, so he told himself he'd intended it as a kind of warning to her, probably because he could feel the attraction lighting up between them.

I am not the settling down kind of guy.

And yet, no matter what reason he had confided in her, after he had felt oddly lighter, as if he had been carrying a burden he didn't even know he carried. The way she had looked at him, the way her hand had rested so lightly on his arm, had made him feel as if the power of the sun had intensified.

Now, it felt as if he was seeing his world through her eyes, and it was hard not to find her delight in things that he took for granted contagious.

When she screamed when the chandelier fell, it was the most natural thing in the world to take her hand in his.

But what made him lift it to his lips and kiss the inside of her wrist? He told himself it was not a romantic gesture, but a chivalrous one.

I'm here. Don't be afraid.

And yet, when she went still beside him, when he turned to acknowledge the wideness of her eyes with a steady look, he was not so sure that anything had ever felt quite so good as being there for her.

So, he kissed the underside of her wrist again, before tucking her hand into his side. He resisted the temptation to stroke the inside of her palm with his thumb, because that would take things to a whole different level that would give an entirely different message than *I'm here for you, your protector in the big city.*

Still, with her hand in his, it felt like a good thing he had seen *Phantom* before, because he was so conscious of her beside him, that not a single thing that unfolded onstage pierced that awareness.

He knew the impossibility of flagging a cab after a show had just gotten out, so he had arranged for a driver to be waiting for them.

He should have thought of this when he was laying tender kisses on the inside of her wrist: she was coming home with him.

She looked adorable snuggled under his jacket in the back seat. He moved as far away from her as the car seat would allow. He could see kissing her wrist in the darkness of the theater, suddenly and with excruciating clarity for what it had been: *temporary insanity.*

"Would you like a drink?" he asked her.

Now what part of that would move them back toward sanity?

"I'd usually say no," she said, "but how often am I going to be able to sit in a limo on Broadway in New York City having a drink?"

"What would you like?"

When she hesitated, he could tell she rarely drank. She didn't even know what to ask for. She must have realized what her hesitation was telling him, because she said, breezily, "Whatever I had yesterday is fine."

Just yesterday? She had only been part of his life since yesterday? How was that possible when everything seemed so changed?

He poured her a little sip of cognac, and poured himself a more bracing one. Why was he acting like a man under threat?

Thankfully, they made the trip from Broadway to his apartment in about twelve minutes.

He brooded all the way back to his place. He'd let his guard down. He'd wanted to be a good host, and try to erase her awful first impression of New York. He'd felt, quite naturally, protective of her. But he had crossed boundaries.

He'd gone shopping with her. That was an activity reserved for people in committed relationships, now that he thought about it. Why hadn't he thought about that sooner?

He'd taken her for lunch and supper. He'd strolled through Central Park with her. He'd taken her to *The Phantom of the Opera*.

No wonder she was looking at him with *that* terrifying expression on her face.

He'd been treating this whole day as if it was some kind of date. She was in a vulnerable position. He might end up being her boss.

He contemplated that.

Her boss.

One day with her had him feeling as if his whole reality was shifting. What if she decided to take this job? His life would be brushing up against hers, day in and day out…

"I think the car has stopped," she told him. Her voice was husky. Her eyes were half-lidded.

He scrambled out of the car, and managed, just barely, not to bolt up to the safety of his apartment, leaving her to find her own way.

Running away was not an option.

For Pete's sake, he lectured himself, he had dated some of the most desirable women on the planet. This little lady from Lumber—no, Timber—Falls was not a threat to him. He held out his hand to her to help her out of the car.

The dress slid up, revealing a mouthwatering glimpse of legs that went on forever. He let go of her hand as soon as he had extracted her from the car. He stood as far away from her on the elevator as he could. When the door opened he managed, just barely, to let her out before him. And then he got out, and went by her, making a beeline for the sanctuary of his bedroom.

"Jamie?"

He turned and looked at her.

Her makeup was a little smudged. Her hair was falling out of the twist it had been in. While he watched, she shrugged out of his jacket, revealing herself to him: the long legs, the bodice that clung like mist, the gentle curve of her shoulders.

His mouth felt dry.

"You'll be wanting this," she said.

He stared at her. Her voice had that same husky note to it that he had noticed in the car.

Note to self, he told himself, *do not give Jessica Winton cognac ever again.*

If he told her to just put the jacket down, she was going to *know* she was having an effect on him.

It seemed imperative that she not know that, that he maintain the balance of power.

He sauntered back to her, held out his hand for the jacket.

She placed it in his hand, and then moved in close to him.

"I can't thank you enough for today," she said. "It is the closest I've ever come to having a perfect day."

He reflected on that. They hadn't done anything very spectacular. He, on the other hand, had done spectacular things. He had experienced days that could be called perfect; skiing in St. Moritz, snorkeling off the Kona Coast, trekking in South America. He had been to the final game of the World Series, not once, but twice, and been on a photo safari in Mozambique.

And yet, looking at Jessica, it suddenly seemed as if she was correct. Everything else in his history paled in comparison to today.

She moved toward him. Her intent was obvious. She was going to kiss him. He presumed on the cheek, one of those nice *thank you* busses that his mother gave him after they had experienced a lovely outing.

He wasn't quite sure what changed: the position of his cheek or her intent.

Because the sweetness of Jessica Winton's lips missed his cheek entirely. And connected with his mouth.

For the first fragment of the first second, he might have had the power to move.

But then he was lost.

Her mouth was as sweet as a strawberry that had ripened under the sun. Her kiss transported him to the mountains from where she came. She had a taste to her, what he imagined the fine spray of water cascading over a rock would taste like.

He had deluded himself that he had some knowledge of what a perfect moment was.

Because it was not until the softness of her lips sought his that Jamie knew, fully, completely, unequivocally, exactly what perfect was.

He was in the thrall of something now. For a man who had always prided himself on self-control, he would chide himself—later—for how quickly his had dissolved.

Because suddenly it was just him and her.

The whole world was only him and only her.

There was no tony address in Central Park South telling him he'd arrived, there was no thrum of the city outside his window, there was no great job, holidays to plan for, new and heady successes to achieve.

It felt as if he had lived all of that for this single arrival.

Her.

Jessica's mouth opened against his, soft, moist, beckoning him yet deeper into the enchantment that was her.

Far in the back of his brain, some rational part, called to him. Wrong time. Wrong place. Wrong woman.

Wrong. Wrong. Wrong.

But the primal part of his brain was having none of it, crying, just as loudly.

Right. Right. Right.

He lifted his hands to the sides of her face, bracketed it, looked into her wide eyes for permission, which he found. He dropped his mouth over hers, explored the willing, beguiling sweetness with increasing urgency.

He let his hands move, he let them tangle in the silk of her hair, and he pulled her more closely to him.

It was her whimper of pure pleasure, discovery, someone who had never quite experienced this depth of passion before, that brought Jamie harshly to his senses. When she had told him about her fiancé, for one crazy moment in time he had *wanted* this. He had wanted to be the one to awaken this in her. That was why he hadn't backed away from her invitation when he should have.

It was greedy and selfish and unconscionable. He had known this woman just a little over twenty-four hours. Of course sometimes, in his world, things progressed quickly.

But not in hers.

He yanked back from her and stepped away, watching her, utterly appalled with himself. She was not a woman from his world. She was not anything like any woman he had ever taken out before.

As he watched, he could see her breath was rising, moving too quickly in and out. Her eyes were wide. Her lips looked thoroughly kissed.

Both her eyes and those altogether too tempting lips begged for more.

"I'm sorry," he managed to choke out.

"Sorry?" she whispered, as though he had insulted her.

"Yes, sorry," he reiterated firmly. "I can't imagine what I was thinking. That was completely inappropriate."

She nodded, once, biting the lushness of that lower lip.

He was pretty sure, watching her work that lip, that his strength had never been tested quite like this before.

"Good night," he said, his voice a rasp of pure need. He turned away from her before he broke and ran back to her, swept her up in his arms, finished what he had so foolishly started.

He managed to get in his bedroom and close the door. He leaned against it and shut his eyes.

But it didn't matter that his eyes were shut. All he could see was her lips.

CHAPTER SEVEN

JESSICA FOUND HER way to her room in a daze. She realized she was humming "The Point of No Return" from the musical. But when she lay down in her bed, Daisy's song replaced it inside her head. "Nothing is Impossible."

She realized, mutinously, she did not care if Jamie thought that kiss was inappropriate. For her, it had been the perfect ending to an absolutely perfect day. She hoped she would dream of his lips on hers, and she did wake in the morning with a lovely sense of bliss.

She chose her outfit carefully from her purchases from Hennessey's. Today would be all business and she dressed for that in the pencil line skirt, the white blouse, the flat shoes. But at the last moment, she undid a button one daring level lower than she normally would have, and she left her hair loose.

Jamie was up, the breakfast selection already put out on the island. He took in her loose hair and the button position on her blouse and his eyes darkened. Then he looked at her lips—lightly outlined with gloss, as Meredith had showed her—and his gaze lingered for a full two seconds before he looked at his phone.

"Big day today," he said, apparently studying their agenda.

Jessica realized Jamie was as awkward with her as if something quite a bit more substantial than a kiss had occurred between them. She probably should have felt some shame—after all, she had instigated that "inappropriate" kiss with a man who could be her boss—but she felt no remorse at all.

In fact, she was a bit delighted that she, an unsophisticated woman from a small town, had managed to rattle the super suave Jamie Gilbert-Cooper. She made a point of "accidentally" touching his hand as she reached for a bagel. He yanked his own away as if he had been burned.

Before they were done eating breakfast, a courier arrived, with funds for her from the insurance company, and a temporary replacement for her credit card.

Her whole world felt rosy!

She tried to repay him, on the spot, for the shopping trip, but he told her to hang on to her cash, in case she saw something else she wanted, and to send him an e-transfer when she got home.

They took the car to his office, which was in the Financial District, and he pointed out the sights to her, his tone conversational, but in a deliberately tour guide kind of way. They whisked by the statues of the *Charging Bull* on Wall Street, and the *Fearless Girl*. He pointed out the 9/11 Memorial Plaza, and Museum, and Saint Paul's Chapel.

And then they were at his office. From the moment she entered the doors, she realized this sumptuous space, with its incredible view toward the Empire State Building could be her office one day, too.

The day went by in a whirl. It was as unlike yesterday as a day could be. Jamie introduced her to his business world, and to what her future job might entail. It was unbelievably exciting: bringing her skill set with her bookstore to a wider application, which would include liaising with publishers and bookstores, and with bookstores and authors. It would include setting up events and seminars to help independent bookstore owners to achieve the same results she had.

She and Jamie had lunch with a publisher and an author. At first, she thought she would feel awkwardly out of her depth, but as soon as the talk turned to books and bookstores she was right at home. She had a growing sense, not just of being able to hold her own in this environment, but of being so at home with it. After lunch, they visited two bookstores who were current clients of JHA, and despite being in the middle of New York City, Jessica was, again, right at home.

This was her forte: bringing vibrancy and a sense of life and verve to a bookstore. She and the owners clicked immediately over their shared love of books, and the feeling that a bookstore should really be at the heart of any community.

She was aware, as the day went on, that the awkwardness that kiss had caused between her and Jamie dissipated somewhat. She was quite pleased to see a growing respect for her in his eyes.

But why was he surprised? Why had I been asked to consider the job if they didn't already know what my skill level was?

She brushed the question aside when Jamie handed her his phone. "Canadian Consulate," he told her.

She took it and learned she would be issued temporary travel documents early tomorrow afternoon. It meant she could catch her return flight as scheduled tomorrow evening.

Why did she feel almost disappointed? She realized she felt as though she had just begun to explore this world, and that she didn't just want more, she felt as if she couldn't get enough.

It felt as if it was ending before it had really begun.

This could be my life, she thought.

"I'll be going home on schedule," she told him, keeping her tone deliberately neutral, as she handed him back his phone.

Something flashed across his handsome features that could have been regret. Or maybe it was relief.

"Is there anything you wanted to see before you go?"

"I have to see the New York Public Library," she told him, "nerd that I am."

He looked at her solemnly. "I don't think you're a nerd, at all." His eyes rested on her lips for a moment. "I have some things I have to do this afternoon. So, why don't I put the driver at your disposal, and you can take in whatever sights you want? I'll meet you back at the apartment and we'll figure out something truly spectacular for dinner for your last night here."

It was when she went out to the car that she realized, instead of reveling in the awkwardness she had made Jamie feel by kissing him, she should be thinking of a way to thank him for all he had done.

He had not just come to her rescue, he had completely turned a horrible situation around. When she thought back on this time in New York, the theft of her luggage would be just a hilarious footnote to what had been a wonderful time.

And maybe it was because the choice she had to make— about whether to accept the position or not—suddenly felt so overwhelming that she realized exactly how she could thank Jamie and get her own feet back on the ground at the same time.

She could give him, the man who had everything, the one thing he didn't have.

A sense of what a home could feel like. She had money, she had a credit card and she knew exactly how she wanted to spend some of it.

Instead of asking the driver to take her to the New York

Public Library, she asked, "Where do you buy food here? If you want to cook?"

An hour later she arrived back at Jamie's apartment with everything she needed to make the best home-cooked meal ever.

She had a moment's doubt, then. She suddenly felt foolish. Why would she think anything she could offer him could compete with the culinary delights that were just outside his door?

Well, unless she was planning on trying to put a prime rib roast down the in-sink garbage disposal, she was committed.

Jamie stepped off the elevator into his apartment and stopped short. Jessica was behind the island, tongue caught between her teeth, peeling potatoes. He was fairly certain a potato had never been peeled in this space before.

He sniffed the air. It smelled heavenly. Like roasting meat and pies. It smelled like coming home.

She glanced up at him and smiled tentatively. She had a bib apron that said *Life is Short, Lick the Spoon* on over that super sexy outfit she had worn today. How was it possible she looked even sexier?

"What are you doing?" he asked her, and heard the caution in his voice. "I thought you were going to the library."

"I decided that could wait. I wanted to thank you for all you've done for me. I tried to figure out what to give the man who had everything, and a home-cooked meal topped the list."

He contemplated that. She had given up one of the things she wanted to do most to give something to him.

He was unbelievably touched by that. Besides, what man wouldn't want to come home to something like this?

"I actually got to use the double ovens," she said, nodding

at the pies cooling at her elbow. All of New York outside his door, and she was thrilled that she had used a double oven?

As Jamie looked at Jessica, he was aware of feeling a strange longing, a longing for the life he had not chosen. How easy it suddenly was to picture children tumbling across the room toward him, happy to see him, crying *Daddy*.

The vision was as shocking—and compelling—as imagining her in a field of lavender. What was it about this woman that so bewitched him? That made secrets he had kept, even from himself, thrust their way up to the surface?

Claim you have a meeting you forgot and get out of here, he ordered himself.

Instead, Jamie found himself drawn into the warmth she had created in his space. As he drew closer to her, he was acutely aware that the life he had chosen suddenly seemed empty—filled with things and lacking soul—and it made him feel alone in a way he had not felt before.

"What can I help with?" he asked gruffly, coming around to her side of the kitchen island, not wanting to reveal to her the full extent of the feelings clawing up through him.

"I've got an extra potato peeler."

How could that invitation possibly sound sexy? And dangerous? When he took off his suit jacket and joined her at the sink, he knew why it was both sexy and dangerous.

"Here," she said, "let's get an apron on you. It will protect your clothes."

"I don't have an apron," he protested, but she took a folded piece of cloth off the counter and shook it out.

"You do now."

What was this *let's* put the apron on? He had been dressing himself since he was two. Plus, she had obviously *planned* to get him involved, even knowing full well what had happened between them last night. But, no doubt on purpose, she had wisely chosen a very wholesome activity.

He should have backed away, but instead he ducked his head so that she could put the loop of the apron over it. She was so close. It reminded him of that kiss last night. It would be so easy to...

He steeled himself against unwholesome thoughts. They had no place in this most wholesome of activities.

He tilted his head down and read, upside down, the phrase on his apron. It said *I'm cute AND I can cook.*

"I think I got your apron," Jamie said. "This is a lie."

"Only half of it," she told him with a sassy grin.

Was she flirting with him? He frowned at her. Hadn't she got the memo? Flirting had no part in a wholesome activity!

Jessica went behind him and tied the apron securely. The apron snugging up against his waist and her hands at his back increased both the sense that there was potential here for unwholesomeness and the sense he had entered a scene of domestic bliss. She handed him a potato peeler.

"Your weapon," she told him.

He looked at her lips, her weapon. He turned quickly away from her, grabbed a large potato and focused furiously on removing the skin from it.

They were shoulder to shoulder. Her scent was blending with the smell of a roast cooking and pies cooling. Her hair was shiny and begged his fingers to tangle in it like they had last night. Who could have imagined peeling potatoes could be so much fun and such an exercise in discipline?

An hour later, they sat down at his dining room table to eat. The roast was overcooked and the potatoes were lumpy because she had not considered the possibility he would neither have milk to mash them, nor an implement created specifically for that purpose. The gravy had not thickened properly and the apple pie was sour enough to make him pucker.

"Well, that was a disaster," she said, sadly.

"Really?" he said. "I think it's easily one of the most exquisite meals I've ever eaten. With the best company."

"That's a lie," she said.

"Only half of it."

And there was the laughter, again, springing up so easily between them.

"So, it's your last night in New York. Is there anything I can do to make it special? To thank you for this?" He gestured at the table, littered with the remains of dinner.

Her eyes found his lips, and skittered away.

"No, no," she said hastily, "you don't have to thank me for this, this was to thank you. Oh, geez, I sound like those chipmunks who are always trying to outdo each other in politeness. *After you. No, after you, I insist.*"

He laughed at her great impression. "And then they end up fighting!" he reminded her.

And then they were both laughing at the absurdity of it.

"Come on," he coaxed her, "what's on your New York wish list?"

"Oh, no, I—"

"It's an order."

"Now you sound like Beast."

He cocked his head at her.

"As in *Beauty and the Beast*?"

"I'm not familiar with it."

"You are so! Belle is the town bookworm."

"Like you?"

She blushed. A man could live to make her blush. He made her tell him the whole story, pretending it was all new to him.

"I can't believe you've never seen that movie," she said when she had finished.

He laughed and sang, "'No one's as slick as Gaston, no one's as quick as Gaston—'"

She scowled at him. "Why did you let me go on and on about it?"

"You were so earnest. My sister made me watch that with her, over and over again, when she got chicken pox, not long after my dad died."

Jessica looked at him, and the loveliest smile tilted her lips. A man could live to make her smile. "And you think you failed in some way?" she asked softly.

And a man could live for that, too. For a sense of his flaws being filtered through a gentler, more forgiving light than the one he held on himself.

"Pick something," he insisted, now more determined than ever to give her some precious memory to take home with her, since, of course, he had no intention of giving in to the desire to do everything he did for her—for her blush, for her smile, for that light that came on in her eyes that made him feel ten feet tall and bulletproof.

She hesitated. "You'll think it's corny."

"Cornier than my apron?"

"Maybe."

"Try me."

"I wanted to go on the horse-drawn carriage through the park."

"You know, I've lived here all my life, and I've never done that."

"I told you, corny."

"I think it's about time I did," he told her softly. If his sister could see him pulling out his phone to check availability for the carriage ride tonight, she would no doubt repeat what she had said to him when he had texted her that first night that Jessica had arrived.

Who are you and what have you done with my brother?

He shushed that voice and pushed a single button to book the carriage ride. An hour later, Jamie watched, amused, as Jessica introduced herself to the horse. She blew into his nose, and despite her beautiful clothes, she didn't even step back when he blew back on her. In fact, she threw back her head and laughed.

Jamie thought a world without her laughter to look forward to was going to feel empty in a way he had not realized the world could be empty just forty-eight hours ago.

"She knows horses," the carriage driver said approvingly.

"Do you?" Jamie asked Jessica.

"Oh, sure. Timber Falls is rural. I always had a pony when I was growing up. Horse-crazy teenager, all that stuff."

A reminder, as she settled in beside him, of what she was. *Wholesome.* Ponies and pies. Not the kind of woman a guy like him should tangle with any further than he already had. But what was he going to do? Jump off the carriage and tell her to have a good time, he had just thought of something he needed to do?

Surrender, he told himself.

This was about her. Not about him. She was here only a short time more. And then what?

Was she leaving forever? Or was she coming back? Would she be working with him, day in and day out?

He took his place beside her in the carriage. He tried to keep some distance between them, but she shivered, and tonight he didn't have a jacket to put over her shoulders.

He surrendered yet again. He moved closer to her, throwing what he hoped was a companionable arm over her slim shoulders.

"What are your thoughts about the job?" he asked. It was a desperate and pathetically late effort to keep all of this in some way businesslike. That already seemed hopeless. But he had to try.

Jessica felt like Cinderella, with Jamie's arm around her shoulders, the steady clip-clop of the horse's hooves, dusk falling over Central Park. She felt as exquisitely alive as she had ever felt, as if the night air was creating tiny explosions of sensation against her skin.

She wished Jamie wouldn't have mentioned the job!

"I don't know yet," she said. "There's a lot to think about. It's not just my own business, though of course that is part of it. Who would look after it? And a big part of it is my mom and dad. They aren't old—both in their late fifties—and they're in good health and active, but they rely on me quite a bit."

"In what way?"

"Technology baffles them. I think I get a call or a visit once a day at the store with questions about their television, or their phones. Don't even get me going on their recent purchase of matching tablets!"

He laughed.

"My mom has taken to social media, though," she said ruefully.

Even as she said it, she realized these sounded like weak reasons to put a life on hold.

"I think they would want you to do what is best for you," he said.

"You're right, of course. If you met them, you would see that instantly."

Jamie Gilbert-Cooper meeting her parents? She couldn't imagine what circumstances that would cause these two very different worlds to collide.

A wedding, something sighed within her. She instantly banished the thought as both embarrassing and ridiculous. Despite feeling she *knew* Jamie, the truth was she did not. This sense of intimacy was because he had rescued her. He had invited her into his life. He had treated her like a princess. Conversation flowed easily between them. They laughed together. There was definitely chemistry!

All that was not a reason to start humming *someday my prince will come*, even if she was riding in a horse-drawn carriage!

It probably was showing her that Aubrey and Daisy were absolutely right: Jessica had made her world too small. Her reaction to this close proximity to such a confident, charming, gorgeous man was a result of not having nearly enough encounters with men of any sort.

Not since Devon had died. Not since the fiasco with Ralph in Copenhagen. Ralph should really serve as her lesson: her romantic notions could get her in trouble.

Though, a voice insisted on pointing out, Jamie was the opposite of Ralph. Her illusions about Ralph had collapsed as they had spent more time together. The more time she spent with Jamie, the more enamored she felt!

"You must be leaning one way or the other, though," he said. "The clients you met today loved you."

"Did they?"

"Unequivocally."

She wanted someone else to love her unequivocally! She ordered herself to stop being so teenager-with-a-crush.

She realized, in terms of the job, she didn't have any idea what was best for her. It was all too heady, like trying to make a decision when you were full of champagne.

"I need to go home," she said. "I have a place, beside the Falls, where I like to sit when I have a decision to make. It's free of distractions. No phones, no computers." Of course, she didn't have those things now, but she did have the biggest distraction of all: Jamie.

"The right answer always comes when I'm there."

"I envy you having a place like that."

"You could come one day, and see it." What was she doing? Trying to keep him in her life, even if she said no to the job? Trying to see what they would have left if they did not have this fabulous backdrop behind them?

"I could," he said, and she scanned his face. Was he placating her? Being polite? Or would he really like to see Timber Falls? She felt as if she would genuinely like to see him on her home ground. It would help her know if the strength of her feelings for him were real.

But it was complicated, because if he did meet her parents, if he did ever come to Timber Falls to see her, her mom and dad would jump to the conclusion it was serious. Knowing her parents, they would start picking names for grandchildren, and sharing them with him!

She'd known the man two days. Yes, she had to go home and get her head on straight. There would be no making a rational decision under these present circumstances.

So she might as well just enjoy the experience while it lasted!

When they got in, it was late, and yet Jessica could not help but notice that he was as reluctant to say good-night as she was.

They cleaned up the kitchen together, and then went into his living room. He put on music, and then patted the couch beside him.

"So little time left," he said. With relief? Or regret? Or some combination of both? "Tell me everything there is to know about you."

She laughed. "I wouldn't know where to start. And it's not interesting."

"Start at the first day of school, when you told me you met your guy. And let me decide if it's interesting."

And so she found herself telling him about growing up in a small town, surrounded by people who knew you and were related to you. She told him about swimming in mountain lakes, and decorating the trees in their teachers' yards with toilet paper rolls, and picking huckleberries on hot summer days, riding their horses down tree-shaded trails.

She told him of her and Devon, always together, best friends.

"It was such a perfect life," she said, and heard the wistfulness in her own voice. "And then when he died, there was an awareness I had never had before. That life was not safe, that everything you loved could be taken from you in a blink.

"The bookstore was my grandmother's. I had never considered owning her bookstore, though I had always worked there. But then she wanted to retire, and Devon had died and it seemed like a natural choice."

"A way to make your world safe again. Predictable."

Trust him to see that, so quickly, and so completely.

"Yes," she said, with tears forming in her eyes. "Yes, I've played it very safe ever since Devon died. And it seems every time I've tried to step away from that safety net, all my fears about life are proven entirely correct."

"Tell me about that."

"I've hinted about my online dating disaster. The truth was, I didn't really feel ready to meet anyone. I think it was a reaction to everyone in town suggesting it was time to get over it. One of the joys of small towns is that everyone knows your business, and weighs in on everything about your life, usually without an invitation."

"So, you met a guy online, which takes the pressure off.

Shows people you're getting on with things, without really changing anything."

"Quit being so astute! Anyway, it was a catastrophe. I finally decided to meet him. At the Annual Ascot Music Festival. Have you heard of it?

"Oh, yeah."

Of course he would have heard of it! He was cosmopolitan.

"Well, I hadn't. But I decided to meet him. It was all on the up-and-up. I paid my own way, and insisted on my own room."

"He let you? Pay your own way?"

"I insisted!"

"Okay," he said in a tone that let her know that's not how it would have happened with him.

"And anyway, I was glad I did, because then I didn't owe him anything. And in person, he was an absolute jerk. Full of himself and self-centered. There was a lady at the music festival who had lost her dog and was hurt, and he acted as if he was more important than that. As if it was a big inconvenience to him. I made a decision, on the spot, to not let it go any further with him."

"Good for you. So then you came home and licked your wounds until now?"

"Yes."

"A perfect excuse to play it safe some more?" he suggested, his tone gentle.

She wasn't used to this, someone *seeing* her so clearly.

"Well, that might be true, but I did meet two women who have become lifelong friends."

"Uh-huh."

"More safety?" she guessed from his tone.

He lifted a shoulder at her.

"Anyway, there is nothing wrong with playing it safe.

Look at this time! I took another chance, and another catastrophe."

"Really?" he said, softly. "I would think this is about the furthest thing from a catastrophe that I could imagine."

He was right. He was 100 percent right. She was living an absolute dream.

"Maybe the message from life," he suggested, "is that bad things happen. They happen to all of us. And we survive. Sometimes, if we look closely there can be a gift hidden in our worst moments."

She looked deeply at him, and his eyes so full of wisdom, and felt herself falling deeper. Tumbling toward him and what he offered.

A world that rewarded bravery.

A world where she could trust someone to be honest with her.

She could feel herself leaning toward him, leaning toward the adventure. And he leaned toward her, too.

Their lips met. Two souls who knew each other, who had known each other since the beginning of time and would know each other until the end.

He tasted of what he was: strength and calm.

But that strength, that she loved, and that was so obvious about him, was also what made him pull away from her.

"You know we can't," he said softly.

"If I don't take the job, can we?"

He laughed softly. "Now there's as poor a reason for making a career decision as I've ever heard."

He got up from her reluctantly. He stood over her for a moment, then reached down and cupped her cheek in his hand. He gazed at her face as though he were trying to memorize it. And then, he bent, placed one more gentle kiss on her lips, turned and went down the hall, into his bedroom. The door clicked shut with a kind of firm finality.

CHAPTER EIGHT

IT WAS JESSICA'S last day in NYC, and already it was show-ing every sign of being perfect. To her surprise, after put-ting her off last night, Jamie had joined her this morning.

From the moment he had introduced her to Patience and Fortitude, the marble lions that guarded the main en-trance to the New York Public Library, Jessica had been enchanted. They had joined a tour, just leaving. Jessica had been enraptured with every square inch of that iconic building,

And the truth was, not just with the building.

It was having another incredibly memorable experience with Jamie at her side. It was remembering his lips, the taste of them, it was the potential, in the air between them for *more*.

It was her last day here. Jessica could already feel a sense of loss—and something else.

She was going to say yes. She was going to say yes to this incredible opportunity that was being offered her. She was going to say yes to the adventure. Maybe not forever. She distrusted forever.

But what would the harm be in trying it?

And did the sizzle between her and Jamie have anything to do with her saying yes?

If anything, she saw it as a complication. He really was going to be her boss. He probably wasn't going to be avail-able to act as her tour guide, to eat pizza with, to take her to shows, to cook homemade meals for, to go on carriage rides through Central Park.

But he would be part of her life.

And she wanted that. She wanted to know him better. She could see the fabric of their lives weaving together. Perhaps fate had even ordained this. Even the theft, forcing them closer together, destiny having its way with them...

She stopped suddenly.

She was making plans for her whole life without checking in with a single soul. She had not checked in since she got here. She had not looked at any of her social media accounts and, apart from that first phone call to her parents, she had not talked to anyone.

Not being connected had felt freeing, and amazingly so.

But now, she couldn't help but wonder if she was living in a bubble. Jamie Gilbert-Cooper was just the kind of guy who could make a woman erase every other thing from her reality.

She needed to check in with her real life. She needed to ground herself. And just as she was recognizing that, she saw one of the library workstations—with a computer— come available.

Jamie had been emailing her pictures of their excursions. She could pick them up, and make a few posts. She could message with her mom and dad, and Daisy and Aubrey.

She suddenly recognized how momentous a turn in the road she had come to. She *needed* the input of those closest to her. She needed to know she had not given herself over to a fantasy, a fairy tale.

"I should use one of those computers," she said. "Can you give me half an hour?"

"Of course. I'm not sure if you have to be a member, but I can sign you in if you do."

Jessica signed in under Jamie's library account, and picked up the photos he had been emailing her. She could feel the delight unfolding in her as she looked at each of them. It confirmed her decision. She would take the job. She would move here. She would embrace the unknown.

I will let myself finish what I have started, which is falling in love with Jamie Gilbert-Cooper.

But that was the problem, wasn't it? Was she basing her decision on any of the right things?

She opened the message app on her favorite social media account. She sent her mother a picture of her with the lions in the background and a quick note saying she had seen *Phantom of the Opera* and been to the Russian Tea Room.

It was as if her mother had been waiting—which she probably had, Jessica realized guiltily.

Her mother wrote back.

So exciting. What's the job like? What are your thoughts?

Jessica replied that she was undecided and, after a little more conversation with her mother, reviewed some of her other social media accounts.

Jessica saw she had messages from both Daisy and Aubrey, but before she could open them, Aubrey saw she was online and popped up on chat.

How is it going? Why haven't we heard from you?

Awful incident at the airport. All my luggage, my computer and phone stolen. Haven't posted anything about it, as I don't want Mom and Dad to worry. I'm using the computer at the New York Public Library right now. So much to tell you!

And Daisy and I to tell you!! We have both been given the most extraordinary gifts. Daisy got a house in Italy.

What?

Yes! And I've been given the funds to have the most grand adventure of my entire life. I can afford to circle the globe, travel, have adventures. I feel as if I've won a lottery!

I don't really understand.

We don't either. We've been waiting for you to check in, because we think your job offer is related, too.

In what way?

Well, doesn't it seem just a little too coincidental that all three of us are being given these opportunities? Not just gifts, really, but life-changing chances?

Jessica could feel something in her going cold.

From who?

But then, she knew. There was only one thread connecting the three of them. That little old lady and her dog that they had helped in Copenhagen. The three of them had talked about that before: how Viv had said she wanted to keep in touch, but though Aubrey, Daisy and Jessica had, Viv had not. While she had accepted their friend and contact requests, her social media accounts had never been used and she had never responded to messages or inquiries after her health.

Daisy and I think she might be Vivian Ascot.

I don't think I recognize that name.

Yes, you do. Ascot Corporation. They were the big sponsors of the music festival. It's one of the biggest corps in the world. They're into everything from ducks to doughnuts. Didn't you say your job interview was with Jensen, Henry and Ascot?

Aubrey had underlined Ascot to make her point. Jessica stared at the screen and felt as if the bottom was falling out of her world. It was a worse shock than having her things stolen. She'd been tricked. Deceived.

Oh, no doubt Viv—if this was Viv behind all this—thought she was doing a good deed, repaying some perceived debt or act of kindness.

But it meant that Jessica hadn't been chosen for this job because of her qualifications, or her know-how.

She felt a fool. How could she have believed, even for one second, that the owner of a miniscule bookstore in a town no one had ever heard of, which did not even deserve its own dot on the map, had come to the attention of an international firm like JHA?

No wonder she had been picked off at the airport! She might as well have had "easy mark" tattooed across her forehead.

And he was part of it! Jamie was part of it.

She'd planned to abandon her parents. And her bookstore. And her community. On the power of a kiss! She was deeply ashamed of herself.

And she was shocked by her lack of discernment. Last night, she had felt as if she could trust this man almost more than anyone else she had ever met! She wasn't just so naive they could pick her off at the airport, she was an immature fool.

I've just about got interim travel documents in place, so I'll be heading home soon. I'll call you and Daisy when I get there.

We haven't talked about your job yet! Or NYC.

Her job. Jessica felt unnaturally irritated that Aubrey hadn't picked up on it. It was a joke. A sham. There was no job. It was a creation of some little old lady with way too much time on her hands and way too much money. You didn't shape people's lives as if they were children's modeling clay just waiting to be molded!

She logged off the computer, resisting a temptation to try a seedy site while she was signed in under Jamie's name. What would happen? Alarms go off? An investigation into him? His reputation smirched? It would be a stupid, childish, "take that" gesture.

As she got up from the computer, she saw him coming toward her.

He was every bit as glorious as the first time she had laid eyes on him. It could make a woman weak when she desperately needed to be strong.

"What's wrong?" he said, as he came up to her. He took her shoulders in his hands. "Jessica? What's happened? Did you get bad news from home?"

"Bad news," she said, shaking out from under his hands, "but not from home."

She turned away from him and went out the main exit, past Patience and Fortitude, the magic of meeting them dissipated.

The magic of this city dissipated.

Suddenly it didn't seem energetic and vibrant and as if she could never get enough.

It felt dirty and noisy and crowded and she just wanted to go home.

"Jessica—" he put his hand on her shoulder and she spun around. "What's happened?"

His face, the genuine concern that darkened his eyes, made her feel as if she could be made of steel, and still melt. She had to be strong! She drew in a sharp breath and jerked out from under his hand.

"Does the name Vivian Ascot mean anything to you?"

"You know Ascot is part of our company name," he said, his tone guarded.

"I did know that. What I didn't know was that a little old lady that I told you about last night—the one I helped at the music festival in Copenhagen—had that name. I knew her only as Viv. But you know her, don't you?"

"Not really. She's mostly a silent partner. I met her once."

"The whole thing—the whole job offer—is some pathetic act of charity, isn't it?"

"No! Not as far as I know."

"What I want to know is what is your part in all of this?"

"Look, I admit, at first I thought the old gal was off her rocker, recommending you for a job."

Off her rocker.

"Was there a job? Or did she create one?"

His look of discomfort was all the answer she needed. "What was your part in it?" she asked again. Jessica could hear something dangerous in her voice. And so could he.

He hemmed uncomfortably.

"Be honest with me," she said, of the man that just last night she had thought was one of the most honest she had ever met. "If you are capable of it."

He flinched from that. "Okay. I wasn't sure why she picked me to meet you. I admit I thought it was a punishment."

"Meeting me was a punishment?" she asked. Her voice was shrill enough that a few heads turned toward them.

"That came out wrong."

"Did it, now?"

"I crossed swords with her. I didn't like her name for the music festival in Copenhagen. I don't even remember it now."

"Carlene to Celine and Everything In Between."

"That's it," he said with a wince. "Really, it was so trivial I thought she'd forgotten it. But then when I got the order I was supposed to personally meet your plane and look after you when you got here, I thought it was payback time."

"So, Miss Ascot got me here on a false pretense, and I was some kind of revenge to you against some slight against her?"

"That's what I thought. But I was wrong, Jessica. Really wrong. When I saw you meet our clients, I realized she knew what she was doing. You have something. You—"

"Oh, spare me. How would I know you were telling the truth?"

He looked like she had slapped him, and she was glad!

"Everything we did was about looking after me, wasn't it? From the Russian Tea Room to *The Phantom of the Opera*—"

"No, it wasn't," he told her tightly.

She barely heard him. "Your grand obligation, your need to win back Viv after a fall from favor. You should be very pleased with yourself. I actually thought you were enjoying spending time with me. Last night? I thought I could trust you to tell me how it really is. Isn't that a laugh?"

"Jessica—"

But she was beyond listening to him. "Even the clothes were part of the grand lie, weren't they? Those clothes from Hennessey's. How much were they really worth?"

He was silent.

"They were worth a fortune, weren't they? You had Meredith make up a bill that coincided with what the insurance company said they would give me."

"It was just making you so happy. I wanted—"

"Lies do not make people happy!" she said. "I'm an adult. Do you get that? I don't need you, or anyone else, to look after me, to decide the course of my life for me."

His mouth opened to protest and then closed again.

"When you get back to your apartment," she told him, "you can box all those clothes up and take them back. Some things still have the tags on. Anything I wore can go to Goodwill. But I'll pay for it all. I'll send you the e-transfer as soon as I get home. I don't want it anymore."

"Look, we're both going back to the apartment, and we're talking this thing through."

"Again, you're going to make all the decisions, as if I'm a child who needs your guidance? What exactly is the point of talking it through?" She cocked her head at him. "You think I'm gullible, don't you?"

"That's not how I would put it."

"And that's not a no. I bet you've found this all quite hilarious—small-town girl's infatuation with super suave you!"

He cocked his head at her. He frowned. "Infatuation?" he asked softly.

And then she realized she had said way too much, and revealed way too much. Unable to bear one more moment, afraid her anger was going to turn to tears, she turned and ducked into the crowd.

"Jessica!"

But she spotted the rarest thing you could ever see in New York City—an empty cab—idling at the curb, waiting for a customer.

She jumped in and closed the door.

"Where to?"

She could see Jamie racing toward them. Where to? "Take me to the Canadian Consulate office," she said, and the cab pulled away, leaving Jamie standing there. She was pleased to see the faint look of panic on his face.

His charge had escaped him.

She hoped he would have fun explaining that to Vivian Ascot!

As the cab squeezed out into traffic, she turned and looked at Jamie one more time. And an awful truth nudged her.

Was this really about Vivian Ascot?

Or was this a convenient excuse to run? To not face her deepest fear.

Which is? she asked herself. No answer came.

Jamie watched helplessly as the cab pulled away. He felt afraid for her. It was a big city and she had few skills for navigating it.

He saw another cab coming, lifted his arm to flag it, and then, slowly put it down and turned away.

It was more of the same, it was more of the very same thing she was accusing him of: not treating her like an adult, taking charge, protecting her. As much as it bugged him, he had to trust her to find her own way.

He went to work and tried to clear Jessica from his mind. It was not that easy. Her parting words about *infatuation* clawed at his insides. She cared about him. She had trusted him. And he had blown it. He had blown it, even though he cared about her, too.

Which was just proof he was unsuited for the whole serious relationship thing. He didn't have a clue how to navigate any situation that required any depth. Jessica required depth.

Why was he even thinking about her in terms of a serious relationship?

He cared about her, yes, but he barely knew her. They barely knew each other. And yet, even as Jamie tried to convince himself of that, he sensed the lie.

They knew each other. There had been a serious, serious connection between them. In that light, it was good that she was gone. No, more than good. It was *great*. She was the kind of woman who could make even a hedonistic self-centered guy like him put his life under the microscope. Look hard at it. Find it—and himself—lacking.

She was the kind of woman that could make a man long for something more, feel his whole life was a desert of shallowness and meaninglessness, and that she held an answer, she could guide him to the oasis.

Jessica Winton could do that after two days! He was *glad* she was gone.

But when he entered his apartment after work, it seemed dark and lifeless and empty. He found himself in the bedroom she had used.

Her scent was in the air again—lavender. It made him ache, which made him feel furious with himself. That fury propelled him to the closet. He would do exactly as she instructed. She wanted to be an adult? She wanted to be in charge? Fine, he'd send all that stuff to Goodwill, just as she requested. He'd do it right now—he'd banish her from his space and from his heart.

He opened the door and saw *that* dress, the cocktail dress, in wisps of blue so insubstantial the dress might have been constructed of fog. It was the dress that she had worn to *Phantom of the Opera* and memory flooded him.

Memories of every single moment they had shared crowded around him. He went into the closet and buried his nose in the fabric.

He thought about how much she had loved that dress. Most women would have wanted it, would have taken it, especially if they were mad. All the women he'd ever met kept his gifts when it was over. But she wanted to give them away?

Somehow he knew, despite her ability to think of someone else, even when she was in distress, he knew he would not be sending that dress, or anything else of hers, to Goodwill.

He also knew she was the kind of woman who would require him—any man she was with—to be a better man.

"Not up for that," he said out loud, as if somehow that would make it true, as if it would take away the unexpected longing to be the kind of man worthy of a woman like Jessica.

He told himself, again, he was glad she was gone.

The words rang as hollow as a tree that had had its insides burned clean out by a lightning strike.

CHAPTER NINE

"JESSICA, YOUR FATHER and I have to talk to you. Can we come over?"

Jessica sighed. This was the problem with living in a little cottage in your parents' backyard. Of course they could come over, they were steps away. She couldn't even pretend she wasn't home. Her mother's kitchen window looked right at her house. They would have known the second she returned from the bookstore today.

Funny how since she'd returned from New York, she was so aware of the "problems" in her life. Town too stifling, parents too close, house too small, bookstore not challenging. Her trip to New York had triggered a deep sense of dissatisfaction in her. Which explained why she had been avoiding her parents. It made her feel guilty that she suddenly yearned for things she had never yearned for before.

Including the taste of a certain man's lips.

But still, all those "problems" seemed like they might only be distractions from the real issue. And yet, she recoiled from the question that pressed at the edges of her mind every time she lay down to go to sleep: What was the *real* reason she had run away from Jamie?

If she craved the taste of his lips, if she wanted him in her life, why hadn't she stayed and talked to him? Heard his side of things? At least given whatever was happening between them an opportunity to grow? Should she call him? Should she apologize?

Before she could go too far down that road, there was a knock on the door. Jessica realized she should have offered to go over to their place. Her small space was something it had never been before—a disaster! Since her return, looking after her own space seemed like too much of an effort.

She opened the door and her mother and father filed in, looking very solemn, casting worried glances at her and the state of her house, on the way to her kitchen table.

"Jessica," her mother said, without preamble, "you've been home a week. Your father and I can't help but notice you seem depressed."

Depressed? Did it go that far? She looked around her tiny home: empty ice cream buckets on the counter, dishes piled in the sink, clothes on the floor. Good grief! This was not her.

"We know you told us you were robbed in New York. We were wondering about post-traumatic stress. Maybe some counseling—"

Jessica bit her lip. It was the first time she had felt like laughing since she got home. "Mom, I'm okay. I don't have PTSD. Honestly, the robbery…" she hesitated. What could she say? Led to the best experience of her entire life? "…just didn't affect me that much."

If that was true, if it had led to the best experience of her life, why had she been so quick to run, to slam the door shut behind her?

"But something has!" her mother wailed. "Your father and I have talked about it. Another possibility we thought of was that you fell in love with New York, didn't you?"

For a heart-stopping moment, Jessica heard *you fell in love in New York, didn't you?*

She didn't say anything, so her mother rushed on.

"If that's what's bothering you—if you want to go there—we support you 100 percent. We would miss you dreadfully, of course, but we are still young people, quite capable of looking after ourselves. We're not doddering old fools, even if we can't run our phones. Or the TV set."

"Don't forget the tablets," her father added, pleased to be of help.

Her mother shot him a look.

Jessica saw, between them, in that look of exasperated affection, everything she had always wanted. Comfort, companionship, love that had survived many tests and challenges, a deep *knowing* of another human being.

Her parents, she knew, from their stories, had been just like Jessica and Devon: lifelong companions, soul mates who had grown up next door to each other.

But in New York, Jessica had glimpsed something far more terrifying than their steady love, something that burned brighter and hotter.

There was that fear again, flitting around the edges of her mind. She shoved it away.

"What your mother is trying to say is that we would never want you to put off an opportunity out of a sense of obligation to us."

"Yes, that is exactly what I wanted to say. Just think! We could visit you in NYC. It's on my bucket list."

They were both looking at her so hopefully, wanting so desperately to fix anything that was wrong in her world.

Jessica could feel tears forming in her eyes. Her parents were setting her free, giving her their blessing. But in her heart, she knew it wasn't a sense of obligation to her parents holding her back.

That was just one of her many excuses.

"Thank you," she told them softly.

Her father took that as a signal to leap up from his chair and get away from a conversation that was not about an old car, so therefore was uncomfortable.

"I have to work on that lock thing," he said, and hauled his phone out of his pocket. "Look, Jessica, I can lock the doors of the house from here. I'm trying to hook up the bookstore for you, but—"

Her mother gave him a nudge and a warning look.

"But I can do it myself!" he said. "No need for you to help, Jessica. At all."

After they left, she looked at the clock. There was time, before dark, to go to the Falls. She had told Jamie that she always went there when she needed an answer, but she had been making the hike almost daily, and still no answers came.

New York had shown her an uncomfortable truth. Jessica had outgrown her hometown. Now what? Obviously, New York had not worked out, but should she be actively seeking out other opportunities? Thinking of selling her bookstore? Moving on?

She might have normally sounded out these ideas on Aubrey and Daisy. She had come to trust their judgment deeply. They were definitely her "go-to" when she needed to share a confidence.

But this time, they were in a tizzy of excitement over the shocking gifts they had been given.

Neither of them would entertain the notion that their gifts—Daisy, a villa in Italy, and Aubrey, funds to go on a grand adventure—were very different than hers. Neither of their gifts was directed at their professional competency. While their gifts seemed only to reflect the generosity of the giver, seemed to be only about embracing *fun*, Jessica felt the weight of a judgment in the gift of a job opportunity, as if Viv had sniffed out a failure, as if the opportunity she had directed toward Jessica was based in pity.

Aubrey had scoffed at the idea, and Daisy had been silent when Jessica had said it, which Jessica assumed was disagreement. So, she had gone quiet online, feeling, not quite betrayed by her two friends, but not understood, either.

Suddenly, she had the feeling. *They knew.*

Aubrey and Daisy knew that Jessica's feelings of up-heaval may have been precipitated by the unexpected job offer, but they had not been caused by it.

Indeed, it might have all brought her to this place she most needed to be.

Facing the fear that was at the core of her being, and that directed every single other thing in her life.

Jamie swatted at a mosquito. He felt as if he had been on the longest journey of his life, and it had brought him to the very edges of the earth.

Timber Falls was not an easy place to reach. It had taken nearly two days to get here, including the flight and renting a car from the nearest airport. After driving through a wil-derness of towering trees and soaring mountains—country so endless and magnificent it made a man feel small and lost—his GPS had finally delivered him to Timber Falls.

It was a town out of a postcard: against a backdrop of ragged-edged mountains and deep green forests, was a wide valley that held neat and tidy streets, lined with pastel-painted cottages and Victorian houses in historical colors. There were shady porches, with swings on them, fenced yards with patches of lush green grass that begged for bare toes to wiggle in it. He caught glimpses of garden plots with neat rows of furry green growth poking up through rich black soil. Everywhere were lilac trees, in full blooms of white, lavender, deep purple. The summer air was per-fumed with their scent.

He passed two churches, small boxes of buildings with soaring spires, and a water park where children squealed as they squirted each other with cannon-like guns and as a bucket on a post filled and then spilled over on top of them. The elementary school and the high school shared grounds, the soccer fields and baseball diamonds empty, the swings in the play yard deserted for the summer.

The outlying neighborhoods gave way to a quaint main street, baskets overflowing with colorful petunias hanging from old-fashioned streetlight standards. At two stories, the tallest buildings were the town hall, and the Royal Bank.

It was all exactly as Jamie had pictured the town Jessica would come from.

He drove slowly, passing the hardware store, a restaurant, a bakery, a hair salon. And there it was. Sandwiched in between a false-fronted ice cream store and a sandstone art gallery was a narrow old house that had been converted into a bookstore.

The plate glass window had a graphic in Baskerville Old Face that declared it was Jessica's store, The Book and Cranny.

Jamie could feel his heart begin to beat faster in anticipation of seeing her again. How would she react? Surely she would not slam a door in his face when she knew how hard it was to get to this place?

He was here on official business, but if that was completely true, his heart would not be beating nearly out of his chest at the thought of seeing her.

He got out of his car and was blasted by early-summer heat. He hurried across the sidewalk and opened the door of her store.

A bell rang when the door opened. The store should have felt dark after the bright sunlight of outside, but it didn't. He had expected he might feel closed in by shelves of books, but instead the space felt open, cheery, light-filled and wonderfully cool.

He could see Jessica's touch everywhere: in the beautiful

little nook that the store had probably taken its name from, which was filled with colorful pillows, in the sunflower-yellow wall hung with framed posters for favorite children's books: *Where the Wild Things Are, Love You Forever, Goodnight Moon.*

A well-loved copy of *Are You My Mother?* was open on its spine on one of the pillows. He scanned the space and saw only four people: a mother with two children, and a middle-aged man flicking through the newspaper selection.

No Jessica. In fact, there was no evidence that anyone was employed here. He walked around and looked at hand-lettered signs on the walls.

We can book you without an arrest.
Odds are we're your favorite bookie.
Caught you read-handed.
We're all about buy the book.

Then a door opened, and he held his breath, then let it go again when an elderly woman came out from an office area and set some books on the service counter. He craned his neck to see into the office, but she frowned at him and closed the door.

He walked over to the counter. "I'm looking for Jessica Winton."

The woman lowered half-glasses to the tip of her nose and regarded him silently for a long moment. "She's not here. She left early. She's been leaving quite early every day since she came back from New York City."

She said this in a faintly accusing tone, as if she could read where he came from, from a mile away. As if Jessica had returned to them changed, and she saw that as his fault. Had she returned changed?

Reading way too much into it, he told himself sternly.

He was here on business. He couldn't very well ask where she lived, could he? Or maybe he could, since it felt like the pretense of business, not that he could afford any more pretense around Jessica!

"When will she be back?"

"Tomorrow morning."

Did he look as deflated as he felt? Because the woman's expression inexplicably softened, and she pushed her glasses back up on her nose.

"You could try the Falls," she said. "I've seen her going up that way several times."

Small towns, where everyone *knew* what everyone else was doing and weren't afraid to share it, either. What if a stranger was seeking Jessica for nefarious purposes? He wanted to say something to the woman about revealing her boss's whereabouts, but Jamie reminded himself, as he exited the store back into the heat, that Jessica had not appreciated his feeling protective of her.

The Falls. She had told him that was where she went for answers. What answer did she seek since she had returned to this place?

Swatting at mosquitos, it occurred to Jamie that he was in her home territory this time. It might be that he was the one needing protection. Weren't there bears around here? His shoes didn't seem particularly well suited to this activity either. How far were the Falls?

He heard them before he saw them, a roar in the distance that grew louder and louder until he could see mist in the air. He came around a final twist in the pathway and stopped short.

Jessica was sitting on a large, flat rock, facing the Falls. Her eyes were closed and her face was lifted to the mist that fell around her. Her knees were drawn up to her and her arms were wrapped around them. She had on a sleeveless white tank top, belted khaki shorts and sturdy hiking boots. In the time she had been back here, her skin had become sun-kissed and was the warm golden brown of a loaf of bread fresh from the oven. Her hair was in a braid that hung over one shoulder.

She did not look like the same woman as he had spent time with in New York: she seemed more natural, completely at home with herself, more stunningly beautiful, if that was possible.

She must have sensed she was no longer alone, because she dropped her head, opened her eyes and turned to look at him.

For one moment, in her eyes, he saw surprise, followed by unbridled joy.

He was aware a man could live for such a look from a woman.

But then the look was gone, so quickly he wondered if it was a trick of light and mist, an illusion created by the rainbows that danced in the air around her.

"Hello, Jessica," he said, having to raise his voice to be heard over the thunder of the Falls.

She slid off the rock, brushed off the seat of her shorts and faced him, her arms crossed over her chest.

"What are you doing here?" she demanded, the look a man could live for gone completely from her beautiful face.

Jessica could not take her eyes off Jamie. He was out of his element, and impossibly it made him even more gorgeous! That beautifully cut suit, the jacket hooked over his shoulder with his thumb, made him look like a model ready for a photo shoot in a rugged location. His hair was falling sexily over one eye, and he looked as confident as he had on the streets of New York.

She had been coming here for answers since her return

from the big city but the Falls had been stubbornly silent. How could she have known him for such a short period of time, and her heart whispered *beloved* when she saw him?

When Jamie had come out of the mist, he had seemed as if he could be her answer.

But wasn't he the kind of man who a lot of women probably thought was their answer? By his own admission his very own sister said he had made capturing hearts a game. Besides, here was the truth: people needed to provide their own answers!

She had to steel herself against that abundance of charm and confidence. She had to steel herself against the cry of her own heart.

"What are you doing here?" she asked him again.

"I was sent here. To talk to you."

Sent here. She was still some kind of assignment. "Oh," she said, and tossed her braid over her shoulder, *"punishment."* You let the charity case get away."

His expression darkened. "It was never like that. Vivian Ascot has amazing instincts. She hasn't gotten to where she is in business on her inheritance alone, believe me. You have something she wants, and I've been sent to get it."

Jessica actually felt disappointed. He was here for business, not because he had missed her. Not because he had thought of her every day. Not because those thoughts had crowded out all else and filled him with an insane sense of longing. Not because his life had suddenly felt as it was lacking and as if he needed to change everything.

"What does she want?" Jessica had tried to get in touch with Vivian since she and Daisy and Aubrey had figured out that was who their benefactress was. They all had. But as Daisy had put it, *"You'd think she was the Queen."*

Her security was impenetrable. They couldn't even tell if

Vivian knew about their multiple social media attempts to reach her, or if they had all been relegated to the spam pile.

"She—we, JHA—want to see, firsthand, how you are making that bookstore such a phenomenal success. If you won't come to work for us, we'll come to you. We're hoping you'll agree to let us use your bookstore as a model. We'd compensate you, naturally."

The only part that interested her was the *"we."* JHA. Not *me.* Not *I.*

"It's unnecessary to compensate me," Jessica said stiffly. She also realized she was slightly miffed that he wasn't here to beg her to change her mind. "And it was unnecessary to come here. I could have sent you any information that you needed."

"You could have," he agreed.

"But that wouldn't have been a punishment, then, would it?"

"This isn't a punishment. I asked to come. I wanted to see you in your own environment."

She studied his face, and found she could not meet the steadiness of his gaze. She could feel her heart spinning crazily. He was here because he wanted to be. A woman not as determined to find her own way as Jessica was could read way too much into that.

She, accidentally, looked at his lips. She remembered the taste of them and felt dizzy with longing, weak with a need to throw herself at him, feel his arms come around her, cover his face with tiny kisses, tangle her hands in the silky gray of his hair.

Instead, she brushed by him and headed back down the trail, fast.

"Those shoes are ridiculous for a hike in the mountains," she called to him over her shoulder.

"Believe me, I already figured that out."

"You want to see how my bookstore works? You want to use it as a model? Fine. How long are you here for?"

"I thought I'd stay the whole day tomorrow, and leave the following morning," he said, his tone cautious.

"Perfect. You can get some firsthand experience with the *model*—and not the kind of model I assume you're used to, either."

"What kind would that be?"

"Long-legged, photogenic." She noticed he did not deny it. Of course he was the type that dated models! No surprise there. "Story time is tomorrow at ten. You can lead it."

"I'm not that good with kids."

"You have a nephew."

"At a distance!"

"That's just sad."

"Look, Jessica, I'm trying to tell you I'm not a kid person."

Maybe what he was really trying to tell her was that he was not husband material. Good grief! Was she looking at him like he was husband material?

"You read them a story. You don't have to be good with them."

"How old are they?"

"Three to five."

He looked nonplussed. "Don't you need a criminal record check, or something? To work with kids?"

"Working with them is overstating it. Don't worry, their mothers will be there."

Ogling the super cute guy from the big city who had I date models *written all over him.*

"Is there a gang of them?"

"We don't have gangs in Timber Falls," she told him, straight-faced. "Expect five or six kids."

Then, knowing in those shoes he could never catch her, she started to jog down the trail.

"Are there bears out here?" he called after her.

"Yes! And cougars."

"Cougars?" he said, and inserted a theatrical hopeful note into his voice.

"Not that kind, you pervert."

"That's right! A pervert. I should not be asked to work with children."

She wanted to be indifferent to him, but it was impossible. "Also, the odd wolf. Definitely coyotes."

"You'll be sorry if I get eaten, Jessica Winton! Who will lead story time then?"

She didn't turn back to him. She didn't want to let him see her smiling. She didn't want him to know just how easily she was charmed by him.

"Are you going to at least offer to take me out for dinner?" he called. "I did that for you."

"You thought of it as a punishment," she reminded him.

"You can think of it the same way."

Somehow, she could not. "I have plans for tonight." This was not exactly the truth, unless watching TV was considered a plan, but there was no sense him thinking she was just going to set her life aside since the big, important man from New York had arrived.

"Oh," he said. He sounded disappointed. Which was elating. He also sounded as if he had not even considered the possibility she might have a life here in Timber Falls. Which was insulting.

He made her life complicated without even trying, she thought grumpily.

"Go to Henry's for supper," she told him. "They have the best burger in town. And try the B and B on First Street. I bet they'll let you check in without ID."

"As they should. I'm a completely trustworthy person."

"Ha. Tell that to someone who wasn't offered a fake job by you."

"We need to talk about that. Obviously it—"

She realized he was engaging her, even though she had decided not to be engaged by him. "Tomorrow at ten," she interrupted him, and then broke into a jog down the familiar trail, literally leaving him in her dust.

That night, lying in her bed, sleepless, because she knew he was just down the street—probably had charmed the socks off all the local girls at Henry's tonight—she warned herself against feeling the way she did.

Alive. Tingling with the delight of having seen him again, the anticipation of spending the day with him tomorrow.

I am falling in love with him, she realized, shocked. It was like nothing she had ever felt before, certainly it was not the cozy-as-a-comfortable-shoe feeling she had had with Devon. It felt as if he was air, as if she needed him in order to breathe.

It seemed imperative that he not know this. She had already let it slip once that she was infatuated with him, but now she had to keep this secret to herself. He could never know she *regretted* not joining him for dinner.

In her head she made a complete schedule for him for the next day: he could lead story time, send emails to people she had tracked down books that she thought might interest them, play chess with the Court Chessters in the afternoon. Serendipitously, the Smitten Word met here tomorrow night, and he could be the guest speaker. She'd surprise him with that one.

Professionally, she'd throw everything she had at him in hopes it would keep the personal stuff at bay!

CHAPTER TEN

"I LOOKED UP books last night," Jamie told her in the morning. "*Truck in the Muck* is a current favorite of the under-five set. Have you got that?"

She slid him a look. He was dressed in jeans. That was a first. And a casual shirt, also a first. If he had any lingering trepidation at all about leading story time, it did not show now. He was, obviously, one of those highly adaptable people, who could rise to any challenge. He looked extraordinarily handsome—and at home—in her space.

He was also freshly shaven, and she could smell soap and aftershave, and it made her feel as if she had been drinking champagne. So much for keeping the personal stuff at bay!

She realized her bookstore—her safe place, her hidey-hole in all the world—was never going to feel the same.

But, in fact, it hadn't felt the same since she had returned from New York, anyway.

He also looked rested, not as though he had tossed and turned, and wondered endlessly what to wear today!

She had chosen casual, because really she did not have much to choose from. She longed for her dress with the poppies on it, but settled for a knit tank top and capris.

"I have it. You can't read that one, though. I bring in a dozen copies of the book we read at story time and today's story is *How Do You Do, Suzie Q?*"

"A dozen?"

"Some of the moms who come today will buy one for their own child, or to put away for a gift for later, or for the book bag."

"The book bag?"

"Not every family in Timber Falls can afford a brand-new book, and so I created the book bag. You buy one book for yourself, and another to donate that will find its way to a child who is in need."

"You know all the kids in town?"

"No, of course not. But as the idea caught on, people tell me, in confidence, which kids might be struggling a bit. They'll slip me a note, or call anonymously. So-and-so has a birthday coming up. Or not much under the Smith family tree this year for Christmas. Or John Doe has been invited to a birthday party, and his mom can't afford for him to bring a present."

He stared at her for a long time. "It's brilliant. But it's more."

She cocked her head at him.

"It's beautiful," he said softly. "It's like feeding the homeless, only better. Feeding minds and souls instead of bodies."

"You're making too much of it."

He looked at her steadily. "I don't think I am."

And she felt herself blushing as though he had said, not that her idea was beautiful, but that she was beautiful.

Because he was looking at her as if she was.

Thankfully, Phillip Morrison chose that moment to burst through the door, having freed himself of his mother. She would never tell Jamie—or anyone else—but his mom was a struggling single parent, and he was one of those kids who benefited from the book bag.

"Could we have *Truck in the Muck* today?" he asked, his voice loud, his eyes already darting around looking for things to wreck. Thankfully, she had done her best to Phillip-proof the kids section.

"A kindred spirit," Jamie said in an undertone to Jessica.

"Who are you?" Phillip demanded.

"You can call me Jamie. I'm reading the story today."

"I want *Truck in the Muck*," Phillip said, his voice getting shrill.

Jamie contemplated him for a moment, and then sank onto his heels so he could look the little boy right in the eye. "That's what I want, too," he said in a confidential tone. "Tell you what, if you will be my assistant for the first story, we will have two stories today."

Jamie had been here five minutes, and he was changing the rules. And yet, as she watched, a small light came on in Phillip, so starved for male attention, and the worst possible thing happened to Jessica.

"So this is my first time," Jamie said, rising to his feet, "what do we do?"

"Set out the pillows in a circle, here," Phillip said and raced off to the nook to grab pillows.

Jamie's eyes met hers, so filled with *knowing* about that little boy's life. As something hard around Phillip melted as Jamie and he set up the mom chairs, something hard around her heart melted, too. She could picture Jamie as a father. As each of those children came in, and appeared equally awestruck by their new story time leader, the vision intensified.

She should find something else to do.

But instead, entranced, she sat down with the moms in a circle of chairs behind the children.

He was a magnificent storyteller. He used different voices. He paused theatrically in all the right places, he lowered his eyebrows and raised them up. He controlled Phillip with firm ease that made Phillip putty in his hands.

"Oh, my goodness," Doris Anderson whispered to her. "I'm in love."

Even though Jessica shot Doris an exasperated look that reminded her she was a very happily married woman, secretly she knew exactly how Doris was feeling.

Exactly.

As promised, Jamie read the two stories, and then was swarmed by small people wanting hugs—Jessica had forgotten to tell him about that traditional ending for story time. He handled the unexpected assignment delightfully: uncomfortable, obviously, but soldiering through.

Normally, the mothers would grab a copy of the book that had been read today from the available stack, leave their children in the children's section and wander off to peruse a book for themselves.

Today, they surrounded Jamie, wanting information.

"Where are you from?"

"What are you doing here?"

"How long will you be here?"

He handled it all with grace and humor, and soon had those women around him laughing.

He's bad for sales, Jessica told herself crankily, even as she could not take her eyes off him.

He saw Phillip and his mother slipping out the door, and excused himself from the women he was talking to.

"Hey, buddy," he called.

Phillip turned around.

"This is for you." And he squatted down to eye level and presented him with the copy of *Truck in the Muck* that he was still holding.

Phillip stared at the book, and then threw himself into Jamie's arms with such strength he nearly bowled him over. Then he let go and ran out the door after his mother. Jamie's pristine shirt looked faintly grubby, and he didn't even brush at the stain the child had left on it. He looked down at it, with a funny smile on his face.

Jessica went to the till, where a line was forming. She had been wrong about Jamie being bad for sales. She sold eight children's books, three romance novels, a cookbook on dinners for two, and a dusty copy of the *Kama Sutra* that she had not been aware was in inventory. She was unable to meet Doris Anderson's eyes as she shoved it quickly in a bag.

The last person in line was Jamie, with his wallet out. He had another copy of *Truck in the Muck*. "Please ring up the one I gave him, and put this one in the book bag."

She did, as unable to meet his eyes as she had been when Doris Anderson bought the *Kama Sutra*, afraid of what he would see.

The awful, awful truth.

Falling. Falling. Falling.

Jamie found himself immersed in Jessica's world. It was a magical place. He quickly discovered people loved her bookstore. And why wouldn't they? It was warmly welcoming, a place to drop by for a chat with neighbors, a book browse, a quick look at the calendar of upcoming events that she posted and put a copy of in every single book bag that went out of there.

In the next month she was hosting two readings by authors, one "Summer Fun" theme night for teens and one for eight-to-twelve-year-olds. She had live music here every Thursday where she showcased local talent—and sold their CDs.

As well as hosting story time once a week, the bookstore hosted the chess club, whom he would be meeting this afternoon. She also provided evening meeting space for AA—now those people bought books; toastmasters—also book buyers; as well as a host of other local clubs, interest and support groups. She even brought in a fortune-teller twice a year.

She tracked people's buying habits and, without any pressure at all, she would show them a book she had discovered in their area of interest.

"Mr. Thompson, I came across this book on common fossils of the Rocky Mountains. Would you like to have a look?"

Or, "Pam, I found this book about elderly parents and Alzheimer's."

"Sheila, is Freddy still going through his dinosaur obsession? You might like this for him."

But none of this interest in her customers was the least bit mercenary—even though she sold a ton of books. She cared about these people. They were her friends, her neighbors, her relatives, people she had gone to school with, people her parents had gone to school with.

It was very evident to him as he shadowed Jessica through her day, that the people of her town loved her, and she loved them. Despite the fact she didn't sell any beverages or food—bad for the books—the bookstore was their gathering place, the heart and soul of their community.

She had managed, as far as he could see, to do the rarest of things. She mixed compassion, concern and genuine caring for people with her business. The Book and Cranny was not a repository of dusty tomes, but alive with energy and enthusiasm.

And it was Jessica at the heart of all that.

Jamie thought they could probably use her "model" all they wanted. They could package her procedures and document her successes and show her numbers in a glossy-covered report and distribute them to all their clients. But it would be missing the secret ingredient: Jessica Winton. Without her, would it be successful?

When he was with her, he couldn't help but remember how she had made him feel in New York: happy, engaged. Her company was imminently enjoyable. Could he revisit the possibility of her working for JHA?

But there was that other thing going on between them, too, just below the surface. Awareness of each other. A desire to touch—to brush hands, to graze shoulders. He tried to avoid looking at her lips, because every time he did he was nearly swamped by the memory of that taste of them.

So, how could they revisit her coming to work for JHA? He would be her boss. He didn't want to be her boss.

He wanted to be...

He was stunned by the word his mind filled in. *Lover.*

He wanted to be Jessica Winton's lover. He wanted her eyes to rest on him with hunger, and he wanted his touch to make her long for him. He wanted to taste her all over. He wanted to possess her in every way it was possible for a man to possess a woman.

And he wanted her to possess him the same way.

"What?" Jessica asked him, turning back from the door to look at him. She had just ushered the last customer out, and put out the closed sign.

"Nothing." Too sharply, too quickly, too defensively.

"You were looking at me oddly."

"Was I?"

She gave him a quizzical look. "Never mind. We have time for a quick dinner, and then I have a group coming in tonight."

They left the store, and she locked the door behind her with a code. "Don't tell my dad," she told him with a laugh. "I'm supposed to be able to lock it with my phone. I don't have the heart to tell him it's not working right."

Her *dad*, he reminded himself. She was not the kind of girl a man could give himself over to having lascivious thoughts about!

But even with that stern reminder to himself, dinner was a torture of being aware of her. A hamburger! Not pheasant under glass, not Le Bernardin, not anything special at all. But that little speck of mustard at the corner of her lip made awareness of her snap along his spine as though he was touching a live electrical wire.

This was what life would be if Jessica was in it: everything would become special, every moment lit from within. That was what she had done with that bookstore. She had infused it with her spirit and her sparkle and people were drawn to that.

As he was.

He had to get out of this place, and he had to get away from her. From the very beginning she had been an enchantress, waving a wand, and not changing the world, but changing the way he looked at it.

Back at the bookstore, she tried to use her phone to unlock the door, but it didn't work. She used her key and they went in.

Moments later, a woman arrived in a flurry of breathlessness.

"You must be our guest!" one of them—she reminded him, unfortunately, of Debbie of Gidgets Widgets fame.

"Your guest?" he asked.

"I'm Bailey Turnbull, president of the Smitten Word. We're a group of women who meet to discuss our favorite topic—romance!"

His mouth fell open. He shot Jessica a look, only to see she was smiling gleefully.

"That's a topic about which I know nothing," he said firmly.

"Nonsense. Have a seat here at the head of the table. The rest of the girls will be here shortly."

There wasn't a girl among them, naturally.

"This is Jamie Gilbert-Cooper," Bailey introduced him. "He's here from New York City and he's going to speak to us tonight on the topic of romance in the city."

He shot Jessica another look. She was busy setting up a table by the counter with stacks of the current Harlequin bestsellers, but her shoulders were shaking with mirth.

He'd like to show her a thing or two about romance.

"I haven't really prepared anything," he said, hoping for a short meeting.

"Oh, well just tell us what you would do if you were wooing a girl," Bailey encouraged him.

He narrowed his eyes at Jessica. "I'd eat pizza on a deck overlooking Central Park with her," he said slowly. "I'd take her shopping. We'd watch the kids float boats in the Conservatory Water in Central Park. I'd take her out for a nice dinner, at a restaurant in the Theater District called Le Bernardin. Then I'd take her to see *Phantom of the Opera* after. It has some scary surprises in it that practically guarantee a woman will be clutching your hand. We'd see some sights in New York, but there would definitely be a horse-drawn carriage ride."

"Oh," the women seemed to sigh in unison.

But Jessica had gone very still.

Possibly he and Jessica were both asking themselves the same question. It was supposed to have been a job interview.

But when he looked back over their time together, he didn't remember much about the business parts of it. Only the wonder of being with her. Was that wooing, then?

And why was he really here?

It occurred to him: *I can't stand the thought of a life without her in it.*

The ladies had lots of questions about New York City, his marital status, what he did for fun, what his ideal woman looked like—wasn't that her standing over there—and he did his best to be funny and engaging without revealing one personal thing about himself.

Thankfully, after the heat of the day, a terrible thunderstorm was brewing, and it knocked out the power. They were quite willing to wait and see if the power came back on, but Jessica insisted they go before the rain started.

Jessica had to usher the reluctant ladies out the door into the pitch-blackness of a town that did not have a single light burning in it except for the headlamps on cars.

When she closed the door, it made a loud clicking sound, and they both looked at it to see the dead bolt turning on its own.

"Good grief," she said, trying the handle, "I think we're locked in." She tried to open the dead bolt. It was stuck fast. Then she pulled out her phone and opened an app. She pushed something. Nothing happened. She handed him the phone. He pushed something. Nothing happened. She turned on the flashlight feature and they both looked at the door. There was no place to insert a key from the inside.

Now they were alone, locked in the bookstore. He could think of worse things.

"Good one," he said softly. "Me the guest speaker at a romance group."

"I just knew they would find you exotic and intriguing and delightful."

"You could have warned me."

"I could have," she agreed with an impish grin.

Lightning lit up the sky, and her face. Despite the grin, he could see something beneath it.

The hunger.

"Do you?" he asked her softly. "Find me exotic and intriguing and delightful?"

The world went dark again, but her voice came through the darkness.

"Yes," she said, hoarsely, "yes, I do."

And then he could not stop himself anymore. He reached through the pitch-blackness and his hand found the softness of her cheek. He heard her soft intake of breath, and he moved in closer to her.

His eyes adjusted to the darkness, and her face, illuminated by the odd flash of lightning, was possibly the most beautiful thing he had ever seen.

"That look you're giving me," he said gruffly, "it seems distinctly come-hither."

"Oh, it is," she assured him.

He could not resist her anymore. Not if he used all his logic. Not if he used all his strength. With the thunder rolling as the perfect background music to what was happening to his heart, he dropped his head over hers.

Tenderly, he took her lips. Outside the rain began to fall with drumming intensity.

It might have started as conquest, but it quickly became something on the opposite end of the spectrum. He felt the surrender in himself. He felt the surrender in her. He knew what was going to happen next.

It was all so wrong. She was not that kind of girl. A bookstore was not the ideal place to make love for the first time.

And yet, as he scooped her up in his arms, and took her back to that cushion-filled nook, nothing had ever felt so right.

Ever.

Not in his entire life. He laid her down in the pillows, and the lightning flashed as she held open her arms to him. He fell into them.

It felt as if every moment since he had met her had been leading to this one: finally, finally, he had her in his field of lavender, her sweet curves crushed beneath him, her scent enveloping them both, her lips tender and welcoming under his.

If he had expected reticence he had been wrong.

She was a woman who knew what she wanted. And she wanted him. A side of her he had not expected came forward: bold, adventurous, willing to explore.

And her lips explored him. They explored his face and his earlobes, her teeth nipping lightly. They explored his lips and then moved on again, down his shirt, her fingers finding his buttons and undoing them. Her hands closed around the sides of his ribs, and her lips moved down the column of his throat to his chest, grazing over one nipple and then the other.

A groan of the pure pain of wanting her escaped him. She stopped kissing him. Her eyes dark on his face, she reached up and opened the top button of her blouse.

"Jessica," he said hoarsely. "Are you—"

She nodded. "Sure. I'm sure."

And then he took her fingers away, and tenderly he undid the rest of the buttons. He flicked her blouse open and gazed at the wonder of her. Then he lowered his head and began the same exploration she had done on him: lips, ears, column of her throat, anointing her with the fiery brand of his kisses.

Something banged. He lifted his head. She drew his attention back to her. "The storm," she whispered.

But it was not the storm.

The bookstore door banged open with force, all the sounds of the storm—thunder and pounding rain—coming in with it.

Jamie pulled away from Jessica, blocking her body with his own. A flashlight beam caught him in the eye.

"Who the hell are you?" a man's voice asked.

"I think the question is who the hell are you?" he shot back, shoving himself up.

Behind him, he sensed Jessica frantically doing up buttons, doing something to the mess of her hair.

"Dad," she said, "this is Jamie Gilbert-Cooper."

Her dad, understandably, looked less than impressed.

Jamie did not know he was capable of the feeling that overcame him. Guilt. A terrible sense of remorse.

What did he think he was doing? Well, no that wasn't the question. He knew exactly what he was doing.

What he had forgotten was *who* he was doing it with.

A young woman from a small town. Beloved to all. Adored by her family. Protected by her father.

Jamie had known all along that she was wholesome and traditional.

How could he have done what he just did?

She wasn't the kind of girl you had a tryst with. She wasn't the kind of girl a man had an entertaining dalliance with.

"Are you from New York?" her father asked, as Jamie quickly did up the buttons on his shirt.

"Yes."

"And are you the reason she's been so unhappy since she got back?"

Startled, Jamie looked at Jessica.

He could tell he was the reason.

Why had he come here? Why had he chased her down? It wasn't at all as he had said. Yes, Vivian Ascot had read the riot act to his boss, and yes, he had been sent to get Jessica's model for her bookstore.

But really? Anyone could have come.

But he'd insisted, like a man who had sipped an elixir that he couldn't get out of his head. That he couldn't get enough of.

She made him powerless.

But that was only an excuse—and a pathetic one at that—for not controlling himself. Her father had arrived in the nick of time. Before Jamie had managed to fuel this thing between them until it burned them both down.

Not daring to look back at her—afraid he would be haunted forever by what he saw in her eyes—Jamie brushed by her father and went out into the rage of the storm.

He felt empty and bereft.

CHAPTER ELEVEN

IT TOOK EVERYTHING Jessica had not to chase after Jamie. She turned to her father and he shoved his hands in his pockets.

"Dad! Really?"

He had a mulish look on his face. "I wanted to know if he's the one who hurt you."

"No one hurt me."

"When you came back from New York—"

"That's none of your business! And you shouldn't have come barging in here!"

"I came to check on you. I might have accidentally set the lock on the store. When you didn't come home I was afraid I locked you in."

"I would have called you if I needed you."

"It's bad out there tonight," her father said stubbornly.

"For Pete's sake, he wasn't my date for high school prom! I don't have a curfew! I'm an adult. You know what the problem is with Timber Falls? I can't grow up here. I can't grow at all!"

The words had come out in a rush of feeling. She saw she had hurt her father, and she was instantly sorry, even if it was so true that a complete stranger that she had met only for a few moments had seen it. Vivian Ascot had seen it before she had seen it herself. Jessica was trapped in a cozy, lovely life. If she wanted to be alive—fully and completely alive—she had to outgrow everything she had ever known.

She had to face her fear.

She left her father and went to find Jamie. She wanted to finish what they had started. Somehow it felt as if her life depended on it.

But when she got there, he had already left the B and B.

"I told him it wasn't a good night to go," Ethel Clariman said, worried, "but it seemed as if he couldn't get out of here fast enough. He left something for you, though."

Ethel went back into the office and came out with a large garment bag.

Jessica took it and got out of there as quickly as she could, hoping she had not looked as shaken as she felt that he was gone.

The hard truth was that he regretted what had happened between them as intensely as she embraced it.

He couldn't get out of here fast enough.

She went home, opened the garment bag and slowly put on the blue dress. She twirled a few times in front of the mirror. This was the woman she could be. This was the woman she wanted to be. How much courage would it take to get there?

She went to bed in the dress. She let the tears come.

And the fear came out of the misty corners of her mind and showed itself to her.

She recognized the core belief that had ruled her entire adult life, had shaped every single decision, that had made her choose safety and security over boldness and full engagement.

In her mind, love equaled loss.

In her mind, the avoidance of pain had become paramount.

In her mind, love equaled the potential for the destruction of the entire world as she knew it.

It occurred to her it was not Jamie she had not trusted.

It was herself. If the loss of Devon had crippled her for so long, what could the love of Jamie, so much hotter, so much brighter, do to her?

Leave her in ashes, obviously.

She had not trusted herself to be strong enough, and resilient enough to cope with what life and love gave her. To cope, to become more courageous, and more confident in her ability to survive.

So, each time life had given her a gift, she had turned away from it.

No thanks, that might hurt me.

Jamie had been a gift.

It was time to find what was at her core. It was time to rise to the challenges of life instead of shrinking away from them.

It was time to embrace love in all its capriciousness. In all its uncertainty.

In the morning, she picked up her phone and, with no hesitation whatsoever, she dialed his number.

It went straight to voice mail, which, given the complexity of the journey to Timber Falls, was not unexpected.

She listened to his voice. She listened to the beep. Jessica took a deep breath.

"I am not afraid to love you," she said, and then ended the call.

She slipped the phone into her pocket. She didn't feel as if she was waiting for a response. She felt as if she had set herself free.

For the first time in so, so long, she was not afraid.

Because she knew she was strong enough to handle whatever life gave her next. Three days passed, and she heard nothing. Still, her belief in what she had discovered did not flag. There was an ultimate gift in loving someone and in being open to love: it didn't rip you down, it didn't destroy you.

It made you better than you had ever dreamed you could be.

And then, after a week had gone by there was a tap on her cottage door.

She opened it and was stunned to find Jamie standing there. It wasn't until that moment when it started beating again that Jessica realized her heart had stopped when she had left him that message. Her heart had been waiting, even as she went on.

Jamie looked beyond haggard. He looked haunted. And uncharacteristically disheveled, his shirt wrinkled, his hair a mess that made her want to fix it with her fingers.

She was in her pajamas, she remembered suddenly, the ones with ducks on them. They did not make the statement about the new bolder, braver her that she wanted to make! She wanted to just close the door in his face, at least until she went and changed, but there was something there that was so tortured about him, that she could not.

Love told her this was not about her.

"Jamie?"

He looked as if he was going to reach out and touch her cheek, but then rethought it, and put his hand in his pocket. "I have a proposition for you," he said, his voice hoarse.

"Like a business proposition?" she said, and could not help but feel disappointment. It was just more of the same. Except it wasn't. Jamie would not be looking like he was looking for it to be just more of the same.

She thought of those lions at the library. One urged her to patience.

"Kind of like that."

"You should have emailed, then. It's a long trip." One that required fortitude.

"Can I come in?"

But she moved back from the door and he moved into her little space. It was so different from what he lived in, she wondered if he would laugh.

But he didn't. He looked around, and then back at her. He took in the pajamas and smiled. Even though his smile was tired, it lit the room and her heart. "It suits you."

She hoped he didn't mean the damned ducks on the pajamas.

"Not as much as it once did," she told him.

She gestured to a chair. It seemed too small for him. She took the couch facing him. Whatever his proposition was, she was saying no. Unless it was an indecent one, and then she would consider it.

"JHA wants you."

As she had suspected. Was he going to ignore the message she had left him?

"Vivian Ascot wants you."

Getting worse and worse.

"What about you?" she said, amazed at her own boldness.

"Well, therein lies the problem. I want you, too. Only I don't want you in the way they want you."

Her mouth went dry. "W-what?"

"I want you in a way that is completely inappropriate for a boss to want an employee. So we can't offer you a job, Jessica."

She realized she didn't care about the job.

"And of course I can't have you in the way I want you, either."

"Why not?" she stammered shamelessly.

"Ah, Jessica, we both know you aren't that kind of woman."

"I could be," she said.

"No, you couldn't. I realized that when your dad came in and found us. That you weren't that kind of woman and that you never would be. That you would compromise something integral to you if you tried to be."

"Maybe that's not for you to decide."

He sighed. "I felt sick with shame that night. I nearly did something I would have regretted forever. But I want a chance to try again. Only to do it right this time. To see if I can be the kind of man worthy of a woman like you."

"I'm afraid I don't understand."

"I want to be a man you never have to be afraid to love. Worthy of what you have held out to me. I proposed to JHA and Vivian that we give you a private contract as a consultant. You can do everything you do best—run seminars and training sessions for bookstore owners—but you can still own your bookstore, too. You can go back and forth between New York and here. And I can go back and forth between New York and here. Because I've fallen in love with your world."

Her *world*, she told herself firmly. But then he went on.

"And I am falling for you. Unlike you, I'm afraid as hell of it. But I have a feeling you could teach me the meaning of courage, if I give you the chance."

It dawned on her, that's why he was here.

They were going to give this thing—this powerful, mysterious force that was blossoming between them—a chance.

"Because you don't work for me," Jamie continued softly, "and I won't be your boss, I can romance you the way a woman deserves to be romanced. Wooed, as the gals of the Smitten Word called it.

"I want to be that man, Jessica, the one who takes it slow and woos you and sees if what we have both been feeling over the last few days can go to where I want it to go. Where I hope you want it to go, too."

"And where is that?" she whispered.

"I'm hoping, one day, you'll be my wife. I'm hoping, soon, I'll be the guy so in love—so unafraid of love—that I'll buy the most expensive engagement ring in the store window."

It was a pinch-me moment. She began to weep. And then to laugh. And then she wept some more. She had never felt joy as all-consuming as the joy of Jamie finding his way back to her, saying yes to all the possibilities love held out to them.

And then he was on the couch beside her, and he lifted her into his arms, and cradled her against the solidity of his chest and whispered love songs into her hair.

This was what she knew in that moment: this was the gift of having the courage to say yes to love. This place, her cottage, her parents, Timber Falls, none of these were home any longer. She did not need them, any longer, to feel the world was safe. And New York would not be home, either.

Home, that place of ultimate safety, where you were accepted and celebrated for yourself, would be, from this day forward, wherever love led them.

EPILOGUE

I READ THE report in front of me with a good deal of pleasure. For a while it seemed as if my attempt to repay Jessica Winton her kindness to me that day in Copenhagen was going to backfire. I got a number of emails from her, snappy in tone, letting me know she was not happy with an old lady meddling in her life.

She even called me that. An old lady! Imagine.

"It's quite funny, isn't it?" I said to Max. "I thought she was going to be the easy one."

Max seemed quite bored with the discussion, and looked longingly at his cookie jar. The doctor has said I have to cut down on his cookies.

"Half," I told him, breaking one in two. He nearly took my hand off as he grabbed it and gulped it down. He acted as if he was starving, as if he had been doing doggie obstacle courses, instead of lying on my lap all day.

I hadn't planned the romance part of it. Of course, I wouldn't plan that. A romance is always a complication that, in my experience, life does not need.

And a romance with that man, the hyphenated name one. Even though I consider myself jaundiced about the topic, the thought of those two together—Jessica and Jamie, as I found out his first name is—pleases me in some way. Some people, maybe even most people, given time, seem to bring out the worst in each other, but somehow I believe those two will beat the odds.

I think they will bring out the best in each other.

"I'm getting soft in my old age," I told Max. I could see from his hopeful expression he thought that meant the other half of the cookie.

I felt a sudden and completely unexpected longing for the life I had not chosen. Family, that most complicated of things, and children.

I shook off the thought.

Family, to me, has always been a source of great pain, not an experience I was eager to repeat once I had escaped my own. The constant worry about the health and welfare of my doggie companions has shown me I didn't have the constitution to raise a child. The worry would have never stopped. If I'd had a child when I was twenty, that child would be in his or her fifties today, and I bet I would be as worried as the day they were born.

Maybe I would have had grandchildren, a forlorn voice inside me said wistfully.

No, I am better off alone. Me, with my gift for seeing so clearly what other people need, should have every confidence I have made the right choices about my own needs.

Still, I hope the other two young ladies are going to be easier, and not create such a sense of longing in me for the paths I had not taken.

Aubrey has been sick, poor thing. Not that there's any good person to get sick, but she's absolutely the wrong one: so independent and spunky. Her well-meaning brothers probably nearly suffocated her in their clumsy love. Well, hang in there, dear, all the adventures you ever longed for are coming at you soon.

And Daisy!

I've given Daisy the old house in Italy. She thought what she needed was success, as so many of us do, but I can tell you that it is not what it's cracked up to be. What she needs most is a place to call home.

Extravagant some people might say, but I don't see it that way.

With no family to leave all this to, why not be extravagant? I could walk down the street and give one-hundred-dollar bills to strangers for a whole week and not even make a dent in my fortune.

Maybe I'll do that. Next week. Me and Max.

But today, I feel ready for a nap. All this meddling, as Jessica so unkindly called it, has left me quite exhausted.

* * * * *

IN SEARCH OF
THE LONG-LOST
MAVERICK

CHRISTINE RIMMER

For Callie Brazzell and her cat, Fury.
Fury was found beside the dumpster
at Zaxby's Chicken and is the inspiration for
the sweet, wild-eyed black rescue kitten, Homer,
in this story. As all you Montana Mavericks fans
have probably already guessed, Homer the kitten
is named after eccentric moonshine-making
Homer Gilmore, who has been delighting
Montana Mavericks readers for many years now.

Prologue

Melanie Driscoll let out a shriek of dismay as the bride's bouquet came flying right at her. It hit her in the face. She put up both hands just in time to catch it before it dropped to the grass.

"Lucky girl!" cried a woman right behind her.

"No fair!" whined someone to her left. "I *never* catch the bouquet."

"Mel! You go, girl!" shouted her high school friend, Sarah Turner Crawford.

Mel blinked down at the gorgeous creation of sunflowers, asters, cornflowers and delphiniums and wondered what she was doing here at this relentlessly romantic outdoor wedding in Rust Creek Falls Park.

She shouldn't have come.

But Sarah had insisted. "Come on, Mel," Sarah had coaxed. "Believe me, I know exactly what you're going through." Sarah did know. She'd had some big troubles with men in the past. But now she was happily married to one of the five brothers of the groom. "It's going to be fun," Sarah had promised. "And you need to get out."

Fun. Right. Mel sneered at the bouquet.

"It's official," another of Mel's high-school friends announced with a giggle. "You're next!" Everybody started clapping.

Mel knew she should just roll with it. She should smile and pretend to be thrilled that her "turn" was coming right up.

But it wasn't coming up. Not a chance. Her life was a mess and a man was to blame. And as for smiling sweetly and pretending to be pleased as everyone applauded and hugged her and patted her on the back?

No way.

Mel tossed the damn thing back over her shoulder. She felt bitter satisfaction at the gasps and shouts of shocked surprise that followed.

Then a childish voice cried, "It's okay! I got it!"

Mel turned. Wren Crawford, the flower girl and daughter of the groom, came running toward her, ribbon-braided pigtails bouncing, the giant bouquet of flowers clutched between her two small hands and her flower basket swaying on her arm. Wren skidded to a stop in front of Mel. Big blue eyes stared up at her accusingly. "You threw the bouquet away."

"Yes, I did."

"Don't you want to be the next bride?"

No, she did not. But the pretty little girl was only six or seven. Mel couldn't quite bring herself to say anything that might spoil Wren's innocent fantasies of love and happy-ever-after. Instead, she gentled her expression and answered softly, "You keep it. I don't have anyone special in my life right now."

One of the other single women muttered, "Well, if that kid is next, I'll be forty before *my* turn comes around."

Everybody laughed.

Except Wren and Mel. Frowning, the child continued to gaze up at her. "You came to the ranch with my aunt Sarah last week, didn't you?" Wren's branch of the Crawford family had moved to town the summer before. Her uncle Logan was now Sarah's husband.

"Yep. That was me. I'm your aunt Sarah's friend and my name's Mel."

"Mel, do you really want me to have this bouquet?"

"Yes, I do."

"Then I have something you are going to need."

Wren turned and headed for a wooden bench several yards away.

Mel couldn't think of a single thing she might need from the little girl, but she trailed after her anyway—partly to get away from the crowd and partly out of curiosity.

"Sit down." Wren hopped up on one end of the bench, the organza skirt of her ivory lace dress fanning out around her like the petals of a delicate flower. Mel sat beside her. "Here." Wren held out the bouquet.

"No, thanks."

"Just for a minute. Please?"

Reluctantly, Mel took possession of the bouquet again. She watched, intrigued in spite of herself, as Wren folded back the swatch of ivory silk covering her flower basket and pulled out an old book. Of brown leather, it was studded with gemstones and stamped with a giant *A* on the front cover.

"It's a diary," Wren explained. "My uncles found it under a floorboard at the Ambling A." The Ambling A was the ranch where Wren lived with her dad and now her new stepmom, the bride, along with her grandpa and more than one of her dad's five brothers and their new brides. "Here." Wren held out the diary. "It's for you."

Mel's free hand seemed to open of its own accord. She looked down and the diary was firmly in her possession.

Wren hooked her flower basket over her arm again and held out her hands. "I'll take my flowers now." Still puzzled as to how, exactly, she'd allowed the child to give her the diary, Mel passed the flowers back. "Thank you," the pretty child said.

More than a little bewildered, Mel watched as Wren slid off the bench and started to walk away. "Wait!" She held out the old book. "You forgot your diary!"

Wren only smiled. "It's yours now."

"Huh? Wait. No…"

"Yes. It will bring you good luck in love. Just ask one of my uncles. They found the diary and they're all happily married now and so is my grandpa Max. And now, my daddy is married, too." Wren beamed, clearly thrilled that her father, Hunter Crawford, had tied the knot with Merry Matthews. "Ask my uncle Wilder," the little girl suggested. "Uncle Wilder will 'splain everything to you."

"But I—"

"He's right over there." Wren tipped her blond head in the direction of the uncle in question. "Bye." And off she went.

Mel jumped up to follow, but then changed her mind and headed for Wilder instead. If the child wouldn't take the old book, surely her uncle would. It looked like an antique and was probably quite valuable.

But Wilder Crawford shook his head when she tried to hand it over. "Mel, the diary is yours."

"No, it's not."

"You caught the bouquet and I'm thinking that means you're meant to be the next one to find love. The diary will help you with that."

Apparently, this branch of the Crawford family was a few screwdrivers short of a tool kit. "Wilder," she said patiently, "love has not been good to me and I have absolutely no interest in finding any more of it."

Wilder crossed his lean arms over his broad chest. "Open it."

"I just want you to—"

"Humor me. The diary. Open it."

She huffed out a hard breath to show her impatience with him and his adorable niece and the bride and the groom and just generally everyone and everything that had anything to do with love and forever and all that crap. Wilder was not impressed. He simply stood there, waiting for her to do what he'd asked her to.

"Fine." She opened the diary and Wren's uncle uncrossed his arms long enough to show her the place in the binding where a letter was hidden. A never-mailed letter, apparently. The wrinkled, dog-eared envelope was addressed to Winona Cobbs at a psychiatric facility in nearby Kalispell.

Mel was stunned. "*Our* Winona Cobbs?"

Wilder nodded. "Who else could it be? Rust Creek Falls is a very small town."

Mel knew Winona Cobbs well and was fond of the old woman, who had shown up in town the summer before Mel lost both of her parents in a car accident. Wise and kindly, Winona was in her nineties now. Some considered her a little off in the head. Others believed she was psychic. Pretty much everyone had enjoyed her newspaper column, "Wisdom by Winona."

"It's a short letter," said Wilder. "Go ahead. Read it."

Mel tucked the diary under her arm, took the letter from the creased envelope and smoothed it out between her suddenly shaky hands.

My dearest Winona, please forgive me. But they say you will never get better. I promise you that your baby daughter is safe. She's alive! I wanted to raise her myself, but my parents forced me to have her placed for adoption. She is with good people—my parents don't know, but I have figured out who they are. Someday, I will find a way to bring her back to you.

Yours always,
Josiah

Mel refolded the letter. "Who's this Josiah person?"

"Josiah Abernathy. He was the son of the original owners of the Ambling A. He wrote the diary."

She had heard the old stories of the Abernathys. Years and years ago, they'd put the Ambling A up for sale and left town suddenly, never to be heard from again. "I know it seems unlikely that another Winona Cobbs lived in town all those years ago, but really, that has to be the case."

"Why?"

Mel stuck the letter in the envelope and eased it back into its hiding place in the binding of the old book. "Because *our* Winona has only lived in the area for the past six years." Mel held out the old diary for him to take. "I remember when she came to town." It was only a few months before Mel's parents died. "I met her that first summer she moved here. And then that fall, when my parents died and I came back from school to bury them, she was right there at my side, helping me any way she could, so kind and understanding and wise and loving. She made it possible for me to get through a very tough time."

"Everyone loves Winona," Wilder said gently. Then he shrugged. "And she could have lived here decades ago, moved away and then returned—and stop pushing that diary at me. It's yours now."

"But have you talked to Winona? Did you show her the letter?"

Wilder shoved his fingers in his hair and raked the thick, dark strands back off his forehead. "Look. My brothers and I have gone around and around about whether to approach Winona with this. But you know the situation. Winona's so old and she's been sick a lot lately. We just weren't sure if it was a good idea to go there with her. It could be a big shock and we all agreed that a shock is the last thing she needs right now."

"What about the psychiatric hospital in Kalispell where Winona was supposedly sent? Did you check with them?"

He nodded. "I did look the hospital up."

"And?"

"It burned down forty years ago—and I doubt we would have gotten anywhere trying to question the people there, anyway. Patient confidentiality laws would've barred them from revealing anything to me or anyone else who came nosing around."

"Translation—you've essentially done nothing."

Now he seemed kind of sheepish. "Yeah. That's about the size of it."

She held out the old book again. "Please. I'm not staying in town. I'm taking a job in Bronco, starting a week from Monday."

"Doesn't matter," said Wilder. "Wren gave you the diary and I'm not taking it back."

Mel ended up bringing the old book home to the too-empty house she'd grown up in.

Todd Spurlock, her cheating ex-fiancé, texted her around ten. He'd been doing that, trying to get her to engage so he could beg her again to come back. She was fed up with that, so she blocked his number. That should do it for Todd.

And then, to distract herself from angry thoughts of the man who had messed up her life on too many levels, she picked up the old diary and started reading. It was pretty absorbing. She didn't stop until she read it through to its tragic end, using up half a box of Kleenex in the process.

The old book contained the sad story of Josiah Abernathy and his love affair with a woman he called "W." It was a story as old as time, really. The rich boy and the poor girl, the boy's disapproving parents. A forbidden love and an unplanned pregnancy—an "out of wedlock" pregnancy, as they used to say in whispers so long ago.

What became of the baby? In the diary, Josiah wrote that the child he and "W" named Beatrix had died at birth. And that "W" had suffered a breakdown at the loss. Josiah's parents had arranged for

"W" to be cared for in a Kalispell psychiatric facility.

Late in the night, after she'd studied Josiah's journal cover to cover, Mel got out the envelope with her dear friend Winona's name on it and re-read the letter that claimed baby Beatrix had lived.

By the time she finally went to sleep, it was nearing daybreak.

First thing Monday morning, Mel headed for the Rust Creek Falls Library and the archives of the *Rust Creek Falls Gazette*. She was looking for evidence that the Winona she knew and admired had been anywhere near Rust Creek Falls all those years ago.

Much to her surprise, she found a picture of a very young Winona waving a flag. Mel felt her throat clutching and a tear trailing down her cheek, just to see the pretty, vibrant woman Winona had once been. The photo was taken on Main Street during the annual Fourth of July Parade more than seventy years ago. The caption read "Miss Winona Cobbs waves the red, white and blue."

Mel visited Winona that afternoon. She found the old woman resting on the couch in her small living room. The network of wrinkles on her pale cheeks deepening with her welcoming smile, Winona sat up and reached for a hug. She let Mel brew them both some tea. They sipped and chatted about inconsequential things while Mel tried to find the right moment to bring up the story she'd read the night before.

She'd yet to find a way to broach the strange and difficult subject when Winona set her teacup and saucer aside. She had that look, the one she got when she knew something was bothering Mel.

For a moment, Mel felt eerily certain that her friend was about to announce that she, Winona, was the "W" of the journal, that she'd once loved Josiah Abernathy and ended up in the hospital when her baby was lost to her.

But then, very gently, Winona asked, "How's Todd?"

And Mel realized that Winona had picked up on the *other* thing that was bothering her. "You don't really want to hear."

"Yes, Mellie. I want to hear."

"Well, I don't want to go into detail about all that went wrong."

"That's all right, too. I just want you to know I'm here and ready to listen if you need to talk it over."

"Thank you. The downstroke is that Todd and I are over. I moved out of his house and I'm never going back to him."

"Where are you living?" Winona frowned.

"Somehow, I don't see you moving back home to stay..."

Mel had lived in Bozeman for the past eight years, coming home in the summers and for holidays the first two years when her parents were still alive and less frequently after that. "No, I'm just in town for a few days. I've left Bozeman behind for good, though. In fact, I've got a temporary job waiting for me in Bronco. I start next week."

"Bronco," Winona echoed teasingly. "Aren't you the fancy one?"

In the heart of Montana, Bronco was a five-hour drive southeast from Rust Creek Falls. The town was well known as home to some of the wealthiest people in the state. "I'll be managing a new restaurant for DJ Traub."

"DJ Traub of DJ's Rib Shacks?"

"That's him."

"You worked in a Bozeman Rib Shack all through college, didn't you?"

"I did, yes. The Bronco DJ's is more upscale, though. It's called DJ's Deluxe and it's in Bronco Heights."

"Where all those rich people live."

"Yes, Winona," Mel said with a grin. "In the posh part of town."

"And you said the job in Bronco is temporary?"

"That's right. At the end of the year, I'm moving

to Austin. I've already got something good lined up there. A company that tried to hire me more than once while I was in Bozeman is expanding into Texas. I'll be their finance and insurance manager. I have to tell you, I'm more than ready for a real change."

"You are such a go-getter." Winona gave her that strange little smile—the one that always had Mel thinking the old woman knew a lot more than she was saying. "But as for your move to Texas, we'll see, won't we?"

"It's happening, Winona. I'll be back now and then to visit you, and to look after the house." Though she had no plans to live in her hometown again, Mel had never been able to bring herself to sell her parents' house, so she rented it. Her last tenant had moved out a month ago—which meant it had been waiting for her when she'd left Todd. The property manager she used had a new tenant moving in on August 1st. In the meantime, Mel had scheduled painters to freshen up a couple of the rooms and a handyman to take care of a couple of necessary repairs over the next few weeks.

"You won't move back to Rust Creek Falls and I understand that. I can see you're ready for something new. But Montana is your home," Winona insisted with a challenging gleam in her eyes. "I don't really believe Texas is where you're meant to be."

There was little point in arguing with Winona

when she'd made up her mind. Mel settled for giving her friend a noncommittal smile. "As you said, we'll see…"

"You belong here in Big Sky Country, dear," Winona said gently. "You'll figure that out, I think." And then she seemed to sag a little. "Oh, I do get tired these days."

"Lie down, then. Get comfortable."

With a weary little sigh, Winona slipped off her shoes again and slowly stretched out. Mel got up and settled the afghan over her. As she leaned close, Winona reached out and brushed a hand, light as a moth's wing, against Mel's cheek. "You're a sweet girl, Mellie."

The diary, Mel thought. She still hadn't managed to bring it up to Winona—but really, where to even begin? So many questions had backed themselves up in her throat.

And Winona looked so frail. If the story Josiah Abernathy had written in the journal was true and Winona was his beloved "W," how would she respond to the startling news that the baby she'd believed had died so long ago might have lived, after all?

Wilder Crawford was probably right. Dumping something like that on a weakened woman in her nineties could cause a stroke or a heart attack.

And what good, really, would dredging up a tragic past do for Winona now?

* * *

Mel left Winona's little house without revealing what she knew.

First thing the next morning, she packed up her Audi Q7. The U-Haul she'd rented in Bozeman was already full of the few pieces of furniture and necessary household goods she'd taken from the house she'd shared with Todd. By 9:00 a.m., she was on her way to Bronco, where her interim job at DJ Traub's new restaurant was waiting, along with a studio apartment in a great building in Bronco Heights.

She took the old journal and its hidden letter with her—and no, she had no plans to pursue the mystery of Winona and Josiah and the lost baby Beatrix any further. But Wilder Crawford wouldn't take it back, so what else could she do?

Chapter One

Gabe Abernathy loved his family. But sometimes they made him a little bit crazy. Especially his dad. George Abernathy knew how a ranch should be run: *his* way. He didn't like anybody suggesting anything new or different—and "anybody" included his own 32-year-old son.

Mostly, Gabe let his dad run the ranch. He pitched in when needed and put his focus on his investments and property deals. Abernathy was an important name in Bronco and Gabe knew all the heavy hitters in the area. Luckily for his bank account, there were a lot of rich men—and women—in

Gabe's hometown. And Gabe was on a first-name basis with most of them.

He still lived on the family ranch, though. He'd built his own place in a beautiful spot not far from the main house. Proximity to his parents had its benefits. It kept their family bond strong and he was there if they needed him. But living a few hundred yards from their front door also meant it was pretty much a given that now and then, he and his dad would lock horns. Gabe tried to pick his battles, but sometimes a man had to say what he thought.

Today had been one of those times. He and his dad had had words, an argument about overgrazing that went nowhere, as usual.

In the end, Gabe had tacked up Custard, his palomino gelding, and ridden out on the land to cool off.

The ride helped. The day was warm and breezy with a few cottony clouds floating around up there in the endless Montana sky, the kind of day that made a man count his blessings. Gabe was strong and smart and rich. His dad got on his last nerve now and then, but Gabe had nothing to complain about, really.

He clicked his tongue at Custard, stirring him to a canter and then to a gallop as they climbed the next rise. "Whoa, boy..." He drew the horse to a stop at the crest and leaned on the saddle horn.

Someone was trespassing.

Below, on the side of one of the winding dirt roads that crisscrossed the ranch, sat a silver SUV. It looked empty from Gabe's vantage point.

He clicked his tongue again and Custard took him down the other side of the hill to the vehicle.

He dismounted and circled the car, peering in the windows as he went. A yellow sweater was draped over the back of the passenger seat—a woman's sweater, soft-looking, with little pearl buttons. Through the passenger window, he spotted what looked like a zebra-patterned pouch in the side compartment of the driver's door. Makeup essentials, most likely.

Girlfriends on an adventure across private land? A definite possibility. They were probably harmless, but it never hurt to let tourists know that cattle could be dangerous and a working ranch was not a public park.

Right away, he found the footprints. There was only one set of them, after all. Leading Custard by the reins, his loaded rifle in his free hand, just in case, he followed the tracks of a pair of female-sized boots up over the next rise.

On the other side, the land sloped gently down to a copse of cottonwoods and the banks of Little Big Bear Creek, a narrow, swift-running stream that wound its way over a good portion of the Abernathy spread.

Maybe ten feet from the creek, a small blonde woman in jeans and a silky shirt the color of a ripe apricot sat on a blanket with a picnic basket at her side. She had her head in her hands. Her slim shoulders shook. Gabe could hear her sad little sobs.

As a rule, crying women made Gabe as uncomfortable as the next guy. He considered turning around and going back the way he'd come. But she looked so pitiful, her shoulders all hunched over in misery, her pretty wheat-colored hair falling in thick waves down her slender back. He had the strangest urge to comfort her at the same time as he felt he had no place intruding on a total stranger's private misery.

Then Custard let out a nervous snort.

The woman jumped up and whirled to face him, her streaming eyes widening at the sight of his rifle. Slowly, she put up her hands.

"Hey," he said gently, trying on a sheepish smile. "I'm not going to hurt you."

"You know what?" She dropped her hands with a forlorn little sigh. "Go ahead and shoot."

"Aw, now. You don't mean that…"

For a long moment, they simply regarded each other. Finally, she sniffed. "So you're *not* gonna shoot me?"

He engaged the safety and stuck the rifle back in the scabbard. "There. Just being cautious, that's all."

She tipped her head to the side as she regarded him. "Who *are* you?"

"I'm Gabe. I live here."

That brought a sad little laugh. "Just a lonesome cowboy, huh?"

"Pretty much." Yeah, okay. He was a long way from a poor cowpoke, but the woman was upset. The last thing she needed right now was some rich guy bragging about how much money he had. "Is it all right if I come down there?" When she gave him a slow nod, he led Custard on down to her, stopping a few yards from the blanket. "Mind if I join you?"

A tiny crease drew down between her sleek gold-kissed eyebrows. "Why?"

"You look like you could maybe use some company."

With a sniffle, she swiped tear tracks from her cheeks. "I came out here to be alone."

"Ah." The silence stretched out as they stared at each other. Even with her eyes and nose red from crying, she was gorgeous. He considered informing her that she was trespassing on private property. But really, it was obvious she only wanted to sit by the creek and cry in peace. "All right then, you be safe." He started back the way he'd come, Custard following placidly after him.

"Wait!" she called. When he paused and glanced back at her, she said, "On second thought, yeah."

"Yeah, I should join you?"

"Well, I mean, if you still want to."

"All right, then." He led his horse down to the creekside. It took only a minute to hitch Custard to a cottonwood. When he glanced at the woman again, she had dropped to the blanket. With a brave little smile, she patted the space next to her.

Not wanting to spook her any more than he already had, he approached her slowly and took the spot she'd indicated, setting his hat on the blanket between them.

A little smile tugged on the corners of her soft mouth. Kind of devilish, that smile. She could get up to trouble, this one. And she had a look in those tear-damp blue eyes that said she wouldn't be putting up with any man's crap. He might have caught her in a weak moment, but if he thought he could get one over on her, he had another think coming.

He glanced up at the sky. "Pretty day."

She gave a little snort-laugh. "That the best you can do?"

He doubled down. "It's a *beautiful* day." And it was. That gentle breeze was still blowing, and the cottonwoods were kind of whispering together. The creek burbled in a cheerful way, glittering in the sun. A few clouds had gathered, creating dappled shadow on the ground as they drifted by overhead.

"I'm Melanie Driscoll. Call me Mel."

He looked at her again. It was a pure pleasure to do so. "Good to meet you, Mel."

"I'll bet you want to know why I've been bawling my eyes out, don't you?"

"I do want to hear, if you want to tell me."

That brought a small laugh and a long sigh. "I have to admit, there's something oddly safe about telling a stranger the things you don't have the heart to say to people you've known most of your life."

"I'm listening."

She blew out her cheeks with a hard breath. "It's nothing new or different. In fact, it's the oldest story in the book. A couple of weeks ago, I came home at lunch to find my fiancé, Todd, in bed with another woman."

"A cheater. Tell me you dumped his sorry ass."

"You bet I did. I threw his ostentatious diamond ring in his cheating face, packed a bag and left. He followed me out the door, swearing it was nothing, promising that it would never happen again."

"You didn't believe him." It wasn't a question.

"No, I did not. There *had* been others. I'd seen the signs, but I'd been kidding myself. Long story short, a few days later I went back to collect what few belongings I had. But I was definitely done with Todd. I quit my job with his family's company— because, yeah. Todd was the heir to the business where I'd been working my butt off since I graduated from Montana State. It was a job I loved, by the way. I'd made it to the top of the finance and insurance department." She pulled her knees up to her chest, rested her chin on them and stared off toward the creek. "Our plan, Cheating Todd's and mine, was to buy out his parents and run the place together. It was a tractor dealership. Spurlock's Farm Machinery."

Gabe knew of Spurlock's. A family business, a successful one, in Bozeman. "So then, you're from Bozeman?"

She shook her head. "Born and raised in Rust Creek Falls."

"Pretty country up there—and I'm sorry," he said. "At least about the job. Sounds like getting rid of Todd was a damn good move."

"Thank you, Gabe. I couldn't agree with you more." She stretched out her slim denim-clad legs, leaned back on her hands and spent several seconds regarding the thickening clouds overhead. "I went home to Rust Creek Falls for a few days. It's never been the same there for me, though. My folks were killed six years ago in a head-on collision with a long-haul trucker who fell asleep at the wheel."

"That's rough." He really did want to comfort her and had to remind himself not to reach out and touch her—maybe stroke her silky-looking hair or wrap an arm around her. He felt powerfully drawn to her, but he needed to remember that he didn't really know her and he had a responsibility to respect her space.

She shrugged, her face still tipped up to the sky. "Thus, the crying jag. And now, I'm in Bronco till the first of the year, here to temporarily manage the new DJ's Deluxe restaurant in Bronco Heights—*and* put A-hole Todd firmly in my poor, broken heart's rearview mirror." Finally, she glanced his way.

He returned her wobbly smile with a relaxed one of his own. "What happens at the first of the year?"

"I'm moving to Austin, taking a job as F&I manager for a company similar to Spurlock's. Getting a whole new start in Texas, if you know what I mean."

Was it crazy that he was already thinking he didn't want her to go? "Maybe you'll discover how much you like it here, decide that Bronco is the right place for you."

"Not likely, Gabe. I'm ready for a major change."

"You'll miss Montana. The winters won't be long enough and the summers in Austin—way too hot and sticky."

They were looking at each other and they both kept on looking. It felt easy to him, not awkward or strange. It felt like they were sharing secrets with their eyes.

She broke the extended silence. "I have a picnic."

"I noticed the basket."

Those jewel-blue eyes glinted with humor. And invitation. "I'm willing to share."

"I would like that."

"All right, then." She pulled the basket closer and turned so she was sitting facing him. Moving the basket between them, she set out cheese and crackers, apple slices and grapes. She had a bottle of white wine and a corkscrew. "Do the honors?" she asked.

He opened the wine and poured it into the plastic Solo cups she'd brought.

They shared a toast to new beginnings. He was having a great time, his frustration with his father all but forgotten in the pleasure of just being with her. This was one of those great things that happen now and then in life—a magical encounter with a complete stranger.

She nibbled on a cracker and said what he was thinking. "This is kind of magical, Gabe. I don't really even know you, but you've made me feel so much better about everything without really saying much of anything." She laughed, the sound soft and sweetly self-deprecating. "So far, I've done way more than my share of the talking."

"I like listening to you talk."

She sipped from her Solo cup, a thoughtful expression on her beautiful face. "We'll probably never see each other again…" She caught her lower lip between her pretty teeth. He longed to lean close and bite that lip for her.

As he considered his chances of stealing a kiss, a giant raindrop plopped on the basket. It was quickly followed by more.

They both glanced skyward—and with a flash of lightning and a hard crack of thunder, the heavens opened up in a downpour. They'd been so wrapped up in each other, neither of them had noticed that the clouds had grown thick and dark.

Mel let out an adorable shriek of surprised laughter as Custard gave a nervous whinny. "I'm soaked to the skin already!"

"Let's get out of here!"

She laughed again. "Good idea."

He helped her reload the basket, feeling a twinge of regret as she dumped the remaining wine out on the now-streaming ground.

He put on his wet hat. "I'll get the blanket." She stepped off it as he grabbed it up. "Come on. I'll take you to your car." Tossing the soaked wad of vinyl-backed flannel in front of the saddle horn, he untied Custard's reins. "Give me the basket."

"Wait—there's not enough room for both of us in that saddle."

"I know." The rain was a solid sheet of water pouring from the sky, loud enough he had to raise his voice to be heard over it. "I'll *walk* you to your car."

"It's not necess—"

"Yeah, it is." Gently, he took the basket from her and tied it to the saddle. "Okay then. Let's go."

She took his offered hand, her skin cool and soft and dripping wet. They started up the rise, the rain a curtain all around them, Custard right behind them. It was a very wet walk, but at least it was quick.

At her Audi, she pressed her key fob to open the back hatch as he untied the basket. He handed it over and then gave her the muddy blanket. She tossed both inside and pressed the fob again to shut the hatch.

"Thank you, Gabe!" She stood there under the continued onslaught of the rain, gazing up at him through thick, wet eyelashes as water plastered her hair to her head and shoulders. It also streamed down her cheeks and over her chin and neck.

"Anytime," he said, not caring in the least if the two of them just stood there forever, practically drowning, having sex with their eyes.

"Can I give you a ride?" she asked.

"Nah. Me and Custard'll make it home just fine."

"You made a bad day so much better. Thank you."

"Yeah?" He couldn't stop looking at her mouth, so plump and inviting, shiny with the water pouring down over it.

"Oh, yeah—and I'd better get going..." She started to turn. He let Custard's reins drop and caught her arm before she could escape him. Those blue eyes got bigger. "What?"

"Give me your number."

A small sound of regret escaped her. "I am so tempted."

"Give in, then."

"Oh, Gabe..."

She really didn't need to say more. He got the message and reluctantly accepted it. Scooping off his streaming hat, he dropped it on the roof of the car. Now the rain poured directly on him again. He didn't care in the least. "If I can't have your number and I'm never going to see you again..."

Her gaze searched his face. "What?"

"I've been dying to do this." And he dipped his head to touch his wet lips to hers.

She sighed against his mouth, her breath warm, scented of apples and wine.

It was all the encouragement he needed. He dared to gather her to him, pulling her up to her tiptoes so he could feel her soft, slim body pressed nice and close.

But somehow, not close enough. He pulled her in even tighter and tasted her deeply.

It was magic, that kiss, everything he could have hoped for. A little crazy, kind of wild, beneath a streaming sky. He wanted it to last forever.

But it couldn't. When she pulled away a second time, he made himself let her go.

"Bye," she said, and turned away again. That

time, he didn't try to stop her. A moment later, she had the driver's door open and was sliding in behind the wheel.

He grabbed his hat off the car's roof as she turned the engine over. And then he stood there, hat in hand, and watched her turn around and drive away. The Audi disappeared from sight and still he stood there, with the rain coming down in buckets, his eyes trained on the spot where she'd disappeared from his view, his arms feeling much too empty, his lips still tingling from the taste of that kiss—until Custard grew impatient. With a snort, the gelding butted him gently between the shoulder blades.

Gabe mounted up and turned Custard for home.

Mel drove toward Bronco in kind of a daze. Gabe the lonesome cowboy had kissed her!

And she'd let him. And it had been perfect. The kind of kiss that had a girl thinking maybe she didn't hate all men on principle, after all.

Very quickly, the rain slowed to a drizzle and then stopped altogether. The sun appeared and the clouds just melted away.

If she hadn't been soaking wet and sitting in a puddle behind the wheel, she might almost wonder if her picnic with Gabe and their kiss in the pouring rain had really happened.

It seemed like a dream to her. Magical. Unreal.

She felt almost breathless—because she was. She wished she'd just gone ahead and given him her number. Or at least that she'd gotten his last name.

But she hadn't. And really, wasn't that for the best? She was swearing off men indefinitely, focusing on *her* life and her own future. Even the hottest cowboy in Montana couldn't be allowed to distract her from her plans.

Still, her lips seemed to tingle all the way to the sprawling, upscale apartment complex in Bronco Heights where she would be living for the next six months or so.

It was called BH247, the complex. BH was for Bronco Heights, of course. And the 247? The street number on Serpentine Drive.

The complex pretty much had it all—indoor and outdoor pools, hot tubs, a big clubhouse and a fitness center. Her cute little studio even had a gorgeous view of the mountains.

She parked the Audi in her reserved space in the underground garage, gathered her soggy picnic stuff from where she'd tossed it in the back and took the elevator up to her floor.

On her own little service porch, she shoved the wet blanket into the high-efficiency apartment-sized front-loading washer. Next, she took off her mud-caked boots and then peeled off the rest of her clothes, adding the clothes to the load. Tossing in a detergent pod, she started the wash cycle.

Her boots she hauled back to the main room, where she dropped them in the sink. From there, she went straight to the bathroom for a long, lovely shower. After piling her acres of wet hair up into a haphazard knot, she pulled on shorts and a tank top and returned to the main room.

Twenty minutes later, she'd cleaned off her boots and unpacked what was left of the picnic. The boots and the drenched picnic basket she carried out to her small balcony to dry.

"Hey, neighbor," said a friendly female voice. It was coming from the balcony that adjoined hers.

Mel gave the picnic basket a nudge to tuck it under the eaves, where it would be safe from any future surprise downpours, and straightened. "Hi."

The gorgeous, pulled-together woman on the next-door balcony grinned at her. "I'm Brittany Brandt." She offered a smile.

They exchanged basic information. Mel explained that starting Monday, she would be managing the new DJ's Deluxe.

Brittany was unemployed. "Well, as of a couple of days ago," she said. "I'm an event planner. I was working for Evan Cruise—you know him?"

The name sounded vaguely familiar. "I think I

saw his picture on a billboard on my way into town the other day. Dark-haired and intense-looking?"

"That's Evan."

"He does ghost tours, or something?"

"Yes, he does," said Brittany. "There are lots of supposedly haunted places in Bronco Valley—abandoned mines, rusted oil rigs, tumbledown ranch houses with ghosts running around in them, that sort of thing. Evan does a big business with his tours. Unfortunately, he's a hard man to work for and he doesn't pay enough."

"So you quit?"

"Yes, I did. I've already got something new lined up, so I'm not complaining. Right now, I'm taking a short but much-needed break. And I was just about to drag my roomie away from her laptop and head out to the pool, get a little sun. Come with?"

Mel cast a wary glance up at the sky. "You think it'll rain again?"

Brittany laughed. "What's the worst that can happen? We'll already be wet."

"Good point." And it would be nice to get to know her new neighbors a little. "The outdoor pool, you said?"

"Yeah. Put on your suit. We'll meet you there."

By the time Mel joined her neighbors at the giant outdoor pool, the sky had cleared completely and the late-afternoon temperature was a balmy 80 degrees. Brittany and her roommate, Amanda Jenkins, had saved her one of the comfy cushioned poolside loungers.

Amanda was self-employed, a marketing manager who did most of her work on her laptop at home. She focused on social media campaigns and outreach for her clients. She and Brittany were both brunettes with brown eyes, but the similarity ended there. Tall, willowy Brittany had light-brown skin, an air of glamor and sophistication about her and an outgoing personality, while Amanda was petite, softly pretty and kind of quiet.

Mel liked them both. A lot. She found them fun and easy to talk to. For the second time that day, she said more than she probably should have about her cheating ex-fiancé and the great job she'd had to leave behind.

She even told them about her chance encounter with Gabe—because why not? They were good listeners and the good-looking cowboy was definitely on her mind.

"So there I am," she said, "with my pity-party picnic, out in the middle of who-knows-where, crying my eyes out over my lowlife, cheating ex and the great life I had to walk away from, when who should appear but a handsome cowboy, a rifle in one hand, leading a gorgeous palomino with the other."

Amanda seemed mildly alarmed. "Why the rifle? You don't look all that threatening to me."

"He was just being cautious, I think. He put the rifle away and asked if he could join me. I said yes."

"So this mysterious cowboy of yours wasn't the least shy, then." Brittany's low voice held more than a hint of irony.

"Not shy, but really sweet and understanding. And did I mention hot?" Mel pretended to fan herself. "And an amazing kisser, too."

Brittany gathered her glorious mane of natural curls in one hand and wrapped an elastic band around it, anchoring the thick mass into a high ponytail. "Has Gabe the Cowboy got a last name?"

"He didn't mention it." Both women looked puzzled. "Hey, it was just one of those things, you know? A great moment with a guy I'll never see again."

"But maybe we know him," argued Brittany. "Bronco's not as small as your hometown, but it's small-ish. And Amanda's got mad web skills. You give her Gabe-the-Cowboy's full name, she can find out way more than you ever wanted to know about him."

"But I don't need to know anything about him. That's the point. I'm not going to go looking for him. I've had enough of men to last me into the next decade, at least. But I had a great time with him and meeting him made me feel better about guys and life and everything, you know?"

"What did he look like?" asked Amanda.

"Does it matter, really?"

Brittany eased her designer sunglasses down her nose a fraction and gave Mel a long look over the top of them. "Humor us."

Mel threw up both hands. "Fine. Tall, lean, wide shoulders. Late twenties to early thirties. Light blue eyes, slightly spiky dark blond hair..."

"Well, that really narrows it down," Amanda said drily. "The good news is, the name Gabriel didn't become popular until the last twenty years or so."

Brittany was still looking at Mel over the top of her sunglasses. "Meaning there aren't a lot of Gabes who are the age you think *yours* is," she clarified.

"Gabe the Cowboy is in no way *mine*," Mel felt driven to insist. "And come on, Amanda, how can you even know that about his name?"

"Too much time online," said Brittany.

Amanda tapped the side of her head with a finger. "You'd be surprised the number of off-the-wall facts I've got stored in here."

"Ladies." Brittany clapped her hands sharply. "Can we please stay on task? Mel, we need more details. Close your eyes. Picture the guy..."

Why not? Mel played along. "Um, well, his silver belt buckle had a big *A* on it."

Brittany suggested, "Last-name initial, maybe?"

"Hold that thought." Amanda jumped up and headed for the building behind them.

When Mel shot a baffled glance at Brittany, she said, "Laptop."

"Ah."

A few minutes later, Amanda was back. She sat cross-legged on her lounger, her fingers flying over the laptop keys. "Hm," she said. "Yeah." She turned the laptop so that Mel and Brittany could see. "This shot appeared in the *Bronco Bulletin* last December—"

"That's him!" Mel cried. The picture had been taken at some sort of white-tie event. Gabe wore a tux, of all things—and clearly not a rented one. He stood beneath a wrought-iron chandelier looped with Christmas garland and twinkly lights. A gorgeous redhead in evening dress clung to his arm.

"This was taken in the ballroom at the Association," said Amanda. "I know the venue because I did some outreach for them a few months ago and they gave me a tour of the buildings and grounds."

"It's a country club," said Brittany. "Or maybe you could call it a cattlemen's club. Seriously exclusive. Costs a fortune to join, but just having lots of money won't do it. To get in, you have to be sponsored by someone who's already a member."

Amanda was nodding. "Your *poor* cowboy, Gabe? He's from one of the richest families in town. The man has it all going on. Looks. Charm. Brains. Big money. And he's a heartbreaker, too. Lots of girls have tried to tame him, but he's never settled down."

"Of course, he hasn't," Mel muttered bitterly. At the same time, she couldn't help recalling how sweet and tender he'd been with her and—hold on just a minute.

What was the matter with her?

He was rich. Rich men were dangerous.

Plus, hadn't Amanda just said he was a player?

A player who'd lied to her, letting her think he was only a poor cowpuncher when in fact he had money to burn. The last thing she needed was another lying rich guy in her life.

Not that Gabe was in any way *in* her life. It was a chance meeting and they'd both agreed they would probably never see each other again.

Amanda went on, "The Abernathy spread is the second largest in the Bronco area."

Abernathy?

Mel popped bolt upright on the lounger. "Wait. Abernathy, you said? Gabe's last name is *Abernathy*?"

"That's right." Amanda closed her laptop. "And Gabe's not only a rich rancher's son. He's branched out into property development. Made quite the success of it, too."

Brittany reached between their loungers and patted Mel's arm. "You okay?"

"Yeah, fine. It's just…" She thought of sweet, old Winona, who might or might not be the tragic young girl in Josiah Abernathy's diary. Could there actually be a connection between Gabe's family and the Rust Creek Falls Abernathys?

No.

Really. There were people named Abernathy all over the country and it was just a bizarre coincidence that Gabe was one.

Her new friends watched her with worried expressions. "What's the matter?" Amanda asked softly. "Are you okay?"

"Sorry." Mel played it off. "It's just, you know… men. Lying liars who lie."

"Oh, honey." Brittany shook her head with a sigh. "We hear you."

"And really," said Amanda, "maybe we shouldn't judge the guy."

"Please," Brittany scoffed at her friend. "You're too forgiving. You always have been."

But Amanda was insistent. "No, really. Look at it this way, Mel. Maybe Gabe *liked* that you thought he was just some ordinary cowboy—and yet you were interested in him, anyway."

By now, Mel just wanted to leave the subject of Gabe Abernathy behind. "I think I'll just stick with my first take on what happened with Gabe. He was

kind to me when I was feeling low and I'm grateful for that."

At least she'd had sense enough not to give the
guy her number. She'd been much too attracted to
him and it would be way too easy to let him get
under her skin.

Mel spent the next day purposely not thinking
of Gabe Abernathy or any other guy. She puttered
around her apartment and went out to dinner with
Brittany and Amanda. Saturday was Independence
Day. Mel attended the town parade and watched the
fireworks from her balcony that night.

Sunday night, she climbed into bed early. She
wanted to be fresh for her first day at DJ's Deluxe.
It would be a long shift tomorrow. She would go in
around noon and meet the current manager, who
would introduce her to the rest of the staff and bring
her up to speed. Dinner service was the main event,
so of course she would be there for that.

Sleep was elusive, though. After a couple of
hours of punching her pillow and tossing around,
she ended up turning the light back on, propping her
pillows against the headboard and pulling open the
nightstand drawer, where she'd stuck the diary that
Wilder Crawford had refused to take back.

In the lamplight, the gemstones on the front glit-
tered at her as if in welcome. She reminded herself

that she'd already read the sad story cover to cover. She needed to shut the drawer and turn off the light.

But she didn't. She got out the diary and read it again. It was just as sad the second time. She cried at the end. And then she blew her nose and dried her eyes and read the brief letter addressed to a girl named Winona who had the same last name as the kind old woman who lived up the street from her parents' house in Rust Creek Falls.

She fell asleep like that, with the lamp still on, the diary open across her knees and the creased letter in her hands.

In the morning, her neck ached from sleeping sitting up and she had to go heavy on the concealer to cover the dark circles beneath her eyes.

DJ's Deluxe had a whole different feel than the DJ's Rib Shacks that had made DJ Traub famous. Instead of picnic-table ambiance, the interior was all rich woods with accents of hammered copper and brushed nickel. The long bar was a shiny expanse of gleaming teak. Somehow, the restaurant managed to be warm, inviting—and exclusive. The place had a casual feel, but in a very upscale way.

Mel spent the day shadowing the current manager, who left at six.

Gwen Fox, the assistant manager, took over. Mel followed Gwen around the front of the house until seven, greeting customers, making sure everyone was happy with the food and the service. It was your usual Monday night in the restaurant business, meaning the pace was slower than most nights, a good night to train.

At seven, she left Gwen to handle the front of the house and went into the kitchen where the chef, Damien Brutale, ruled. Her plan was to help expedite if necessary, but really, she just wanted to observe, watch the staff get the food out, see how efficiently they worked together, get a feel for everything they were doing right as well as for what might need improvement in the future.

She'd been in the kitchen for five minutes, max, when Gwen came racing down the hallway from the dining room. "Mel." Mel left the serving line and went to her. "A customer would like to speak with you."

"They asked for the manager?" Since Mel was training for the next few nights, Gwen would logically have dealt with any customer issues.

"No. He asked for you by name."

"Has this customer got a name?"

Gwen leaned a little closer. "It's Gabe Abernathy."

Chapter Two

"I know you're new to Bronco," Gwen said, keeping her voice low. Confidential. "Do you know Gabe?"

Annoying butterflies danced a ridiculous jig in her belly, but Mel kept her voice noncommittal. "We met the other day. Briefly."

"You don't know him well, then?"

"No. Not at all, really." Okay, yeah. She *had* laid practically her whole life story on him and then kissed him with some serious tongue. But still, that didn't mean she *knew* the guy.

"Heads up, then. The Abernathys are an important family around here."

She knew that already, courtesy of Amanda and Brittany. And why had she made the mistake of telling him her full name and where she would be working? "Thanks, Gwen."

"He's at the bar."

"I'll just go and see what he wants, then…"

Mel found him sitting alone at one end of the bar. Looking all kinds of gorgeous in dark-wash jeans, a crisp white shirt and a lightweight jacket, he already had a whiskey, neat, in front of him.

As soon as he spotted her, his fine mouth quirked with a grin. He patted the empty stool next to him.

She moved close but didn't take the offered seat. "Gabe." She leaned an elbow on the bar. "Got a problem with the service?"

"The service is excellent."

"How was your meal?"

"Right now, I'm just enjoying a drink—and admiring the view." His gaze skated over her black pencil skirt and white silk shirt. "Very professional."

"Thank you. So then, no complaints on the service and you haven't ordered yet. What can I do for you?"

Those clear blue eyes made a bunch of intimate suggestions. "How's the new job going?"

"Surprisingly smoothly for a first day."

"Glad to hear it."

"Gabe, why are you here?"

"I like this place. I eat here often."

"Well, all right. Tonight, I'm training. Gwen is the one you should ask for if there's anything special you need."

He seemed to be studying her. The silence between them spun out. Finally, he asked, "When's your first night off?"

She considered refusing to tell him. But he would only keep after her until she gave it up. "Thursday." She knew what was coming next.

And she was right. "Let me take you out to dinner Thursday night."

"It's not a good idea."

"Why not?"

She glanced at the bartender, who seemed to be minding his own business setting up drink orders for one of the waitresses and taking care of the customers at the other end of the bar. "Are you pursuing me, Gabe?"

He gave her that killer grin again. "Damn straight."

"Well, pursuing me will get you nowhere. Remember that cheating fiancé I mentioned the other day?"

"How could I forget?"

"He chased me. I knew it wasn't smart to get involved with the boss's son. I kept saying no. He kept asking. Took him a year to get a date. My mistake. I never should have said yes to him. Todd Spurlock was a lesson I won't forget."

"I'm not Cheating Todd, Mel. I think you know that."

She held his gaze and kept her voice low and firm. "I mean it, Gabe. It's not going to happen."

"I like you. I want to see you again."

She wrapped her arms around her middle to keep from gesturing wildly with them. "Have you heard a word I've said?"

"Yep. You have my undivided attention." The quietly spoken statement caused more of those fluttering sensations in her belly.

"What I'm trying to make you understand is that this time, I'm not letting myself be caught. Chasing me will get you nowhere."

He picked up his drink and took a sip, setting the glass back down with care. "How many ways can I say it? I'm not Todd."

"But you did lie to me. You pretended to be a broke cowboy."

"No, I didn't. You asked who I was. I gave you my name."

"Just your *first* name," she accused.

"If you'd asked, I would have told you my last name, too. But you didn't. I said that I lived there—

and I do. Did you know you were on Abernathy land?"

She'd had no clue. "No, I did not."

"Well, there you go. Then you called me a lonesome cowboy and I said that I was. I can rope and ride and I've been working around cattle since I learned how to walk. The way I see it, that makes me a cowboy. As for the lonesome part, sometimes I do feel kind of lonely, so I qualify on that score, too."

She scoffed. "You're a rich guy from an important local family."

He picked up his glass again and kind of wiggled it at her. "You sure you don't want a drink?"

"No, thanks."

"So about Thursday night? I'll pick you up at seven."

Did the man ever give up? "You're not getting it. There's also a big problem with your name."

"What? Now you don't like the name Gabe for some reason? My full name is Gabriel. You can call me that."

"I like Gabe just fine. It's your *last* name I'm not comfortable with."

"Okay, I'll bite. What's wrong with Abernathy?"

"There were Abernathys in Rust Creek Falls."

"There are Abernathys a lot of places."

"Well, in Rust Creek Falls, so the story goes, the Abernathys sold off their ranch and left town suddenly, without a trace. Like in the dead of night, never to be seen or heard from again. At the time, there was a lot of whispered speculation about the things those Abernathys got up to, the kinds of things that would make a whole family run away in the night. They were a shady bunch, the Abernathys of Rust Creek Falls."

He gave a low laugh. The sound made the nerve endings tingle up and down her spine. "That's quite a story, Mel."

"It's a known fact that you can't trust an Abernathy."

"You're just yanking my chain," he accused in a low, sexy rumble.

She had to press her lips together to keep from smirking. "You can take it."

"Have lunch with me tomorrow out at the ranch. I'll introduce you to Malone. He's been the family cook for longer than I can remember. You'll love him. You can ask him anything you want about me and he'll give it to you straight. Malone knows where all the bodies are buried."

"There are bodies?" Should she be alarmed?

"Settle down, Mel. It's just a figure of speech."

"I'm serious," she insisted. "I'm not falling for any of your lines."

"Lunch." He kept pushing. "Just lunch…"

Actually, she *was* kind of curious to see his

ranch. And maybe this Malone person had Abernathy family secrets he would share. Maybe the Bronco Abernathys had some connection to the ones who had vanished from Rust Creek Falls. Maybe the answers to the questions posed by Josiah's diary had been right here in Bronco all this time, just waiting for her to come and root them out.

Yeah. Hardly likely.

However, having all the dirt on Gabe could be fun. She really wasn't going to date the guy. But her so-called lonesome cowboy was wildly attractive and she very much enjoyed giving him a bad time. Lunch at his ranch could present any number of delicious opportunities to rattle his cage.

Then again, being near him was kind of like wandering into Daisy's Donuts back home and ordering a dozen of their amazing maple bars—all the while promising herself she would only eat one. The man was too tempting by half and the whole idea was *not* to fall for another smooth-talking rich guy.

No, she reminded herself. *Just tell him no*. But when she opened her mouth, what came out was, "Lunch. Tomorrow. At your ranch. But it's not in any way a date. I'm just, you know, curious about what the Bronco Abernathys are really like."

That got her his full-on smile. It was nothing short of a secret weapon, that smile. All of a sudden, her cheeks felt hot. Was she blushing? The gleam in his eyes said she was. "Give me your number and your address," he instructed. "I'll pick you up at—"

"Uh-uh. I'll drive myself."

"I'll still need your number to text you directions."

She should grab a napkin and tell him to write the directions down. But maybe that would be skirting a little too close to out-and-out bitch mode. "Give me your phone," she said.

He picked it up off the bar, unlocked it and passed it over. She sent herself a text. Her phone buzzed in her pocket.

"Be there at eleven," he said. "I'll show you my place and then we can walk over to the main house to eat. It'll be casual, buffet-style. But Malone always puts out a good spread. I'll arrange for you to talk to Malone privately, so you can find out all my dirty secrets. You can also meet my dad and mom—don't freak." Had he seen the panic in her eyes? "I get it. You're not in the market for a boyfriend and you don't want to meet *any* guy's parents. But they live there and lunch in the main house is kind of a thing. You can ask them questions, make up your own mind about the Bronco Abernathys. You're going to find we're not as shifty as you seem to think."

The next day, Mel had no trouble finding her way to the Abernathy ranch.

It took maybe twenty minutes to reach the turn-off from the state road. A few minutes later, she was driving right past the spot where she'd parked for her impromptu picnic the other day.

The ranch was beautiful—rolling, open land where cattle grazed peacefully under the endless sky. Fields of wildflowers stretched off toward the mountains, small stands of cottonwoods and the occasional tall pine dotting the landscape here and there.

It was almost eleven when she made the final turn down the long, graveled driveway that led to a cluster of buildings in the distance. Up ahead, one of those fancy iron ranch signs arched over the road, with rustic split-rail fencing running off into the distance on either side. On the rolling prairie land beyond the sign, she could make out giant barns, several sheds and a few large houses scattered about on low, rolling hills.

Gabe and his family had clearly done all right for themselves.

Her pleasure at the sheer beauty of the setting vanished completely, though, when she got close enough to read the sign.

In black wrought iron, stretching over the road with a wagon wheel mounted to either side, was the name of the ranch.

The Ambling A.

The sight had her hitting the brakes hard enough that she bumped her head on the rearview mirror.

"Ouch!" For a minute, she just sat there with her foot on the brake, the car idling in the middle of the graveled road, rubbing her head, more than a little creeped out.

How likely was it that a random family named Abernathy in Bronco would call their ranch by the same name as the Abernathys who had suddenly vanished from Rust Creek Falls?

Didn't it make more sense that the Abernathys from her hometown were related somehow to Gabe's family, that they'd named their ranch here after the one in Rust Creek Falls—or possibly the other way around?

She would have to look into it. Maybe. As soon as the hair on the back of her neck stopped standing on end every time she thought about it.

Maybe Gabe's family had heard of the other Ambling A and decided they liked the name. But if they had, wouldn't Gabe have said something last evening when she'd given him a hard time about those other Abernathys running away in the dead of night?

And wait. Was she making a really big deal out of nothing at all?

Probably.

Easing her foot off the brake, she drove on, under

the sign, past an ostentatious log-cabin mansion to a slightly smaller place of natural stone and cedar, with log accents and lots of big windows.

Gabe greeted her at the wide, rough-hewn front door wearing faded jeans, rawhide boots and a worn plaid shirt with the sleeves rolled to the elbows. He looked more like the lonesome cowboy she'd met that first day than the rich man who'd shown up at DJ's last night.

For a long, sweet minute or two, he just stood there in the doorway, grinning like the sight of her had made his day. "Right on time."

There ought to be a law against men as good-looking as Gabe. "I had excellent instructions. And Google Maps."

He stepped back and ushered her inside, where a lean, brown-spotted dog sat looking up at her hopefully through big chocolate-brown eyes.

"Who's this?" she asked.

"Butch."

"German shorthair?"

"Most likely. And Lab and maybe beagle. Butch is a little bit of everything. Go ahead and say hi."

The mutt let out a whine of happiness as she knelt to stroke his head and give him a good scratch down his back.

"He's one of Daphne Taylor's rescues," Gabe explained. "Daphne's a rebel, I guess you might say.

The Taylors are arguably the most influential family in town. They have a hand in just about everything that goes on around here, but Daphne's kind of turned her back on all that. She runs an animal sanctuary called Happy Hearts. You want a dog or cat or maybe a goat, a chatty parrot or a really good-natured pig, I'll introduce you to Daphne."

A pet? She hadn't had a pet since her senior year in high school when her childhood cat, Bluebonnet, headed off to that big scratching post in the sky. Todd, the cheating jerk, had been allergic to pet dander—or so he'd always claimed. "I'm not sure they even allow pets in my building. But an animal sanctuary, that sounds interesting."

"Say the word. I'll take you there." He was giving her that look again, the one that melted her midsection and lowered her IQ by several points.

"Not going out with you," she reminded him, her voice strangely husky to her own ears.

"It's not a date if we go to Daphne's animal sanctuary. It's me helping you to put an end to your sad state of petlessness."

The man was just way too good at this. He elevated flirting to a high art. "I'll think it over."

"Can't ask for more," he said mildly.

"Right." He could and he would and they both knew it, too. "Your house is beautiful."

"I had it built a couple of years ago. The main

house has plenty of room, but my dad and I get into it now and then. It's better having my own place to go to. Come on. I'll give you a quick tour."

He led her through the rooms. The living area had floor-to-ceiling windows, vaulted wooden ceilings and a huge natural stone fireplace with a mantel made of a giant log. In the rustic-style kitchen, she admired the gorgeous granite counters and chef-quality appliances. As for the master suite, you could fit her whole apartment inside it with room to spare. The bath in there had heated slate floors, dual vanity sinks, a walk-in shower and a big clawfoot tub.

"You live here alone?" she asked as he led her back to the living room.

"Just me and Butch. But I'm open to sleepovers."

"I'll bet you are."

He took a step closer. "I'll even let you soak in my clawfoot tub." His quiet, slightly rough voice stirred her, made her think of long, wet kisses shared in a big, comfy bed.

She could smell his aftershave, clean and woodsy, and his mouth looked so soft, in perfect counterpoint to his sculpted jaw and hard, lean body. It would be so easy to sway toward him. His sky blue eyes promised that if she kissed him again, she wouldn't regret it.

No. Uh-uh. Not happening. "Nope. No sleepovers."

He looked at her so tenderly. Patiently, too. As though he could wait forever for her to say yes. "The offer's open if you change your mind."

At lunch, she met Gabe's mother and father, George and Angela, and his grandfather, Alexander. Alexander, she learned, had three brothers. Each of those brothers had children and grandchildren. There was even a great-grandchild or two. Gabe not only had a large extended family in the area, he also had a sister, Erica, who lived in Denver and rarely visited her family in Bronco.

After they loaded up their plates at the buffet, they sat clustered together at one end of the long dining room table under an antler chandelier and facing a big window with a spectacular view of tall peaks in the distance. Mel considered casually mentioning that there was an Ambling A Ranch in Rust Creek Falls, too, and that a family named Abernathy had once owned it.

But she knew that if she started in about the Rust Creek Falls Abernathys, she wouldn't sound casual at all. She might end up blurting out everything— telling these people she'd just met about her friend Winona who might or might not have loved a man named Josiah Abernathy, had his child and ended up in psychiatric care when the baby died—except, maybe the baby hadn't died, after all...

No. It just wasn't a conversation to be having over lunch with people she'd never met before. Mel needed time.

She needed to mull over this eerie turn of events, to deal with the uncomfortable sense she was getting that Wilder Crawford might have been right—not about her finding true love. That was not happening. But about the mystery of the missing baby Beatrix.

Had fate somehow handed her the diary and then guided her to the place where the mystery might be solved?

It seemed way beyond far-fetched. But still, it had also started to feel eerily possible, somehow.

Not long after they sat down, Gabe and his dad got into a minor dispute over bison, of all things. Gabe was pushing to introduce a small herd to the ranch.

Bison meat was becoming more and more popular in stores and restaurants, Gabe argued, and raising bison beat out cattle in terms of the cost and sustainability. Bison could live on wild grasses and didn't require special shelter in the cold months. Plus, they didn't congregate by ponds and creeks like cattle did, flattening the grasses and sometimes contaminating their water sources.

"We're a cattle operation," George said sternly. "Always have been, always will be." Alexander bobbed his white head in agreement with his son. "No self-respecting rancher raises bison, my boy. A bison is a wild animal."

"Exactly," Gabe agreed. "And a wild animal does a lot better job of taking care of itself and the land that it grazes on."

"Mel." In a clear bid for a change of subject, Gabe's mom cut in. "Tell us a little about yourself. Where are you from? What brings you to Bronco?"

Mel explained briefly about her upbringing in Rust Creek Falls and the loss of her parents. She said she'd lived in Bozeman for several years. From there, leaving out her job at Spurlock's and the disaster that was her engagement to Todd, she skipped right on to how she'd come to Bronco to work at DJ's Deluxe.

Gabe's mom had more questions, about her education and her life in Bozeman.

Gabe cut in. "Mom. Enough. You'll scare her away."

Angela laughed and let it go.

"I like your folks," Mel said later, when they'd finished lunch and Gabe had led her out to sit in the log chairs on the long front porch, just the two of them, with Butch snoozing nearby.

"My dad's kind of stuck in his ways and my mom gives the FBI a run for its money when she starts in with one of her interrogations."

"Just like parents everywhere."

"True."

"And you're lucky you still have them," she reminded him softly.

"You're right." He gazed at her in a warm, steady way that almost made her want to forget she'd sworn off men. When he looked at her like that, she was seriously tempted to announce that she'd love to go out with him, and yes, a sleepover in his bed and a long soak in his clawfoot tub sounded like the best plan ever. Especially if he would be climbing in the tub with her.

The front door opened and a tall, craggy-faced cowboy who looked a little younger than Gabe's grandfather came out. He had a mustache and graying hair.

Gabe stood. "Malone. There you are. I want you to meet Mel."

Not sure whether to feel relieved or disappointed at the interruption, Mel got up, too. She shook the old man's leathery hand. "Lunch was delicious."

"I'm glad you enjoyed it."

Gabe said, "I'll leave you two alone for a while."

She grabbed his arm, which was solid and strong, just like the rest of him. "Wait." He glanced down at her hand on him and then up into her eyes. She felt her cheeks coloring as she let go. "You sure? I can ask anything?"

His mouth hitched up in a smile that curled her toes inside her ankle boots. "Anything." He nodded at Malone. "Tell her the truth about me."

"You know I will," said the old man.

And Gabe went inside, leaving Mel standing there trying to decide what questions to ask. She dropped back into the giant log chair. "Have a seat."

"Don't mind if I do." Malone lowered himself into the chair Gabe had vacated. "Ask away."

"You're, um, the expert on Gabe, then?"

"Well, now, I *have* been with this family for more than twenty years. I've seen all the Abernathys in action, you might say. And I've known Gabe since he was a knobby-kneed youngster."

She couldn't resist teasing the old guy a little. "But can I trust you to tell me the truth about him?"

"I make it a point to shoot straight. Ask any man who knows me."

"Well, all right, then. Is Gabe a liar?"

"He is not."

She shook a finger at him. "When I met him, he pretended to be a poor cowboy."

Malone sat up straighter. "He told you right out that he was broke?"

"Well, no. But when I called him a lonesome cowboy, he didn't say he wasn't."

"Young lady, I do not see how you can call that a lie. Gabriel Abernathy has been ropin' and ridin' since he was knee-high to a gnat. If that doesn't qualify him as a cowboy, I don't know what does. And as for the 'lonesome' part—"

"Okay, okay." She patted the air between them with both hands. "That's pretty much what he said when I jumped all over him about it."

"Then why are you askin' me?"

"It never hurts to cross-check a man's story."

Malone gave her a long, squinty eyed stare. "I don't mean to offend, Mel, but you got trust issues, I think."

Why deny it? "Oh, yes, I do."

"Well, I stick by my previous statement. Gabriel Abernathy is no liar."

"Has he ever cheated—on a test, over money, on a woman he was seeing?"

"'Course not."

Actually, this was kind of fun. "Is Gabe an ass?"

Malone gave a low snort of laughter. "No, but he's pretty damn sure of himself. All the ladies seem to love him."

"So I've heard," she muttered.

"He's yet to find the girl for him, so I see no problem there. A man has a right to keep searching till he finds what he's looking for."

"Some men do find what they're looking for— but they keep on searching, anyway. Just for the fun of it, I guess."

"You mean they cheat."

"That's right."

"I'll say it again. Gabe is no cheater. As long as he hasn't promised his heart, he has every right to step out with any pretty lady he likes—that is, given that the lady in question is willing and unattached."

"Has Gabe ever been in love?"

"I do not believe so."

Her phone buzzed in her pocket. "Excuse me." She took it out and saw she had a text from a number she didn't recognize.

You blocked me. Why?

Todd. Suddenly, her stomach felt twisted and she wanted to break her own phone. She thumb-typed a swift response. Leave me alone. I will block you again.

How can you be so unforgiving? I love you. You're the only woman for me.

You mean aside from that woman I found in our bed with you? Never mind. Don't answer that. Goodbye, Todd.

She blocked that number, too, and put the phone away.

When she glanced up, the old guy was watching her. "I'm sorry, Malone. Where were we?"

"You look mad as a peeled rattler. What was that all about?"

She almost played the question off, but that would be lying and she'd just made a big deal about her contempt for liars. "It's my ex-fiancé. He cheated on me and I left him and now he won't stop trying to convince me he deserves another chance."

The old guy reached out and gently patted her hand. His kind touch had her eyes misting over. "Once a man cheats," Malone said, "it gets really hard to trust him again."

"I will *never* trust him again."

"And, though I've always believed in second chances, I can't help thinking you're wise. Stay strong, Mel." Gently, he added, "But don't be afraid to give a better man a chance."

She drew a slow, slightly ragged breath. "Where were we?"

Malone launched into a cute story about the first horse Gabe had trained himself. "That pesky horse kept throwing him, and Gabe just climbed right back on—and got thrown again. The horse gave up first. In the end, that horse was a marvel. Bred as a cutting horse. Gabe trained him right and he lived up to his potential, had that uncanny ability to read each and every move of any given cow. Pure poetry, watching that horse work."

Mel asked, "Was Gabe a troublesome kid?"

"He was curious. Determined. He got into scrapes and then managed to find a way to get out of them, mostly without major consequences. He was honest. Even as a child, anyone could see he had a good heart. You could do worse, Mel."

"Too bad I'm not looking for a man," she replied and hit him with more questions. Malone answered each one thoughtfully, with a touch of charming humor.

When Gabe, with Butch at his heels, emerged from the house, Malone got up. "I did my best. She's a tough customer, this one."

"That was fun," she said, once Malone had gone back inside.

"So?" Gabe spread his arms wide. "What's the verdict? Hit me with it."

"I'll say this much. You don't suck."

He let out a low laugh. "Is that all I get?"

"Hey. Malone works for you. How can I be sure he's going to tell me the worst about you?"

"Give a guy a break, Mel."

"I like you, okay?" She *more* than liked him. But it didn't matter. She refused to get anything started with him. "It's just not going to happen."

"But you *do* like me."

"Didn't I just say I did?"

He dropped into the chair at her side again. "The way I see it, I'm bound to get through eventually."

"I'm a bad bet."

"Don't say that. It's not true."

"Yes, it is. I'm still bitter about my rotten ex—and anyway, I'm leaving in a few months, remember? You should probably just give up on me now."

Undeterred, he shot her that gorgeous grin of his. "Aw, Mel. I'm no quitter. Malone should have mentioned that. And from now until January is a very long time."

Chapter Three

That night at DJ's, the bar was packed until after seven. Mel stepped in to help the bartender with set-ups and to serve beer and a few of the simpler drinks.

When things slowed down a little, she went back out on the floor. She'd just made the rounds of all the tables and dropped in at the hostess station to make sure all was well there when she glanced over at the now-quiet bar and saw Gabe sitting on the same stool as last night, watching her. When their gazes met, he gave her his slowest, sexiest smile, the one that almost had her seeing rainbows and unicorns.

Ridiculous. Truly. You'd think she would have learned her lesson by now. Rainbows never lasted.

They appeared in that too-brief moment after a storm—and then vanished as though they'd never been. As for unicorns, they didn't exist in the first place.

As soon as she had a spare minute, she went over there, sliding into the space between his stool and the next one, just like the night before. "Two nights in a row." She wore her most professional, impersonal smile. "You must really like it here."

"I do." His sky-blue gaze swept over her. "The food is excellent, the atmosphere manages to hit the perfect middle ground between comfortable and exclusive. And the bartender knows my drink." He toasted her with his glass of whiskey.

"Just here for a drink, then?"

"I'm meeting some business associates for dinner."

"Ah." A business dinner. Nothing to do with her. Good. He'd gotten the message. She should be relieved. And she was—relieved, not disappointed. Not disappointed in the least. "Well, have a productive meeting, then."

"Mel." His warm fingers brushed her forearm as she started to turn. Heat bloomed at the light touch and flowed upward, to her shoulder, over her neck. Her cheeks felt hot.

Oh, this was bad.

Chemistry. Why did it have to be so hard to ignore? She blasted him another plastic smile. "Yes?"

He leaned her way just a little. "Have dinner with me. Thursday night."

So then. He might have a dinner meeting, but he was here to see her, too. A little thrill shot through her. She just knew her blush was deeper than ever.

Really, what was the matter with her? She was becoming one of those women, the kind who said they wanted one thing—while wishing way too hard for another. "I'm not going to do that. You have to stop asking me."

"Sorry. But I'm not ready to give up on you yet, Mel. I'm just not. See, I have this really strong feeling that giving up on you would be a big mistake."

She scoffed, but the sound was weak. "Oh, come on. You make it sound like life and death. It's only a date."

"Exactly." He gave her that smile that somehow annihilated her will to resist him. "Only a date. Not a big deal. You just need to say yes."

"No. Really—and I have to go now. I'm working."

"I'm not giving up."

"Enjoy your dinner, Gabe." That time, when she turned away, he let her go.

The rest of his party arrived a few minutes later. Mel was much too aware of where the hostess seated them, of the occasional sound of his low laughter in response to something one of the others at the table had said. The dinner meeting went on for a couple of hours. Mel switched places with Gwen at nine thirty and the next time she emerged from the kitchen, he was gone.

But he came back on Wednesday. She turned around at a little before seven and there he was, in the spot she'd already come to think of as his, at the end of the bar.

She really tried not to go over there. But she didn't try hard enough.

Ten minutes after she first spotted him, she slipped into the space between his stool and the next one over. "Another business dinner?"

"Nope. Tonight I'm just here to see you. Tomorrow's your night off. Spend it with me."

Yes. The word kind of bounced around in her brain and almost leapt out her mouth. But she kept her lips pressed together and shook her head slowly.

He studied her for a long, intense minute or two. "You off all day tomorrow?"

Still half-afraid to say anything for fear she'd find herself agreeing to go out with him, she nodded. And then he was grinning. And then suddenly, they were both laughing. Because she refused to answer his question and he seemed to have a pretty good idea why.

Then he asked, "How about a visit to Daphne Taylor's animal sanctuary? We'll go in the afternoon. It won't in any way be a date. You might find a pet. Or you might just enjoy having a look around."

She really was curious about that animal sanctuary...

"Come on," he coaxed. "You know you're curious about Happy Hearts."

Now he read minds? "How can you possibly know that?"

He was definitely smirking. "It'll be fun. And you'll love Daphne."

She made the mistake of opening her mouth yet again. A yes popped out. "All right. What time?"

"I'll pick you up at noon."

"You don't have my address."

"Text it to me."

This was the moment to insist she would take her own car.

But really, if she was meeting him there anyway, why not just ride with him? She pulled out her phone and sent the text.

His phone, right there on the bar by his elbow, lit up. He shot her a grin. "Great." And then he pulled some bills from his pocket, dropped them on the bar next to his glass and grabbed the phone. "See you at noon."

"I don't need a pet," she warned, though it just so happened that yesterday as she was leaving for

work, she'd seen a calico cat basking in some unknown neighbor's window at BH247. The cat had
her thinking of her sweet, lost Bluebonnet again,
feeling a little wistful, maybe. It wouldn't be such
a bad thing to have a furry friend to keep her company. This morning, she'd checked her lease. Her
building allowed cats and small dogs, though the
lease required that pet owners pay a rather hefty
deposit for possible damages—not that it even mattered. She was *not* getting a pet.

Gabe wore a serious expression, but humor
danced in those beautiful eyes of his. "No pets for
you. Got it."

"And this isn't a date," she reminded him.

"Not a date, no way," he agreed.

"Just so we understand each other."

"We do, Mel. We understand each other perfectly."
With a last nod, he turned and headed for the exit.

Daphne Taylor came right out to greet them when
Mel and Gabe arrived at Happy Hearts Animal Sanctuary.

The daughter of the richest man in Bronco,
Daphne was slim and serious, her pretty face free
of makeup. She hugged Gabe, greeted Mel warmly
and then gave them a tour of the farm where she
made a home for a wide variety of animals in need.

Mel loved the place. She petted the horses and laughed at the antics of the baby goats.

After Daphne left them to their own devices, Gabe led Mel to a big barn not far from where he'd parked his giant four-door pickup.

"This barn is just for the cats and dogs," he explained as he led her through the entry door.

The big, wood-sided structure had cat quarters on one side and a place for the dogs on the other, each area with its own separate outdoor enclosure attached. Daphne had helpers, mostly volunteers, who cared for the animals and supervised the dogs whenever they were taken out to play.

The cats' yard was screened on the sides and above. It had comfy spots for basking in the sun and a series of cat runs going every which way.

And there were kittens. Lots of kittens. They had their own room in the barn. Until the kittens were weaned, their mamas lived there with them. The kitten room was filled with randomly stacked hay bales for the little ones to climb and play on.

Mel and Gabe stood at the glass wall that kept the kittens contained and watched the action on the other side. "There are so many," she said.

"Yeah. A lot of people abandon pregnant cats. Anyone who adopts a Happy Hearts cat pays a discounted amount upfront for spaying or neutering."

"Good."

Beyond the glass wall, kittens jumped around on the hay bales, playing with each other, getting in little tussles, rolling off the bales and then leaping right up and climbing them again.

"You want to go in?" Gabe asked. He was standing very close, close enough that she could see the darker rims around his pale blue irises and breathe in his woods and citrus scent.

"It's okay?"

A teenager in a Happy Hearts T-shirt lugging a giant bag of kibble paused on his way to the adult cats' feeding area. "Just be sure to keep the door closed and the kittens inside."

"Come on," said Gabe. "You know you want to." His expression seemed to hint at more than just petting kittens.

They went in and a few of the kittens came prancing right over to them. "They're all so adorable." She scooped up a long-haired gray one with fluffy white paws. It was already purring. "Aww. Little sweetheart…" Perching on a hay bale, she held the kitten close and buried her nose in its thick, hay-scented fur. "My cat, Bluebonnet, was gray, with big blue eyes."

The kitten glanced up at her. This one had luminous amber eyes. Gabe dropped down on the hay bale with her, close enough that she could feel the warmth of him. His thigh brushed hers, denim on denim, sending a heated little shiver racing over her skin. "It's a cutie, that one."

"Sure is…" But she was not getting a cat. Not now. Her life was in flux and she needed to remember that. Six months from now, she'd be starting over in Austin. If she still wanted a furry companion in January, she'd visit a shelter in Texas and adopt one then. There was never a shortage of cats needing homes.

The kitten wiggled in her arms, ready to get down. With a last kiss on its fluffy gray head, Mel let the little furball go.

More kittens ventured near. She petted them and laughed when they batted at her with their tiny paws and jumped about on the hay bale stacked behind the one where she sat with Gabe. A gray tabby fooled around at their feet, hopping into the spaces between their boots.

Yeah, okay. She really did like cats. They were cuddly and self-sufficient, the perfect pet for a professional woman. And every one of these kittens made her long to be a cat owner again. Especially now that she'd shed the cheating fiancé and his supposed allergies to cat hair. What, really, was stopping her from choosing a Happy Hearts fur baby for her own?

Gabe leaned in closer. His clean scent seduced her. "You know you're tempted," he whispered.

Tempted. That was exactly the right word. And not only when it came to the kittens.

But her job right now was to resist. No kitten of her own until she got to Austin. And no hot, not-so-lonesome millionaire cowboy in her bed, either. Now was her time to work hard for DJ, make plans for her new start in Texas and generally avoid anything that might in any way become an entanglement.

She met Gabe's eyes. "Not getting a kitten," she said patiently as they shared a long, way-too-intimate look that upped the temptation quotient by a factor of ten thousand.

"Whatever you say." He caught a lock of her hair and casually guided it back over her shoulder. All at once, she was breathless. The man was a menace—in the best sort of way.

He put his arm around her. She let him, even though she knew she shouldn't, that it would only encourage him.

And then she went even further and leaned her head on the hard, warm curve of his broad shoulder. "I'm really, truly not getting a—"

And right then, she saw him. *The one.*

A skinny little stick of a black cat with short, scruffy fur and enormous, spooky gray-green eyes. He sat very straight over by the viewing wall, his impossibly long, sparsely furred black tail wrapped around his tiny feet—and he was staring right at her.

How did she know *he* wasn't a *she*? Not a clue from this distance. But somehow, she did know.

With her head on Gabe's shoulder, his lean arm around her, Mel stared that wild-eyed black cat down. Neither she nor the skinny cat blinked.

Homer, she thought. *For some crazy reason, that wild-looking little guy reminds me of Homer.*

"Who's Homer?" Gabe asked.

She must have said his name out loud. "He's this old guy who lives in Rust Creek Falls. Kind of a mystery man, you might say. He's in his seventies, at least, and probably older. He's likeable, really, and kind, too—but also weird."

The little black cat sat, calm and alert, his big eyes locked on Mel. She gave him a grin—and he rose on all fours and arched his bony back in a slow, luxurious stretch.

Gabe squeezed her shoulder. "Weird, how?"

The black cat came toward them in a slow saunter as Mel explained, "Homer makes moonshine. It's very special moonshine, the kind that somehow always has people shedding their inhibitions, often along with their clothes."

"Interesting."

"Oh, yeah. One time, he spiked the punch at a wedding in the town park. There was a Rust Creek Falls baby boom nine months later."

"You're not serious."

"Honest truth." The black kitten reached their hay bale and sat at her feet, gazing up. The look in those strange, sweet eyes said he was hers and she was his and she might as well just go ahead and learn to live with that. She said to Gabe, "Nobody really knows where Homer actually lives. He might pop up any-where, most likely when you're least expecting him."

There was no point in kidding herself one second longer. She could not resist. She patted her lap. With a single "Reow," the little cat leapt to the hay bale, and from there to her lap. Purring now, he curled himself into a ball and closed his eyes.

She petted him in slow strokes for a minute or two. Then she lifted her head from Gabe's shoulder and met his eyes. "I'm adopting this one."

He didn't even say *I told you so*, just, "Let me guess. His name is Homer."

There were forms to fill out before she could take Homer with her. At Daphne's special animal farm, they didn't hand over rescue animals to just anybody. Mel paid for Homer's neutering, which had already been taken care of. The woman who handled the paperwork said he was estimated to be eleven weeks old. The time for various vaccinations was coming up and Mel would be seeing to those.

"Pet store, right?" Gabe asked when they—and

Homer, in a soft-sided cat carrier Mel had bought from Happy Hearts—got back in Gabe's crew cab.

Mel hesitated. After all, the deal was just the visit to Daphne's animal sanctuary, and then he would take her home.

He must have known what she was thinking. "Why not?" he coaxed. "You need to outfit the little guy. Might as well get on that."

Really, he did have a point. "You sure you don't mind?"

One arm draped on the steering wheel and the other stretched out along the back of her seat, he countered, "Do I look like I mind?"

Homer was not a good traveler. He yowled all the way to the pet store. Mel couldn't bear to leave him alone in the truck, so she took him inside, propped his carrier in the baby seat of the shopping cart and wheeled him up and down the aisles with them. He didn't make a peep as they filled the cart with every cat necessity she could think of. Apparently, he liked riding in the shopping cart a lot better than in a fancy pickup. As soon as they got on the road again, he started crying. At least it was a short drive to her place, where she went straight to the manager's office to pay her exorbitant pet deposit.

Gabe helped her carry Homer's gear in. They filled the litter box and set out food and water bowls and the cat bed, along with a variety of toys. Homer christened the litter box, drank some water and clawed at the large scratching post/play structure Mel hadn't been able to resist. And then, after nibbling a few bites of kibble, he jumped right up on Mel's bed and settled in for a nap.

Gabe said, "I'm guessing that nice cat bed you got him is not going to see a lot of action."

She parroted what her mom had told her way back when. "It really is better for him to sleep in a cat bed while he's little."

The twitch at the corner of Gabe's sexy mouth told her he was quelling a laugh. "Okay, then. Good luck with that."

A long moment elapsed. They gazed at each other. It felt way too good, just staring at him as he stared at her. She was trying so hard not to let things go too far with him. What she needed to do was start steering him toward the door.

But honestly, he'd been amazing, taking her to Happy Hearts where she found Homer, driving her straight to the pet store, letting her take forever choosing everything Homer might possibly need. It only seemed right that she at least offer him a beer and maybe some nachos.

They ended up sitting at the little café table out on the balcony, chowing down on chips drizzled in nacho cheese sauce and sprinkled with olives and jalapeños. She was laughing at something he'd said when Amanda appeared on the balcony next door.

Gabe and Mel got up and joined her neighbor at the low wall where their balconies met. Mel introduced them.

"Amanda Jenkins," Gabe said. "Marketing, right?"

Amanda granted him a cautious smile. No doubt she was thinking of the other day, when she'd tracked down a certain "lonesome cowboy" online for Mel. "That's me."

"I've heard good things. You did that campaign for the Association. Great work—and you also do outreach for Happy Hearts, right?"

"Clearly, I have no secrets," Amanda said wryly. "And thank you. I like thinking my clients are satisfied."

"They are. I can testify."

"Gabe took me to Happy Hearts today," Mel said. "And I tried, but failed, to come home empty-handed."

Amanda's smile widened at the news. "Mel. You adopted a pet?"

"Yep. A kitten." Amanda offered a fist bump and Mel took her up on it. "Come on over and meet him."

"I would love to, but it's worktime. I just took five to stare at the mountains and clear out the cobwebs, you know? Gotta get back to it."

"Come over when you finish, then?"

"Definitely." She gave Gabe a jaunty little salute and then vanished into her apartment.

Mel stared after her, feeling simultaneously regretful and determined. Amanda's appearance was kind of a wake-up call. Somehow, the sight of her new friend had snapped her back to hard reality. She and Gabe were not and would never be a couple.

And yet, here she was, driving out to his ranch for lunch, spending her day off with him, sitting on her balcony with him, sharing a beer. Was she giving mixed signals, or what?

Slowly, she turned to him.

Judging by the expression on his face, Gabe had a pretty good idea of what she was thinking. "Worn out my welcome, have I?"

Right at this moment, she didn't like herself much. "I really think that we…" She thought that they *what*? She had no idea how to finish her own sentence. "I just don't understand what I'm doing, you know?"

His eyes said, *Yeah, you do.* But he kept his mouth shut.

She tried again. "I like you, a lot. I really do. But I've told you over and over this…whatever it is with us, Gabe, it's not going anywhere."

He answered cautiously. "All right."

"What does that mean?"

"It means I get it."

"I don't think so. If you get it, why do you keep asking me out?"

He took several endless seconds to answer. She was starting to wonder if he ever would when he said, "Someone very important to me once told me that if you have to ask, the answer's no."

Huh? "Well, then why do you keep asking?"

Staring down at his boots, he raked at his spiky hair with a big hand. "Yeah. Not what I was getting at. It means that when you've met the right person, you just know it."

The right person? Where did that come from? She couldn't help blinking at him, baffled—and suspicious, too. "Gabe, we've known each other for a little more than a week. How can you possibly know I'm somehow the 'right' person?"

"Because I didn't have to ask."

"Ask *what*, exactly?"

"Mel." His eyes were warm, full of dangerous affection. "I think you know what."

How did he do it? He stood there before her, all tall and strong and smart and kind and generous. And handsome. Way too handsome. He could break a woman's heart so easily, tempting her until she said yes, and then letting her down.

He probably wouldn't mean to disappoint her. But that wouldn't matter. She'd be wrecked all over again.

She didn't need any more heartbreak, thank you very much.

"You're being purposely vague," she accused.

"And you've had enough for one day." He headed for the slider and pushed it open, stepping through into her apartment and striding straight for her front door.

She trailed after him, wondering what exactly was happening, wishing he wouldn't go, yet knowing that his leaving was exactly what she'd asked him for. "Gabe, I just don't understand you…" *Or myself, for that matter.*

He grabbed his hat off the small table by the door. "I think we're done for now. I had a good time today. I'll see you tomorrow."

"Huh? Tomorrow? I don't—"

"DJ's as usual, probably around seven."

"You're not listening to me."

"Yeah, I am. And I hear you, loud and clear."

"Gabe, we have to stop this. You just need to stop asking and I need to say no and mean it…" By then, she was speaking to the door as it closed quietly behind him.

Chapter Four

"I think you like him. And there is nothing wrong with that." Amanda, lying on her side across the bed, dangled a feather on a wand for Homer. The wild-eyed little cutie lay on his back, furiously batting at the feather as she lowered it teasingly and then jerked it away.

"What's *wrong* is that my plan is not to like *any* guy. Not for at least a hundred years."

Amanda chuckled as Homer managed to grab the feather in all four paws. He chewed at it madly, front paws clutching, back paws kicking, until she gave it another sharp tug and he lost it again. "Yeah, well. Good luck with that."

"You said yourself he's a heartbreaker, dating lots of women, never getting serious with any of them."

"Maybe heartbreaker was too strong a word. Face-to-face, he comes across as a great guy. And besides, you're not looking for anything serious anyway, are you?" Homer gave the feather one more good swipe, bounced to his feet and darted off the end of the bed. "Love your cat, Mel."

"He's a handful." Mel scooped him up off the floor and nuzzled his neck. But Homer was a busy guy. He squirmed and she let him go. He leaped from her lap and went to give his scratching post some serious attention. "Back to Gabe."

"I'm just pointing out that he seems like a great guy and it's beyond obvious he's gone on you. You ought to seriously consider giving the man a break."

"I'm confused. Weren't you the one who looked him up online and then warned me off him?"

"I just provided information. Yeah, he's been out with a lot of girls. He's considered local royalty. Everyone wants to date the prince, right? Especially if he's tall and hot and very, very charming."

"I don't need that kind of trouble."

"Mel. You like him. It's obvious—and it's not a crime to like a guy. Okay, he's never been married. Maybe he just hasn't met the right woman yet. Would you give him a chance if he was divorced?"

"Why are we talking about this?"

"Think about it. It wasn't me who just said *back to Gabe*. Maybe he's like you and doesn't plan to get serious for at least another century. Why is that okay for you and not for him?"

Mel couldn't help laughing. "Whose side are you on, anyway?"

"Yours, of course. The Prince of Bronco has a thing for you. Why shouldn't you enjoy him while it lasts? Nothing wrong with a great rebound."

"A rebound?"

"You need to look it up?"

Mel executed a blatant eye-roll. "I know what a rebound is. Too bad I can't say whether it's a good thing or a big mistake, since I've never had one."

"Hey, me neither." Amanda gave Mel a look from under her lashes. "But lack of experience has never stopped me from having definite opinions."

Mel found herself thinking how easy things were between her and her neighbor—both of her neighbors. Brittany as much as Amanda. She'd known the two women for exactly a week, yet it felt like she'd been friends with them all her life.

Amanda went on, "When you take advice from me, consider the source. I spend too much time online. In my spare time, I read a lot. I'm kind of rusty at real life. And that's the thing. See, I Internet-stalked Gabe for you when maybe I shouldn't have.

Nothing I found online was really that bad. And in person, I like him."

"I like him, too."

"I noticed. And it's because you like him that you keep letting him convince you to hang out with him. There is nothing wrong with hanging out with him. Why make it so complicated when it really isn't?"

Gabe spent Friday rounding up strays in a couple of far pastures on the Ambling A. It cleared his head to work out on the land, to play the ordinary cowboy he'd originally let Mel think he was.

Mel. He couldn't stop thinking about her, going back and forth like a damn seesaw, telling himself he ought to do what she'd asked him to and leave her alone.

Except…

Those jewel-blue eyes of hers told another story altogether. They said he shouldn't give up, that eventually she would give him a chance, offer him a little trust. Invite him in and *not* turn right around and ask him to go.

He should talk to Gramps about her. And he would, soon. He tried to get out to Snowy Mountain Senior Care at least once a week. It would be good to have a long heart-to-heart with the great-grandfather who'd been his idol since he was old enough to toddle around after him in diapers.

Nowadays, Gramps didn't answer much when Gabe talked to him. Advanced dementia made him unresponsive much of the time. Still, Gabe wanted to believe that Gramps was listening, taking everything in, mulling it over in that careful, serious way he used to have. Now and then, Gramps *would* answer back. But even when he never said a word, it always did Gabe good just to sit with him. Gramps had always been the one Gabe could tell his troubles to. That hadn't changed.

So, yeah. Sometime in the next few days, he needed to get his ass over to Snowy Mountain Senior Care.

As for the irresistible Ms. Driscoll, he would be there at DJ's Deluxe tonight just as he'd promised her—or maybe warned was more like it. He needed to give it one more try with her. Maybe she wasn't the one Gramps had always said he would find someday. But there was still something about her that made it really hard to walk away.

It was after nine when Gabe arrived at DJ's. Friday night in a popular restaurant tended to be busy, so he'd waited to come in until things were likely to have quieted down a little.

He wanted some face time with Mel, to tease her a little and have her give it right back to him the way she had the other times he'd dropped in to see her at work. Also, he needed a quiet moment when he took his best shot at finally coaxing her into an actual date. He wouldn't get that shot if she was running around dealing with the hundred-and-one things that needed her attention during the dinner rush.

There was one other reason he came in later than before. He kind of enjoyed the idea of making her wonder if he was going to show up at all. She kept saying he needed to stop chasing her. Fair enough. Let her suspect for an hour or two that he'd taken her word for it and given up on her.

Was he a fatheaded, entitled SOB to imagine she cared whether he showed up or not? Pretty much. But the way he saw it, he *knew* she cared. Showing up later might give her a nudge toward realizing that.

His stool at the bar was taken when he walked in. He found that kind of annoying at the same time as he grinned at his own damn ego to expect a certain bar stool to be there, empty and waiting for him, whenever he wanted it.

But then as it turned out, he was not only an entitled SOB but also a lucky one. As he scowled at his occupied stool, the woman sitting on it and the guy next to her got up and left. He sat down and the bartender served him his usual whiskey, neat.

He hadn't eaten since noon and was looking over the menu, trying to decide between a T-bone and

DJ's famous ribs, when the woman he'd been waiting for spoke from behind him.

"I was beginning to wonder if you'd changed your mind about stopping by tonight."

He turned on his stool and—bam. Just the sight of her hit him like a shot of adrenaline straight to the heart. Tonight, her black skirt clung to her curvy hips and flared out around the hem. Her white shirt was tailored, pintucked to fit her snugly, showing off her little waist and the round perfection of her breasts. The undone button at the neck hinted at everything he hadn't seen.

Yet.

"Miss me?" he asked.

"Was that your plan?"

"My great-grandma Cora always said it's not nice to answer a question with a question."

She tipped her blond head at him, considering. "So it *was* your plan."

"Maybe." He held up his thumb and forefinger with a half inch of space between them. "Just a little. Did it work?"

Her gorgeous smile bloomed wide. "I'm not even going to answer that one."

Right then, the restaurant's assistant manager appeared from the hallway that led to the kitchen. She signaled Mel.

"I'll be back," Mel said.

"I'm counting on it."

Twenty minutes later, as he was polishing off his appetizer, she reappeared. He asked how Homer was settling in.

She shared some of the little guy's crazy antics and admitted that she'd let the kitten sleep with her last night. "It's not like I have much of a choice. I put him in his bed and he jumps right out and leaps to *my* bed. It's a studio apartment. What am I going to do? Lock him in the bathroom?"

"That is a puzzler…"

She folded her arms under those breasts he was trying hard not to overstare at. "I know what you're thinking."

"You might be surprised. Hint. It has nothing to do with that crazy little cat you adopted."

She tried to look disapproving, but then ended up laughing. He laughed, too.

And then she was gone again, off to deal with some minor crisis or other.

She came back as the bartender served him his T-bone. "Looks good."

"Want a bite?"

"I'm tempted. But not while I'm working. It's not done for the manager to eat off the customer's fork."

"I would tell you to make an exception this once. But I know you won't."

"You're right—and please. Eat. Don't you dare wait on my account."

He leaned a fraction closer and lowered his voice to a slightly more intimate level. "I don't mind waiting. Not as long as I'm waiting for you."

She didn't say anything. The bloom of color in her soft cheeks and the shine to her eyes spoke for her.

He took his time cutting a bite of his steak, chewing it slowly. "Excellent, as always," he said once he'd swallowed.

"That's what I want to hear."

"I liked your friend, Amanda."

"Isn't she terrific? She's got a roommate, Brittany. I feel like I've known them both forever."

"Brittany Brandt? Works for Evan Cruise and his Bronco Ghost Tours?"

"That's the one. But Brittany and the ghost tours have parted ways. She's got a job with Bronco Heights Elite Parties now. She loves it so far." Mel tipped her head to the side, thinking. And then she said, "It means a lot to have friends in a new town." She looked really sweet when she said that, kind of innocent and vulnerable.

"I'm sure it does. You might discover you love Bronco so much, you can't leave in January, after all."

She gazed at him steadily now. It was as if they

could have whole conversations while just standing there, staring at each other. He liked that about her—liked it a lot. That feeling of connection that went deeper than words.

But then she did speak and the words weren't encouraging. "I'm leaving at the first of the year, Gabe. A new start with a great job in a whole new place. It's what I need, it really is."

He wanted to argue that Bronco was better and if she wanted a job in finance and insurance, he could see that she found the right one here in town. But he didn't. January, as he was constantly reminding himself, was a long way away. "Got it. When's your next day off?"

"Tell me you're not going where I think you're going."

"What day are you off next?"

"You're like an EF5 tornado, you know that? Relentless. Mowing down every objection in your path, all while looking like sin on a stick, with that easy, confident smirk on your face."

Sin on a stick? That meant she thought he was hot and that was just fine with him. He wasn't a smirker, though. Was he? *Stay on task, man. She's softening.* "What day?"

"Fine. Monday."

"Works for me. Dinner. I'll pick you up at seven thirty."

She gave him another of those long, speaking looks, after which she finally said, "Okay. Have it your way. Seven thirty." He barely had time for a mental fist pump before she added, "Now, eat your steak. I've got a restaurant to run." He watched her walk away, a perfect, petite dynamo of a woman, slim shoulders held proud and straight, curvy hips swaying.

She didn't come back. But that was okay. He smiled to himself all through his solitary dinner and allowed himself a second whiskey, as well. He figured he had a right to celebrate.

Mel Driscoll had agreed to an actual date with him.

Monday evening, Mel answered the door in a short, sleeveless dress of cream-colored silk. The silk was covered in lace the dusky purple color of the rose of Sharon that Gabe's mom grew in her back garden. That dress had a nice, deep V-neck and her shoes were a mile high, showing off those strong, sleek legs of hers.

Unfortunately, she had all her emotional walls back up again. Her first words were, "I can't believe I said yes to you."

He whipped out the fistful of sunflowers he'd picked up at a flower shop on his way over. "You look beautiful."

Her stern frown vanished and she sighed. "And you are much too handsome. Plus, I love sunflowers." She accepted them from his outstretched hand. "Thank you—and you'd better get in here before Homer realizes the door is open."

Inside, she brought down a pitcher to use as a vase as Gabe pulled out one of the two chairs at her tiny table. The moment his butt hit the seat, Homer leaped to his lap. "Hey, little guy. What's up?"

The kitten stared at him through those perpetually astonished gray-green eyes and was silent. He allowed Gabe to pet him for about twenty seconds. Then he shot to the floor and attacked his scratching post.

Mel put the pitcher of cheery yellow flowers in the middle of the table. "All set." She grabbed her small purse and off they went.

"The Association," Mel said as Gabe rolled his Cadillac CTS-V to a stop in front of his club. "I've heard about this place."

The valet, in black dress pants, a dressy red Western shirt and string tie, pulled Mel's door open and tipped his hat at her. "Welcome."

"Thank you."

To Gabe, he said, "Mr. Abernathy, how are you?"

"All good, Jack. How *you* doin'?"

"Can't complain, sir." Jack ushered Mel out and

shut the door, after which he ran around to Gabe's side and opened the driver's door. "You have a good evening, now."

Gabe got out. "I will, thanks." Once Jack drove away, Gabe went to Mel and offered his arm.

She took it as the Cadillac disappeared behind the sprawling clubhouse of wood and natural stone. "What happened to your ginormous pickup?"

"It's at the ranch. I like the Caddy now and then." He bent to her. "Is that a disapproving expression you're wearing?"

She stole his breath with a dazzling smile. "Not at all. That Cadillac is perfect for a night like tonight."

Pleasure stole through him, just to have won her smile. "Come on. Let's go in."

Mel found the Association clubhouse every bit as impressive as Amanda and Brittany had hinted it would be.

A pretty dark-haired woman greeted them in the foyer with its high beamed ceiling. "Gabe. So good to see you. Right this way."

She led them through a series of lounges filled with oversized leather sofas, dark wood tables and fine craftsman lamps with mission-style glass shades. Men and a few women greeted Gabe with nods and waves as they went by.

Giant, heavily framed windows looked out on the shadows of the high mountains in the distance. Closer in, the gorgeous landscaping was lit by in-ground lanterns. Every room had a stone fireplace large enough to roast a side of venison, each one with a rustic wood mantel the size of a tree trunk, much like the one in Gabe's living room on the Ambling A.

The woman led them onward, through the lap of rustic luxury that was the bar area and the main dining room to a private room with just one table. The window on one wall had the usual gorgeous mountain view.

"Thank you, Ariana," Gabe said after they'd been seated. As she went out, an old man came in. He wore a Western-style tuxedo and reminded Mel faintly of the butler in *Downton Abbey*.

The old guy greeted Gabe warmly, poured them water from a crystal carafe, took their drink orders and rattled off the dinner choices. Gabe asked for a couple of appetizers and the old man left, returning quickly with their drinks.

When he left again, Gabe said, "Rex has been here for as long as I can remember. He moves a lit-tle more slowly than he used to, but he takes great pride in doing the job right."

"I can see that." Mel sipped her lemon drop cocktail. It was perfect, both sour and sweet. "You know, a girl could get used to this kind of luxury."

Those chambray-blue eyes gleamed. "That's what I'm talkin' about." He leaned in across the table. "You're too far away."

For that, she gave him a one-shouldered shrug and surprised herself by suggesting, "Then move closer." The words got out before she could edit them.

Not that she really wanted to take them back, anyway. Gabe was a great guy. Why shouldn't she thoroughly enjoy every moment she spent with him? She'd made it way more than clear that whatever happened between them could only be temporary and he didn't seem the least concerned about that— and why should he be? So far, he'd shown no inclination in his own life to find the perfect woman and settle down.

And as for moving closer, he didn't need to be invited twice. Sliding his elaborate place setting to the head of the table, he took the chair in front of it. She scooted her own chair toward him. Now they were just around the corner from each other, in easy whispering distance.

Not that they really needed to whisper. It was just the two of them, cocooned in this beautiful little room.

Rex uncorked a bottle of wine and filled their

wineglasses. He served their appetizers and left them alone for a long, sweet time.

They spoke of their childhoods. Mel explained that she'd always wanted a little sister or brother. "But not desperately. I also liked having my parents' undivided attention. I was kind of spoiled and that suited me just fine."

He said his dad was strict. "But my mom's a pushover. And when I needed a man to talk to, there was always my great-grandfather. Gramps taught me most of what I know about horses and cattle." He grinned. "Not that my dad didn't try. He and I just always ended up butting heads, somehow."

Their entrées appeared. Once Rex had left them again, Mel asked, "What's your sister like?" She was watching Gabe's face and saw the slight frown that creased his brow. "You...disapprove of Erica?"

He sat back away from her. "What makes you think that?"

"I don't know. Suddenly, you're frowning. And you're tensed up. Right here." She reached out and brushed two fingers between his eyebrows. It felt good to touch him. Maybe too good. She started to pull her hand back.

"Don't." He caught her wrist. His grip was firm and warm, the skin of his palm and fingers a little rough. Suddenly, her breath was all tangled up in her chest.

He pried open her fingers and pressed her palm to the side of his face. His warm skin was smooth, freshly shaven. Her breath hitched at the contact. "Don't be afraid of touching me, Mel. I like it when you touch me."

She felt thoroughly seduced, somehow, and tried to gather her scattered wits. "Wariness is not the same as fear."

"Why are you wary?"

"You know why. I don't think you really need to hear all that again."

"Do you want me to let go?"

Never. "Um, yeah. I think you'd better."

He turned his head just enough to touch his warm, soft lips to her palm. Heat skated along her arm, flared across her shoulder and up over her throat. Only then did he release her.

Rex appeared again to ask if they would like dessert and coffee. They both said yes and he brought them a decadent chocolate mousse to share. Mel enjoyed every bite and then settled back to sip her coffee.

Gabe said, "You asked about my sister…"

"I did, yes."

"She's completely absorbed in her life in Denver, with a longtime serious boyfriend and a great job in a growing company."

"Sounds pretty good to me." A lot like her own

life in Bozeman—until Cheating Todd showed his true colors.

"Yeah." Gabe seemed a little sad now. "If she'd only come home every once in a while. She's been in Denver for twelve years, and every year we see less of her. We lost Great-Grandma Cora five years ago. Erica barely made it home for the funeral. My great-grandfather is not well. This is my sister's last chance to spend some time with him while he's still around."

For once, Mel was the one reaching out. She took his hand and wove their fingers together. She needed the contact—to show him support. "Hey…"

"Yeah?" He leaned closer, blue eyes warm as a bright summer day.

Drawn by the clean, intoxicating scent of his skin, she leaned in, too. "Cut her some slack," she whispered in his ear.

"Good advice," he answered ruefully.

"And sometimes that's the hardest kind to follow?"

"Yeah, pretty much…" He brought her hand to his lips and pressed a tender kiss to the back of it. She didn't pull away.

Was she sending the wrong signals? Probably. But this little room tucked away by itself seemed like a place where real life couldn't touch them. Where she could forget all the reasons she shouldn't let herself get too close to Gabe. She liked him so very much.

Every moment she spent with him just made it more difficult to remember why those reasons even mattered. It grew easier and easier to imagine crossing the line between a carefully controlled friend zone and something more.

More. It didn't have to mean forever, did it? When, in her whole life, had she ever taken a chance on having a little fun with a guy, having it be just for now?

The answer to that was a big, fat *never*.

Before her parents died, she'd known she wanted what they had—a loving relationship with a life partner, the kind of relationship that weathered the years, and children to cherish together. She would find a man she could count on, one who could count on her in return. Along with the right man, and the children he would give her when the time was right, she intended to have an interesting and challenging career.

After she lost her folks, she still wanted those same things, but even more so. Without their steady love and unwavering support, she'd felt cast adrift. Untethered. She'd needed to ground herself, to carve out a place for herself, make a new family after losing the family she'd loved so much.

By the time she'd said yes to Todd's marriage

proposal, she'd been absolutely certain that he was the right man, the one she was meant to share her life with. The one she could count on to cherish her and love her as she would cherish and love him for the rest of their lives, the one she could trust to have children with.

And then Todd blew her trust all to hell.

Was there really any coming back from that for her?

Maybe not.

Not every woman ended up half of a couple with children around her. She might just be destined to go it alone.

What if that ultimately turned out to be the case for her?

The thought that it might caused a deep, echoing sadness within her, as well as a need to reach out and grab hold of the good things. She was no longer waiting for *the one*. And tonight, with Gabe, she couldn't stop asking herself a different kind of question.

Why couldn't she have something wonderful just for now?

She glanced down into her empty coffee cup.

Gabe asked, "More coffee?"

She sent him a grin. "This was perfect. Nothing more, thanks."

A few minutes later, they waved goodbye to the

pretty hostess in the front foyer and went out into the summer darkness where the Cadillac was waiting.

"Come out to the Ambling A with me," he offered as they left the Association behind. "Just for a little while."

It had been such a great evening. She really didn't want it to end. And she didn't have to be at DJ's until late afternoon tomorrow. "All right. I would like that."

"Where's Butch?" Mel asked as Gabe ushered her in the front door. "I thought he'd be right here waiting at your door."

"He's over at the other house. He likes to hang out with Malone and my folks when I'm not around. They spoil him rotten, not that I mind." He led her into the big living room. "Brandy?"

"Brandy sounds just right."

He tapped at his phone and music played. It was country, a slow song. They settled on the sofa. She sipped her brandy, enjoying the warmth and the heady flavor.

"It's so good," she said. "This evening. The dinner. This brandy...you."

He set his glass on the beautiful burled wood coffee table in front of them, then gently took hers from her hand and set it down, too. She didn't object. She was much too eager to find out what would happen next.

And she was not disappointed.

He touched her cheek and then traced her jaw, his big, warm fingers sliding under the waves of her hair to gently cradle the nape of her neck.

"Melanie." He said her given name rough and low, lingering over it, as though savoring the taste of it. She preferred to be called Mel. It was short, sweet and strong, and that was how she saw herself. But tonight, well, the way he said her full name worked for her in a big way. "All night, I've been hoping I might just get a chance to do this…"

He gathered her into him. For a long, sweet span of seconds, she was looking in his eyes, feeling lazy and easy, arousal curling through her, smoky and warm as the taste of the brandy on her tongue. Then he covered her mouth with his.

She let her eyes drift shut as she opened for him. The kiss bloomed into something hotter, more urgent, as his tongue swept in to taste her.

Beneath his crisp white shirt, his broad chest was hard and hot to her touch, and his arms held her so tight, like he would never let her go. Images danced on the insides of her eyelids—his smile that first day when they met out by the creek, the patient look he'd given her every time she'd told him no, those nights at DJ's when she would spot him at the bar as he glanced up and saw her looking his way.

Whatever this was, this heat and energy that always arced between them whenever he was near, she wanted more of it. She wanted it now.

He leaned back enough to capture her gaze again. "I'm thinking you really need to spend the night here with me."

Okay, yeah. She'd been thinking pretty much the same thing.

Pulling the trigger on that, though—it was another big step altogether. "Really not sure that's such a great idea."

He kissed her, soft and quick. "That's okay. I'm sure enough for both of us."

She fondly combed his spiky hair back with her fingers. It was silky to the touch. "I am so tempted."

"Excellent." That smile of his was downright combustible. "And you know what they say…"

She lifted up from her lazy slouch against the cushions to press a kiss to that sculpted jaw of his, lingering long enough to nip him lightly with her teeth. "Tell me. What *do* they say?"

"The best way to get over a cheating rich guy is to jump right in with an honest man."

"You mean someone like you?"

"That's right. You should jump right in with me, Mel. You should do that right now, tonight."

"You, the rich guy who pretended to be a poor cowboy when I met him?"

"We've been over that. Let's not go there again."

She laughed, the sound low and husky to her own ears. "But it's so much fun to razz you about it."

"Fair enough. Go ahead. Razz me all you want, just as long as you…" He nuzzled her neck. "Stay." He breathed the tender word against her skin. "I want you, Mel. Here. In my arms. All night long."

And then his mouth found hers again and they were kissing, endlessly kissing. He slid a questing hand down her body, under the curve of her bottom and on along her thigh, over her short skirt to the bare skin midway to her knee. Every inch of her flared with heat and yearning in the wake of that long, slow caress. His palm skated lower, over her knee and down her calf. When he reached her ankle, he eased off her high-heeled shoe. She heard a soft *thunk* as it hit the floor.

The other shoe followed right after.

No doubt about it. All the so-valid reasons she had *not* to go where she was going with him right now were blown away. By his touch. By each and every teasing conversation she'd indulged in with him at DJ's in those evenings he'd shown up to sit at the bar. By the way he always looked at her as if she was the only other person in the room.

Right now, it didn't matter in the least where this

might be going. She was swept away by his manliness, his great sense of humor, that burning look in his summer-sky eyes. Somehow, he'd done it, thoroughly seduced her. And tonight, she was ready to relax and enjoy this for what it was—the magic of true chemistry, the pleasure she might find in one perfect night with a man like Gabe.

There was no tomorrow. Only now. Only Gabe and his captivating kisses, his bold, burning touch. For once in her life, she was going for it, giving herself up to the delicious decadence of it, a wild night with the right man—not a man for forever, but the perfect man for right now.

And as for tomorrow?

Tomorrow could damn well take care of itself.

Chapter Five

Gabe couldn't believe it. It was happening at last.

He had Mel in his arms and he wasn't letting go.

He kept kissing her, greedy for her. He wanted to claim every inch of her with the heat of his mouth. She was eager, ready. Every signal she gave him said yes.

She clutched his shoulders and surrendered her mouth to him, moaning so sweetly when he kissed his way down the V-neck of her dress, into that soft, perfect valley between her pretty pale breasts. She urged him on with eager sighs and softly murmured encouragements.

"Yes," she cried low as he nibbled her collarbone.

"Please," she begged sweetly as he swept her heavy, fragrant hair aside to get to the long zipper at the back of that sexy little dress. With a sizzling purr of sound, the zipper parted.

"Gabe. Anything, everything," she whispered as he pulled the dress down her arms, revealing a purple lace bra and more smooth, kissable skin.

He pressed his hungry mouth to the tiny satin bow between the perfect swells of her breasts.

She let her head fall back. "Yes," she said again, her long hair falling every which way, curling down her back, tumbling over her satiny shoulders.

He kissed his way up over the top rim of the lace, a chain of kisses, first one breast and then the other. When he couldn't wait another moment to uncover her, he undid the clasp and the bra fell away.

She stared up at him, open to him, her eyes a jewel-blue sea of want, of yearning. "Gabe," she whispered. "Oh, please. Yes…"

He took one hard, pebbled nipple and then the other in his mouth as she clutched him close, crying his name again, begging him, "Gabe, yes, more…"

More sounded very, very good to him.

But not here.

He wanted to stretch out with her. The leather sofa was a big one, but not big enough.

He tipped up her chin and she gazed at him dazedly. "Hmm?" she asked sweetly.

"Bedtime."

A quivery little breath escaped her. "Um. Okay."

Oh, he could get used to this side of her. So soft and innocent. Not the sharp and guarded Mel he sparred with at DJ's. This was a softer Mel. Vulnerable and yielding.

Rising, he caught her hand and pulled her up to stand with him. The skirt of her dress still hung around her hips. She glanced down over her bare breasts and then back up at him. "I guess I don't need this right now, do I?" And she pushed the dress down. It fell in a satin and lace puddle around her bare ankles, leaving her standing there in nothing but tiny purple panties.

He indulged in a long, slow look. At all of her, from her strong, slender legs to the outward curves of her hips, the fine indentation of her waist, the womanly beauty of her round breasts. There wasn't an inch of her he didn't want to kiss, to hold, to worship all night long.

Her hair spilled down over her shoulders, golden, wild and curling. She was glorious. A sight to behold.

"There." She stepped out of the dress, snatched it up and tossed it across the back of the sofa. Gently, she nudged her shoes with a toe until they were under the coffee table. And then she held out her hand to him.

He took it, but only to turn her and scoop her

high against his chest. With a low, happy sound, she twined her arms around his neck and dropped a sweet little kiss at his jaw.

"Ready?" He kissed her plump, delicious lips, thinking of how long he'd waited. To find her. To hold her. He'd dated a lot of women, gotten himself something of a rep for never sticking with even one of them. Slowly, he'd reached the sad conclusion that Gramps didn't know what he was talking about. There was no special woman out there for him, no one who was *the one*.

Well, Gabe got it now. He was a believer. Gramps was right. With this woman, he didn't have a single doubt. He truly didn't even need to ask.

"Let's go," she said softly.

Cradling her close, he headed for the master suite.

In his room, he carried her straight to the bed, which was already turned down by the housekeeper who came in daily to whip everything into shape.

"Where are you going?" she demanded when he gently set her on the white sheets and took a step back.

"Nowhere." He unbuttoned his shirt, impatiently enough that two buttons went flying. "I'm staying right here with you." He tossed the shirt at a chair, turned and dropped to the side of the bed to pull off his boots.

As he was tugging on the second one, her smooth, cool hands came around him from behind. "I like it better when you're close." She pressed her naked breasts to his bare back and the silky skin of her slim arms encircled him. For a moment, he forgot how to breathe. He felt her lips against his shoulder.

And then those clever hands of hers got busy unbuckling his belt.

He chuckled at that, turning his head to share a kiss with her over his shoulder—a long, sweet one. His eager tongue met hers, tangling. She moaned into his mouth. It was possibly the sweetest, hottest sound he'd ever heard.

The boots were off in a matter of seconds. Socks, too, as he kissed her. She undid his belt and whipped it away. Her nimble fingers dealt with his fly.

He hated breaking their long, sweet kiss. But it had to be done for him to get out of his pants and boxer briefs. He stood and shoved them down, groaning a little when his erection got in the way.

Finally, though, everything was off. He turned to her and his heart stopped. She'd dispensed with those tiny panties. On her knees on his bed, her hands on her creamy thighs, her golden hair all over the place, she was an invitation to sin. Those eyes were cobalt-blue right now, full of longing and secrets, deep and dark as a hidden pond in some magical forest glen. He loved the look of her, so small and strong and perfect, without a stitch on.

She caught her lower lip between her pretty white teeth, the way she did when she was uncertain. "Gabe. What's the matter?"

He gave her a slow smile. "Not a thing."

"You sure?" She was chewing on that lip a little now, adorable and nervous.

He bent, put a finger under her soft chin and used his thumb to pull her lower lip free. "If anyone's going to be biting those pretty lips tonight, it will be me."

At last, she smiled again. "You looked so serious there for a moment."

"You're beautiful." He kissed her quick and hard. "All of you. I'm very serious about that."

"Oh, Gabe…" She came up on her knees, reaching for him.

Best invitation he'd ever had. He went down to her, wrapping his arms around her good and tight, rolling her little body under him.

She felt like paradise, like she'd been made just for him.

They kissed, one of those kisses a man can get lost in, the kind where he hoped he would never be found. Her hair tangled around them, silky. Wild. And her soft hands stroked his shoulders and strayed down his back, pausing in the dip of his spine, rubbing there as she made the sweetest, softest, hungriest little sounds that echoed pleasurably inside his head as their endless kiss continued.

He wanted more—to get his mouth on every inch of her. She whimpered in protest as he broke their long kiss and then sighed in delight as he kissed his way across her collarbone and then back to that little notch at the base of her smooth throat.

From there he went down, stopping to worship each pink-tipped, round breast, and then moving lower, dipping his tongue in the tender well of her navel, but not stopping there.

Oh, no. He wanted—*needed*—to kiss the secret heart of her.

But he took a small detour first, down to the tender groove where her hip met her body. He kissed her there, pausing to scrape his teeth against the sweet jut of her hip bone. She stirred restlessly, making little pleading sounds that only got him more determined not to rush a single caress during this first time with her.

He began on the other side, lavishing equal attention there, too, as she begged, "Please, Gabe," and clutched at his shoulders, fisting her little hands in his hair.

Still, he refused to hurry. He lingered, nipping

and kissing, so close to the feminine heart of her, but always, just barely, *not* there.

"Please, Gabe. You're making me crazy, you know that?"

He did know. And he was glad. Every moment with her was better than the last and he refused to miss an inch of her. She needed kissing all over and he was the man for that job.

He scattered a curving, twisting line of kisses down her to knees and over each shin. He kissed her pretty ankles and even the tips of her turquoise-painted toes. She begged all the harder, complaining that he was pushing her over the edge.

"I'll never come back," she cried. "I'll just end up trembling in a corner chanting your name."

He chuckled over that. "Shh, sweetheart. It's going to be all right. Just be patient a little longer."

"Patient! You can't purposely drive a girl out of her mind and ask her to be patient while you're doing it."

By then, he was kissing his way back up the inside of her left leg, lingering on the tender inside of her knee. She moaned and cried out, encouraging him to keep moving upward. He did, slowly. So slowly...

When he reached the core of her, he lifted those slim legs of hers over his shoulders and settled in to enjoy the wet, musky taste of her.

She cried out sharply, grabbing his head between her clutching hands. And when she shattered, he stayed with her, using his fingers as well as his mouth, kissing her endlessly as her body crested, shuddered and then went limp and lazy.

A low, throaty laugh escaped her, followed by the sweetest little whimper of mingled satisfaction and disbelief. "How did you do that? That was... Oh, Gabe... I don't have the words. Get up here where I can kiss you properly." She was pulling at his shoulders.

He gave her what she wanted, easing her thighs back to the mattress, sliding up to take her in his arms again.

She grabbed his face between her hands and laid one on him, a long kiss, one that promised more pleasure to come. Then she rolled on top of him and rested her head in the cradle of his shoulder. "I think I'm going to need a minute or two to catch my breath."

He smoothed a shiny, wheat-colored curl away from her cheek. "Take as long as you need. We've got all night."

She sighed. "Homer will be pissed."

"He'll live."

She snuggled in a little closer. "At least I left him plenty of food, a full bowl of fresh water and a clean litter box. He should be fine."

He stroked an idle hand down the silky slope of her back and then traced her spine, set on memorizing her body, on learning every inch of the curvy, delicious perfection of her.

She sighed, kissed his shoulder and rubbed a soft hand up and down his arm. "You know," she said in a soft, happy tone, "I've never had casual sex before."

Casual—wait. What?

She went on blithely. "I can't wait to have more of it. I can really see now how this rebound thing can help push a person down the road to realizing she's truly over her cheating ex." She lifted up, stacked her hands on his chest and braced her chin on them. Those gemstone eyes gleamed. "So, thank you." She granted him her sweetest smile.

Gabe kept his game face on. He might be falling for her hard and fast and pretty damn deep, but he'd set himself up for where she was taking this. After all, an hour before, he'd been the one to suggest that the best way to get past what her douchebag ex had done to her was to spend a hot night with a man who would treat her right—namely, him.

How could he get on her for taking him at his word?

True, for him, this thing between them wasn't casual in the least. And her cheerful, offhand words hit him where it hurt.

But he needed to look on the bright side. He had

her in his bed now. And no matter how lightheart-edly she spoke of having herself some hot rebound sex, he knew she wasn't a woman who shared her body casually. This night was special. Someday she would admit that to him.

He could wait. Take his time with her. Give her plenty of space to come around to the real mean-ing of this night on her own. He cupped his hand around the back of her head and urged her up so their lips could meet. Closing his eyes, he lost him-self in her kiss.

When he looked at her again, her eyes had gone hazy in the best kind of way. "Oh, Gabe…" And then she blinked and said hesitantly, "I forgot to ask…"

He knew the drill. "I've got a clean bill of health and condoms in the bedside drawer."

She gave a shy little laugh. "Me, too—on the clean bill of health. And I'm on the Pill."

"Then we're golden." He tugged her closer and covered her irresistible mouth with his.

After that, they didn't need words. He lavished kisses everywhere his hungry mouth could reach. And she sighed and pulled him closer, kissing him so deeply, her soft hands roaming everywhere.

When he pulled away long enough to deal with the condom, she stared up at him dreamily, so ready. So sweet. Once he'd rolled on the condom, she pulled him close again. Her hands moved over his skin, stroking him—down his arm, over his chest, as though she couldn't get enough of touching him.

He understood her need to have her hands on him. He felt the same about her. That he needed to be closer to her, to have his hands all over her, to lose himself in the scent and feel and taste of her.

Taking the lead, she pushed him to his back and eased one slim leg over him. She wrapped her pretty hand around him, held him in position and slowly lowered herself down to him.

They groaned together, eyes locked on each other, as she took him fully into her.

After that, things got frantic, desperate in the best sort of way. Hard and fast. Wild and out of control. He knew he would lose it, but somehow, he held on.

The rhythm changed, going deep, rocking long and slow.

He rolled them, so he was on top—and then rolled again. Face-to-face, on their sides, it went on and on.

Finally, she broke. He watched her let go. It was the most beautiful thing he'd ever seen, the wild spots of deep color on her satiny cheeks, the hot flush rushing up her slender throat, the transported expression on her amazing face. He managed to wait for her to hit the peak before following her over the edge of the Earth.

* * *

Around midnight, as Mel was settling in, closing her eyes, drifting toward sleep, Gabe nuzzled her ear.

"I have a question." His deep voice set off sparks along her nerve endings, reminding her of the pleasure he'd just brought her—three times.

Clearly, she'd been missing out. Having sex with Gabe Abernathy was like no sex she'd ever experienced before. If this was rebound sex they were having, well, she never wanted to have any other kind.

Not only had Todd been a cheater, he'd been a slacker in bed.

But maybe she had been, too. Having sex with Gabe took sex to a whole other level for her. He not only did glorious things to her very willing body, he made her want to do fabulous, naughty things to him right back.

And she had. Oh, she definitely had. She could feel her cheeks turning pink just thinking about the things they had done. And she could not wait to do them all again.

She might be insatiable now. And guess what? She was just fine with that.

He was up on one elbow, grinning at her. "What are you thinking?"

She grinned right back. "I'll never tell. You said you had a question?"

"I do. What is your opinion of Ben & Jerry's?"

She levered up enough to kiss the tip of his nose. "Okay, now you've done it. Do you *have* Ben & Jerry's?"

"I might."

She poked at his rocklike, sculpted shoulder. "Now you're teasing me. It's not nice to tease the woman you've worn out with fabulous, hot sex, three times. A woman in my condition really needs some Ben & Jerry's. Any flavor—as long as there's plenty of chocolate in it."

He traced her brows with a lazy finger. "We'll have to get up and go to the kitchen, have a look in the freezer."

"I don't feel like putting my dress back on."

"Who said you had to?"

Five minutes later, they stood at the kitchen island eating Chocolate Fudge Brownie straight from the carton, sharing the spoon, Gabe in an old pair of jeans, Mel in his white dress shirt from earlier tonight.

Really, she was having the best time. Gabe was not only great in bed, fun to hang around with and generous and thoughtful to a fault, she just really, really *liked* him.

As he handed her the spoon again and she scooped up another decadent, delicious bite, she thought of the diary that had once belonged to a young man named Josiah, a young man with the same last name as Gabe. That young man would be in his nineties now, if he still lived. He'd loved someone named Winona, who might or might not be the Winona Mel knew and admired. And what about the baby who hadn't died, after all? Was Beatrix still alive somewhere, in her seventies now? With no clue that the family she'd grown up in wasn't the one she'd been born into?

Mel had so many questions when it came to the diary and the heartbreaking story it contained. She kept telling herself to leave it alone, that it was none of her business, really, a mystery that would never be solved. And then, as soon as she denied the diary's hold on her, she would start wondering again, longing to find out what really happened to the young lovers and their child.

It hurt her heart to think of those long-ago lovers, lost to each other, so old now, or gone forever. Or to think of their baby, Beatrix, who could be anywhere now—if she was still alive.

"All of a sudden, you look so sad." Gabe stuck the spoon in the carton and set the carton on the counter. He tipped her chin up with a finger. "What is happening in your beautiful head, sweetheart?"

Sweetheart. She could really get used to him calling her that.

"Hey, now…" He framed her cheeks with his big hands. One had been holding the ice cream. It was cold against her skin. "It can't be that bad."

"It's what you said, just sad, that's all."

His lips descended. He tasted so good—of cold chocolate and banked desire. She opened to him and the kiss went on for a while. Slow. Lazy. Tender. Achingly sweet.

When he lifted his head, he suggested, "Talk to me about it."

Did she dare? Before, it had always seemed somehow foolish to even go there with him or his family. If his family was the family who had fled her hometown in the dark of night decades ago, wouldn't he have mentioned it or at least looked uncomfortable when she'd razzed him about the Rust Creek Falls Abernathys vanishing into the night?

She had way too many questions and very few answers. And the whole thing with the diary was a sore point with her. Wilder Crawford should have taken the diary back when she tried to give it to him. This was not her quest. She was a reluctant sleuth at best.

But then, well, tonight happened. Yes, she'd called tonight a rebound. But it didn't matter what she called it—tonight had changed things between her and this man who was turning out to be a whole lot more than she'd bargained for.

"I think you do want to talk about it, whatever it is." His eyes held hers, waiting for her to open up and explain herself.

"You might be sorry you asked. In fact, you'll *probably* be sorry you asked."

He gave her that smile, the one that made her want to move in closer and beg for more kisses. "Try me."

Standing there in bare feet, wearing only his shirt, she shivered a little and wrapped her arms around herself.

"You're cold." He stroked a slow hand down her hair, smoothing it back over her shoulder. When she shivered again, he pulled her close. "I'll put the ice cream away and we'll turn on the fire."

They sat on the stone hearth right there in the family room off the kitchen. The fire there was gas. He turned it on with a remote.

"Better?" he asked.

The heat quickly soothed her. "Much." She met his eyes—and started talking. "A week before I moved to Bronco, I went to a wedding in Rust Creek Falls Park…"

Gabe listened, not once interrupting, as she detailed catching the bouquet, her encounter with Wren Crawford and the "gift" of Josiah Abernathy's diary that Wren had insisted she take. She repeated the information Wilder Crawford had shared with her, including the letter tucked away in the diary's binding. She explained her friendship with the old woman who had the same name as the girl to whom the never-mailed letter was addressed. She told him that she had gone as far as to check the archives of the *Rust Creek Falls Gazette*, where she'd found a picture of a young Winona that proved her elderly friend had been in Rust Creek Falls about the time the events in the diary had taken place.

She shared all of it, everything she knew about the long-ago love story and its tragic ending.

And when she was finished, he still didn't say anything.

In fact, he seemed…distant now. Far away from her, and much too quiet.

"Gabe?" She put her hand on his rock-hard bare arm. He didn't pull away, but it seemed to her that he stiffened. "Gabe. What's wrong?"

His eyes focused in on her face. "My great-grandfather…"

"The one you call Gramps, right?"

His head dipped in the slightest of nods. "Gramps's given name is Josiah. Josiah Abernathy."

Chapter Six

With the fire at her back, Mel wasn't cold anymore.

That didn't stop her from shivering, though, to hear that Gabe's beloved Gramps had the same name as the young man who'd written the diary.

Gabe was staring at her, his expression distant now, hardened. "Gramps was married to Great-Grandma Cora for seventy years. They had four sons together. They were devoted to each other. There was never any other woman in Gramps's life. My family has lived in the Bronco area for generations. No one's ever said a word to me about Gramps and his parents fleeing here from Rust

Creek Falls for some shady reason having to do with this Winona Cobbs woman and a disappearing baby."

"You're angry."

"No, I'm not." He glared at her.

"You sure seem like you're angry."

He drew in a slow breath and then bent forward and braced his forearms on his spread knees. "Look. I'm sorry. I know I'm overreacting. But if Gramps *is* the same Josiah as in this diary you talk about, that would mean he's not the man I thought I knew."

She dared to touch him again. He let her take his hand. She held it between both of hers. He didn't try to weave their fingers together and neither did she. "Gabe, if your Gramps *is* the Josiah I just told you about, it was before he ever met your great-grandmother. It's not as if he had a secret life or he cheated on his wife or anything. The events of the diary happened over seven decades ago. Josiah was hardly more than a boy—a boy in love with a girl in a very different time than ours. He really did want to do the right thing. His parents were the troublemakers. You have to see that."

He pulled his hand from hers and raked at his spiky hair with his fingers. "I just don't believe that the Josiah in your story is my Gramps. I don't. It's a coincidence, that's all. A weird coincidence."

Mel felt terrible. She'd known she should keep her mouth shut about the damn diary. But no. She'd just *had* to lay it all on him and make him question the character of a man he'd always idolized—not to mention, his family's history. "You know, maybe it would help if you read the diary and the letter for yourself."

He turned those hardened eyes on her again. "Look, Mel. The last thing I want is to go digging for dirt on my family in some old diary some guy I've never met found in a ranch house more than three hundred miles from here."

She hard-swallowed at his cold tone. "I, um, understand." He turned and stared straight ahead. Anywhere but at her, apparently. She should get the message, she knew that. But she couldn't stop herself from making one more pass at the Josiah question. "You know, a conversation with your great-grandfather just might clear everything up. I would love to meet him."

He still refused to look at her. "You don't get it. The thing with Gramps is complicated."

"How so?"

Gabe shook his head. "He lives in a senior care facility. He's a fragile old man, far gone in dementia. He's withdrawn. Uncommunicative. Most times when I go to visit him, he doesn't speak. I can't tell if he even really knows I'm there."

"But maybe if we—"

"Mel. I'm just not comfortable taking you to see him, okay?"

"Um. Yeah. I get it. And I'm sorry. I should have just…let it be."

"It's not your fault. I encouraged you to tell me what was on your mind." His words were more than reasonable. But he still wasn't looking at her.

She really, really wished she'd driven her own car tonight. "I'm kind of thinking I've worn out my welcome here."

"No. Of course you haven't." He did look at her then, but not exactly with warmth.

"Do you think you could maybe drive me home?"

He stared at her. She dared to imagine he might urge her to stay. But then he only said, "All right. Let's get dressed."

The ride into Bronco Heights was anything but chatty. To Mel, the summer night, thick with stars, seemed empty and endless beyond the windshield.

Gabe pulled into one of the guest spaces in front of her building. She thanked him for the evening and tried to say good-night, but he insisted on walking her all the way to her door.

"'Night, Mel," he said when they got there. For a moment, she thought she might get a good-night kiss, that he was going to loosen up a little and leave her with hope that things would be all right between them.

But he only stared at her kind of wistfully for several awkward seconds, brushed her cheek with his warm hand and left her standing there trying to figure out how in the world such a beautiful evening could go so bad so fast.

Inside, she flipped on the light to find Homer sitting three feet from the door looking up at her through those buggy gray-green eyes of his. "Honey, I'm home," she said in a lame attempt at humor. Dropping her keys and purse on the table against the wall, she scooped up the little black cat.

He purred when she nuzzled that sweet space between his pointy ears. "It's for the best, I guess," she whispered to the kitten. "I mean, the last thing I need right now is another man in my life. I was getting in too deep with him, anyway." At the bed, she kicked off her shoes and stretched out on her back, resting Homer on her chest. For once, he didn't leap up and dart away, but settled in comfortably.

It was nice, feeling his purr right over her heart. Soothing. "We had a beautiful dinner at Gabe's private club. And then later, we had sex." Homer purred at her, his eyes low and lazy. "The sex was fantabulous. Even if it did all go to hell shortly thereafter." Homer stretched out a paw and batted at her chin. "Oh, really. Don't worry about me. I'm fine. Just fine."

She stared up at the ceiling, feeling kind of forlorn.

When Homer suddenly leaped to his feet and took off for his water bowl, she rolled to her stomach, wrapped her arms around her pillow and shut her eyes.

Gabe had said that Josiah lived in a senior care facility. It was probably right here in town. How hard could it be to track the old man down?

But no. That wouldn't be right, to go against Gabe's wishes and snoop around behind his back that way.

However, there was no one stopping her from a little Googling of the local Abernathy family and maybe a visit to the Bronco library to have a look through the archives of the *Bronco Bulletin*. The Abernathys were an important local family. They probably got their names in the paper all the time...

The next morning, she looked around on the internet. Mostly, she just found current stuff about Gabe and his rather large extended family. There were several pictures of Gabe at local events, always with a good-looking woman on his arm. That was kind of depressing, actually. It was way obvious Gabe would have no trouble finding a pretty woman to take to dinner at the Association any time he chose to go.

She did find the obituary of Josiah's wife, Cora, from five years before. She'd died peacefully in her sleep at the age of ninety, after being married to Josiah for seventy years.

Nothing in that obituary made it impossible for Josiah to have been in Rust Creek Falls around the time that the author of the diary fathered a child with a woman named Winona Cobbs.

At a little past eleven, Mel headed for the library. In the archives of the *Bronco Bulletin*, she found Cora and Josiah's wedding announcement, complete with a grainy photo of the groom and his bride. Gabe's great-grandfather had been a tall, lean man with a serious face. Did she see a certain sadness in Josiah's eyes—or was that just her overactive imagination? The young Josiah looked a bit like Gabe, she thought, especially around the mouth and in the determined set of the jaw.

There were other articles that mentioned Josiah— at the baptisms of his four sons, the death of Cora's mother a few years later and the dedication of a new courthouse building fifty years ago. As a respected member of the Bronco community, Josiah had been asked to do the ribbon cutting.

Eventually, she ran out of hits on Gabe's great-grandfather. She started searching for information that might tell her approximately when the Abernathy family had moved to town.

No luck there. She also couldn't find a single mention of the Bronco Abernathys in the *Bulletin* until after the time the Rust Creek Falls Abernathys would have fled her hometown—not that that necessarily proved anything.

Mel left the library feeling kind of discouraged. A whole morning's work had brought her no closer to knowing if the Josiah in the diary might be the same man Gabe called Gramps. If she really wanted to find out what had happened to the Josiah of the diary, she should probably hire a PI or someone like Amanda who knew her way into all the nooks and crannies of the internet.

Mel was getting nowhere in the search for the truth about Beatrix. And she felt awful about the way she'd left things with Gabe. That evening at DJ's, she felt anxious all through the dinner service. Her gaze kept straying to the bar, where customers came and went. But Gabe never appeared. What if he never contacted her again?

Just the thought made her heart hurt. Longing burned through her.

Seriously? What was the matter with her that she went moping around over Gabe? She had not come to Bronco to fall for a man. And if it was over with Gabe after their one spectacular night together, that was a good thing. Bronco was only a stopover on her way to her new life in Austin, after all.

Still, she kept checking her phone. Not a call. Not a text.

Wednesday night was the same. No calls, no texts. No Gabe.

Thursday was her day off. More than once, she got out her phone and punched up Gabe's number. Somehow, she managed to keep her finger from hitting the call button. She kept herself busy, shopping for groceries, straightening up the apartment. She invited Amanda and Brittany for dinner that evening at her place. When the subject of Gabe came up, she waved a hand and said she really didn't expect to be seeing him again.

"What did he do?" Brittany demanded, instantly pissed off for Mel's sake.

Mel played it extra cool. "He's great, but it is what it is, you know? I like him, but I'm not looking for anything serious and I'm guessing he's not, either."

Amanda was watching her much too closely. "Translation—whatever went down, you don't want to talk about it."

Affection washed through Mel as she gave a low laugh. "You guys. How can you possibly know me so well in such a short time?"

"Seems like we've known you forever," said Brittany with an elegant shrug. "And you're still not going to tell us what happened with you and the crown prince of Bronco, are you?"

She shook her head. "I don't really want to get into it."

Amanda reached across the small table and gave her arm a comforting squeeze. "We're here and ready to listen if you change your mind."

Brittany picked up the bottle of red Mel had opened to go with the pasta. "In the meantime, you need another glass of wine."

Gabe somehow got through Tuesday without calling Mel. That night, after dinner, he joined Malone on the front porch for a couple of hours. They didn't talk much. After about half an hour, Malone asked what was eating him. He lied and said nothing. Malone gave him a disbelieving look, but at least the old man let it go.

Wednesday was harder to get through than Tuesday. Gabe almost convinced himself it would be okay to head over to DJ's and see Mel.

Somehow, he kept himself from going there.

Thursday, he woke up thinking he couldn't take it anymore. He *had* to see her.

By the time he'd had coffee and breakfast, he'd changed his mind. She'd probably want to talk more about that guy with the diary who had the same name as Gramps. Gabe just wasn't ready to go there.

Maybe he never would be.

And really, it was about damn time he paid a visit to Snowy Mountain Senior Care. He should've gone days ago. But first he'd been busy and then Mel had blindsided him with that crazy story about the diary and the missing baby and the star-crossed young lovers, one of whom had Gramps's name.

None of that justified his staying away. He owed Gramps a visit and he damn well would go. Today. No excuses.

North of Bronco Heights, Snowy Mountain was a rambling series of brick buildings surrounded by manicured grounds crisscrossed with walkways. The facility offered a full range of services, from independent living to end-of-life care.

Josiah lived at Snowy Mountain West, a wing of the complex devoted to seniors with varying degrees of dementia or Alzheimer's. It was a big, open building, easy to get around in, where Gabe's great-grandfather got round-the-clock care.

"Hi, Gabe! Right on time," said the chatty brunette behind the desk in the sky-lit foyer. "Josiah has been for his walk and he's chillaxing in the lounge."

"Thanks, Linda." He gave her a smile as he went by.

Gramps was sitting quietly on a big sofa, his watery hazel eyes focused straight ahead. Gabe greeted him and refused to be too disappointed when the old man gave zero indication he knew that Gabe was there.

"Come on," Gabe coaxed, taking Josiah's thin arm. "Let's go where we can talk." It only took a gentle tug and Gramps rose. Gabe tucked the wrinkled, heavily veined hand in the crook of his arm and led Gramps to his rooms, which were attractively decorated in blues and grays and included a living room, bedroom and bath. The living room boasted big windows facing a pretty stretch of lawn with a winding path and a lilac tree.

Gabe led Gramps to the sitting area, guided him down to the big recliner and took the love seat across the low table from him. Gramps rarely spoke anymore, so Gabe filled the room with the sound of his own voice. He talked of everyday stuff, some property he'd just sold for top dollar west of town and the going price of beef this year. He confided that he was still trying to convince his dad to let him try a small bison herd on the Ambling A.

"So far," he said wryly, "the old man says no followed by a big hell, no."

And then, well, he went ahead and got into the stuff Mel had laid on him Monday night. He said how it had really pissed him off that she could even suggest that Gramps might be the kid from Rust Creek Falls who'd filled a diary full of entries about some woman he called "W," whose full name turned out to be Winona Cobbs—a woman the young Josiah's parents did not approve of.

"This Winona person," Gabe said gently, "had a baby as a result of her love affair with the kid named Josiah. Then, when Winona thought the baby had died, she couldn't deal. She had to be hospitalized in a mental health facility in Kalispell.

"But a letter tucked in the diary said the baby, whose name was Beatrix, had survived. Beatrix is missing to this day—or so the story goes. Mel is very fond of a woman about your age in Rust Creek Falls whose name just happens to be Winona Cobbs. Apparently, the Cobbs woman isn't well and nobody has been willing to tell her what they've found out. They're afraid it might be too much for her to take."

Across the coffee table, a long sigh escaped Josiah. Gabe fell silent. He watched Gramps closely, hoping against hope that maybe today would be one of those rare days when his great-grandfather spoke to him, or even recognized him.

But the sigh was all he got. Other than that, Josiah didn't make a peep. He continued to stare in the general direction of a family portrait hanging on the wall across the room, one taken at least fifty years ago. It included Great-Grandma Cora and all four of their boys.

"I told Mel it couldn't be you, Gramps. I know Great-Grandma Cora was the only woman for you."

About then, Gabe realized he'd jumped right into the bizarre story of the diary without telling Gramps about Mel herself.

"And I guess you're kind of wondering who the heck this Mel person is." A nervous chuckle escaped him. "Her full name is Melanie Driscoll. I met her when she wandered onto the Ambling A not long ago. And since I've met her, well, I'm always trying to figure out ways to get close to her, you know? Last Monday night, I thought we were really onto something, Mel and me. Then she laid all this crap on me about the diary and the woman named Winona and the lost baby Beatrix and, well, I haven't called her since."

Gabe braced his elbows on his spread knees, linked his hands between them and stared down at his boots as he confessed, "But I want to call her, Gramps. I want to call her so much it hurts. With her, it's like you always said. I don't have to ask the question. When it comes to Mel Driscoll, somehow I already know. I'm in love with her, Gramps. She's the one for me." Stunned at his own words, he glanced up.

Josiah's eyes were empty. Gabe felt that emptiness echo in the center of his chest. He would have given the world right then to have Gramps look directly at him, to hear him say that he understood exactly how Gabe felt about Mel—or to set him straight if Gramps thought he somehow had it all wrong. Until the past few years, Gramps had always been the one to give Gabe exactly the advice he hadn't known he needed.

Now, though? Gramps just sat there, still and staring, making Gabe wish for the impossible—to turn back the clock, have a real conversation with the Gramps he used to know.

Gabe was halfway back to the Ambling A before he let himself admit what he'd just done.

Whether Gramps had heard him or not, he'd said it out loud.

He'd told his great-grandfather that he was in love with Mel.

And that scared the crap out of him. He'd never been in love before, not really. It had always seemed easy for him, to enjoy spending time with a woman, but not to get in too deep. He'd savored his freedom, maybe even felt kind of smug that he wasn't one of those guys who got his heart all tied in knots over a girl.

Gramps had always warned him that one day it would happen. That one day, he would finally meet the one for him and after that, well, he'd learn what it was to belong to another.

So was this it, then? This longing that wouldn't stop? This feeling of missing some big part of himself when he tried to stay away? This sense that he should be with her and the world wouldn't be right until he'd broken down all the barriers between them?

Damn. If this really was love, he wanted nothing to do with it. It had been one thing to pursue her relentlessly when he didn't comprehend the depth of his own feelings. Until today, the possibility that he would end up with his heart in pieces hadn't even occurred to him. After all, until now he'd never been with anyone who could leave his heart in shredded bits.

But now? Everything had changed for him.

For Mel, though?

Not so much.

She constantly insisted she was leaving in January. Even worse, the other night she'd made it crystal clear she considered him no more than a rebound, a diversion, a pleasurable way to thumb her nose at her cheating ex-fiancé.

She was leaving and she didn't take him seriously.

Where did that leave *him*, but with a broken heart?

Uh-uh. No way. He needed to stop moping around like a long-gone fool. He wasn't *that* far gone. Not yet. He needed to forget her.

And one way or another, he would.

Chapter Seven

Once again, on Friday night, Gabe failed to show up at DJ's. Mel hadn't seen him since their night out on Monday, the night they'd made perfect love— and ended up barely speaking.

He'd never even bothered to call or send her a text.

She was constantly reminding herself that his radio silence was for the best. But it didn't *feel* like the best. Not by a long shot. She missed him, damn it.

She missed him a lot.

And then she started thinking that maybe something had happened to him. Maybe he was really sick. Or what if someone in his family had been in an accident or something? And here she was thinking evil thoughts about him when life had thrown him a curve and he didn't know how to deal with it. He could be suffering. What kind of a friend would she be if she let him suffer without lending her support in any and every way he might need it?

And yes, she *did* consider Gabe a friend. They hadn't known each other long, but she liked him so much.

And she couldn't stop thinking about their one amazing night together. Really, they needed to get past her oversharing about the diary. If she'd upset him, she needed to know so that she could make it right between them again.

By Saturday morning, she'd had enough of not hearing from him.

She paced the floor as she discussed the situation with Homer.

"Really, what's the matter with me?" she asked the bug-eyed cat, who sat in the middle of her bed watching with that special look he had of startled interest as she marched back and forth a few feet away. "I'm not shy. I'm not afraid to call a guy I like. I'm not one of those women who waits by the phone but doesn't have the guts to take the lead and make the call herself." She halted, turned and glared at the kitten, who lifted a leg and started cleaning what was left of his man-parts. "So why have I been acting like some shy wallflower?" The cat rolled to his back and began chewing on his skinny black tail.

"Alrighty then, Homer. It's clear I'll get no answers from you." She marched to her small kitchen counter, grabbed her phone, punched up Gabe's number and held the screen toward the kitten. "If you don't stop me, I'm calling the guy now."

Homer said nothing. He did roll back over and sit up, though. Low-eyed and lazy-looking, he just sat there and purred at her.

"So, then, I'll call him." She hit the call icon.

It rang four times.

And then, just as she was wondering if the damn thing would ever go to voice mail, he answered. "Hello, Mel."

"Gabe!" she said, way too loud and downright frantic. "Is everything okay?"

"Yeah. Sure." He sounded…beyond calm. More like bleak. Or possibly bored.

Her skin felt too tight, her face kind of clammy, and her heart pounded like she'd just run a couple of miles uphill. "It's only, well, I hadn't heard from you and I was wondering if you were okay and… everything." Inside, she was cringing. Could she possibly sound more desperate, more lame?

"I'm fine, really. Everything's fine." He did sound bored. Yes. Definitely. She was boring him.

"Okay. Well, great. I just thought I'd, y'know, check in, thank you for the other night, which was beautiful—I mean, until I brought up the diary thing. If I've upset you with anything I said, I wish you would just tell me and let me try to make amends. I really didn't mean to be intrusive. Maybe I shouldn't have asked to meet your great-grandfather. I totally get why you're protective of him. I should have given the situation more thought before dragging an innocent old man into something that probably has nothing to do with him and might very well be a wild-goose chase, anyway. I apologize if I, well, stepped over the line, you know?"

"It's fine."

"Gabe." She wanted to reach through the phone and shake him—or maybe strangle him. "You don't *sound* fine."

"Look, Melanie…"

Melanie? It was down to him calling her *Melanie* now? That did it for her. "You know what, Gabe? Never mind. Just delete my number. Pretend we never met. You won't hear from me again. Goodbye." She disconnected the call.

She was standing there, vaguely stunned, feeling terrible about what had just happened, when the phone rang in her hand. For a fraction of a second, her heart lifted. She dared to hope it was Gabe, calling her back to apologize for acting like a coldhearted jerk. But then she looked at the screen and the flare of hope died. She didn't recognize the number.

Answering calls from unknown numbers was rarely a good idea. But right at that moment, she was so upset over the way Gabe had just blown her off that she swiped up without thinking.

"Yes?"

"Mel. My God. At last."

"Todd," she muttered grimly.

"Oh, Mel. It's so good to hear your voice. I've missed you so much. Mom and Dad have missed you, too. I need you. *They* need you. Spurlock's needs you. The numbers have really dropped since you've been gone. It's bad. I'm a wreck. Mom and Dad are on my case. They love you so much, honey. *I* love you so much. Where *are* you, Mel? Up in Rust Creek Falls? I'll come to you, right away. If we could just talk, face-to-face, I'm sure you'll see reason and come back to me, to us, to the good life we've made together."

"Todd," she said again, taking great pains to keep her tone even and reasonable.

Todd let out a long sigh. "Ah. At last. There's my girl—yes, Mel. Anything. Whatever you want."

"I want you to quit trying to contact me, Todd."

"I can't quit. I *love* you."

"I *don't* love you, Todd. I'm not your girl."

"You're just saying that."

"Because it's *true*. Whatever I might have felt for you once, well, you killed that, Todd. Killed it stone dead. I am completely and totally through with you. I want nothing to do with you. When are you going to accept that it's over and move on?"

"It's not over. I need to talk to you. Just give me an hour, you and me, face-to-face. I'll make you see—"

"I've seen all I needed to see—a naked woman who wasn't me in our bed. With you. There's no coming back from that, not in my book. You need to let it be and move on."

"Just tell me where and when to meet you. Just let me—"

"Not a chance. It's over. Deal with it. I never want to talk to you again. I'm going to block this number and any other number you try to call me from. Stop wasting your time. Nothing you can do or say will change my mind. Give it up. Let it go. Move the hell on. Goodbye." She ended the call and blocked the number.

On the bed, Homer was still watching her. She sat down next to him. He rose from his haunches to crawl into her lap. She petted him slowly, soothed by the motorboat sound of his sweet purr. "Men," she said glumly to the kitten, since nobody else was there. "When you're done with them, they won't go away. And when you want them, they're no longer interested."

* * *

Mel was wrong about Gabe.

He was very interested. And acting *un*interested had been a bad idea. He realized that now. He'd freaked and tried to tell himself he needed to forget her.

Unfortunately, forgetting her wasn't happening. She filled his mind and heart.

So sue him. He'd never been in love before. He had a right to be bad at it at first. Didn't he?

Would Mel understand if he tried to apologize after not calling for four days, and then being a hopeless jackass when *she'd* called *him*?

No. She wouldn't understand. Why should she understand? Mel was a proud woman. She wasn't going to put up with a guy who treated her like she was wasting his time when she called to ask if he was okay. He would hate it if she put up with a guy like that.

Even if the guy was him.

He'd lost her without having ever really had her.

What was he, thirteen again? He was certainly acting like it. Gone on a girl, being an idiot about it.

Disgusted with himself, he went to the stables and spent a few hours mucking out stalls with only his dog, the gruff head groom and the horses for company. The dirty job didn't improve his attitude any.

He returned to the house, cleaned up and put on

a suit. He had a business dinner at the Association. Over good whiskey and a blood-rare porterhouse steak, he tried to keep his mind on the prospective project at hand: two blocks of luxury townhomes in Bronco Heights, which could be very lucrative for everyone involved.

But keeping his mind on business wasn't easy. His thoughts kept wandering to Mel. Had he totally blown it with her? If he showed up at DJ's again, would she even speak to him? If he knocked on her apartment door, would she refuse to answer?

He really didn't need a damn broken heart—and that had kind of been why he'd behaved so coldly when she'd called.

It was a case of seriously flawed reasoning. He was already in love with her. Being rude to her, trying to push her away, wasn't going to make his love go away. It only made *her* go away, which didn't help in the least.

He was miserable. Heartbroken already. And he'd brought it on his own damn self. He needed to do something to make things better, somehow.

Even if Mel would never give him a real shot at winning her heart, that didn't stop him from stepping up and apologizing for acting like a jerk when she'd been nothing short of a sweetheart, calling to find out if he was all right, trying to clear the air between them, wanting to let him know she wouldn't push him about the diary if he wasn't willing to go there with Gramps.

And as far as that whole thing with the diary, well, why not help the woman he loved clear up an old mystery if he could? What if the impossible turned out to be true and Gramps actually was the Josiah she was looking for?

Yeah, his first response to the story in the diary had been a defensive one—defensive for Gramps, for the family name, for the history of his family as he understood it.

But wasn't the truth supposed to set everyone free?

It had all happened decades ago. A baby had been lost, stolen from her rightful parents. What if that baby—older than his own grandfather now—still lived? What if he had a great-aunt he'd yet to meet who'd lived her whole life never knowing the family she'd been born to? What if a very old woman in Rust Creek Falls could be reunited at last with the daughter she'd lost at birth?

Gabe got home from his business dinner at a little after midnight. He felt edgy, uncomfortable in his own skin. For a while, he sat at his laptop in his study, trying to go over the numbers on the townhome project. His heart wasn't in it, though. He mostly just stared at the columns of figures and thought about how he'd messed up with Mel.

He didn't go to bed until after two.

And he was up before dawn. When he woke, he realized he'd made a decision.

Mel wanted to meet Gramps. And even if she was never going to let herself love him, Gabe loved *her*.

Real love equaled trust. And he needed to trust her enough to take her to his great-grandfather, to give her that shot at finding out the things she longed to know about the past. Whatever did or didn't happen between the two of them, Gabe could at least be the man who helped her get what she wanted.

But there was still Gramps to consider. Would it be damaging to Josiah, somehow, to bring Mel to Snowy Mountain and let her quiz him about what could be the most painful secrets of his past?

Hell if Gabe knew. When he'd brought the subject up Friday, Gramps hadn't responded in any way—beyond a deep sigh, which might or might not have had anything to do with what Gabe was telling him. Chances were high Mel wouldn't get anywhere with the old man, either.

And really, what *did* Gabe know about his own family in the distant past, anyway?

Not a lot, now that he thought about it. Offhand, he couldn't even recall the names of his great-great-grandparents—on his father's *or* his mother's side.

To him, the family history began with Gramps and Great-Grandma Cora.

Maybe he ought to start with lunch at the main house. He could ask his dad and grandfather about Gramps's parents and find out how the Abernathys had come to settle in Bronco.

Unfortunately, though the spread Malone put out was delicious as ever, information-wise, lunch was a bust. Both his dad and Grandpa Alexander said that the Abernathys had "always" lived in Bronco. Grandpa Alexander did at least recall his own grandmother and grandfather. Josiah, Sr. and his wife, Noreen, had both passed away in their fifties.

"I hardly knew them," said Alexander. "They weren't the kind of grandparents who get down on the floor and play with the kids. They always seemed kind of distant. And strict. We all had to be on our best behavior when Grandfather Josiah and Grandmother Noreen were around."

So much for learning about the family from his dad and grandfather. Gabe considered approaching Malone, seeing if the cook knew anything. Malone really was like a member of the family, and he did seem to know things about the Abernathys that no one else had a clue about. But Malone had only been around for a couple of decades. To Gabe, twenty-plus years might seem like a long time. But the events that concerned him now had happened long before Malone became a fixture at the Ambling A.

Not knowing what else to do, Gabe decided to try again to talk to Gramps before taking the big step of bringing Mel to visit him. Maybe this time, his great-grandfather might show him some kind of sign that he heard and understood...

Gabe arrived at Snowy Mountain at a little past three that sunny Sunday afternoon.

Gramps was in the exercise room with several other residents. A fit-looking gray-haired lady led them through a simple routine of chair stretches followed by basic balance exercises and a few modified push-ups and sit-ups. Gabe waited near the door until the class ended. Gramps didn't really participate, but neither did some of the others. Nobody seemed to mind either way.

When the session was finished, Gabe led Gramps back to his room, settled him in the recliner and took the love seat for himself.

He wasn't much encouraged that this visit would go anywhere. It was another of Gramps's "far away" days, as Gabe had come to think of them. Lately, most days were of the "far away" kind.

Josiah stared off toward the family portrait across the room, his eyes vacant, his expression unreadable. Gabe talked to him about everyday stuff to begin with, filling Gramps in on what had been going on with him since his last visit two days before.

Did any of it register with the old man? Hard to tell.

Gabe needed to keep his attitude on straight. If nothing came of this visit, so be it. He reminded himself that it was good, just to be here, him and Gramps. Together.

He leaned in. "I got a problem, Gramps. That woman I mentioned the last time I was here, the one I can't stop thinking about? The one who…" Why the hell was he stalling? He needed to just come out and say it, for God's sake.

He tried again. "Mel. Her name is Mel and I really am in love with her, Gramps. It's finally happened for me and I'm kind of freaked about it, if you want to know the truth. I'm in love with Mel and Mel has had a bad experience with a cheating douchebag ex-fiancé and she says she's through with men. She's got a job waiting for her in Austin at the first of the year. She says she's taking that job, moving on, not coming back. I'll probably have to learn to let her go, Gramps. Plus, I kind of treated her coldly when she called yesterday, which only made my chances worse with her."

Gabe paused for a breath and to judge Josiah's reaction. What he saw wasn't encouraging. Gramps was still staring off into nothing, his face an empty mask.

"Okay, so I'll get to the iffy part. I mentioned this last time, but just in case it didn't register with you, or whatever…" That sentence wandered off into nothing. He started again. "It's like this, Gramps. Mel has this idea that you're originally from her hometown of Rust Creek Falls. She thinks that maybe you loved a woman named Winona there, that Winona had your child and, somehow, Great-Great-Grandpa Josiah and Great-Great-Grandma Noreen arranged to take the baby, Beatrix, away from her mother and to arrange for a secret adoption."

Nothing. Zero response.

Josiah stared into space, same as Friday.

Who did Gabe think he was kidding? There was no point in continuing this one-sided conversation. He wasn't going to get any answers from Gramps.

He reached across the coffee table and gently clasped his great-grandfather's bony shoulder. "It's okay, Gramps. I love you."

It would be wrong to bring Mel here. Gramps was lost somewhere inside his own mind and he couldn't say yes or no to a visit from anyone.

Gabe got up, circled the coffee table and bent to give the old man an awkward hug. Gramps sat passively as Gabe wrapped his arms around his thin shoulders, gave a gentle squeeze and then straightened. "I'm letting this whole crazy story go now. I won't bring it up again, I promise you."

Easing back around the coffee table, Gabe turned for the door. When he got there, he paused with his hand on the knob. "I'll be here again next week, just to check in, visit a little, see how you're doing." He pulled the door wide.

And right then, his great-grandfather said in a rough, rusty voice, "Don't give up on love. Bring her to me."

Gabe stayed for another hour. He spent the whole time trying to coax a few more words out of Josiah. He got nowhere. Gramps had reverted to a silent, staring shell of himself.

It hurt to give up, but what could Gabe do? He left reluctantly.

At the Ambling A, he sat at his desk in the study for a while, feeling kind of low about everything.

When he picked up the phone to call Mel, he wasn't at all sure she would answer.

She didn't. He hung up without leaving a message, though he was pretty confident she would call back if he admitted he was ready to take her to Gramps. A visit with Josiah was probably all she wanted from him now. And that grated.

Yeah, he had no one to blame but himself that she wouldn't take his call. He wanted to fix that— before he said anything about taking her out to Snowy Mountain.

And it had occurred to him that there was one solid clue he could probably track down as to when the Abernathy family might have first come to Bronco. He would follow through on that before trying to reach out to Mel again.

For the rest of the day, Mel constantly reminded herself that she was *not* returning Gabe's call.

He hadn't even left a voice mail. If he wanted to talk to her, he could damn well do her the courtesy of leaving a message, giving her at least a clue of what he needed to talk to her about.

But no. The prince of Bronco was above leaving voice mails explaining himself. He simply called and hung up and his loyal subjects fell all over themselves calling right back to beg for a chance to do his bidding. Whatever *that* might be.

She was buttoning up one of her many white shirts, getting ready for work, when her phone, on the dresser, pinged with a text. She was on it like a shot.

It was from Gabe: I was an ass when you called. I'm sorry. Give me a chance to explain myself?

Her shirt half-buttoned, her ridiculous heart doing something resembling a happy dance inside her chest, she stood holding the phone, her fingers itching to reply.

Nope. Uh-uh. Not happening. She dropped the phone back on the dresser—and it lit up again.

Please?

Somehow, she managed not to grab the damn thing and start typing an answer. It was just better not to go there. They'd had one glorious night and she refused to regret that.

But as for giving him another shot, no. He was much too attractive for her peace of mind and he ran hot and cold. If she accepted his apology this time, how long would it be before he blew her off again?

She just didn't need that kind of grief.

"It's a minute of your time, Mel," argued Gwen. It was seven thirty that night. Mel and her assistant manager were huddled in the hallway between the kitchen and the dining room. Waiters and other staff bustled past them going in both directions, carrying orders and dirty dishes back and forth. "And he *is* Gabe Abernathy…"

"Of course, he is," Mel muttered angrily.

"Give the guy a smile and a quick hello. It's not going to kill you. You've had no trouble dealing with him the other times he's stopped by."

"Yeah. Don't remind me."

Gwen was frowning, confused at Mel's change of

heart when it came to the Abernathy heir. But then she shrugged. "Okay. You're the boss. I'll tell him you're in the middle of something important and can't be disturbed." She turned for the dining room.

Mel grabbed her arm. "You know what? You're right. I'll talk to him."

Gwen hit her with a wide grin. "Excellent. I really wasn't looking forward to telling Gabe Abernathy that the manager didn't have time for him."

Mel emerged from the hallway and saw Gabe right where she expected him to be—at the bar. He'd already spotted her. As their gazes locked, a slow, gorgeous smile spread over that heartbreaker-handsome face of his. He wore a Western-cut jacket over a dark blue dress shirt, his spiky hair just begging her to shove her fingers in it.

She strode toward him with a rising feeling of pure anticipation. She'd missed him so much. The ass. "What can I do for you?" she asked, ladling on the irony, as she slipped into her usual spot between his stool and the next one over.

"Pick up the phone, for a start," he said downright tenderly.

She resisted the urge to fold her arms across her middle in a clearly defensive gesture. "I was reluctant to bore you, the way I obviously did the last time we spoke on the phone."

"You have never once bored me, Mel."

"If you weren't bored, then what?"

"Crazy 'bout you, Mel, and frankly scared of my own damn feelings."

Warmth stole through her. She stiffened her spine, but her anger had fizzled. She asked, a plaintive note creeping in, "Really, Gabe. What do you want from me?"

He answered without having to stop and think about it. "A little while alone, just you and me. Somewhere other than here, someplace quiet, where we can talk privately." His eyes were steady on hers. She believed him, believed his sincerity in this moment, even though she wanted to wrap herself in a protective shell of doubt and suspicion. "Are you off tomorrow?"

Her throat felt tight. She gave a little cough to clear it. "I am, yes."

"Meet me at noon. On the Ambling A. Same spot along the creek where I found you that first day?"

There were so many reasons she shouldn't. But none of them mattered in the least—not against the hungry, deep beating of her heart and the longing she couldn't seem to shake. "All right, Gabe. Noon tomorrow, that spot by the creek."

He tossed some bills on the bar, got down off the stool and leaned in. His breath warmed her cheek as he whispered, "See you then."

She watched him walk away, so tall and broad-shouldered, proud and strong. The last thing she'd planned to do was give the man another chance.

Yet, she'd agreed to meet him. She should probably be having second thoughts about that decision.

However, the mere sight of him had reminded her sharply that she really had missed him. It was hard to stay mad at him when every cell in her body yearned to be close to him again.

Chapter Eight

By noon the next day, when Mel pulled her Audi in behind Gabe's giant black pickup on the dusty ranch road, all her doubts had resurfaced. She really shouldn't be here, yet somehow, once again, she'd let him convince her they needed to...

What?

She didn't even know what this meeting was about. Some men were just plain dangerous to a woman's heart and mind and, well, general equilibrium. Gabe Abernathy was the premiere example of that kind of man. She ought to just start up the car again and drive away.

But she'd said she would meet him here and she

was a woman who followed through on her commitments.

At least, that was the excuse she gave herself as she emerged from the car and climbed the dirt path that led to the spot by the creek under the cottonwoods where they'd first met. She crested the gentle rise of the hill and there he was, below her. He sat on a blanket beneath the dappled shade of a cottonwood, next to a picnic basket, facing the creek.

How was she supposed to stand firm against him when he showed up with a picnic—and at the spot where they'd met and shared their first kiss, no less?

Squaring her shoulders and reminding herself that she had to be strong, she descended the hill.

Gabe heard boots on gravel. Rising, he turned to greet her.

Damn, she was beautiful, in rolled-cuff jeans that fit her curvy hips like a glove, those cute short boots she favored and a silky shirt splashed with a swirling blend of pink, purple and jewel blue. "Hi."

She stopped on the edge of the blanket. "Hey." Her gemstone eyes spoke of doubts and her plush mouth twisted down at the corners.

Refusing to feel the least discouraged, he offered a hand. She took it with obvious reluctance. He reminded himself that at least she was here, her hand cool and soft in his.

"Come on," he coaxed. "Sit down." She dropped to the blanket and he settled in beside her. A few feet away, Little Big Bear Creek burbled cheerfully. The sweet, high warble of a meadowlark rose from the wild grass somewhere nearby and Ambling A cattle grazed beyond the fence across the rippling ribbon of water. The sky was cloudless, an endless sheet of pale blue. No rain in the offing today. "Malone makes this chicken salad with grapes and pecans and all kinds of stuff you wouldn't think of when you think chicken salad."

At last, she gave him a smile. Suddenly, the world was a brighter place. "I love chicken salad with grapes and pecans."

"On crusty bread, with chips and a wine cooler?"

"Perfect."

He flipped open the basket and served her lunch. Except for the intermittent serenade of that lone meadowlark and the babbling of the creek, they ate in silence. As each minute passed, his feeling of dread increased.

He'd asked her to come here to the exact spot where they'd met so that he could tell her he'd fallen in love with her. But she held him at a distance with her careful silence. He had a sinking suspicion that a declaration of love from him right now would have her leaping to her feet and sprinting for her car.

Clearly, he needed to slow the hell down to baby

steps with her. No sense in making his big declaration if it was only going to send her running for the hills.

"That was so good," she said, once he'd put the remains of the food back in the basket. She took another sip from her wine cooler, carefully set the half-empty bottle on the blanket beside her and leaned back on her hands. Almost shyly, she turned those deep blue eyes his way. "So, um, you had something you wanted to talk to me about?" Her mouth was softly parted. He wanted to kiss her so bad, to wrap her up good and tight in his arms and never let her go.

But she gave off a definite vibe, one that said he'd better keep his lips and grabby hands to himself. "I can't stop thinking of our night together. I really have missed you, Mel. I want another chance. I want to spend more time with you."

She tugged at a loose thread on the blanket and dragged her gaze up slowly to collide with his. "Have you forgotten how you couldn't wait to get rid of me that night?"

"You have to know, that wasn't about you."

"You *acted* like it was about me. When I tried to apologize for upsetting you, you said it wasn't my fault. But your eyes were cold and when I said I should go, you couldn't hustle me out the door fast enough."

He wanted to keep denying his own behavior, but he knew that wouldn't cut it with her. "You're right, about all of it. Will you let me explain?"

She answered with a half shrug. "Go ahead, then."

"It got to me, got to me bad. Just the idea that my family might have a whole other story I never knew a damn thing about, that my Gramps might have loved someone else before he loved my great-grandmother, that my grandpa Alexander might have a half sister he's never met. It was a lot to process and I did kind of blame you—you know, like that old saying. I wanted to shoot the messenger.

"I knew at the time I was in the wrong, but I wanted so bad *not* to know what you'd just told me. It was completely unfair of me, Mel, to blame you for telling me something I didn't want to hear. And I really am sorry. I only hope that maybe you'll forgive me for being such a jerk about it."

For several uncomfortable seconds, she simply stared at him. And then slowly, she nodded. "Okay, yeah." The word was more breath than sound. "I do understand. It's hard information even for me to deal with—that the Winona Cobbs I know and love in Rust Creek Falls might have this tragic past she's never said a word about. Gabe, I didn't even *want* that diary. Lately, I feel like this heavy burden has been laid on me. I try to ignore it, but it nags at me, you know? The questions echo in my head. What really happened all those years ago? And did it happen to strangers—or to *your* great-grandfather and *my* Winona?"

He caught her hand. She let him, so he went further and wove their fingers together.

She held his gaze. She wasn't smiling. "You didn't call."

"No, I didn't. And that was wrong, too." A humorless laugh escaped him. "And then *you* finally called *me*. You were so sweet."

"You weren't." She scowled at him.

"Most men are fools." *Especially when it comes to love.* He thought that last part, but somehow kept himself from saying it. "I'm sorry, Mel. I'm beggin' for another chance here, but I have to admit, if you say no, I can't really blame you."

She squeezed his hand. He told himself that had to be a good sign. When she spoke, though, he wasn't so sure. "I just… Gabe, I don't want to give my heart again. I really don't. My heart broke when I lost my parents. Todd broke it a second time. My poor heart just doesn't have another break left in it."

He wanted to swear he would never hurt her—but he already had, hadn't he? And as for the whole love thing, well, how could he bear to say he loved her when she'd just said she was through with love?

He brought their joined hands to his lips and kissed her knuckles one by one.

His hope rose again when she leaned her head on his shoulder. He wrapped an arm around her, brushed his cheek against her silky hair and breathed in her perfect scent of vanilla and roses.

She glanced up at him with a sad little sigh. "Oh, Gabe. If any man could tempt me now, that man would be you."

He pressed his lips to her hair. "How 'bout this, then? Could you be with me for right now? You're not going anywhere for months, right? There's plenty of time for us to just be together. We could see where it goes between us. All I would ask is that you try to keep an open mind and heart."

"It seems so dangerous…"

"Most good things involve an element of risk."

She chuckled. It was the sweetest sound. "Gabriel Abernathy, you are far too convincing, you know that?" They stared at each other.

He dared to suggest, "So, that's a yes?"

When she didn't say no, he saw his chance and lowered his mouth to hers. She didn't pull away.

He gathered her closer, grateful for this, at least—the feel of her small, soft body in his arms again at last, for her kiss that was sweet and tender, with a promise of more.

He lifted his head sooner than he wanted to, just

to show her he understood the meaning of restraint. "Yes?" he asked again.

Her eyes were deep as oceans. "What do you do to me?"

He smoothed an errant lock of hair away from that irresistible mouth of hers. "Everything. I hope. If you'll let me."

She put a hand to his chest. He wrapped his fingers around it. "Okay. We'll, um, try again." And she dipped her head a little shyly. "Whatever that means."

He tipped up her chin so she was looking in his eyes again. "How about we start with right now and the whole afternoon and on into the evening?"

She laughed and playfully pushed him away. "You're not wasting any time."

"Hell, no."

"It is nice here." She lay back on the blanket, laced her fingers behind her head and stared up at the shifting leaves of the cottonwood overhead. "So the plan is to just hang out by the creek, you mean?"

He thought of Gramps and the other information he'd uncovered yesterday. She'd just agreed to give him another chance. He almost wanted to forget the diary and the sad story it contained.

But she'd asked to meet Gramps. And for a moment, Gramps had blasted through the wall of his own silence. He'd commanded Gabe to bring her to

Snowy Mountain. There seemed no choice now but to go forward, to do what he could to solve the old mystery. "Well, there is something else I've been meaning to talk to you about…"

She'd shifted her gaze from the leaves above to his face. "What's going on?"

He stretched out beside her, bracing up on an elbow so he could look down at her and hold her gaze. "I've been out to see Gramps twice since our night together—last Friday and then again yesterday afternoon. I really have been thinking about the story of Josiah and Winona and the missing baby Beatrix."

"Did something…happen?"

"Not on Friday. I told him about the diary that day, and a little about you. He didn't respond. I got nothing, you know? It's the way he is most times now, like the lights are on, but nobody's home."

She reached up and laid her hand on the side of his face. "I'm sorry. I know how much you love him. It must be so hard."

He caught her fingers and kissed the tips of them. "Yeah—but anyway, then you called on Saturday and I was a jerk. After that, I couldn't stop thinking about you, about what an idiot I am and about Gramps, too, and the story of the diary. So I went to see him again. I talked about you and the diary. He was silent. I got nothing. But then I got up to go and he spoke. Just a few words. He said, 'Bring her to me.'"

A small gasp escaped her. "He meant me?"

"Yeah. He meant you." Gabe almost told her the rest of it.

Don't give up on love, Gramps had commanded.

But no. The way Gabe saw it, at this point those words were just for him. She wasn't ready to hear them yet.

She sat up. "Does that mean you're taking me to meet him?"

He nodded. "If you still *want* to meet him."

"Oh, Gabe. Yes. I do."

"There's more…"

Her eyes widened. "Tell me."

"All right. I started thinking of ways to find out if the Abernathys of Rust Creek Falls might have anything to do with my family. At lunch yesterday, I asked my dad and my grandfather about the family history in Bronco and about my great-great-grandparents, Gramps's mother and father. My dad and Grandpa Alexander weren't very helpful. They both insisted that the Abernathys have 'always' lived in Bronco. Grandpa Alexander didn't remember a lot about Josiah's parents, except that they were kind of distant and strict. Later, it occurred to me that property sales are a matter of public record. And if my family showed up here seventy-plus years ago and bought the ranch that is now our Ambling A, there would have been a deed, proof of the sale and when it happened."

"You mean, at the county offices somewhere?"

"Well, as it turns out, I didn't have to look that far. My grandfather has the information in the safe in the office at the main house. He's very proud of the fact that it's a fireproof safe, impervious to burglars and whatever. Also, he assures me the deed is duly recorded at the assessor's office."

"So then, when did your family acquire the Ambling A here in Bronco?"

"In 1920, my great-great-great-grandfather, a wealthy speculator from back east, bought up several parcels from poor farmers who'd gone bust after claiming the land in the land run a few years earlier."

"Wait. So then, you're saying your family has owned the ranch here in Bronco since 1920? Are you trying to say that proves they *aren't* the Abernathys who vanished from Rust Creek Falls?"

"No."

She sat up and slapped him playfully on the arm. "Gabe. What are you getting at?"

He sat up, too. "My family has owned the land for a hundred years. But they didn't incorporate it into the Ambling A until seventy-five years ago. My great-great-grandfather, Josiah Sr., did that."

Her sweet mouth dropped open. "That would

have been about the time the Abernathys in Rust Creek Falls disappeared."

He grinned. "It doesn't really prove anything."

"I know. But it does kind of give me the shivers."

"Yeah. I have to admit, I got a shiver or two myself when I saw that the dates match up."

"So then, you told your grandfather about the diary?"

"I didn't need to. As an Abernathy heir, I'm expected to take an interest in the ranch and everything else my family owns and/or controls. I also have the combination to the safe. My grandfather Alexander didn't question me when I said I wanted to look over the articles of incorporation."

"I think what you're telling me is that you didn't explain to your grandfather about the diary because you were afraid that if you shared the real reason for your interest, you might upset him. Is that right?"

"Pretty much. You saw how *I* reacted when you told me—and really, didn't we just agree that nothing is in any way proven yet?"

"Fine. I get it. Until we have a better idea of what really happened in the past and if your family might be somehow involved, why take the chance of getting everyone stirred up?"

"Yeah. I'm thinking that at this point the story of the diary ought to be on a need-to-know basis."

She was frowning. But then she nodded. "Okay, that makes sense—yet you did tell Josiah."

"Because he might be the key. Somewhere deep down, he might know everything. As for my dad and my grandfather, though, I really do think they're completely in the dark about what happened seventy-plus years ago. I'm not ready to go there yet with them."

"Yet. Meaning you will in the future?"

"Meaning, let's talk to Gramps first and then take it from there."

She was tugging on that loose thread in the blanket again. "I feel a little guilty. I confess, I can't make myself ask Winona if she might be the woman in the diary."

He stilled her hand. "It's done, Mel. I talked to Gramps about the old story. He said to bring you to see him."

"You're braver than I am."

"Naw. But I *am* curious. Very curious. So? You up for meeting my Gramps today?"

Mel wanted to pick up the diary on the way to Snowy Mountain West. That worked for Gabe. He needed to have a look at the old book and the letter, anyway.

He followed her to her place, where Homer greeted them at the door. The kitten jumped on

Gabe's boot and started chewing on it. "Hey, buddy. Easy there…" He picked up the little guy and Homer instantly began to purr. "I think he really likes me."

"No doubt about it." Mel dropped her keys on the entry table, crossed the room to the bed and took a worn, leather-bound volume from the bed-side drawer.

Gabe set the kitten down and Homer darted away. With the diary pressed against her chest and apprehension in her eyes, Mel returned to where Gabe stood at the door.

"Do I get to see it?" he asked when she stopped in front of him. She nodded and held it out. He took it. "Bejeweled, no less."

"Fancy, huh?"

He traced the tooled letter *A* centered on the cover. Different-colored stones encircled it. He opened the book to the first page.

"Is the handwriting familiar?" she asked.

"No. But I don't recall ever really noticing Gramps's handwriting."

"Maybe if we could get a sample of something he wrote, we could take it and the diary to a handwrit-ing expert." She gazed up at him through hopeful eyes, her soft cheeks pink with excitement.

"Maybe."

Her expression turned rueful. "I guess I shouldn't go getting ahead of myself here, huh?"

She looked so sweet and sincere. He wanted to drop the old diary on the table next to the keys she'd put there and pull her into his arms. They could spend the day in her bed instead of trying to coax information from an old man who rarely spoke anymore.

Could she read his thoughts in his eyes? It sure seemed like it. "Oh, Gabe," she whispered. "I keep saying I'm leaving at the end of the year, that I don't want to get anything started with you, but this past week, I couldn't stop thinking about you. Even though I was mad at you, I really did miss you. So much."

He set the book down by the keys, after all, and eased a hand around the silky nape of her neck beneath the glorious tumble of her long, blond hair. "And I missed *you*—everything about you. From the sound of your laugh to that sharp tongue you've got. And then there are those unforgettable blue eyes." He brushed his thumb across her cheek. "And this naughty dimple right here. I missed this dimple so damn much."

The dimple in question deepened with her radiant smile. "Yeah?"

"No doubt about it." How could he resist? He swooped in and claimed that gorgeous mouth.

She swayed closer and he wrapped her up tight in his arms, her scent of flowers and sweet vanilla making his head spin and his blood run hot in his veins. The kiss kind of took on a life of its own. She opened to him and he swept his tongue into the wet heat beyond her parted lips. He could have stood there, kissing her endlessly, into the next decade and beyond.

But finally, she pulled back a fraction and drew in a slow breath. "Okay. Enough of your amazing, distracting kisses, Gabe Abernathy. We're on a mission today. I want to meet your great-grandfather. Please?"

Regretfully, he set her away from him and picked up the diary. "All right."

She hesitated. "I didn't show you the letter. Do you want to read that first?"

"Later. Right now, let's just go." She picked up her keys. He caught her hand. "You're riding with me."

Did he expect the usual pushback? Yep. But he was pleasantly surprised when she said, "Fair enough. But I do need one of these keys to lock the door."

"I'll allow that." With a finger, he eased a heavy lock of hair behind her ear. And then he couldn't resist bending closer, brushing his lips across hers just one more time.

She made the sweetest, softest little sound of pleasure, like a moan that got caught on a sigh—

and then she pressed her hand with the keys in it against his chest. "We can't stand here all day, kissing at the front door."

He brushed his mouth across hers a second time. "Oh, no?"

She gave another sweet sigh—and then pushed against his chest a little harder. "Out the door, mister. Now."

Gabe felt a rising sense of anticipation as he ushered Mel into the reception area at Snowy Mountain West.

"This is nice." She gave him one of those glowing smiles of hers. "It's open and inviting."

"Snowy Mountain is the best around. Especially for memory care. The environment is secure and comfortable with open rooms and wide hallways that are easy to get around in. Residents are monitored round-the-clock. Staff-to-patient ratio is excellent, too."

"Hi, Gabe." Linda gave him a wave from behind the front desk. She glanced down at the big laptop screen on the desk. "Let's see…ah. Josiah has just finished his supervised afternoon walk. He'll be in his room."

"Great." Gabe turned to Mel. "I just want to go see how he's doing first, before I introduce you."

He gestured at a sofa and chairs near a picture window. "Have a seat. I'll come right back for you."

"Sure." Mel exchanged smiles with Linda and took one of the chairs.

Gabe found Gramps in his rooms, as promised, sitting quietly in his recliner. "Hey." He bent close. "How are you doing today, Gramps?"

As usual, Gramps gave no response. His shirttail had come out of his belt on one side and his collar was slightly askew.

Gabe gently tucked in the loose section of shirt and tugged the collar straight. "There. You look great. And today, you're about to meet the woman you asked me to bring to you—you remember, don't you? Her name is Mel Driscoll and she's *the one*, Gramps. But remember, she's not ready for love yet. So don't tell her that I know she's the one for me." Gabe dared to look into those hazel eyes then.

Nothing. He saw nothing at all.

And that hurt. It hurt like hell every single time he had to face anew that the man who'd taught him how to *be* a man was never really coming back. Gabe would gladly offer up his big house and the fortune he'd made for himself in the past decade just to have his Gramps grin and give him a wink the way he used to do.

"Don't move," Gabe said with forced cheer. "I'll be right back."

As he retraced his steps to the welcome area, he wondered if he was doing the right thing. What if the sight of the diary upset the old man? Now and then, Gramps did get agitated. He would shout nonsense, even throw things. Gabe would have to call the staff to settle him down. Gramps had never hurt anyone physically, but it always broke Gabe's heart to see the calmest, kindest man he'd ever known lose control.

Mel had the diary. She held it close to her body, same as she had back at her apartment, as she rose and came toward him. When she got to him, she gazed up at him searchingly. "You look...unsure. Did something happen?"

"No. It's a day like any other day. He's in his room, staring into space. You really shouldn't get your hopes up that you'll find out much from him."

"I understand."

No, she didn't. But she would soon enough. "Okay, then. This way..."

Gramps was right where Gabe had left him, sitting motionless in his favorite chair, his eyes blank and staring.

"Gramps, this is the woman I told you about yesterday. This is Mel."

After no response from Josiah, Mel said, "I'm so pleased to get to meet you, Mr.—"

"Call him Josiah."

"Um. Josiah, then. Hi, Josiah." She gave the expressionless old man her prettiest smile, after which she sat where Gabe indicated, on the love seat across from Gramps. Gabe sat beside her. She held out the diary and started to say something, but then set it down on the coffee table and turned to Gabe. "I'm not sure how to begin…"

He doubted it would matter what she said. But she was here now, and they were set on a course. There was nothing else to do but proceed. "I already told him the basic story you told me. He didn't respond. You never know, though. Maybe if *you* tell him, the story will get through."

"Yes. All right." She launched into a brief version of the ill-fated love affair between Winona Cobbs and the young man with the same name as Gramps. "Winona had a baby," she said, holding out the diary again, explaining that the whole story was inside, including a letter tucked in the binding, written by Josiah Abernathy, who was also the author of the diary itself. "The letter says the lost baby didn't die, after all, but was somehow taken by Josiah's parents and given up for adoption. The letter claims Josiah knew who the adoptive parents were. Josiah, would you like to see the letter?"

Gramps didn't answer. He didn't even move. His eyes seemed focused on nothing and everything at once.

Mel shot a worried glance in Gabe's direction.

What could he say? "Sorry. I don't think he's going to be responding today." He reached across the distance between the love seat and the recliner and clasped Gramps's shoulder. His old bones seemed to poke right through his skin. "Okay, Gramps. Maybe some other day?" Gabe started to stand.

Mel's light fingers brushed the back of his hand. "Let's stay. Just for a little while."

"He's not going to suddenly have anything to say." Irritation gave his tone a cold edge. He was angry at his own foolishness to have brought her here, made her a witness to a helpless old man's painfully diminished capacity for even the simplest sort of human interaction.

Her smile was as sad as it was angelic. "I get it. But we're here. It seems rude to just get up and run out." That cute dimple in her cheek kind of winked at him. "Sometimes, when I go to see Winona, I have a tall glass of water or a cup of tea and we just sit, you know, not saying a word, nice and quiet, enjoying the moment of being there. Together."

This woman. She drove him a little bit crazy, what with wanting her so much and trying not to lose hope that she would ever be his. She also bugged the crap out of him now and then. In addition, she kind of amazed him. Not a lot of women would want to hang around for any longer than necessary with an old man who rarely spoke and stared blankly at nothing for hours on end.

Gabe couldn't help but grin. "You want a tall glass of water, is that what you're saying?"

"Water would be perfect, Gabe. Thank you."

The room had a tiny rudimentary kitchen area—a bit of counter, a sink, cabinets containing plastic glasses and plates, a drawer with some flatware. There was also a mini fridge with an ice maker in the dinky freezer area. Gabe took down three glasses, dropped some ice cubes in each and filled them with water.

He carried them back to the sitting area and deposited them on the coffee table.

Mel pushed one over in front of Josiah and one in front of Gabe's seat. The third, she sipped from. "Thank you, Gabe. Very refreshing."

He wanted to grab her and kiss her for being so sweet about this, for wanting to sit and visit with an old man whose visiting days were behind him. "You're welcome." He dropped down beside her and drank from his own glass.

Mel relaxed against the cushions and glanced around. Her gaze landed on a large wedding portrait on the wall by the window, behind Gramps's chair.

"That's Gramps and Great-Grandma Cora on their wedding day," Gabe said. Gramps wore a baggy suit with enormous lapels. His bride wore a forties-style satin dress with a long, white veil.

Mel frowned a little. "They look so serious."

They did, as a matter of fact. "Great-Grandma Cora was a quiet woman," he said. "It was hard sometimes to know what she was thinking. She made the best buttermilk biscuits, though. I've never tasted any to compare. And she played the piano. Holidays, we'd gather 'round, including all my uncles and aunts and cousins. Great-Grandma would play Christmas carols and we'd all join in singing."

"My mom played the piano." Mel's eyes shone bright. "She was talented, a natural musician. I thought, since my mom had a talent for music, that of course, I would play, too."

"Do you?"

She laughed. The sound was sweet and kind of goofy, too. It tugged on a tender place down inside him. "Nope." She popped the *p*. "Frankly, I suck at it. I mean, we are talking no musical talent whatsoever."

He grinned at her. When he glanced across the coffee table, it seemed to him that Gramps had settled more comfortably into his big chair. He still stared into nowhere, his plastic glass of ice water untouched in front of him, but he seemed more relaxed about it, somehow.

The strange little visit continued in the same vein. Mel noted personal items around Gramps's room and Gabe explained their significance. She talked more about her mom and dad. It was so obvious she'd loved them very much and the loss of them remained fresh and painful for her.

Gramps didn't say a single word. He never made eye contact with Mel or with Gabe. But somehow, it felt like he was there with them, enjoying a nice visit, a little small talk and a cool drink.

If Gabe hadn't already been in love with the woman sitting next to him, he would have fallen right then, on that sunny Monday afternoon in his great-grandfather's quiet living room at Snowy Mountain Senior Care. She was not only sharp and smart and strong. Mel had a good heart, a deep and natural kindness that made her even more beautiful than her pretty face and curvy little body.

They ended up staying for over an hour. When they got up to leave, Josiah had yet to respond to their presence in any way beyond seeming to relax slightly in his chair. He sat silent, his arms stretched out, resting on the chair arms.

As Mel rose, she took the diary in one hand. With the other, she reached across the coffee table to give the back of Gramps's hand a quick, fond touch. "I'm so pleased to have met you, Josiah."

It happened right then. Gramps blinked two

times and turned his hand over, palm up. His bony fingers closed around Mel's. Gabe saw it happen and heard Mel's tiny gasp. He felt a burst of pure joy—that Gramps had responded, that he *saw* Mel, even liked her.

But then alarm jangled through him. Had Gramps frightened her?

No. Her blue gaze met Gabe's and she smiled her dazzling smile. "Do you see?"

Gabe nodded, relieved Gramps hadn't scared her, glad to see her pleasure at the old man's reaction. "I do."

Mel turned her bright glance to Josiah again.

But the moment of connection had already passed. Josiah had released her. His hand lay limp—palm still turned up, fingers curled inward like a dying leaf.

"Josiah?" Mel asked softly, with the sweetest, saddest note of fading hope. "Come back…"

But Gramps's face gave her nothing. His curled hand didn't move again.

"Love you, Gramps," said Gabe quietly, hating the resignation in his own voice. "See you soon."

Chapter Nine

A few minutes later, out in the parking lot, Gabe opened the passenger's side door for Mel and she climbed in. He went around and got up behind the wheel. They hooked their seat belts simultaneously.

And then they both sank back in their seats. Maybe it was just him, but sorrow seemed to weigh down the air around them. Gabe stared out the windshield at an empty bench beneath a pretty sugar maple several yards from the hood of his F-450.

"For a moment there I really thought he might smile at me," Mel said.

"Yeah, well. That rarely happens anymore.

Sometimes he speaks, but not much and usually in kind of a flat voice."

"I'm so sorry, Gabe."

"I really do think he's still in there somewhere, but most of the time I have to admit that he's just… not." Was he being overly negative? She gazed at him as though she had no idea what to say. "On the plus side, the staff here is amazing. They kind of get him going on an activity and he'll sort of carry through. But it's all as though he's on automatic pilot. Going through the motions by rote."

She wrapped her hands around the diary, which she'd laid on her lap. "I guess I was foolish to think he might have all the answers to this old mystery, huh?"

"Not foolish. Just hopeful. And there is nothing wrong with having hope. I'm glad you came to meet him, even if it didn't play out the way you might have pictured it." And there he went, being a downer again. "Look at it this way, Mel. He did seem at ease around you. You were good with him. And hey, it could be worse. I'm grateful for every minute I get with him. I visit him at least once a week and we talk—well, *I* talk and sometimes I really do get the feeling that he understands everything I say."

She shut her eyes and turned away.

"Hey, hey. What'd I do wrong now?"

Slowly, she turned to face him again, her eyes open now. Her smooth throat worked as she nervously swallowed. "Nothing, Gabe. You did nothing wrong. On the contrary. I'm just feeling a little humbled right now, that's all."

"Humbled? Why?"

"You, Gabe. Sometimes we get crossways, I know. But you are a good man. You've got a lot of heart. And wherever things end up with you and me, well, I'm glad I went trespassing on Ambling A land that first day we met."

It was far from the declaration of undying love he wanted from her, but for now, he would take it. He leaned across the wide console and ran a finger down the velvet skin of her cheek. Sweet color bloomed in the wake of his touch. "It's your night off. Share it with me. Come out to the ranch. Give my mom a thrill and have dinner at the main house. Then we'll go back to my place, just the two of us."

She tried to back out. "I don't know. I'm not exactly dressed for dinner with the parents."

"Weak excuse, Mel. It's a working cattle ranch and it's just dinner. Malone will cook and that means the food will be great. But it's not like we dress up for dinner every night. You're welcome just as you are." When he pulled her closer, she let him, and he took heart from that. "I don't want to let you go." His lips just barely brushed hers. "Not yet. Indulge me."

"I feel the same," she confessed in a whisper.

He kissed her, a slow kiss that gradually deepened. When she sighed in surrender, he wished they were anywhere but here, in broad daylight in the parking lot of Snowy Mountain Senior Care.

"Say you'll have dinner out at the ranch," he commanded gruffly against her parted lips, fully expecting more objections.

But she surprised him—in a very good way. "Yes."

He pushed his luck. "Yes, what, exactly?"

She gave a low, sweet laugh. "Yes, Gabe. I would love to come to dinner tonight at the Ambling A."

Dinner at the main house went pretty much as Gabe expected.

Malone outdid himself with his famous standing rib roast and Yukon Gold potatoes. Gabe and his dad argued over just about every subject that came up. Alexander made pronouncements concerning how nothing in the world went the way it ought to go anymore and everyone under fifty was spoiled and self-centered, unwilling to work hard to achieve their dreams.

Gabe's mom had a whole lot of questions for Mel, all of them geared toward pinning Mel down as a prospective daughter-in-law. Gabe had to cut in when she started talking about her favorite wedding venues.

"Mom. Nobody at this table is planning a wedding," Gabe reminded her, mentally adding *yet*.

His mom waved him off with a flick of her hand. "It's idle conversation, Gabriel. Relax. I was just wondering what Mel thought of an outdoor wedding. They can really be something glorious if done right—don't you agree, Mel?"

Mel took his mother's shameless matchmaking in stride. "I do, yes. We've had several weddings in the town park up in Rust Creek Falls. Everybody in town is always invited. Sometimes things do get a little crazy after dark, though."

Gabe remembered the story Mel had told him the day she adopted Homer. "Yeah, some old moonshiner spiked the wedding punch once. Things got pretty wild."

His mother looked vaguely concerned. She suddenly had other ideas. "Maybe a barn wedding. Or one at the Association. They really put on the most gorgeous weddings there. So elegant. Just unforgettable. I'm hoping I can have the Association do Erica's wedding, though she's always vague and distant about it whenever I suggest that maybe it's time for her and Peter to set a date—Peter's her longtime steady boyfriend. He's also the company attorney for his family's business, Barron Enterprises, and Erica works for the company, too. I hope she's not planning to be married there in Colorado. I mean, Montana is her home and she ought to be married here."

"It'll all work out, Mom, don't worry," said Gabe, though he had no idea whether things with Erica would "work out" or not. He just didn't want to get down in the weeds over his absent sister tonight.

"Well, I do worry," his mom insisted. "She should come home more often."

"Yes, she should," his father agreed, rather sternly. Husband and wife shared a speaking glance. Whatever Gabe's dad communicated to Angela in that look, she let the subject of Erica drop.

Once they'd finished the meal, they all went out back to sit on the patio in comfy lounge chairs. They watched the sunset and enjoyed Malone's irresistible lava cake, with brandy-laced coffee.

It was almost nine, still not quite dark yet, when Gabe took Mel back to his place. Butch, who always tagged along when Gabe went back and forth to the main house, trailed after them.

"I should go," she said as he ushered her in the front door and Butch edged around them and kept on going toward the living area. When they'd walked over to the main house earlier, she'd left her purse and the diary on the credenza right there in the front hall.

Before she could grab them up, Gabe captured her hand and pulled her close. He wrapped both arms around her. She felt so right pressed tightly against him. "Stay."

"Oh, Gabe…" Her body said yes—but he could hear the doubt in her tone, see caution in her eyes.

He caught a lock of her hair and smoothed it over her shoulder. "Life's too short. But still, you keep running away. Stay. Just for a little while."

The thing was, Mel wanted to stay. So much. She wanted to spend the night in Gabe's bed.

She wanted it to be more than a rebound with him. She truly did. Every moment she spent with him, she liked him more. *Trusted* him more.

And that made her afraid she was only setting herself up to be hurt again.

"If you hurt me, Gabe…" She let the words trail off without finishing her thought, let her wary expression speak for her.

He framed her face between his warm, rough palms. His eyes burned into hers, begging her to believe. "Not gonna hurt you, Mel."

"I don't *want* to trust you, but then somehow I can't help myself." She pressed a hand to his hard chest. "I'm starting to believe you, Gabe. Starting to think that you are actually for real."

He put his hand over hers, pressing her palm more firmly to his chest. Beneath the layers of muscle and bone, she felt the strong, steady rhythm of his heartbeat. "This is special, you and me," he said. "I'm not messing with you. Yeah, I've never gotten close to forever with anyone before. And I get that people think that's a bad sign, that a guy needs to be practicing commitment from an early age or he's not a good risk when it comes to love. Sometimes people are wrong. Sometimes a guy is just waiting for the right woman to come along."

Her breathing had gone a little ragged and her chest felt tight. "What are you saying to me, Gabe?"

"You really want to know? You want me to say it out loud right now?"

Why was her pulse racing? She gulped, hard. "I don't think I'm ready."

And there it was, his slow, delicious smile, the one that made him almost impossible to resist. "You should get ready."

"I'm not sure I know how."

He lifted her captured hand from his chest and brought it to his lips. She felt his warm breath on her skin and prayed that, whatever this was with him, she wouldn't blow it and neither would he. That they would ultimately be bigger than their fears and their doubts, that neither of them would end up letting the other one down.

And she thought of the diary waiting a few feet away, of Wren Crawford, of the crazy idea the little girl had that the diary brought love to whoever possessed it. She saw herself, not long from now, passing it on.

Passing love to the next person.

After claiming it for herself.

"It's all right." Gabe pressed those wonderful lips of his to the back of her hand and a thrill vibrated so sweetly down the length of her spine. "It's gonna be all right." He said it as a promise, a solemn vow.

Her doubts reared up again. "How can you know that, Gabe? How can you be sure?"

"I know one thing." Oh, those eyes of his. So steady, sky-blue. And true. That was the thing about Gabe. She was honestly beginning to believe that he would know what Todd Spurlock hadn't—how to be true.

"What one thing do you know, Gabe? Tell me, please."

He gazed at her for a long time, his eyes holding hers, before he said softly, "No. Not tonight."

She groaned. "You're a tease, Gabe Abernathy."

"Yeah, probably. But you did say you're not ready."

He was right, of course. She might have begun to wonder if there really was something kind of magical about the diary, but she wasn't ready to hear any brave declarations. Not right now. Not tonight.

He bent close to nuzzle her neck. She let out a low moan as he scraped his teeth down the side of her throat, leaving a hungry trail of sparks in his wake.

"Stay with me tonight." He breathed the gruff words into the tender crook of her shoulder.

She could feel him growing hard against her belly. And that hot shiver running down her spine? It was spreading out inside her, turning slow and lazy like warm honey, touching her everywhere, making her tremble in her boots.

She stretched her neck back, giving him better access. He scattered sweet kisses along the side of her throat. "Well, the more I think about it, the less I want to leave right now." Her voice sounded slow and lazy, hungry and very willing to her own ears.

"Stay as long as you want, Mel." He scraped his teeth along the line of her jaw and nipped playfully at her chin. "Stay forever."

She started to tell him that she really wasn't ready for forever. But before the words took form, his mouth claimed hers. She drank in the taste of him. Their tongues were dancing.

Dancing, yes…

He danced her backward, kissing her as they went—across the entry hall, through the big, open living room with its enormous fireplace, down a wide hallway and into the master suite.

Standing by the huge bed, he undressed her, pressing kisses on the bare skin he revealed as he peeled her clothes away. "You are perfection, Mel. This shoulder…" He kissed the outer curve, where her shoulder met her arm, as he dropped her shirt to the rug. His lips traced a path to the base of her neck and then across her collarbones. "Perfection."

She closed her eyes on a heavy sigh, every inch of her open, willing, deliciously aroused, as he took her bra away and lavished kisses on her bare breasts. She threaded her clutching fingers into his hair, trying to hold him there.

But he was on the move, trailing those lips of his down the center of her body.

Blinking like a sleeper half-awakened from the deepest dream, she stared down at him as he dropped to his knees before her. He was looking up, his eyes waiting. Their gazes met and held.

He took her hand and braced it on his broad shoulder. She held onto him for balance as he lifted her right foot and took her boot away. He peeled off her thin sock and then repeated the process with her left boot.

A moment later, he was pulling down her jeans, taking her little pink thong with them as he went. When her jeans and underwear got down to her ankles, she stepped out of them and lightly kicked them aside. It seemed surprising in that moment that she was totally naked and he still had on all his clothes.

Not that she cared who was naked, who wasn't. He had her completely at his mercy. She was needy and yearning, ready to be his.

And he made her more ready with those clever, stroking hands of his, with that mouth that knew magic spells to cast on her. That mouth was everywhere, taking control of all her most secret places. She welcomed him, opened to him willingly, and she cried out his name over and over as she came.

The second time he took her over the edge of the world, as she was still quaking at the sheer beauty of the things he did to her willing flesh, he lifted her up and set her on the bed. Her body felt heavy and hungry, ablaze with desire. A quivering mess of pure sensation, she fell back, arms and legs limp. Staring up at him through dazed eyes, she watched as he swiftly and ruthlessly stripped away his own clothes.

He was magnificent, looming above her, his body lean and cut, a racehorse of a man, beautifully masculine, his eyes holding hers, not letting go as he took a condom from the bedside drawer. She reached for him with a cry of need and pleasure. He came down to her, wrapping her up in his heat and his strength.

They rolled together, holding on so tight, kiss-

206 IN SEARCH OF THE LONG-LOST MAVERICK

ing so deeply, their bodies on fire. He was ruining her; she knew it. After this, after Gabe, there would never be another man who could possibly compare.

No, she wasn't ready for him. Not ready for the promise of the diary, either. Not ready for any of this, really. She'd had all the right plans once, known just where she was going and how she would get there.

But her perfect plans had come to nothing.

And now she was here, with Gabe. And in this moment, right now, her failure to judge the true character of the man who'd betrayed her didn't matter. None of that mattered, really—all her careful machinations to make the right choices, to engineer a good life with a trustworthy man who'd turned out in the end to be anything but.

Some things, a girl could never be ready for. Some things, a girl just had to give herself up to and hope that happy-ever-after was more than some romantic fool's impossible dream, more than a promise of love in a tattered, bejeweled, leather-bound journal found hidden in a run-down ranch house three hundred miles away—a promise destined to be broken in the most tragic way.

Gabe rose up above her, his eyes blue fire now. She watched him roll on the condom.

She begged, "Please, Gabe. Please, now…"

And then he was there, all around her, holding her, in her, *with* her in the truest way.

True. He was true—in his heart. As a man. And she believed in him.

At least in that moment, she believed. She believed she had everything—Gabe in her arms and hope in her heart.

Her body rose to the crest again. She whispered his name that time, holding on tight as her climax rocked through her. And then she pulled him even closer. He was lost to his own pleasure, moving hard and deep within her. She held him, loving the desperate way he groaned her name as he came.

Mel hadn't meant to fall asleep in Gabe's giant bed with its frame and four posters made of massive, rough-hewn logs.

But every time she started thinking she needed to get up and go, he would pull her close and cover her eager mouth with his—and the heat between them would rise again. Sometime after 2:00 a.m., the night must have caught up with her. She'd closed her eyes, just for a moment...

And when she opened them, daylight was peeking through the blinds.

She sat up and shoved the tangled mess of her hair out of her eyes. It fell right back down again. She blew at it, accomplishing nothing, and finally raked her fingers back through it, until it stayed off her face. "I need to get going."

Gabe didn't answer. She glanced down at him to see if he was still asleep. That was when he reached out, wrapped a hand around her arm and pulled her down on top of him. "In a little bit." He tried to kiss her.

"Hey!" She shoved at his beautifully muscled bare chest. "I mean it. I have to go."

"No, you don't."

She glared down at him, though it was hard to be crabby when he looked so rumpled and sexy, his hair spikier than ever, a sleep mark on his beard-scruffy cheek. "Homer chews on my things when I'm gone too long. I really hope he didn't find a way to get into my closet."

"That cat needs a trainer." He tried to pull her close again.

She fake punched his rock-hard shoulder. "Stop right there, mister. Or you're getting a big dose of morning breath."

"Give it to me, baby. Give it to me now." He pursed his lips at her and scrunched his eyes shut.

She laughed and squirmed away—and then couldn't resist wriggling close once more. He banded an arm around her. For a moment, they just lay there, with her tucked nice and cozy against his side. She could have stayed like that forever, wrapped in the tangled sheets, the two of them, Gabe and Mel.

It felt so right. It felt like this, with Gabe, was how it was really supposed to be, that maybe her whole life had blown up in her face because it was the *wrong* life all along. And the wrong life had brought her to the threshold of the right one.

Sheesh.

She really needed to put a lid on all these romantic fantasies she found herself indulging in lately.

One day at a time, Mel. Yeah, Gabe was a great guy, but that was no reason to go fantasizing about forever.

He dropped a quick kiss on the top of her head. "Coffee?"

She put her silly, romantic musings away and grinned up at him from the cradle of his arm. "I thought you'd never ask."

He tipped up her chin and kissed the tip of her nose. "You got it. I'll go make some." He rolled from the bed, so gorgeous, so naked. She could have lain there staring at him for hours. But then he grabbed yesterday's jeans and yanked them on.

She sat up and blew her sleep-mangled hair back out of her eyes again. "Is it okay if I use the bathroom, freshen up a little?"

"Go for it. I'll look into rustling us up some eggs."

Gabe had the coffeemaker going and was about to grab the eggs from the fridge when his dad spoke from behind him. "Still got company this mornin', I see."

Wincing, Gabe shut the fridge door and turned to face his father, who held the diary in one hand and Mel's purse in the other. "You know it's rude to just bust in without knocking, Dad."

"And you oughta start locking the damn front door."

"I never felt I had to—until right this minute, anyway."

His dad shrugged. "Relax. Your mom and I just happened to notice that you never drove Mel home last night."

"What are you telling me? You two lurked out on the front porch, listening for the sound of my pickup driving away?"

"What can I tell you, son? We're not getting any younger and neither are you. I see the way you look at Mel. I think that girl's special to you and I also think it's about damn time. Can you blame your mother and me for being anxious? Your mom longs for grandkids. Your sister is a lost cause. Even if she married that guy in Denver and they had some kids at last, she would likely never bring our grand-babies home to us. It's your job to give us some babies to spoil."

"You are so far out of line, Dad. This is so wrong."

"See now, I think it's a fine thing for me and your mother to make our wishes known. I like that girl. It's more than clear that *you* like that girl. And it's about time you settled down. You can make an honest woman out of her and make your mother happy, too."

The thing about George Abernathy was he thought he knew everything. And even when Gabe wanted what his dad wanted, somehow Gabe felt all wrong about agreeing with George—and more so than ever right now, when it came to Mel.

Mel was skittish about this thing between them. The last thing she needed was to walk in on his dad with his big mouth, going on about how he approved of her as a prospective daughter-in-law while simultaneously implying she'd be something of a slut if she didn't get Gabe's ring on her finger immediately.

"How many ways can I say this? Stay out of it, Dad."

His dad didn't even blink. "That coffee smells good. I'll have a cup." He set Mel's purse on the breakfast table and held up the diary. "What's this?"

Gabe had no intention of going into all that right now. "It's not yours. Put it down."

"It's old, isn't it? And it's got a big *A* on the cover."

"Thank you, Captain Obvious," he muttered under his breath.

"I heard that. Smart-ass." George flipped back the front cover. "What the hell?"

"Put it down."

"Josiah Abernathy?" He pointed at the first page. "This has Gramps's name in it. And the Ambling A…in Rust Creek Falls?" George's eyes, the same pale blue as his own, accused him. "What's this all about? Are you trying to tell me this is Gramps's old diary from way back in the day?"

"Dad. I'm not telling you anything. Put it down."

George poked a finger at the first page. "Why in hell would Gramps keep a diary? And why does it give a Rust Creek Falls address for the Ambling A? This doesn't make a damn bit of sense to me."

"Good morning, George." Mel, fully dressed, with her hair falling just so and her face freshly scrubbed, stood in the open arch that led back to the master suite. Damn, she was something. It had to be awkward for her, to find his dad in his kitchen after spending the night in his bed.

But Mel didn't seem bothered. She exuded calm confidence.

Gabe's dad glanced up from the old book he should never have touched and smiled—a warm smile. He did seem pleased to see her. "There she is. Pretty as a picture. Good to see you again, Mel."

He brandished the diary some more. "Found this in the front hall, along with your purse."

"Ah. Yes, well…" Mel drew in a slow breath and sent a quick glance at Gabe. Her eyes asked, *What now?*

He gave her a slight shrug.

Really, what could they do at this point but explain the situation? It would most likely all come out in the end, anyway, whether Gramps and the brokenhearted boy who'd written the diary were one and the same, or not.

Mel read his expression as though he'd spoken aloud.

At her slight nod of acceptance, he turned to his father. "Okay, Dad."

George peered at him sideways. "Okay, what, exactly?"

"Sit down, have some coffee. Want some eggs?"

"I could eat." George shot a glance at Mel and then swung his narrowed eyes back to Gabe again. "What's going on?"

"Here's what. I'll pour your coffee and scramble the eggs. Then Mel will tell you a story…"

Chapter Ten

A half an hour later, when Mel finished sharing the story contained in the diary, their coffee cups were empty. Their eggs sat untouched. Mel didn't much like the tense expression on George Abernathy's face. He looked a little pale, too, especially around the mouth.

The big, beautifully rustic kitchen was deadly quiet. Butch, stretched out on the floor by his water bowl, scratched at his ear. The tags on his collar clattered together, the sound shockingly loud in the too-silent room.

Finally, George picked up the diary, which he'd set on the empty chair next to him. He waved it at her. "You're saying all that you just told me is in here?"

"Yes—except for the part about how Beatrix survived and was adopted by some other family, a family never named. That part is in a letter Josiah wrote to 'W,' whose name was actually Winona, at the psychiatric facility she was sent to in Kalispell, a letter he never mailed."

"Where is this letter?"

"In the diary."

George flipped the diary over and ruffled the pages. Nothing fell out. "Where?"

She held out her hand. "I'll be happy to show you." His expression wary, his eyes guarded, George passed her the diary. She folded the front and back covers open until they touched and carefully pulled the flattened, folded envelope from its slot in the binding.

George snatched the envelope from her hand. "Give me the diary, too."

She felt suddenly, ridiculously possessive. She wanted to clutch the old volume to her heart and never let it go—which was beyond ironic. From the first, she'd tried to deny the diary's hold on her. She'd been telling herself it had nothing to do with her, that it wasn't her story, that the old book had been dumped in her lap and all she wanted was an excuse to get rid of it.

Well, George Abernathy, who watched her, narrow-eyed, his mouth a thin line, was offering her exactly what she'd been so sure she wanted, the perfect excuse to walk away.

And yet here she sat, longing with all her heart to hold on, to never let go until she'd found Winona's daughter and reunited her with the frail old woman in Rust Creek Falls—and with Josiah, too.

Because who did she think she was kidding, anyway? She did believe. She believed that Gabe's dear old Gramps had written the diary and that *her* beloved Winona was the missing Beatrix's rightful mother.

Gabe seemed to understand how she felt—her feeling of ownership, that she wasn't finished yet with her part in this. "Dad," he said gently, "the diary doesn't belong to you."

George huffed in outrage. "It's got my grandfather's name in it written in my grandfather's hand."

Mel's heart stopped dead in her chest—and then began racing. "How do you know that?"

"I know Gramps's handwriting like I know my own."

Gabe shook his head. "Oh, come on, Dad. You're exaggerating."

George huffed out a hard breath, glanced away, and then back. Gruffly, he backpedaled. "Well, I'm pretty sure, anyway."

"Dad." Gabe's voice was gentle. "Slow down. Mel's the one who was given the diary. She's in charge of this situation and I'm helping her in any way I can. She and I are dealing with this. You can't just jump in and take over."

"Have you already tried to talk to Gramps about it?"

"We did. We told him everything Mel just told you. But you know how he is nowadays."

George looked so sad suddenly. "Non-responsive?"

"That's right. But we're still on it, Dad. I promise you we won't stop until we've figured out who's really who and exactly what happened."

We? Did Mel like the sound of that too much? Was she getting in way too deep here?

She did. And she was.

George's beefy shoulders slumped a little. "Well. Ahem." Suddenly, he didn't look so proud and imperious. For the first time in Mel's limited experience with the man, it appeared that George Abernathy might defer to his only son. "At least, I would like to be kept in the loop. I want to know whatever you find out."

Gabe glanced at Mel. She realized he was waiting for her answer. "Yes, of course," she agreed.

"There's more," the older man said. "I would like to feel free to share what you've told me with Angela and my father and others in the family. I see no reason that the events chronicled in that diary should be kept a secret."

"You're right," Mel admitted. "Gabe and I agreed to keep the story to ourselves until we knew more. We thought that there was no reason to get everyone excited when we're still not absolutely positive that your Gramps and the author of the diary are one and the same."

"That story shocked the hell out of me, I admit." George pushed his untouched food aside and rested his forearms on the table. "My immediate response was denial. But the more I think about it, the more I realize I don't know that much about my great-grandparents, really. And neither does my father." George turned to Gabe. "As your grandpa Alexander told you the other day at lunch, he found your great-great-grandfather Josiah and your great-great-grandmother Noreen cold and judgmental and impossible to get to know. As for Gramps, he never said much about them, either. There are holes in our family history. And they kind of line up with the events in the diary. I can't tell you much of anything that happened in the family before Gramps married Cora—which reminds me, Gabriel. Your grandfather told me that you'd been asking about the deed to the Ambling A."

"That's right. I was trying to find out what I

could about how the family came to Bronco. I still don't know anything for sure about that."

"Son, the truth is, none of us do. Except maybe Gramps—and he's all locked up now inside his own mind. What we do know is that the ranch didn't formally become the Ambling A until seventy-five years ago. I'm guessing that would be right about the time what's described in the diary took place?"

Mel confirmed that. "Yes, it would."

"So, there we are." George looked ten years older, somehow, than he had when Mel first entered the kitchen and found him standing there with the diary in his hand.

"Nothing is proven," Gabe reminded him.

"Maybe not. But I feel the truth of it down in my bones."

"Okay then. You are now in on this, Dad. You know what we're trying to find out and we can use all the help and information we can get. The best way to do that is to ask anyone who might possibly know something about the past."

"Works for me," said Mel.

"I'm in," said George.

"With one stipulation," added Gabe. "We all agree that information sharing goes both ways. We need to be working together on this. You share whatever you find out," he said to his dad. "Mel and I will do the same."

"Like I said, I'm in," George solemnly replied. He held up the letter to Mel. "I would like to read this now."

"Yes. Please do."

The old paper crackled as George removed the single sheet from the wrinkled envelope and scanned the few lines it contained, after which he carefully refolded the letter, put it back in the envelope and handed it to Mel. She returned it to its place in the diary's binding.

George asked, "Has anyone checked with the hospital in Kalispell where Winona Cobbs was sent?"

Regretfully, Mel shook her head. "Wilder Crawford, whose family now owns the Rust Creek Falls Ambling A, told me that the hospital burned down forty years ago. Back then, all the records would have been on paper, so that's kind of a dead end. Not to mention, if we could find somebody who knew something, they would be in their nineties, at least, and no doubt reluctant to share patient information due to confidentiality laws."

"Well, that's discouraging." George picked up his coffee mug, started to sip from it, realized it was empty and set it back down. "I have another request, Mel. I would appreciate a chance to read the diary for myself."

Again, Mel felt that strange reluctance to part

with it. But in the end, she knew she would have to accept that the old journal was never meant to be hers to keep forever. "Gabe hasn't read it, either," she said, glancing at the man in question. "I'll leave it with him."

Gabe said to his dad, "Once I've read it, I'll give it to you with the understanding that it comes back to me—and then back to Mel—within a day or two." An unwelcome shiver went through Mel as he said that. She was getting the feeling that her time with the old book was ending. She should be happy about that. She'd never wanted it in the first place. But she didn't feel happy. She felt angry and sad and very confused.

"All right, then." George picked up his coffee mug and pushed back his chair. "We're in agreement. I need more coffee. Anybody else?"

A half hour later, George had returned to the main house and Gabe stood at the fancy chef-style range scrambling more eggs to replace the ones they hadn't felt like eating while Mel related the story contained in the diary.

Mel sat at the table, sipping another cup of coffee, her eyes drawn to the man at the stove. His broad, muscled back was to her. He still hadn't put on a shirt and his feet were bare. He looked amazing from behind and right now, he reminded her of the lonesome cowboy she'd believed him to be the first day they met.

Warmth pooled in her midsection and she heard herself sigh as she watched him spoon the eggs onto the plates and pop the toast from the toaster. He was spreading on the butter, the knife scraping across the toasted bread, when the terrifying realization hit her like a bullet straight to the heart.

He turned with a plate in each hand.

I'm in love with this man.

The words took form in her mind and she recognized the absolute truth in them—at the same time as she knew with total certainty that she couldn't go there.

She simply could not. Not now. Not…for the longest time. Maybe never. She wasn't ready.

Not for this. Not for love.

She'd known Gabe for less than three weeks. Just a month ago, she was about to marry Cheating Todd. She'd thought she'd loved *him* at the time. She couldn't just turn right around and fall for the gorgeous man who stood above her now. She was smarter than that.

He set one of the plates in front of her. "You okay?"

"Uh, what? Yeah. Sure. Fine."

"You don't look fine. You look like you just got some really bad news."

"No. Uh-uh." She pasted on a big smile. "It's nothing." And she was such a big, fat liar.

He bent close, brushed her lips with his. Longing speared through her—for everything. A lifetime. True happiness. Forever love.

With *him*.

Oh, dear God. What was the matter with her?

It was one thing to lose her head while he was making her moan his name in bed—natural, really, to get swept away in the moment, to tell herself little fantasy stories about how the diary had done its work and brought her true love.

But to indulge herself in thoughts of love now, the morning after?

Uh-uh. Not good. Not possible. No way.

This was so dangerous. The whole point, after the abject awfulness of her breakup with Todd, was to make an independent life for herself, to find happiness on her own terms, not defined by a man.

Not even *this* man—who was as beautiful inside as out.

The whole point was to have *no* man. To be complete and content, self-sufficient financially and emotionally, all on her own.

"Hey, now," he said softly. "Hey…" He set down his plate, too. Then he took her hand and pulled her out of the chair. She went, feeling numb. Disembodied.

Except for her heart. Her heart yearned. Her heart…loved. Her heart felt like it was trying to batter its way out of her chest to get closer to him.

Even though that was impossible. Even though she could not be in love with anyone right now.

Gabe wrapped those hard arms around her. For a moment, she gave in, let herself lean on him. She drank in the strength of him, the warmth of him surrounding her.

She felt his lips in her hair. "Tell me," he whispered. "What's wrong? Talk to me."

"Listen, I…" She made herself look up at him and then had no idea at all what to say.

Gabe tipped her chin up with a gentle touch. "You're scared. Of what?"

"I…think I feel too much for you."

He gazed at her for the longest time. "Let me be sure of what you're saying. You feel strongly for me and that scares you?"

"Yeah." Her voice was small. Weak to her own ears. She made herself speak with more force. "After Todd messed me over, I promised myself I would find my way, on my own. I promised myself I would make my life—a good, full life—without a man in it. And then you came along and I'm, well, I'm getting ideas, Gabe. About you. And me. Together. In a permanent way."

His smile was slow and oh, so tender. "I would

like that. A lot. More than anything else in this world. It's what I want, Mel. You and me. Together. In a permanent way. Mel, I'm in lo—"

"No!" She pressed her fingertips to his lips. "I can't hear that now."

He wrapped his hand around hers and kissed the fingers that had shushed him. "I don't get it. Why not just hear me out?"

"Because I'm weak. I want to believe you and I can't afford to do that." She searched his face. "I'm sorry, I really am, that we're not on the same page about this. My heart tells me to trust you."

"So listen to your heart." His voice was low, carefully controlled, but charged with strong emotion.

"Gabe. I can't. I have to do what's right for me. I just wish you could understand that."

He dragged in a slow breath. "I'm trying. And I do get it. I hate it, but I get it. Take your time. Think it over."

"Oh, Gabe. I don't know how I'll think of anything else."

He stroked her hair. "You want to run away, don't you? To hide from this, from you and me?"

"Yeah. I do. A little."

He chuckled. It wasn't a happy sound. "More than a little, I think."

"I just, well, the last thing I expected was you."

"Well, you got me. And I guess I'd better not say

more until you're ready to hear it." He took her by the shoulders. "Tell you what."

She caught her lower lip between her teeth. "Hmm?"

"We've already thrown out one batch of perfectly good eggs. Let's eat these before they get cold, too."

She gave him a slow nod. "Yeah. Good idea."

So they sat down and had breakfast. A silent breakfast, during which she couldn't help feeling she was throwing away the best thing—the most important thing. At the same time, she felt bound and determined to carry through with the promise she'd made to herself, to create a life on her own.

They cleared the table and loaded the dishwasher. By the time that was done, the silence between them felt like an open wound.

Had she done that? Wounded him?

He said, "I get the feeling you're leaving now."

"Yeah. I think I'd better go. I need to get in to work early. The boss is coming into town to see how I'm doing." She'd been looking forward to catching up with DJ Traub. He was a good guy and a great boss.

"Right." Gabe picked up the diary from where she'd left it, on the table. "I was watching your face when my dad asked to read this. You seemed uncomfortable with the idea of leaving it here."

How did he know her so well? "I was. I am. I've

grown kind of attached to it. But I know that I need to let go. You need to read it and I think your dad does, too."

"You're sure?"

Dear Lord, he was the most beautiful man. She wanted to grab him and hold him, to drown in his sweet kisses. To never, ever lose him.

And yet, here she was, walking away.

Was getting a little distance from him the right thing to do now—or simply proof of her fear he would break her heart if she gave him too much power over her?

She answered his question about the diary. "I'm sure. I want you to keep it."

"All right." His fine mouth was a bleak line. "I'll get it back to you in a few days."

"No!" The word escaped her of its own volition. She sounded panicked. With considerable effort, she softened her tone. "I mean, really. After you and your dad read it, your grandfather will want to read it, too. And your mother. And what about your dad's brothers? And your cousins? I think a whole bunch of Abernathys are going to want to know about Josiah and Winona. They'll want to try to figure out where Beatrix might be. I'm starting to accept that my part in this old mystery is pretty much finished. Through some crazy twist of fate, I brought the diary to Bronco—to you and your family—where it needs to be. I think it's time for me to let it go. I'm turning the search for the truth over to you."

Something had happened in his eyes. They were no longer warm as a summer sky, but wintry. Cold. "It's one thing to turn your back on me, Mel." His voice chilled her.

She gasped. "But I'm not!" It was a lie. After today, she fully intended to stay away from him, to give herself some much-needed distance from the danger he posed to her vulnerable heart.

And he knew it, too. "You're walking away from me, Mel. And you're a liar to say you're not. I don't like it, but I get it. I know you're scared, though I am not that SOB in Bozeman."

"I don't think that you're like Todd."

"Yeah, well. Could have fooled me. And hey, I understand your fear that I might just do you like he did. I'm willing to wait, back off, give you the time you need to see how wrong you are. What I'm not willing to do is watch you drop this diary on me and walk away. You're in this and you need to stay in it. You're the connection to that woman named Winona in Rust Creek Falls. Are you just going to turn your back on her, too?"

"Of course not."

Those ice-blue eyes said he didn't believe her. "You're lying to yourself as well as to me. That woman believes her child died being born. What if Beatrix is still alive today? What if there's a chance your Winona could be reunited with her daughter? You're just going to walk away from that, dump it all in my lap? What if your help would make the difference, somehow? Gramps and Winona are both in their nineties. They don't have a lot of time."

"I'm aware of that."

"Then what are you doing? What if your walking away slows the whole process down just enough that Winona doesn't live to meet her own daughter?"

"That's crazy. That's not going to happen."

"You don't know what could happen—what *will* happen. Stop kidding yourself. What about that guy named Wilder whose family lives in the house that more than likely once belonged to my great-great-grandparents? What if I need to talk to that guy? Are you going to make me do that without you?"

She drew herself up. "Wilder will be glad to talk to you. You don't need me for that."

He shook his head slowly. "You just won't admit what you're doing, will you?"

She couldn't bear to tell him the truth—so she lied some more. "I don't even know what you're talking about."

He held up the diary, held it right in her face. "This—what's in this old book here—it's a sacred trust and you damn well know it. You didn't want to take it on, but you knew that you *had* to take it on. Why are you suddenly ready to just drop it and run?"

"Gabe, I... Look, I didn't just drop it on you."

"Yeah, you did. You know you did—and no, Mel. You don't get to dump the diary on me and walk out the door to your independent life where no one can ever hurt you again. Not without me first telling you exactly what I think of what you're doing."

Her throat felt tight. She ordered her lungs to draw in a slow, shaky breath. "You're not being fair."

"You're right. I'm not. I don't want to lose you and so I'm not playing fair. I'm not keeping my mouth shut while you walk away and tell yourself you somehow did the right thing by turning your back on me and Winona and Gramps and a missing little baby who never knew who she really was."

"You're way overreacting." She tried to stay reasonable, to keep her voice even and calm.

"Wrong. The truth is, I was *under*reacting. I was trying hard to be understanding. I was going to let you walk out on me without a fight in hopes that you'd realize on your own what a mistake you were making and finally come back to me. But, Mel, you went too far. You dumped the diary on me and said you didn't want it back. You did that for one reason and one reason only—to cut ties with me completely."

Panic rattled through her. She had done exactly that—and now she couldn't stop herself from jumping straight to denial. "No. No, that's not—"

"True? Yeah, it is. You're willing to abandon the truth in order that you won't have to talk to me or have me reach out to you." He shook his head slowly. "I gotta tell you, Mel. I'm not very *understanding* about that. I'm not letting you go without telling you what I think of what you're doing. I damn well am being honest, Mel. And you? You're lying to yourself and acting like a coward, to boot."

She was shaking. She couldn't take any more. "I can't do this. I need to go."

For several truly awful seconds, she was certain he would light into her again. But then he only scooped up her purse from the chair at his side and shoved at her. She took it from him as he muttered, "Fine. Let's go."

With trembling fingers, she hooked the strap on her shoulder. "Listen. Whatever you need from me, concerning anything in the diary—anybody in Rust Creek Falls you need to get in touch with—of course, I'll help in any way I can. You just have to call and I'm on it."

He only stared at her, his cold eyes giving her

nothing. Finally, he shrugged. "I'm not calling you. You want out, you're out. Come on, I'll drive you home."

The ride to Bronco Heights seemed to take forever. Mel stared blindly out the windshield most of the way. Neither of them said a word.

When he pulled to a stop in front of BH247, she didn't know what to say to him. She had this ache in her chest and she had a really bad feeling it was only going to get worse. If she'd imagined she could leave this man and be untouched by what she'd had with him, however briefly...

Well, she'd been deluding herself.

Her stomach churned. Her heart ached with desperate yearning—for the chance she couldn't make herself take, for what she was throwing away. This really was the end for them and, well, she had this sudden awareness that she'd made a whopper of a mistake in calling it off between them.

And now it was too late. He really seemed done with her in a very final way.

And his being done with her was only what she'd asked of him.

It hurt so bad, much more than she'd allowed herself to admit that it might—and she had only herself and her fearful heart to blame.

All it took was one quick glance at his steely expression and the hard set to his jaw to know there was nothing she could say right now to make this moment better.

She unlatched her seat belt. "Thanks, Gabe. For the ride. For…everything."

He turned his head and faced her then. His eyes remained that frosty blue, distant and withdrawn from her and all they might have been, if only she'd been braver, truer. Or at the very least, willing to risk her heart again. "Goodbye, Mel."

She yanked on the door latch and got out of there, fast. Eyes front, she raced for the building. If she so much as hesitated, she might just whirl and run after his big pickup as he drove away.

It took forever, or it felt like it, to get to her door, to let herself in. She shut the door behind her, dropped her purse to the floor and then let her knees give way, until she was sitting there, her back against the door, her breathing ragged and frantic, her heart pounding so hard she almost feared it would explode inside her chest.

Across the room, Homer sat on the foot of her bed. He watched her through those enormous gray-green eyes.

"Hey," she said weakly, still gulping in air.

Homer jumped down and came to her. She held out her hand and he ducked under it. Scooping him up, she cradled him to her chest, pressing her ear against his soft fur so his welcoming purr radiated through her.

For a long time, she just sat there, holding the purring kitten. At some point, the waterworks started. She ugly cried, getting snot and tears all over poor Homer. He didn't seem to mind. He didn't even try to squirm away from her, just let her hold him and cry on him as he continued to purr.

She cried for her parents, cried for all the love they'd given her so freely, all the years of tender care. For all the love she had within her, stored up for them. They were supposed to be there, for her wedding to just the right guy, to be grandparents to her children, to be among the ones she loved and cared for as the years went by and they needed her more.

She missed them still. She always would. The loss of them remained, an empty space inside her, an empty space that echoed with all that would never be.

And what about Cheating Todd? Yeah, she cried for him, too—well, not for the reality of Todd. But for who he was supposed to be. The man she'd created in her heart, the shoes that the real Todd had never actually filled.

And Gabe?

Him, more than anything. She cried for what might have been with Gabe, for the love that she couldn't quite bear to accept from him. Because her heart just wasn't ready. Because after losing her folks and then saying yes to a man who had turned around and betrayed her, well, she just wasn't able right now to trust her own judgment. Not with something so scary and overwhelming as love. She could end up with a big hole inside herself, another terrible emptiness like the one her parents had left through no fault of their own.

Or with a deep and abiding sense of betrayal, an anger that gnawed at her, like the smoldering fury she'd been gifted with courtesy of Todd.

It was too much, what Gabe had asked of her. Too much to ask and much too soon.

She'd been right to say no to him. She would get over this pain. Even though, at this moment, it felt like her heart was breaking for the third time.

Even though now it seemed to her she'd just thrown away everything she needed most.

Chapter Eleven

After a good hour of bawling on the floor, trying to convince herself she'd done the right thing to end it with Gabe, Mel finally dragged herself to her feet and got down to the business of pulling it together enough to go to work.

Hiding the ravages of her long crying jag wasn't easy, but after sticking her face in a sink full of ice water and piling on the concealer, she hoped maybe she looked at least presentable. She arrived at DJ's Deluxe a full hour before she was expected.

DJ Traub was already there, sitting behind his giant desk in his private office in the complex of offices on the floor above the restaurant. His door was wide open, as usual.

Mel pulled her shoulders back and tried to look cheerful and confident as she tapped on the door frame to get his attention. His gaze shifted from his laptop to her at the sound.

"There's my favorite manager." He rose to greet her. "Come in, come in."

In his forties now, Dalton James Traub was a handsome man. He had that steady, boy-next-door quality that made others trust him. A family man to the core, he'd been happily married to his wife, Allaire, for as long as Mel had known him. From the day he hired her to wait tables at his Bozeman Rib Shack, Mel had admired not only DJ's genius as a successful restaurateur, but also his big heart. He was good to the people who worked for him, paying them well, offering decent benefits and reasonable hours.

He came around the desk to meet her and they shared a quick hug. When they pulled apart, she could see by his worried frown that all that concealer hadn't hidden as much as she'd hoped.

"Sit down." He gestured at the seating area over by the tall windows that looked out on the street. Reluctantly, she went over and took a chair. He shut the door and dropped onto the leather sofa across from her. "What's happened?"

She smoothed her hair and crossed her legs and tried to look breezy and relaxed. "Long story. Nothing to do with the job, DJ, I promise you."

"I've been over the books. I know we're doing just fine here—better than fine. And I've spoken with both Gwen and Damien. They have nothing but good things to say about you. You're doing a terrific job, as I knew you would. But I'm not asking about DJ's Deluxe. It's you I'm concerned for."

"I'm fine."

"I don't think so." He frowned. "How long have I known you?"

"DJ, I mean it. I'm okay."

"Just answer the question. How long?"

She glared at him for several seconds, but he didn't back off. "Eight years or so?"

"And I've only seen those haunted eyes I'm lookin' at now one other time."

Mel knew he wasn't referring to her breakup with Todd. When she'd visited his corporate offices in Bozeman last month in search of a job to tide her over until the one in Austin opened up, she'd held it together just fine. Why?

Because I was more angry than brokenhearted over what happened with Todd.

Right now, she felt shattered.

And she hadn't felt shattered since...

Her throat got tight and her lower lip started

trembling. She ordered it to stop and said softly, "You mean the day I got the news about my parents…"

DJ gave a slow, solemn nod. "You don't break easy, Mel Driscoll. So when you do, I notice. I care about what's going on with you. Tell me what the problem is. You never know. Maybe I can help."

"You're the best. But there's nothing you can—"

"Try me."

"It's a relationship thing. You don't need to listen to me whine about my love life, or lack thereof."

"Let *me* decide what I need, Mel. Talk."

She shouldn't. It was so completely unprofessional. But DJ was a good guy and he really seemed to want to help. "I, um, think—well, I've just totally blown it with a very special guy. I'm sad, really sad. I'm also disappointed in myself. I promised myself I wouldn't fall for him, but apparently, my heart failed to get the memo. Now I've broken it off with him and I feel horrible. I've ruined everything with him and there's no going back. It's over. I kind of hate myself, if you want to know the truth."

"Hating yourself will get you exactly nowhere."

"Yeah, well, hating myself may not be constructive, but I seem to be doing it anyway."

"And as far as you and that special guy being 'over,' you might be surprised. It might all work out for you two in the end, after all."

"Of course, you would say that, DJ." She'd seen him and his wife together more than once during the years she worked for him in Bozeman. "You and Allaire have been married for as long as I can remember. You're in love and have been forever and you naturally think everyone's going to end up happily married to the perfect person, too."

"Mel. You don't know the whole story. Allaire and I, we had a very rocky start."

"It couldn't have been that bad. It's obvious you two were meant for each other."

"Allaire didn't think so at first."

That made no sense. "What do you mean?"

"I mean, I always loved Allaire, but she chose my big brother. She and Dax got married right out of high school."

Okay, that was a stunner. "You're not serious."

"As an overcooked tenderloin. My heart was broken. I knew I would never get over it."

"But it *did* work out for you and Allaire."

He nodded. "Her marriage to Dax didn't last. They were divorced within a few years. And more than a few years after that, I came back to my hometown of Thunder Canyon to open a Rib Shack at the resort there. I tried to stay away from my brother's ex-wife. But it was impossible. Within a few months, she had my ring on her finger. Allaire is the love of my life and I can't imagine my world without her in the center of it. So cheer up, Mel. Have a little faith that things will work out just right in the end for you and that special guy."

She longed to believe him. But she didn't. "I'm leaving in January. You know that, DJ. My perfect job is in Austin."

"It's just a job, Mel. And maybe your guy will decide he wants to move to Austin, too."

"Uh-uh. I mean it. He and I are over."

DJ just wouldn't give it up. "We'll see. And there's another possibility we haven't discussed yet..."

She braced her elbows on her knees and propped her face in her hands. "What are you getting at?"

"You know I think you're the greatest. I like to work with the best and the brightest and that means I'm not happy with the idea of losing you again when you head off to Austin at the end of the year. I've been plotting a way to keep you right here in Montana where we both know you belong."

"I'm not staying in Montan—"

"Hold on, now. Let me finish. I've always wanted to boot myself in my own ass for letting you go when you moved over to Spurlock's. I've followed your career, Mel. I know you're a brilliant finance and insurance manager. And I believe you really ought to aim higher."

Cautiously, she prompted, "Higher, how?"

"Would you consider becoming CFO for DJ's, Incorporated? You could work out of the offices here—yeah, you would have to travel to the main offices once or twice a month, but it's not that far and your home base would be Bronco if you want it that way."

She felt suddenly breathless. "CFO for DJ's, corporate…"

"That's right. Our current CFO is retiring. He could work with you starting next month, until you both felt you were ready to take over the job from him. Think about it. Think of what terms and salary and options you would want, what kind of benefits package. Think of how you would see your role as Chief Financial Officer for our restaurants and how you would grow the role. If you're interested, we'll work up an offer and take it from there."

"DJ, I think my head is spinning."

"I can understand that. It's a lot to consider, especially on the heels of what just happened with your special guy. My plan was to be here in Bronco until Friday, but I can stay till Saturday. You can take a break to think things over and I'll cover for you."

"A break? You mean extra time off?"

"Just an extra day or two."

"That's not necessary."

"I say it is and I'm the boss. We should spend some time today going over everything. I want a report from you on our systems and on the front and the back of the house. Just a general rundown on how we're doing at DJ's Deluxe and what could be done better. Then there's the dinner service. We should both be there for that, so I can check on how it's going, and we can consider solutions to any issues that crop up—all of which means I'll need you for the rest of the afternoon and tonight. But I don't want to see you here tomorrow, Thursday or Friday."

"DJ, that's thoughtful of you. But I really don't need two extra days off."

He put up a hand to silence her. "At least take tomorrow. And then Thursday is your regular day off. That will give you two days to clear your head a little, figure out what you want for your future, get closer to a decision about your next step. And, Mel, I sincerely hope that your plans for the future will include working out whatever's wrong with your guy and joining the DJ's team on a permanent basis."

Twice that evening, Gabe realized he couldn't stand *not* to make things up with Mel. Both times, he grabbed his keys and went out the front door, jumped in his pickup and kicked up a cloud of dust heading straight for town and DJ's Deluxe. The first time, he stopped himself at the Ambling A's front gate. The second time, he made it halfway to Bronco before he forced himself to pull over and turn the damn truck around.

Mel was done with him. And he was through with her. He needed to accept that—get over her and move on.

The second time he made himself return to the ranch, he locked himself in the house and got out the whiskey. He would get good and drunk, drown his sorrows at the loss of the gorgeous little blonde with the smart mouth and the naughty dimple in her soft cheek.

But then he only had one drink—a double— and put the bottle away. Because getting blasted wouldn't end his misery. It would only give him a hangover tomorrow, make him more miserable than he already was.

He took a shower and went to bed—with the diary. It wasn't his first choice for a bedmate, but Mel was not available. And she wasn't going to *be* available. He needed to accept that, get used to it, move on.

The diary would have to do. He stayed up all night reading the damn thing, poring over each page, studying the brief letter hidden in the binding. The experience really fit his mood that night. Just what he needed, a sad story of thwarted young love and a lost child, a child yet to be found, seventy-plus years later.

Was the Josiah who wrote the diary really his own Gramps? He couldn't be sure. There was no incontrovertible proof and there might never be.

But he felt strangely certain anyway. Josiah and Gramps were the same person. And the baby named Beatrix, wherever she was now, deserved to be found.

It was after four when he finally dropped into an uneasy sleep. At a little after eight, the ringing of his cell jarred him awake.

He grabbed it off the bed table and glared at it before taking the call. "Erica. What?"

"Good morning to you, too, Mr. Crabby Pants."

"It's 8:00 a.m. and you sound way too cheerful."

"I like to get up and get going on the day. You, on the other hand, sound like you were up all night doing things you shouldn't."

He thought of Mel. Gone. He wanted her back. It was going to be damn hard not to jump in his truck and drive like a bat out of hell straight to BH247 in the next hour or so. And then later, not to just happen to drop in at DJ's Deluxe to see if maybe there was a chance she'd rethought walking out on him and couldn't live without him, after all.

Damn. He was hopeless. He needed to grow a pair and forget her.

"Gabe? You still with me?"

"Right here. Everything okay?"

"Um. Fine. Just checking in, you know?"

Did she sound a little off? "What's happened, Erica? What's wrong?"

"Not a thing."

"You sure?"

"Of course."

"How's the boyfriend?"

A beat of silence, then, "Peter's fine."

"Something's up. Talk to me."

"Stop it. There's nothing. I just called to say hi."

"Let me guess. You're coming home for a long visit."

Another silence. That meant she wasn't. "Soon, I promise."

He wanted to ask why she never kept her promises—not the ones about coming home, anyway—but that would only start a fight and he really didn't want to fight with her. "We miss you. Gramps isn't doing well and you need to—"

She cut him off. "Can you just not get on me about Gramps, please?"

He opened his mouth to insist that she needed to be here, that Gramps needed to see her.

But who did he think he was kidding? These days, Gramps seemed so far away from everyone, trapped in his own head, never really seeming to know the difference between Gabe and any random, helpful Snowy Mountain caregiver.

"Okay," he said. "Sorry. Love you, little sister." And he did—but he had resentments toward her, too. She'd drifted so far away from the family. He worried about her. Sometimes he wondered if everything in her life really was as perfect as she kept insisting it was.

And he didn't know how to talk to her. He wanted to tell her about Mel—loving her, losing her—and the diary and the possibility that their beloved Gramps had a lot of secrets he'd never shared with the family.

But then she said, too cheerfully, "And I love you. How is everything there?"

He played the dutiful big brother and reported that everyone was fine, that Grandpa Alexander could never figure out why young people thought they knew it all and Dad refused even to consider a single one of the suggestions Gabe had for streamlining a few things around the Ambling A. "And you know Mom. She's waiting for the go-ahead to start planning your wedding."

Erica muttered something under her breath.

"What? Didn't catch that."

"Oh, nothing," she answered airily, evasive as ever.

And when she said goodbye a few minutes

later, he heard the line go dead and felt more disconnected from his sister than ever.

The next day—her extra day off, thanks to DJ, who refused to believe that she would prefer to keep busy—Mel knew she would go nuts if she hung around her apartment. She was up at seven and the day seemed to stretch out in front of her, empty and endless. She knew she would only end up knocking on her neighbors' door, interrupting Amanda's workday, crying on her shoulder and then imposing her misery on Brittany, too, when she got home.

No. Mel couldn't bear a whole day of dragging around the complex, playing the sad sack, taking advantage of her new friends' affection and goodwill to moan about how she and Gabe weren't working out. Especially given that she was the dumper and not the dumpee.

She needed action. And she really wanted to get the heck out of Bronco, where everything reminded her of Gabe.

She decided to visit Winona. The long drive to Rust Creek Falls would clear her head—she hoped. Also, she ought to check on the various repairs at her parents' house. The new tenants were moving in on the first and the place had to be ready for them.

Homer could go with her. It would be good for

him to travel a little, start becoming accustomed to being in the car.

Once she was packed and ready to hit the road, she decided she ought to give her friends a heads-up. Brittany and Amanda would worry if she simply vanished for a couple of days—and strangely enough, the thought of how concerned they would be lightened her spirits a little. She might have blown it with Gabe, but she *had* made two true friends during her weeks in Bronco.

Amanda answered the door at Mel's knock. In shorts and a tank top, she had her hair piled up in a messy bun. "Hey, Mel."

Mel recognized her friend's distracted expression. "You're working."

"You know me. I'm *always* working. Come on in."

"No, I won't keep you. I just wanted you to know I got two days off in a row and I'm driving up to Rust Creek Falls. I've got a friend I need to check on and some other stuff I really have to take care of."

Amanda's smooth brow crinkled. "Everything okay?"

"You know how it goes. There's always something."

"You want to talk?"

Mel kept her smile in place. "Thanks, but it's a long drive. I need to get on the road."

After another searching look, Amanda let it go. "So you'll be back…?"

"By Friday. I have to work Friday night."

"Homer?"

"He's coming with. He doesn't care much for car rides, but I'm hoping he'll get used to it."

"I'll be glad to kitty sit."

"Thanks, but I kind of like his company."

"Okay, then. See you Friday. I'll tell Brittany." Amanda held out her arms. They shared a quick hug and Mel found herself thinking that no matter where she ended up at the first of the year, she would be keeping in touch with Amanda and Brittany.

Homer did create something of a challenge. She strapped his kitty carrier in the back seat, and he began wailing in misery the second she started up the car.

Mel drove straight to the pet store and bought a giant tube-shaped cat cage big enough for several toys, a treat dispenser and a soft-sided, collapsible portable cat box. She spent a while introducing him to his new travel space and teaching him how to get his treats, petting him constantly and reminding him what a very good boy he was. And then, once they got back on the road, she stopped every half hour to pet him some more and shower him with praise.

All the stops added more than an hour to the trip, but the extra space, restroom accommodations, treats, toys and attention worked. By the time they reached Great Falls, Homer had stopped crying. She continued to pull over and check on him hourly after that. And he seemed perfectly content in his giant cat tube. He even purred when she praised him.

She arrived at the house in Rust Creek Falls at five thirty and got right to work, bringing in her small suitcase and setting Homer up with his bed, litter box, play structure and food and water bowls. She raided the shed in back where she'd stored her rollaway bed, basic kitchen stuff, towels and toilet paper.

At six thirty, she strolled over to Crawford's General Store to pick up the minimum in food items—eggs, milk, bread, a few condiments, some cheese and lunch meat. The girl behind the counter there was someone she didn't recognize. That made her sad. Always in her memory, members of the Crawford family would be there to greet her any time she shopped at their store.

Back at the house, she ate a sandwich, petted her kitten and inspected the premises. The new paint looked great, the leaky pipe under the kitchen sink had been replaced and the hanging light fixture in the dining area no longer blinked on and off when she flicked the switch. Everything was ready for the next family to move in.

Now what? Her plan was to give Winona a call in the morning. She could just as easily try her now...

But she didn't feel up to dealing with anyone—not even Winona—tonight.

Alone. Brokenhearted. Antisocial. And lonely.

It was not her finest hour.

She ended up, phone in hand, sitting on the rollaway in the empty bedroom that had been hers growing up. As she petted Homer, who was curled in her lap, she wondered what Gabe might be doing. Her longing to call him was so strong it hurt.

Somehow, she kept herself from doing that.

Finally, around nine, she went to bed. Her sleep was fitful. She woke before dawn thinking that it really was time to let go of this house. The happy memories she'd collected here would always be hers to keep. But now it was time to let some other family call it their own.

"Once the new tenants' lease is up, I'm selling this house," she informed Homer as she dished him up some Fancy Feast. Then she sat back on her heels and watched him chow down, waiting for the feeling of panic to rise as it had every other time she'd seriously considered putting the house on the market.

There was no panic. Only a sense of quiet acceptance.

After breakfast, she called Winona, who took four rings to answer and sounded a bit distracted at first. "Mellie? Is that you? What's going on?"

"I'm here, Winona, in Rust Creek Falls. I drove up from Bronco yesterday. I was wondering if I could come over and visit you?"

"Right now? Why, that would be wonderful! I'll get the kettle going."

Mel put Homer in his small carrier and took him along.

Winona was standing in her open doorway when Mel started up the front walk. She looked so thin, fragile as old glass, the network of wrinkles on her face etched deeper than ever. But her smile made the day brighter. She reached out her thin arms and Mel went into them. "Mellie, it's so good to see you." Winona took her by the shoulders and beamed at her some more. "Come in, come in!" She stepped aside so Mel could enter, glancing down at the pet carrier as Mel went by. "What is that you've got—a pet?"

"Someone very special." In the living room, she set the carrier on the floor and unzipped the flap at the top.

Homer popped his head out of the opening. "Reow?"

Winona laughed in delight. "Look at those eyes!"

Mel scooped him up and held him close. He purred against her chest. "His name is Homer."

Winona clapped her hands. "He is definitely a Homer. Perfect choice for a name—oh!" She pressed a hand to her chest. And she was panting.

"Winona?" Mel let Homer wriggle to the floor and jumped up. "Are you—"

"Fine, dear. I am fine." Carefully, her hand still on her heart, Winona lowered herself to the sofa. "There." She drew a slow breath and then another. "Better."

"Let me call your doctor for you."

"No. There's no need. I am fine."

"Winona, you don't seem fine."

"It was just a little breathlessness. It's passed now." Winona positioned a pillow against the arm-rest and started to lie down. But then the teakettle whistled in the other room and she popped back up again.

"Rest," Mel commanded. "I'll deal with the tea."

"I don't mind—"

"Lie down, Winona."

With a sigh, Winona kicked off her shoes and stretched out.

"How about the afghan?"

"No, thank you. I don't need it. I'll just rest for a moment." The kettle continued to shriek from the other room. Winona gave Mel a too-sweet smile. "See to the kettle, dear."

"I will." Mel spoke sternly. "Do not get up."

"I won't."

"I'll be right back."

In Winona's little kitchen, Mel spooned Darjeeling into a tea ball and put the ball in Winona's old Blue Willow teapot. She poured the hot water over it, covered the pot with a hand-crocheted cozy and left it to steep for a few minutes.

Back in the living room, she found Winona asleep. Homer had jumped up on the sofa with her and was curled in a ball at her side. Mel bent over her. She seemed to be breathing normally.

"Don't fuss." Winona's eyes popped open. "I told you. I am fine."

Mel straightened. "I just don't feel right about you living here all alone."

Winona petted the kitten, who purred his approval. "But of course, I'm not alone. I get an endless parade of visitors checking on me daily."

"What visitors?"

"One of the Crawfords is always coming by, and usually a Dalton or two." The Daltons—and the Crawfords, who owned the general store—were well-known local families. Winona scratched Homer's ears. "And this little guy's namesake comes to see me, too. Homer Gilmore drops by two or three times a week. He's just fine, Homer is, in case you were wondering. Still living off somewhere all on his own. No one's quite sure where."

"I'm glad to hear he's doing well. Rust Creek Falls wouldn't be the same without Homer Gilmore popping up when you least expect him."

"What I'm saying, dear, is that I'm *not* alone. Someone is always showing up at my door—and what about that tea? I was thinking Darjeeling..."

"The Darjeeling is brewing."

Winona gave her a wistful little smile. "I've been longing for Darjeeling. And you picked up my mental signal. We've always had that special connection, don't you think?"

"Yes," Mel said affectionately. "We have."

Winona frowned. "If only I weren't so tired all the time."

Mel got up. "Come on, now. Lie back down."

Winona didn't even try to argue that time. She put her head on the pillow and Mel spread the afghan over her.

The tea forgotten, Winona slept.

Mel wandered back to the kitchen and brought in the tea tray. She poured herself a cup and watched over her slumbering friend. Homer jumped onto the sofa again, cuddled up to Winona and closed his eyes.

Mel sipped her tea, her thoughts straying where

she shouldn't let them go—to Gabe. How could she feel such longing for the man she'd run from just the other day?

And the diary...

She decided that when Winona woke up, she would ease into the subject of Josiah and the missing Beatrix.

But "ease in" how, exactly? She had no idea where to start.

And the more she thought about it, the more she feared the shock of the news might have Winona breathless and panting again—or worse.

Really, not much had changed since the last time Mel had visited her friend. Winona was delicate. Startling news might have a devastating effect on her.

No. Mel just wasn't ready to chance sending Winona over the emotional edge. At the very least, Mel needed to find out what had happened to Beatrix before delivering upsetting information to an old woman in questionable health.

But she wouldn't be finding out anything, now would she? She'd turned her back on the diary, left it—and Gabe—behind.

Carefully, she set her empty teacup on the tray. Guilt and shame twisted in her stomach. Gabe had been right. She'd dumped the diary on him and run away—because she was afraid. Of his love.

Of risking her heart again.

The tea had grown cold when Winona opened her eyes and sat up. Homer jumped from the sofa and darted around the room, batting at shadows.

"Oh, my dear," said Winona. "How rude of me, dropping off like that."

"I'm glad to see you resting."

"You are the sweetest girl." Winona frowned at the teapot.

"It's gone cold, I'm afraid. I'll make some more."

"Would you? I would love a cup. Old Gene brought me a red-velvet Bundt cake with cream cheese frosting yesterday." Gene Strickland ran the local boarding house with his wife, Melba. "It's in the upper cupboard on the left. Why don't you cut us each a slice?"

Mel made more tea and served it with the cake. It was after eleven when she put Homer back in his carrier and left Winona's little house.

"Be safe and well and happy," Winona whispered in her ear as they shared a last hug at the door.

Mel walked back to her parents' house, waving at former neighbors along the way, worried for Winona, yet feeling a little less glum to see some familiar faces.

But then she turned the corner and saw the Jaguar parked at the curb in front of the house.

Clutching Homer's carrier tighter, Mel picked

up the pace. A few seconds later, she spotted Todd, perfectly pulled together as usual in Western-cut dress slacks, a crisp white shirt, a butter-soft suede jacket and a pair of high-dollar boots. He was standing on the front porch, waiting for her.

"God, you are beautiful," he said as she climbed the porch steps. His perfect white teeth flashed with his too-wide smile. "I've missed you so much, Mel. You'll never know." He started to reach for her.

She jerked back as Homer hissed in his carrier.

Todd winced. "What's that? A cat? You've got a cat now?"

"Yes, I do, Todd. Why are you here?"

He raked his sleek brown hair back with a manicured hand. "You won't talk to me. I've called, I've texted. I'm at the end of my rope over you. Mel, I cannot live without you." He dropped to a knee and put his hand on his heart. "Won't you please come back home where you belong?"

She couldn't suppress a snort of laughter. "Todd, wake up. I fell for your lies twice. But then you cheated in our bed and I caught you in the act."

"No! I never cheated—I mean, except that one time."

"Stop. You did. You know you did—and so do I. And besides, one time was more than enough."

"But you have to believe me. It *was* one time— the *only* time…" He tried to grab her free hand.

She jerked it out of the way. He sneezed and Homer let out an angry yowl. "Can you put that cat over there?" He pointed to the far end of the porch. "You know I'm allergic."

"Get up off the porch floor and go home, Todd."

"Mel, come on. It was a mistake and I swear on my undying love for you that it was the *only* time."

"Yeah, right. What about that earring I found under the bed a year ago?"

He widened his eyes in a failed attempt to look totally innocent. "It was yours."

"It didn't belong to me and we both know it didn't. And what about that woman, Brandi, the one with the enormous breasts who kept sexting you? You swore it was a wrong number. But it wasn't. Was it, Todd?"

"Why won't you believe me? I was wrong to cheat, I get that." Todd jumped to his feet then. "But I never lied to you. I love *you*, Mel. I've *always* loved you."

"I want you to leave, Todd." She spoke slowly and carefully, as though to a stubborn child. "I want you to go now. If you don't, I'm calling the sheriff's office. In Rust Creek Falls they don't take kindly to trespassers like you."

From the carrier, Homer let out a long, low growl. It was a sound Mel had never heard the kitten make before. She almost grinned. Her little Homer had a protective streak.

"That cat is a menace," muttered Todd.

Simultaneously, a rusty voice from somewhere near the bottom of the steps said, "Git, you durn fool! The lady asked you to leave."

Mel turned toward the voice just as Homer Gilmore rose from the boxwood bushes her mom had planted fifteen years before. "Homer?"

"'Lo, Mellie Driscoll." Homer wore his usual tattered bib overalls and a torn thermal shirt. What remained of his hair had bits of leaves stuck in it. And he had that thoroughly Homeresque expression on his hangdog face—kind of a cross between utterly benign and capable of unimaginable acts of mayhem.

"This is a surprise," Mel said fondly.

"Who the hell is that?" Todd was looking a little alarmed.

"That's Homer Gilmore," Mel replied. "And he doesn't want you here any more than I do."

Homer mounted the steps slowly, those wild eyes of his locked on Todd. "What'd I say to you, city boy?"

"Ahem. Well. I don't—"

"Skedaddle!"

By then, Mel was having to exert a lot of effort not to burst into peals of laughter. And it got better.

Todd kind of zipped around Homer and sprinted off down the steps to his gleaming car.

"You're making a big mistake, Mel!" he shouted as he flung the driver's door wide and got in.

"Git!" Homer roared again and started down the steps.

That was enough for Todd. He revved the engine and sped off down the street.

"Good riddance to bad trash," muttered Homer. "And he better slow down or he'll be spendin' the night in the county jail. Sheriff Christensen's got no patience for rich guys in fancy cars."

"Thanks, Homer." Mel reached out and gently patted the sleeve of his dingy thermal shirt.

He peered at the cat carrier. "What've you got there?"

"Homer Gilmore, meet Homer the cat."

A rumbling sound escaped the human Homer. It took Mel a moment to realize it was a laugh. "You named your cat after me?"

"I did, yes."

"Well. What do you know about that? I believe I am honored, Mellie." He peered more closely at Homer, who peered right back. "He has beautiful eyes."

"Just like yours, Homer."

The old man let out a snort. His scruffy, wrinkled cheeks had turned red. "Now you are embarrassin' me."

She patted his sleeve again. "It's almost lunchtime. Come on inside and I'll make you a sandwich."

Homer put up a gnarled hand. "Thank you, but no. I'm on my way to see Winona. She usually has something sweet for me."

"I think it just might be red-velvet Bundt cake."

"Now, we're talkin'." He went on down the steps. At the bottom, he paused. "You take care now, Mellie Driscoll."

"You too, Homer." She gave him a wave. "You, too."

As she turned for the house, she was thinking of Gabe. Seeing Todd again had brought it all sharply home to her. Gabe was nothing like Todd. Gabe didn't have a cheating bone in his whole big, hot, broad-shouldered body.

"I really messed up," she whispered to no one in particular.

She'd been fighting it so hard, but seeing Todd again had done it, made it impossible for her to keep denying the truth.

Not only was she in love with Gabe Abernathy, she wasn't going to be happy without him at her side. Breaking it off with him had been a terrible mistake.

If only she'd figured that out before she told him they were through.

Chapter Twelve

An hour later, Mel had packed everything up, stored her rollaway and boxes of kitchen and bath stuff in the backyard shed, loaded up the car and gotten Homer all comfy in his giant tube carrier. She hit the road for Bronco.

And she made great time, too, arriving at BH247 at a little after six that evening. It didn't take long at all to bring Homer in, fill his food and water bowls and unpack her suitcase.

"Hey, neighbor!" Brittany called from the next-door patio as Mel sat out at her little cast-iron café table with her feet up on the extra chair, sipping a tall ice water and debating what to throw together for dinner. "I stopped for takeout tacos on the way home," Brittany said. "There's plenty. Join us?"

"Best offer I've had all day."

Mel went next door, where Amanda had whipped up a pitcher of margaritas to go with the tacos.

Mel offered a toast. "To you, both of you. I'm so glad you're my friends and it's good to be home." *Home.* Somehow, so quickly, Bronco had started to be the place she called home. She thought about that "dream job" in Austin. It didn't seem so perfect for her now.

"So how was Rust Creek Falls?" asked Amanda.

Mel gave a quick report of her visit and a blow-by-blow of Todd's unexpected appearance.

"Whoa," said Brittany. "I think I'm a fan of this Homer Gilmore guy."

"Me, too," agreed Amanda. She turned her big brown eyes on Mel. "I can see why you named your cat after him—and I have to ask. You seemed down yesterday. What's going on? Are you all right?"

Mel set down her margarita glass and told her friends the truth. "I'm in love with Gabe—and I broke it off with him."

Brittany looked shocked. "I don't get it. You just said you love him."

"Why break it off?" asked Amanda, bewildered.

Brittany demanded, "What did he *do*?"

Mel let out a groan. "Nothing. He was wonderful. I just got scared when he tried to tell me he loves me."

"You messed up," said Brittany.

"Tell me about it."

"You need to fix this. Go to him, tell him you were wrong and you want another chance."

"It's too late. I blew it. Falling in love wasn't in my plan and I couldn't deal with it. He's been pretty much all in with me from the first and I've been indecisive, to put it mildly, eager to be with him one minute, pulling away the next. He's through with me now and I can't blame him. I need to somehow accept that it's too late. I've blown it with him."

"Wrong attitude." Brittany shook a finger at her. "You just said you love the man. And that means it's never too late."

Amanda nodded with enthusiasm. "You have to keep trying. You have to go to him and admit you were scared, that you know you reacted badly and you want a chance to make it right."

"Tell him how you really feel," Brittany insisted. "Give your love a fighting chance."

Friday morning, Gabe got a call from Roger Dutton, a partner in his latest real estate project.

"We need to firm this deal up," said Roger. "How 'bout tonight?"

"Sure. Let's get everyone together for dinner at the Association."

"I like DJ's Deluxe," argued Roger. "Steaks you can cut with a fork, great service, good drinks and a relaxed atmosphere."

Gabe dropped into an easy chair and stared out his living room window at the mountains and the never-ending blue expanse of Montana sky. Mel would probably be working tonight.

He didn't want to see her. It would hurt like hell, having to watch her in one of those silky white shirts that clung to her pretty breasts and a black pencil skirt that made him want to bend her over the nearest available table. He didn't think he could take having to watch her fly around that restaurant, making sure everything was running like clockwork, scattering her gorgeous smiles to every man, woman and child in the place.

"Gabe? Did I lose you?"

"I'm right here."

"So what do you say? DJ's?"

No way. He couldn't do it.

And that pissed him off.

Yeah, Mel had screwed him over. But Bronco was his town. Damned if he was letting some gorgeous, unattainable blonde keep him from *anywhere* he needed to be. He would buck the hell up and deal.

Starting tonight. "All right. DJ's it is."

* * *

Someone else in Gabe's party had made the reservation, so Mel had no warning that he would be showing up at DJ's that night.

When she spotted him, he was already at his table with three other men and a good-looking middle-aged woman in a red dress. At that point, Mel was making the rounds, checking on the customers, sharing a few words at each table and then moving on.

When she stopped at Gabe's table, he didn't even look at her. Dear Lord, he was so beautiful, in a black jacket and a silver-gray shirt, his sculpted jaw freshly shaven. It was awful, knowing she loved him and having him ignore her. But she managed to keep her smile in place as she asked how everything was going.

One of the men nodded and the woman in the red dress said, "Perfect, as always. This filet is pure heaven."

"Wonderful. Enjoy your evening. And please let me know if there's anything you need." Still smiling, feeling like her face might crack, she moved on to the next table and the one after that.

As soon as she neared the hallway that led to the kitchen, she darted through it and kept going to the employee restroom in the back. It was empty, thank Heaven. She slipped in and shut the door and ended up standing at the sink, staring into her own haunted eyes in the mirror.

She needed...

"To talk to him," she whispered aloud to her own stricken reflection. "I need to talk to him. I need to be brave enough to tell him that I was wrong, and won't he please give me one more chance?" She moaned and squeezed her eyes shut. It was going to be the hardest thing she'd ever done. And he would probably say no.

But Brittany and Amanda were right. She needed to at least give her own happiness a real shot. She'd caused the breakup, ruined things between them. The least she could do was to try to fix what she'd broken.

She glared at her reflection and instructed in a hissing whisper, "You are going to do it. Tonight, if possible. And if no opportunity presents itself tonight, tomorrow you will pick up the damn phone. You will say that you were wrong and you're so very sorry and would he maybe consider—" a soft rap on the door cut her off. "I'll be right out!" she called as she flipped on the tap and washed her hands.

When she opened the door, one of the sous chefs gave her a nod and a smile and darted in as she went out.

In the busy heart of the kitchen, it was organized chaos and chef Damien reigned. He glanced up and gave her a wink and she knew that all was well in the back of the house.

Time to get out on the floor again, do her job—and watch for any opportunity to speak briefly to Gabe. Chin high and shoulders back, she headed down the hall to the dining room.

For the next hour, she kept an eye on Gabe's table. When he excused himself and made his way to the short hall that branched off the one leading to the kitchen, she shamelessly detoured to follow him at a discreet enough distance that no one would notice—she hoped.

She stood out of the way as he disappeared into the men's room. When he emerged a few minutes later, she stepped up to him just before he could escape to the dining room again.

"Gabe." She sounded like a robot—stiff. And mechanical. He looked at her as though he had no idea who she was. "I would like just a minute of your time, please."

"Why?" His wonderful face looked carved from stone.

A waiter carrying a serving tray brushed by her. She dared to touch Gabe's arm. Even through the fine fabric of his jacket, she felt him flinch—and she also felt that special energy, an arc of heat and longing between them.

Did he feel it, too? She couldn't tell. His grim expression gave her nothing.

"Over here." Did she expect him to go where she guided him?

Not really. But he surprised her and stepped back, closer to the wall, so they were out of the way. "What do you want, Melanie?"

Melanie. Well, that was a clue as to exactly how he felt about her now.

She forced herself to carry through. "Will you do one thing for me?"

"What?" His eyes were hard, unreadable.

"Meet me on the Ambling A, the spot by the creek where you found me that first day?" *Our* spot, she was thinking, but lacked the courage to say.

"Why?"

Her heart was a thousand-pound anvil inside her chest, weighing her down with regret and the sure knowledge that he was never going to give an inch. "Please, Gabe. This is neither the time nor the place. But I do want to talk to you privately. Tomorrow. Noon, at the creek. I'll be there. I hope you will, too."

"Is that all?" His voice was as cold as his icy eyes.

She was *not* going to burst into tears right here where she worked. She kept her head up and her spine straight. "Yes." And she whirled and strode blindly up the hallway to the kitchen again, so she wouldn't have to watch him turn away first.

Between that moment in the hallway and noon the next day, Mel second-guessed herself at least a hundred times. She decided there was no point in showing up at the creek—and then she decided that, even if he didn't show, she had said she would be there, and she wouldn't go back on her word. However, five minutes later, she would realize anew that there was no point in going, after all. It went on like that, her heart, her mind, her very soul seesawing back and forth between going and not going.

She hardly slept at all.

But she *was* going. She had no choice, really. She would despise herself forever if she didn't put her heart on the line for the man she loved.

Her first plan had been to bring a picnic. But last night, he'd hardly seemed in a picnic kind of mood. She would be lucky if he even showed. He was going to want to know what she had to say and very likely tell her to forget it, he was done with her.

So, then, scratch the picnic. She wouldn't even take a blanket. She would stand there on the creek bank and wait for thirty minutes. If he didn't appear, well, at least she'd shown up as she'd said she would.

She drove out to the ranch, certain she was heading for an exercise in futility and crushing disappointment.

It shocked the hell out of her to see his pickup sitting there by the road when she drove up. She pulled in behind the truck, turned off the engine, rested her forehead on the steering wheel and forced her breathing to slow to a less frantic rhythm.

Well, okay. He was here. At least she would get a chance to say what she had to say.

Her legs were shaking as she climbed the hill. At the top, she looked down, and there he was, in old jeans and a chambray shirt, facing the hill where she stood, watching her from under the brim of his dusty hat. She met his shadowed eyes, her pulse racing again, her breath sawing wildly in and out.

He was everything, all the *best* things—a cherished dream she hadn't let herself believe in. Gabe, the lonesome cowboy. Just like that first day.

Somehow, she managed to descend the low hill with measured steps. She stopped a few feet from him. He took off his hat—because even though he didn't look happy with her, his mama had raised him right.

"Okay, I'm here," he said. "What's this about?"

She opened her mouth to tell him what was in her heart—and no words came. Her stupid lip was trembling. She bit the inside of it to make it quit doing that.

And…something happened in his face. The carved-in-granite look softened. His eyes weren't quite so icy cold. "Go ahead, Mel," he said, almost gently. "Say it."

Her face got hot and her eyes were burning with tears she refused to let fall. Her racing heart seemed to stop. A ridiculous little bark of a cough escaped her. "Mel. You just called me Mel."

One side of his mouth quirked up. "Talk."

Hope. This was hope. Filling her heart. Making it beat again. "Well, ahem. As you know, I came to Bronco as an interim stop in my life."

"I am aware," he said quietly in that deep, rich voice she loved.

Her mind went blank. She blinked and shook her head and ordered her brain to get back online. "It, um, just never occurred to me that I might fall deeply in love. After the disaster of epic proportions that was Todd, I was so…anti-love. He was a cheater. I had *chosen* a cheater. I realized I couldn't trust my own judgment. I decided the best course was not to give any guy a chance. I never imagined I would end up with the possibility of real happiness staring me right in the face—and Gabe, I can't believe I was such a thoughtless fool, I really can't. I can't believe I called making love with you rebound sex. I can't believe I freaked and ran when you tried to tell me how you felt about me. I'm an idiot, I know it. But

I *can* learn. I really can. And I *have* learned. I've, um, learned that it's *you*, Gabe. You're everything to me. I love you. I do. I was so stupid and wounded and blind. I only hope it's not too late."

He dropped his hat and took her by the shoulders. "Mel." His eyes—they were summer-day blue again. "Mel." It was all he seemed to be able to say. And it was more than enough.

Especially when he gathered her close and lowered his beautiful mouth to hers in a long, searching, perfect kiss.

She melted into him, there beneath the clear sky, by the rushing creek, in the very spot where they had first met.

When he lifted his head, he asked gruffly, "Does this mean you're going to let me say it now?"

She nodded up at him, a tear escaping, gliding along her temple and into her hair. "Please. Yes. Say it now."

He cradled her face in his big, rough hands. "I love you, Mel. You're my one. My only. There never was another. My whole life, I've been waiting. Just for you."

"Oh, Gabe." Now she was crying and laughing at the same time. "Oh, Gabe, I'm so glad. I was so afraid I'd lost you. I... I love you. I really, really do."

He laughed then, a rich, joyous sound. And

then he captured her lips again and kissed her slow and deep.

When he lifted his head that time, he said, "Let's go." He bent and scooped up his hat. Rising again, he wrapped an arm across her shoulders. They headed up the hill, kissing as they went.

When they reached the vehicles, they stood at his driver's door for a half hour or so, holding each other, kissing each other, whispering promises they both knew now they were bound to keep.

"You work tonight?" he asked eventually.

"I'm on at five, yes."

"Follow me to my house now?"

"Yes." She grabbed his gorgeous face between her hands. "Yes, yes, yes!"

At Gabe's, after Mel took a minute to greet Butch properly, they went on to the master bedroom where they stayed for an hour and a half, celebrating their love in the most elemental way.

Later, they took Butch for a walk. George must have spotted them from the main house. He came running out—to say hi to Mel, he said. He'd read the diary and declared himself one hundred percent certain that Gramps had written it. He was all fired up to make plans to find out what had happened to Beatrix.

"We're on it," promised Gabe.

"Good, then. I was going to let your grandfather read the diary, if that's all right."

"That's fine," said Gabe. "Then we'll talk about the next step."

"That'll work." George tipped his hat at Mel. "Good to see you, Mel. Drop by the main house for dinner soon, won't you?"

"I will, definitely," she promised.

"Excellent." With a nod, George headed off in the direction of the stables.

Back at Gabe's house, Mel shared what had happened during her visit to Rust Creek Falls.

Gabe said he understood her reluctance to approach Winona about the diary until they could learn more about the lost Beatrix.

"As for Todd," he added, "I would love to rearrange his face for him, but he's paying for being a cheating fool. He lost *you*—and his loss is the best thing that ever happened to me."

"Oh, I do love you," she whispered, lifting her eager mouth to welcome his kiss.

At four, she had to return to her apartment to get ready for work.

That night, Gabe showed up at closing time. He followed her to her place and slept over. In the morning, they spoke of the future. Mel would be going to work for DJ's as CFO. For now, she would keep her apartment.

But they both agreed she would be moving in with him at the Ambling A sometime in the next few months. Stark naked, he got down on one knee and officially asked her to marry him.

She couldn't say yes fast enough. Laughing with happiness, she threw herself into his arms.

Gabe said his grandfather had read the diary. Alexander was as eager as George to get going on the search for Beatrix.

Mel had an idea. "Amanda is amazing. She can find just about anyone or anything online. I was thinking we might hire her, give her the diary and what information we have, see what she can discover about what happened to Beatrix."

Gabe agreed. "It's a shot. Let's talk to her, see if she's up for playing online detective."

"That sounds good."

"And I was also thinking we should have a look up in the attic of the main house. There are years' worth of documents and keepsakes stored up there in trunks and dusty boxes. Might be something about Beatrix somewhere in all that stuff."

That night, when he showed up at DJ's, Gabe brought the diary with him. He also reported that he, his dad and his mom had spent several hours in the attic of the main ranch house searching for clues to the mystery.

"So far, nothing," he said glumly.

She longed to grab him and kiss him—but the

kisses would have to wait until after work. She folded her arms across her middle to keep them from reaching for him. "It's good that you looked, though. We need to follow every possible lead. Something is bound to turn up, eventually."

He grinned at her. "I do like your attitude lately."

She laughed with sheer happiness. "Must be love giving me a whole new outlook on life."

Monday morning, they knocked on Amanda's door. She was all smiles just to see them together. She offered coffee and they told her the story of Josiah and Winona and their lost child.

Amanda had tears in her eyes when the story was through. She said of course she would help. "I'll find out what I can."

Later that day, back in Mel's apartment, as they sat at her little table eating ham and cheese sandwiches, Mel asked if Gabe would take her to Snowy Mountain Senior Care. "We need to tell Josiah that we're together now, that we'll be married. I just feel that he should know."

"I think he would like that." Gabe pushed his empty plate away. "I didn't tell you before, but that day he said to bring you to him, he also said that I shouldn't give up on love."

Mel got up and went to his side of the table. He pushed his chair back so that she could sit on his lap. She rested her head on his shoulder. "Your great-grandfather is a very wise man. Thank you for giving me a second chance."

Gabe stroked her hair and whispered, "I love you, Mel. You're mine and I am yours. I'm so damn glad you came back to me."

In his small living room at Snowy Mountain Senior Care, Josiah sat in his recliner. He stared blankly into space as Gabe explained that he had found the only woman for him.

Gabe took Mel's hand. "I told you, when it comes to Mel, I didn't have to ask. And I don't, Gramps. I knew from the first."

Mel admitted, "I wasn't so quick on the uptake, Josiah. I've had my heart broken and that made me wary and reluctant to give my trust. I was a fool. I almost ruined everything. But I finally saw the light. Gabe gave me another chance and, well, here we are. Together."

"Forever," added Gabe.

"And always," said Mel.

Josiah said nothing. He stared at the far wall.

Mel and Gabe got up and went around the coffee table to hug him.

"We'll be getting married," said Gabe. "And Thursday, on Mel's next day off, I'm taking her to choose the ring."

Mel kissed the old man's wrinkled cheek. "Tonight, we'll tell George, Angela, Alexander and Malone that we're engaged."

Gabe laughed. "Mom will be so happy." He asked Mel, "Ice water?"

"I would love a glass."

He got their drinks and they sat across from the silent, unmoving old man. Mel talked about the new job she would be taking with DJ. Gabe said he was still working on Erica to come for a long visit home.

When they were ready to go, they carried their glasses to the sink and returned to the sitting area long enough to give Josiah one last hug.

They'd both reached the door when the old man spoke from behind them in his gruff, rusty voice. "Glad to see you two together where you belong. Now find my little girl."

Mel and Gabe turned in unison. "Oh, Josiah," Mel whispered, her eyes blurred with sudden tears.

Across the room, the old man sat, staring straight ahead, still as a statue again.

Gabe was shaken to the core. Gramps had just all but admitted that he and the Josiah of the diary were one and the same. He let the realization sink in and then spoke with calm assurance. "We promise you, Gramps. One way or another, we will find your little girl."

* * * * *

MILLS & BOON

Coming next month

A YEAR WITH THE MILLIONAIRE NEXT DOOR
Barbara Wallace

"Stella…" He breathed her name into her mouth like it was a prayer. She felt his fingers sliding along her cheeks until they cradled her face. He combed back her hair and pulled away.

"Stella," he repeated.

He was rejecting her.

"Well, isn't this humiliating," she said, backing away. "I…"

Linus backed away, too. The tenderness she imagined in his gaze had morphed into embarrassment. "I should go," he said.

"Yeah, I think that's a good idea."

She kept her attention glued to the coffee table while Linus got up and limped toward the front door. "I'm sorry," he said when he reached the landing. "But I don't think either of us wants to do something we'll regret."

Not trusting herself to speak, Stella only thanked God for that. She'd rambled on about her failings and made a fool out of herself, but at least she hadn't done something she'd regret.

*

Linus closed his front door and collapsed against it. That might have been one of most difficult things he had ever done. *Give yourself a pat on the back, old boy. You behaved like a gentleman.* Eighteen months ago, if a beautiful woman threw herself in his arms, he would have kissed the daylights out of her. Lips that soft and delicious? How could he resist?

But he did resist. Had to. It was clear his neighbor needed a friend far more than she needed sex.

I need to prove I'm not a disappointment.

How could the woman with whom he'd spent the evening disappoint anyone? It was inconceivable. She was funny. Beautiful. Smart.

His rejection probably hadn't helped her self-esteem issues. Still, he'd done the right thing. Maybe that meant he was evolving into a better person. Because for once he cared more about helping a woman than seducing her.

Now if he could only stop thinking about how amazing Stella's lips tasted, he'd be fine.

Continue reading
A YEAR WITH THE MILLIONAIRE NEXT DOOR
Barbara Wallace

Available next month
www.millsandboon.co.uk